SILENCE
IN THE
ECHO

JESSICA LYNN MEDINA

SILENCE IN THE ECHO

THE ECHO SERIES BOOK TWO

Printed in the United States of America

First Printing, 2022

ISBN 978-1-7336145-0-4 (*paperback*)
ISBN 978-1-7336145-1-1 (*ebook*)

Library of Congress Control Number 2021923461
Rising Moon Creatives
St. Louis, MO

www.RisingMoonCreatives.com
www.JessicaLynnMedina.com

Editing by Marinda Valenti
Cover Illustration by Allie Preswick

For those who yearn for change and embrace evolution.

Keep fighting.

CHAPTER ONE

Cold water trickled down Avery's neck as she stared at her reflection in the mirror above the sink. Her eyes shimmered, a vibrant gold that she would never get used to. She barely recognized herself.

Grabbing a towel from the neatly folded stack, she dried her face, not wasting another glance at herself. The others were waiting for her. She supposed she was lucky she had been spared these few moments alone at all.

Avery sighed, smoothing the sleek black dress over the front of her thighs. She couldn't hide in a bathroom forever, and her public appearances weren't over for the day. There were still media interviews to give before heading back through the Gate to Echo. Earth wasn't where she belonged anymore.

She touched a keypad on the wall, and the door slid open to an empty hallway beyond, its curving walls accentuated by white lighting that lined the floor. As she headed for the court antechamber, her heels clicked on the floor, echoing around her in a rhythmic staccato.

As soon as Avery emerged from the archway, Petra looked up, leaning casually against a pale marble wall that extended up at least a hundred feet to meet a domed ceiling that widened out over the entire chamber. Grigg and Nova spoke quietly to one another, their bodies alert. Krez stood a few steps away, muscled arms crossed over his wide chest. They were well away from the crowds in the room but still uncomfortable in the Earthen capitol building.

Krez's brown gaze slid to Avery as she approached and she looked away, focusing on the wide wall of windows that encompassed the far exterior wall to the gargantuan gray doors that opened and closed with every new entry or exit.

"Are you ready?" Petra asked, her voice clipped.

"As I'll ever be." Avery cleared her throat and smiled at them reassuringly. Being on Earth, in the heart of the capital, the seat of the Federation itself, was difficult for her—for all of them. "Just glad our role in this thing is over. For the most part, anyway."

"You did great," Nova said calmly, a smile warming her face. Her blonde hair trailed over her shoulder as she tilted her head. "Had them eating out of the palm of your hand."

Petra grunted. "You shouldn't have had to testify in the first place. The Earthen legal system is asinine. We gave them all the incriminating evidence they should ever need."

"You're not wrong," Grigg agreed. "I don't get why humans are so into this whole drama-of-the-trial thing. Feels pretty disingenuous if all they're looking for are the facts."

"Humans don't exactly have telepathic leaders who can ensure the validity of testimonies. Due process is a basic right," Avery reasoned. She lowered her voice before continuing, her eyes flickering to the officials milling about the domed chamber. Sound carried easily, and she wondered for a moment if that was the purpose of the room's design. "If parading me and Finn around will help when it comes to the confidence vote, then I'm willing to do whatever it takes. I just hope that what I said was enough. Klein can't stay in power. Not after what she's done."

"The charges will go through," Nova assured her. "Your statements are already trending in the feeds."

Avery frowned. "What? I didn't realize they were streaming the coverage." That was just what she needed—more attention. Maybe Grigg was right about it being too much.

Everyone knew Avery, on both worlds. They knew her story and recognized her face, whether she was on Earth or across the universe on Echo. She could get around in public fairly comfortably unless someone saw her eyes—then her anonymity went out the window.

Avery never thought she would be longing for the days of lower-level invisibility. She and Gran had possessed little in the way of money or status, but the simplicity of that life had been easier.

Grigg nudged a muscled shoulder into Avery. "Well, they'll have to listen to you now that you're a real celebrity. I wonder how jealous Finn is gonna be after this whole thing." He waggled his eyebrows at Nova.

Petra rolled her eyes, turning away.

Nova grinned. "I'd love to see the look on his face when he watches your final statements. You sounded like a real politician up there."

Krez was quiet. He never said much of anything these days. Not that he did before—but it was worse now, after what had happened to him. To them both. Avery wouldn't allow herself to dwell on the reason for his silence. She never did.

"I wonder how he's doing with the registrations," Avery said softly, her gaze drifting upward, where an expansive mural of the night sky covered the arched ceiling. As though she might see Finn's ship somewhere amid the painted stars. He was back on Echo, leading the efforts to help the humans that remained on the planet after the Federation agreed to withdraw its militia. Once their crew had exposed Minister Klein's duplicity, the Earthen government and its High Council were eager to pause hostilities while a formal investigation was held. It seemed Klein had a few enemies, even among humans.

"If there weren't a block on comms through the Gate, we could ask him ourselves." Grigg waved his wristport at them.

"How sweet." Nova slapped a hand on his arm, smacking against the brown leather. "He'll be thrilled to hear how much you missed him, too."

"Funny," Grigg drawled, making a face at her.

Avery bit her lip, holding back a smile. If Grigg missed Finn, he wasn't the only one. They hadn't seen him in weeks.

Before this trip, Finn had already returned to Earth for nearly a month in a bid to drum up support for Klein's indictment. And then Avery was called to testify just as he was needed back on Echo to help with human refugee coordination. The entire operation to help the humans left on the Reange planet had been Finn's idea to begin with, and he was eager to lead the process. Their new positions kept them both busy. Avery's chest ached.

In a few hours, she would finally get to see him again. It couldn't come soon enough.

Lying about him during interviews had been difficult. After a lengthy discussion with the Elders, Avery and Finn had decided to keep their relationship a secret, fully hidden from the public eye. The hope was that doing so would grant credulity to their individual testimonies. Not to mention that a relationship between a human and a Reange would only stir up controversy.

Species tensions had never been more of an issue on Earth than they had become after Avery's rise to fame. The incriminating vids that Avery and Finn released of what the Federation had done on Klein's orders only fanned the flames of unrest spreading throughout Earth's cities. Many humans had always been wary of Reanges—or Natives, as they were called on Earth—but proof of the unique powers that some Reanges possessed had frightened some of the population. It didn't matter that the Federation had been testing on innocent lives, only that those lives were different from humanity. And that difference was something to be feared.

But if the public was focused on a conflict between humans and Reanges, it would draw attention away from Klein's crimes. And that Avery wouldn't allow. So it was worth the small bit of compromise to keep her relationship with Finn a secret. At least until after the trial.

Avery had no intention of hiding anything after Klein was fully barred from power. She was ready for change on both planets, even if she had to force her way toward realizing progress. Achieving lasting peace between the worlds would require facing the violence that had been used to divide them for decades. Not to mention pruning the leaders who had brought the two worlds to that culmination of bloodshed in the first place.

It was the sole reason Avery welcomed her new celebrity status.

Humans were fascinated by her story: a Reange girl raised as a human and brought out of lower-level obscurity into power, fame, and fortune. She would use that allure to her advantage and show both humans and Reanges that they need not fear one another.

But that would come later, after things had settled.

Petra drew in a sharp breath, a hissing sound that brought Avery out of her thoughts. Petra's shoulders tensed, head dropping as hatred poured out of her, boiling hot and scalding Avery's mind.

Her gaze followed Petra's, landing on the tall doors of the entrance as the once-quiet lull of conversation amplified, bouncing off the curved walls, turning a few dozen voices into what sounded like hundreds. Adrenaline tightened Avery's limbs, her hands balling to fists.

A stately blonde woman strode through the crowd that pushed in to greet her, shaking the hands that reached out to her as she went by. Her smile was easy and friendly, a beautiful face of elegant lines made more so by the satin beige suit she wore. Not a single a hair was out of place, its gleaming length brushed back and falling down around her shoulders. Her blue eyes sparkled.

Klein.

Instinctively, Grigg stepped forward. Krez placed himself slightly in front of Avery, ready to act if needed. Their hostility surged up and over Avery, mingling together until she could barely see through the waves of feeling. They were angry. A deep well of rage bubbled up from them and flowed straight into her. She found it nearly unbearable.

Avery let out a long breath to steady herself. She grabbed on to their minds, infusing them with a sense of tranquility.

Calm down, she spoke internally, opening them to one another in mind. She was grateful for her telepathy, especially during their tour on Earth. It wasn't a full merge, but she hadn't used the entire weight of her powers since she had been forced to do so when facing the Federation in battle months ago. She kept a tight leash on how and when she relied on her gift. *We knew running into her was a possibility.*

Avery could guess what they were thinking. Even if she hadn't just read their minds, she still would have known. Klein was the enemy. The head of a snake that had strangled the Reange people—their people—for centuries. Klein had tortured innocent Reanges, experimenting on them to find the origin of the So's powers—even had tried to do so to Avery. She had manipulated truths and used her own propaganda to fuel a war between their worlds that had raged for decades. So many innocent lives had been lost because of Klein and her agenda.

They could end it all so easily—*Avery* could end it all so easily. This public theater she was forced to participate in, this game that their government insisted she play . . .

One quick strike would be all that we needed to—

No, Avery commanded, imposing her will without any room for opposition. Petra met her gaze, those green eyes full of fire and ready for battle. *We do this the right way.*

Grigg and Nova shared a glance. Avery couldn't bring herself to look at Krez. Of all of them, she feared what she would see in his eyes most.

Klein continued through the chamber, her charisma exuding a sly sense of authority, captivating those around her. She was at ease among the officials, smiles coming to her as naturally as breathing. She was a creature made for the world of politics. And that, at least, Avery envied.

Klein looked up, those magnetic blue eyes locking with Avery's from across the room. They were brighter in person, incredibly light and startling, even from a distance. The edge of Klein's mouth tilted up just before she dipped her chin in a nod. Avery tensed.

And as quickly as she had appeared, Klein went through the doors to the courtrooms and was gone. Heading in for her own questioning. The sentencing would come later.

Avery let out a short breath, her chest tightening further. They needed to leave.

"We're late," Avery bit out, striding toward the massive double doors to the outside world without looking back.

Beneath the open sky, Avery led the others down the hundreds of shallow steps that spread into an elongated terrace. The Federation Court was perched at mid-level in Alexandria, Earth's capital city, nestled between towering skyscrapers that reached up into the clouds above. It was an elegant structure built of dark marble and wide columns, reminiscent of the original government buildings found in the centuries-old district on the ground level. The terrace framed the building beautifully, housing a mirror pool down its center and extending over the drop to the lower levels beneath. It was an ideal setting for speeches and public addresses, one that Klein herself had used often as Council Minister.

And although Avery had seen this place a thousand times before in movies and news reels, she never thought she'd come here herself. In fact, she never thought she'd see Alexandria or any city on Earth. When you were born into a lower level, it was difficult, if not impossible, to ever climb out of it. Her eyes drifted to buildings that rose up around them, to the expensive cruisers glinting light against their curved windows as they zipped through the skyways. She was a long way from New San Fran now, much less that Level 5 apartment that she and Gran had called home.

She stumbled, and Petra caught her arm, steadying her.

"I don't know why you're wearing those idiotic shoes," Petra snapped.

"Megan picked them out." Avery glanced down at the tall black heels.

"What a surprise," Petra said bitterly, before lapsing into silence.

Megan had sworn the shoes would instill confidence, but so far, the wobbling and lack of control made her feel even more out of place. And much to Avery's chagrin, a practical pair of boots wouldn't have really gone with the outfit.

Besides, she was thankful for the whole ensemble a second later as they passed through the anti-bot tech and onto the final landing, straight into the swarm of waiting media bots. Avery prayed they didn't catch a clip of her tripping over her own feet.

Crowds gathered on a lower expanse of the terrace beneath them, where spectators were allowed to congregate between the foot of the steps and the front end of the rectangular pool. Hundreds of humans now filled the space, pressing in against the security line of Federation soldiers, their voices rising up through the air as they chanted or yelled. Many of them held signs above their heads, angling for attention from the cams. A few were painted on scraps of old sheet metal, while others were holoprojections from wristports.

When Avery stepped into view, they cheered, wristports rising to catch vids of her as she stepped forward to the platform's edge. Krez's anxiety touched her mind, a knifelike graze that made her flinch, and she brushed him away. She was nervous enough on her own without his worry. Still, he stepped closer to her side, ready to shield her from any threat. The show of alarm rankled her.

Avery wasn't a fool: she knew there had been attacks over the past several months throughout Earth's cities. The growing support of species integration in the wake of Klein's indictment hadn't been entirely well received, resulting in protests and societal upset. The added danger was why Avery had brought such a large entourage with her in the first place. But she'd be damned if she'd let a few intimidation tactics stop her.

She'd like to see anyone try to touch her. Avery was more than ready.

But what happened on Earth wasn't solely her concern anymore. She would have to trust that the High Council could take care of Minister Klein before any more harm was done to the tentative peace that had already been negotiated. Avery had done her part, to the best of her abilities, and now she needed to give her full attention to Echo.

And she had plans for its future.

A holosign caught Avery's attention, and her stomach flipped. It was her own face, rendered artfully in black and shades of gray. Except for the eyes. They stared out at the viewer, vibrant and glowing and golden. The face had been given the effect of subtle movement via some sort of programming. She watched as her likeness dipped its chin, that piercing gaze narrowing. The phrase *CITIZENS LIBERA-TION* appeared across the bottom of the sign, in a dripping scrawl, as though painted with an invisible brush in a gilded light that matched the eyes exactly.

The woman who held it shook, her whole body trembling as she stared at the real Avery from within the crowd. She was crying. Avery paused, the sight unnerving her enough that her breath caught. The woman was human. And yet Avery's face was on her banner.

Before she could dwell on it, the media bots pulled around in front of Avery, angling for the best shots and effectively blocking her view of the terrace. Right—her part wasn't over quite yet. She still had to give more statements to the news outlets.

Her mind drifted to Finn, conjuring an image of the last time she saw him, in a news feed. He had given similar interviews in the exact spot she was in now, after his testimony a few days ago. High in the sky above, the vague circular outline of the Gate was visible beyond the hazy atmosphere.

Finn would be back on Echo by now, busy with his own work as the newly appointed lead ambassador. Now that Nick was gone, those duties fell to Finn alone.

"Miss Vey! Miss Vey! Over here, Avery! This way, Miss Vey!" Voices filtered in around her from the dozens of media bots filling the air, their hosts calling for attention, drowning out everything else. She squared her shoulders, nodding to the red bot closest to her. She recognized the winged-globe logo of World Public News on its side.

"Thank you, Miss Vey," said a masculine voice emanating from hidden speakers as the interviewer spoke through the bot remotely. The other bots fell quiet, eager for whatever footage they could get, even if it wasn't for their inquiries. "Can you comment on your testimony today and the implications of your statements regarding Minister Klein's illegal activities?"

Avery straightened, clinging to the words she had rehearsed at least a hundred times in the mirror yesterday. "I stand by everything I said in that courtroom. Minister Klein, and those under her direct orders, kidnapped me from my home here on Earth and subjected me to experimentation and torture. She has been lying to the citizens about our role in the war with Echo and diverting funding and resources to fuel her own agenda and violate our rights."

"*Our* rights? Are you still claiming to be a citizen of Earth?"

"A year ago, I would have sworn to you I was entirely human. The rights of Earth's citizens and those of Echo's should be interchange-able." Avery cursed herself for her poorly chosen wording. She had rehearsed to avoid such stumbles.

"Can you comment on your statements regarding the Reange in your party who was killed on direct orders from Minister Klein?"

Krez tensed beside Avery, fury and grief shooting through him and into her mind like a white-hot spear, nearly choking her from within. The brief mention of Fiora, of the loss . . . Avery pulled up a wall to block Krez out.

"I'd rather not discuss it." Avery hoped she sounded steadier than she felt. She clasped her fingers together behind her back to hide her shaking hands. "But Minister Klein is responsible for the destruction of countless lives. If the High Council values the citizens of Earth, then they will move forward on the charges. I believe the footage we presented speaks for itself. And let's not forget the remaining testimonies collected over the course of this trial."

"Speaking of the vids you broadcasted in the spring, do you know anything more regarding Ambassador Lunitia? We're, of course, refer-ring to Nick Lunitia, who disappeared shortly before your incarcera-tion on the Port Station."

"No, I'm afraid not," Avery said succinctly. It was all she could bring herself to say on the matter, and it was the truth. They hadn't heard from Nick since Finn had beaten him bloody in that theater on Echo. They didn't even know if he was still alive. He had vanished.

There was barely a pause on the heels of her awkward response before the host continued. "There's quite a crowd gathered here for you today, Miss Vey. Care to comment on your impact on the social revolution we're experiencing regarding interspecies relations and the development of groups like the Citizen's Liberation Front? And what is your opinion on last week's bombings in Nueva York?"

Avery swallowed back any legitimate answer. "I'm so sorry to cut this short, but I have an appointment to get to, and I'm afraid I'm already running late." She glanced behind her to the others, giving them a terse nod, and Petra moved ahead to lead them away. Avery waved at the bots, plastering her best attempt at an apologetic smile onto her face.

She needed to avoid making waves with social commentary, at least for now. The trial was the most important thing, and Avery certainly couldn't afford to widen the gap of public opinion. Not when the vote of confidence would come down to a popular ballot.

How did I do? Avery asked the others in mind as they continued toward the landing platform on the back side of the terrace. A few bots still followed them, wanting as much footage of their new Reange celebrity as they could get.

Like a real revolutionary, Grigg replied, his pride emanating over and through her.

Nova glanced over her shoulder, to the bots and lingering crowd behind, before she added, *Let's keep moving—I didn't realize there'd be so many people gathered here. Probably not the best decision to have a public statement out in the open like that.*

My thoughts exactly, Petra agreed.

Avery nearly rolled her eyes. They were worse than hovering parents. She would have been fine regardless.

Still, she glanced at the humans once more, hunting for the woman she had seen earlier. Avery understood why she was important to the Reanges, but why would the humans find anything in her to stand behind? The WPN host had mentioned her influence on societal change—was her story that significant, even to humans on Earth?

Elements within Earth's government had never been stable. It functioned on the impression of representation without any real follow-through, since there was little coordination between local government and global rulings. The Federation controlled nearly every aspect of world government, without input from the district officials. The High Council was made up of level representatives from each district, but they could only advise Federation decisions—not mandate them. And even then, higher levels received a larger number of appointed representatives. It was an overt imbalance of power, meant to serve those who already controlled the system.

Which meant things for citizens in the lower levels were bad. Avery knew, better than anyone, what that life was like. What she and

Gran had done to scrape by. And the citizens they had helped along the way, who were in much worse situations than she had ever been. It was why Gran started a healing practice in the first place. She had wanted to help those whom the government would not.

"Avery." Nova said her name gently, almost like a question.

Avery had stopped moving and was looking out over the edge of the terrace, down into the shadows of the levels beneath, where even cruisers ceased to fly. It would be a long drop to the bottom. She had heard that Alexandria's ground level—the District—was one of the worst on Earth. Ironic, considering it was in the capital itself.

"You're right," Avery said quietly, pulling away from the edge to resume her long strides. Or as long as her heels would allow, anyway. "Let's go home."

She resisted the urge to look back at the crowd. And she didn't dare reveal the secret within her heart that curled up in the shadows as though waiting to strike. She could barely even voice it to herself.

For one part of her, Earth would always be home.

CHAPTER TWO

"Is that the last of them?" Finn asked through his teeth, keeping the smile plastered on his face. The couple he'd just finished working with waved at him from the lobby through the glass walls of the conference room. As soon as they were out of sight, he ran a tired hand through his hair, leaning an elbow on the massive table.

"Moons above, I hope so," Markes groaned beside him. "When I agreed to shadow you, sitting in an office interviewing humans all day wasn't exactly what I had in mind."

"You say that like you had a choice in the matter," Linderly pointed out with a laugh. "It was a direct order from Avery, you idiot." She barely looked up from her wristport, attention fixed on the Earthen dramas she had become obsessed with during their time there last month. Megan should never have introduced her to those blazing shows.

But it was true that Avery had left him with the twins while their crew was forced apart by the Elders. In case the Federation tried anything during Finn's media tour, Avery wanted him to have sufficient backup. That, and she hoped the exposure to Earthen culture would help expand the siblings' perspectives regarding human life.

It was only marginally embarrassing that Avery thought he needed two sixteen-year-olds to protect him. But even Finn had to admit that Markes knew more about advanced weaponry than anyone he'd ever met, and Linderly could hack any tech she got her hands on. Plus, they were well trained in combat, thanks to their extremist upbringing.

But after weeks of interviews and public appearances, their days had become fairly perfunctory. Finn couldn't say he blamed Markes for being bored. Not that he could admit that.

"We were supposed to be guarding him from threats," Markes whined. "Not processing paperwork."

"Listen, kid, this is part of the job, too," Finn explained, ignoring the voice in his head that wanted to agree with Markes. "It's not always about saving worlds and blowing shit up."

"See—now *that* sounds like fun."

"Of course it does," Linderly said tartly. "You're a weapons expert—that's his entire point. Making sure the humans have the resources they need, as well as the option to return to Earth, is part of the peace treaty that Avery negotiated."

"Exactly," Finn confirmed, standing up and stretching out the stiff muscles in his neck. "And heading up that process is my responsibility."

"Right—*your* responsibility," Markes said, leaning back in his chair. "I didn't hear my name anywhere in all of that."

"You're welcome to head back to the apartment, Markes." Linderly stood, gathering the tablets that were strewn across the table and piling them into her tattoo-covered arms. The devices had been used for the registrations they'd been facilitating over the past two days. The information they gathered about the humans who were left on Echo would be used for the process of allocating funds and supplies. "Nobody's stopping you."

He scoffed. "And have you rat me out to Avery? Not blazing likely."

"Speaking of, what time is it?" Finn asked, glancing at his wrist-port and cursing under his breath.

Markes grinned. "Worried you won't have time to get all fancied up for her? Trust me, I'd tell you if I thought you'd embarrass yourself."

"Markes," Linderly chastised and roughly shoved his head.

"She's right," Finn said, glaring at him. "Be nicer to me."

"You wouldn't like me as much if I were."

"I like your sister just fine, and she's not a snarky little ass."

"But you don't like her as *much*."

"Hey!" Linderly protested, pulling her face into a frown.

Finn leaned over and ruffled Markes's hair, sending its vibrant yellow into disarray. "You're a real piece of work."

"So you keep telling me." Markes followed the other two as they left the room, smoothing out his hair when he thought Finn wasn't looking.

They each nodded to the few workers still left in the office building as they made their way to the elevators. It wasn't a horrible place to conduct business, if Finn was being honest. Echo's government buildings all boasted breathtaking views of the city from all directions. The trio approached the elevator lobby, where a towering arched window framed the eastern mountains on the horizon, their snowy peaks stained orange in the late afternoon sun. Twilight wasn't too far away now, when they would dissolve into a mottled pink and blue against the bruised sky of early night.

By then Avery would be back in Finn's arms.

The thought almost had him smiling like an idiot, but he bit the inside of his lip to keep from grinning. He missed her. More than he thought he would—more than he thought possible. They'd both been so busy with their new duties, and she had refused to fix her blazing wristport, which meant they'd barely spoken during their weeks apart.

Finn had wanted nothing more than to be with her on Earth, to stand beside her as she gave her testimony and fielded questions from the media. She would be rattled from it. Recounting what had happened to them, what she had gone through, would not come easily. She barely even spoke of it to him. But at least her nightmares had stopped.

Writing her statement had been difficult enough. They had rehearsed it at least a hundred times before he left, and she had still been uneasy about it.

Finn often forgot how intimidating some people found speaking in front of a crowd. That had been the one thing he excelled at. He was good at pretending. He always had been.

Nick had made sure of that. Finn's brother considered lying an art form to be mastered. And to politicians, maybe it was.

"Whoa," Markes drawled, his young voice cracking. "I haven't seen you frown like that since that girl back in Nueva York tried to put her hand in your—"

"Markes!" Linderly snapped, her violet eyes pinning him. "Moons above, leave him alone. He's just nervous."

"I'm not nervous," Finn grumbled. But he was thankful when the elevator arrived and gave him an excuse to move. It flew upward on his command, to the landing platform on the roof where the workers docked their cruisers.

After a few seconds of ascending in silence, Markes said quietly, "Have you given any more thought to my proposal?"

Finn shook his head, a grin pulling at his lips. "Yeah, and my answer is still no."

"Oh, come on, Finn. Why do you need all that extra room in your place? You can't make us go back to that shithole the government provides." He drew down his brows, suddenly serious. "I would make an excellent roommate."

"Given the fact that we just spent three weeks on a ship together, you can't expect me to fall for that line."

Linderly giggled. "He's got a point, Markes. You've always been a slob."

Markes twisted his mouth. "I don't remember asking you. And I know for a fact you hate our place, too."

He wasn't entirely wrong—Finn did have too much room in his apartments. But then, he had never meant to live there alone. He had only bought it in the first place to share with Nick.

Something dark sliced through his gut then, churning its emptiness into nausea. He still hadn't heard from his brother. Didn't know if he was dead or alive. A part of Finn had hoped Nick might resurface once the Elders began advertising the human registration initiative in Milderion. That he would just show up on his doorstep one day, asking for forgiveness.

But there was a good chance he was dead. And if he was, that meant that Finn had been the one to kill him. His last memories of Nick were bloody. Painful. Nick had betrayed him. He had betrayed their position and their family name.

Their father would be ashamed. Possibly of them both.

Finn closed his eyes, pushing the thoughts to the back of his mind.

Every interview he had endured on Earth had brought up the subject of Nick. His brother had been a public figure in his own right. Not as adored as Finn, but that had never been his intention. Nick had taken care of the real work while he pushed Finn into a different role entirely: the irresponsible libertine, the rebellious black sheep. And it had served its purpose, for a time.

But still, the media had taken note of Nick's complete disappearance from public life. And they wouldn't forget him easily. Explaining that, too, was Finn's responsibility. Along with the thousands of humans still left on Echo. It was all on him now.

And he would rather die than let them down.

The Lunitia family had served as ambassadors of Echo since Finn's father had established the position, and it was an honor Finn took as seriously as any military rank he'd ever held. With Nick gone—with the way he'd left—it was more imperative than ever that Finn live up to the Lunitia name.

They reached the roof, the salty wind whipping up around them as they walked to Finn's ship. The smell of the ocean was warm and vibrant, hanging heavy and thick in the air, not a cloud in the soft blue sky above. It would be a clear night, perfect for stargazing. Maybe he'd take Avery out on the terrace and—

"Finn," Linderly warned. She had stopped, turning back toward the exit, her body stiff and alert.

Finn whirled around, experience and training the only things controlling his spike of adrenaline. Armed Reange soldiers filed out of the doorway toward them, two officers clad in gray uniforms at the front of the formation. Finn didn't recognize any of them.

"Shit," Markes muttered, a hand drifting to the blaster on his hip.

"What the blazar is this?"

"Don't touch that gun," Finn said darkly, dropping his chin. That's just what he needed, for this hot-headed kid to shoot some soldier who was only following orders. "They probably just need me to come to the capitol building."

"So they sent a dozen armed guards?" Markes asked caustically, eyeing the officers as they drew closer.

"Why didn't they just comm you?" Linderly asked, her voice barely louder than a whisper.

Finn didn't reply. They were both right—something was off. The officers glared at him as they approached, their faces thick with anger. With rage.

Finn's pulse doubled its pace, instincts firing like mad through his veins. He stepped forward, putting himself in front of the two teenagers.

And he was glad he did, because when the officers finally reached him, they pulled out blasters of their own and aimed straight for Finn's chest.

Avery awoke with a jolt, a sharp sting tugging her ribs and pulling her out of sleep. A quick glance at the port window told her they were in space, the alignment of the stars indicating they had passed through the Gate.

Echo sat just within view from her seat on the bed a vibrant swirl of blue and white nestled against the silent black void. The twinge struck her again, unease swirling with the dormant power inside her veins.

If they were through the Gate, why hadn't the others woken her?

Why are we still in orbit? Avery asked, sending the question out through the ship. She could feel the rest of her crew, gathered together, waiting on the command deck.

You better get up here, Nova replied, her request wrapped in enough urgency to reignite the spark that had brought Avery out of her sleep. She reached out quickly, confirming everyone else was all right. But . . . everyone was fine.

Avery threw on her boots and grabbed her jacket, jogging through the central hall to the command deck. All faces turned to her as she entered, wary and tense.

"What is it?" Avery asked. She brushed against the collective as she connected their thoughts, reading their minds. Her heart stopped. "Finn's not here?"

"No. It's been quiet since we came through the Gate." Nova turned to look at the monitor, as though searching for answers on the map in front of her.

"We've been trying to comm him but haven't gotten a response," Grigg added gravely.

Avery frowned, their anxiety spearing through her. Her palms felt clammy. "Maybe he just forgot?" she suggested hopefully.

"Avery, when it comes to you, Finn doesn't forget anything," Nova replied, the statement flat enough to make Avery blush.

"Except for the fact that you can kick his ass," Grigg added, making Nova chuckle. Even Petra snorted.

Avery's eyes moved to the wide observation windows. Nova was right. Finn wouldn't forget. That stinging hit her midriff again, setting her on edge. Something was wrong. "How long have we been waiting?"

"About an hour," Nova replied.

"What?" Avery couldn't help her brusque reply. They should have woken her sooner.

"It was my call to let you sleep," Petra interjected, breaking the silence. "You needed the rest. And I thought he would have checked in by now."

"What about Markes and Linderly? Has anybody tried them?"

"They're not responding either," Nova confirmed.

Krez said nothing. He was stone, focused on the vision of Echo beyond the windows. Avery could feel him, though. Could sense his growing anxiety.

Avery sent cool tendrils of calm threading throughout the group.

"We shouldn't worry yet. They probably just got caught up in their duties. You know comms don't work inside the capitol building—they're probably just in a meeting that ran late. Let's head in."

Petra turned back to the controls, initiating the engines. Despite Avery's efforts to ease the tension, worry unspooled from Nova and Grigg, winding itself around her and channeling her unease.

They entered Echo's atmosphere, descending swiftly into the heart of Milderion. Buildings rose up around them, arching into the cloudless azure sky, gleaming dark glass against vibrant blue. The Reange population surged to meet her, the presence of so many souls brushing against her mind, the familiarity a marked relief after so many days without. She had missed it. The thoughts and feelings that had once been such a burden to her were now almost a balm.

But still . . . something was different—strange. Like the frequency was off. Altered.

Panic clawed at her, and Avery closed herself off from the group. "Straight to the capitol," she breathed.

"Do you sense something?" Grigg asked, placing himself behind Nova.

"I can't be sure." Avery leaned forward, sending her awareness into the city, searching for something—anything—that would explain the sense of disturbing *otherness*. "Something is wrong."

Grigg's hand went to the gun strapped to his hip, and Nova tensed. Petra and Krez radiated with unchecked energy, ready to fight. But if something truly was wrong, Avery didn't want them anywhere near it.

I'll be going in alone, Avery said to the group.

Like hell you are, Petra argued, her anger a hot wave that crashed against her. *If something's off, then you need us.*

I agree with Petra, Nova added. Grigg didn't have to voice his opinion. He stood with Nova.

Avery frowned, her throat closing. The closer they moved to the capitol, the more the energy intensified, like they were headed for some kind of rift. She prayed she was wrong and that Finn wasn't anywhere near it.

She had to keep the others away. She had to go alone.

An arm grazed hers. Krez. He surveyed the skyline beyond, his features drawn. *I'm going with you*, he said simply. It wasn't a question.

Avery lifted her chin. She'd force him to back off if she had to. She snaked her consciousness around his mind, ready to command his compliance with her power. She locked their connection, holding fast and cementing their bond. Inhaling sharply, Avery widened her eyes as a honed spear of grief stabbed her straight through her chest. The pain radiated outward until she quivered beneath the crushing weight.

Curling red hair. A bright, smiling face. Freckles smattered across a strong nose.

Avery recoiled instantly.

Fiora.

Avery's vision blurred, and she turned away from Krez, unable to face him.

"Fine," she bit out, desperate to get away from that pain. Desperate for relief. She severed connection to the others as well. "I'll take Krez. But the rest of you—head for Gran's and wait there until I contact you."

"You said yourself, comms don't work in the building," Nova pointed out.

"Then I guess it's a good thing I don't need tech to communicate," Avery responded, her voice shaky. "And once I figure out what—"

"Shit." Grigg nodded ominously to the capitol building just ahead. The white structure stood low and wide between the sleek, rising towers surrounding it. "That can't be good."

A monstrous blue banner was strapped across the thick pillars that lined the entrance steps, dark and ominous against the pristine stone, its edges fluttering in the wind. The words *NO HUMANS* were scrawled across it in black ink, as though painted by hand.

"What the blazar is going on?" Avery spat, worry igniting quickly into a fury that tore through her veins. She clung to it, the anger burning away the remnants of her grief—of Krez's grief.

Petra brought the ship down to street level, and Krez was already headed for the hatch, eager for action.

"Make sure Gran is safe," Avery ordered as she backed away to follow him. "And don't come back here until you hear from me."

Be careful, Petra warned Avery privately.

Avery didn't wait to watch them go, climbing the stairs with Krez at her side. They passed beneath the banner, and her eyes trailed upward.

The dark material snapped violently, alive and whipping the wind, the letters distorted by waving ripples. She focused on the heavy stone doors in front of them and what lay inside, ignoring the way her heart flinched at each loud crack of fabric.

CHAPTER THREE

Avery marched through the halls, the sound of her boots reverberating off the white stone, driven by a purpose she hadn't felt in weeks. None of the guards stopped her or Krez, only watching warily as they passed, as agitation tickled her senses.

She frowned, reaching out to the other Reanges in the building, seeking answers. When she left the Elders a week ago, human integration efforts had been fully underway. Finn would have taken over as soon as he arrived, helping to coordinate the registration and keeping things moving while she was away.

The Elders weren't even supposed to be meeting in her absence—there was no possibility anything could have progressed without Avery present. They needed her gifts to connect the Council members telepathically, to ensure transparency and representation in every decision that was made. It was written into the laws that had driven Echo's government for centuries, and before humans arrived, there had been plenty of So's to facilitate it. But now there was only Avery.

Avery's mind reached the Elder chamber ahead, and she stopped short, her body freezing at the presence she felt there. At the one person who was *not* supposed to be there. Her breath lodged in her throat, fear roiling in her belly, quickly hardening into anger. It flooded through her, throwing fuel onto her powers.

Avery charged forward, a swipe of her hand sending out energy that slammed open the thick marble doors, a resounding announcement of her entry as she strode into the room on the wings of her fury.

The Elders looked up in surprise, some jumping in fear, others nearly rising from their seats along the wide table that ran the length of the chamber. Avery ignored them, zeroing in on the one face that she knew was responsible for whatever had happened. The one that would have dared to touch Finn and the peace Avery had brokered with the humans.

Vibrant eyes met her gaze, and there was certainly no alarm in those violet depths. She had known Avery was coming.

Leviathan.

"What are you doing here?" Avery demanded, her voice echoing off the impressive height of the chamber walls. The other Elders in attendance had gone quiet, a few hushed murmurs the only sounds rustling among the silence.

Leviathan said nothing. A single white brow lifted.

Avery could barely focus, rage flooding her body, pooling at her hands in a rush of energy. This was the change—the wrongness she had felt when descending upon the surface. This woman had burrowed her way into the heart of this new government just when it had been finding its legs. Whatever power Leviathan had left, she had used it to poison everything Avery had worked for. There was no other answer. It was staring her in the face.

Avery's power bled from her, pooling outward in the virulence of her rage. The chairs nearest to her rattled ominously, clanging against the floor and heavy table. A few Elders studied her warily.

"Well?" Avery demanded, louder this time, her voice a near yell. "I asked you a question."

One corner of Leviathan's mouth lifted. She stood from her seat at the table's head, leaning heavily on a silver cane. "Must we do this now, Avery?" she asked, voice weary. "We've been reviewing plans all morning, and I must confess, I'm a little overtired."

Avery's lip curled like some snarling animal. She struck out a hand to slash the air, sending a snap of power directly at the old woman.

Leviathan's cane whipped from her hand, soaring across the room and cracking loudly against the wall. It broke on the impact, the pieces racketing to the floor.

Leviathan lost her balance, falling forward on the table with clawing hands. Someone stood to assist her, offering his arm in lieu of the cane. When she looked at Avery again, her eyes were narrowed. Angry.

Good.

"That was a little childish, don't you think?" Leviathan asked sharply, a slight catch in her voice the only indication she was shaken by the display.

"Childish? You mean like waiting for me to leave the galaxy and then staging an extremist uprising in my absence? Where is Finn?"

Leviathan laughed. "You young people are always so quick to reach dramatic conclusions. I'd hardly call it an uprising, my dear." She motioned to the familiar faces seated around her. "Your Elders are still here—we have simply decided to pursue an alternative direction."

"You didn't answer my question," Avery warned, her palm twitching to use her power to finish this now. Just like it had with Klein.

"Oh, your ambassador is fine, I'm sure." Leviathan waved a hand. "Accounted for, at least. Just like the rest of your precious humans."

Avery's eyes caught on a flash of pink hair. Milupe was still here. The Elder Council head had always been peaceful from the day they met, eager to follow Avery's vision for human integration. Avery reached out to her, searching for the familiar bright tether of her mind, the warmth she knew she would find. But she found nothing, only a searing pain that blazed through Avery's skull, vibrating into her bones. She gasped, jerking back in shock and stumbling.

Avery's hand flew to her temple, clawing at the stabbing agony, her eyes squeezing shut against a piercing light that robbed her of all her senses. She staggered backward on another harsh intake of breath, desperate to make the sensation stop.

"Avery." Krez was at her side instantly, his voice deep and concerned, wide hands clasping her arms, the only things holding her upright.

"Leviathan," a level voice warned, registering vaguely through Avery's pain. "You said it wouldn't hurt her."

"Do calm down, Mylan," Leviathan replied. "It's only temporary. As I told you."

Avery peeled her eyes open. She hunched over, shaking in Krez's arms, her cheeks wet from hot, angry tears. The immediate pain had ebbed enough that she could focus, and she zeroed in on Mylan's worried face. He was standing beside Leviathan—of course he was. Mylan had always been her lackey. It had been a mistake to let him join the new Elders after the Federation had left Echo. But Avery had been hopeful and eager to show cooperation, even with the extremist group. She should have known better.

What have you done? Avery asked Mylan, her brain quivering from the effort it took to speak in mind.

"Now, let's not make any more of a fuss, Avery," Leviathan said, clearly losing what little patience she had. She continued directly to Avery's mind, *You'll only make the pain worse if you try to use your power.*

There was no opposition from the Elders around the table. They did nothing—said nothing. Merely watched.

Avery had taken an oath not to use her powers against the Elders. And she had never violated that, had never wanted to. Had never needed to.

But Avery couldn't let this happen. She couldn't sit by and watch as Leviathan used her own power to exploit everything they'd built— to ruin the progress they'd made. And if that banner out front was any indication, it could already be too late. Avery was too familiar with the extremist views of the Origin to doubt what Leviathan's plans for the humans would entail.

Avery had to warn the others. If they came back here for her, they could get caught in Leviathan's web as easily as any of the Elders had. Any Reange would be at risk to Leviathan's manipulation.

Avery reached out to Petra, her power flying across the city, the effort more difficult than anything she had ever attempted. She grasped for that familiar tether between them, feeling for Petra's light. Nothing. There was nothing.

She frowned, confusion mingling with panic and driving her heartbeat into a frenzied staccato.

Avery concentrated harder, ignoring the searing pain as her eyes watered. A fine sweat broke out around her temples. Something was blocking her—if she could just push through . . .

She whimpered, seeing stars from the effort, and finally let go. Her head was on fire, a white-hot blaze scaling her skull from the inside.

She couldn't find Petra. She felt none of the others—not Grigg, or Nova, or anyone else. Couldn't reach out to any part of them. Couldn't feel anything.

Her power . . . It was gone.

Avery panted, glaring at the old woman at the end of the table. "How are you doing this?"

Mylan glanced uncertainly at Leviathan, gray brows drawn low over his eyes. He seemed to be the only one in the room uneasy about the situation. The other Elders sat still and calm, their faces placid, all the picture of meek submission, even Milupe.

"In point of fact, you're doing this to yourself," Leviathan responded cryptically. "You always knew we never had any intention of living alongside humans. It's time you realized your vision for the future is juvenile. No, don't look at me that way." She turned her head to Mylan, adding, "And do stop your moping, Mylan. Avery has demonstrated that she needs a good muzzle until she's properly trained."

Avery looked up at Krez, meeting the deep brown of his eyes. She searched for his presence, for his light. He was standing right beside her. It should be easy.

He frowned, confusion spreading over his face as his breathing grew heavy. He stepped away from her, his whole body starting to shake as though struggling to maintain some kind of control. Terror clawed up Avery's throat.

"What is this, Leviathan?" Avery asked slowly as she turned to the room, hating the way her voice cracked. "Stop it. Leave him alone."

"I think it's clear you need some time to yourself to think," Leviathan said, ignoring Avery's demand. "Krez, if you wouldn't mind." Leviathan motioned to him lightly with the vague request.

Avery whirled as Krez grabbed her. She glanced down at the hand wrapped around her arm, long fingers digging into the pale green of her jacket.

"What are you doing?" Avery asked, shock stilling her as Krez pulled her toward the exit, his broad frame dragging her easily. "Krez! What is wrong with you?" Energy coursed through her limbs, her skin tingling in protest where his hand clamped around her arm.

Energy.

She still had her power. Something of it, at least.

Avery jerked her chin upward, flinging Krez's hand away from her. She shoved his chest with an added boost of energy, sending his body crashing into the stone wall. He slumped to the floor, a low groan emanating as he slipped into unconsciousness.

Her mouth dried. Leviathan was controlling him, and she had no way to fight it. She couldn't wait around to figure it out, not when she was wholly outnumbered. If Leviathan had stripped her of her telepathy, she could easily lose her physical powers next. Avery couldn't stay there. She would have to leave him.

Guards were already running at her from the entrance; she had no time to think. Avery turned to meet them, grabbing the outstretched hand of the first and vaulting the woman over her shoulder and onto the hard floor.

Avery whirled around to Leviathan. She was controlling them. The Elders, the guards, even Krez. There would be no way to talk her way out of this one. Avery needed a diversion and fast.

She looked up to the high ceiling, where three artificial moons hovered above them, spheres of white carved from the same stone that made up the whole building. They were imbued with antigravity tech that allowed them to orbit inside the room, mimicking the celestial movements of Echo's three moons. The sacred pieces were meant to remind the Elders of their responsibility to the ancient powers.

They would be extremely heavy. That could work.

Avery braced her feet, swiping her hand across the air and sending a wide arc of power straight for those moons. It hit them violently, nullifying the weightlessness and bringing the three orbs crashing down to the center of the long table.

Elders scattered, their cries echoing up around them. Mylan dove toward Leviathan and knocked her to the floor, covering her body with his. The weight of the moons cracked the table, its thick glass shattering throughout the room. The whole place erupted into chaos.

And Avery ran.

She made it as far as the main lobby, the wide stone doors beckoning ahead, a glimpse of darkening sky teasing her with freedom, before she went down.

The jabbing pain of electrodarts hit her spine and dragged her to the floor, radiating throughout her bones, turning her inside out in that familiar sensation of agony. Avery clenched every muscle, fighting the pain, willing herself to move, begging her power to compensate for what her body couldn't provide.

But she couldn't.

The darts effectively wiped out any trace of her physical powers, the pain overloading her system until control was nothing more than a distant memory. She spasmed on the floor, helpless. A few feet ahead the main doors were still open to the world beyond.

That blue banner mocked her, its snapping corners striking her ears, stinging her mind, even as the world went black.

CHAPTER FOUR

"Could I at least get some reading material?" Finn rolled over on his cot to face the guard stationed at the doorway. "I've been staring at the ceiling for the past four hours."

The guard ignored him.

"It's the least you can do," Finn tried again. "I can't even use my blazing wristport."

Not that he really expected the soldier to respond. Finn had been trying to get someone to talk to him for the past twenty-four hours. Wherever they had brought him, there was zero connection on his comms. There were only a few places in the city built from the stone of the sacred mountains that blocked any signals from getting in or out. It's what had made the Nos Valuta base so secure, not to mention the Origin, deep beneath the city itself.

Where the blazar was Avery? She should have come through the Gate not long after they arrested him. He nearly grimaced thinking about what she would do when she saw the footage of those soldiers taking him from the building. Whoever gave the order had gone out of their way to make him a public spectacle, dragging Finn into the streets, media bots ready and waiting to broadcast the event across Echo.

It was a calculated move—meant to send a message.

Avery would be livid. Moons above, he hoped she didn't do something stupid. He had to find out what was going on.

He sat up, swinging his legs over the side of the cot on an elongated sigh. "Look, you can't hold someone captive without providing some source of nourishment. It violates the Intergalactic Conventions of 2362. And in case you haven't noticed, I haven't eaten since you guys dragged me in here." The soldier's eyes slid to him. Finn leaned back against the wall, adding lazily, "I'm more than happy to wait here while you fetch some food."

"Ignore him."

The guard turned and spoke to whoever uttered the brief sentence farther down the hallway in hushed tones. Finn leaned forward, trying to catch more of the conversation.

A boy appeared in the doorway, fully dressed in gray militia garb. The guard was gone.

Finn tilted his head, noting the young soldier's slight frame, green eyes, and bluish hair.

The kid frowned darkly under Finn's perusal.

Recognition hit, and Finn let out a bark of laughter. "Moons above, I'd know that frown anywhere."

"Meaning?" The boy straightened his spine, as though trying to appear taller.

"Petra," Finn replied flatly, coming to his feet, peering down the hallway behind him. "You're her brother, right? Tai?"

He nodded quickly, a lock of dark hair falling over his face before he brushed it away. His checked the hallway once more before moving farther into the room.

"I'm technically not supposed to be here," he said, his voice strained.

"Avery didn't send you?" Finn asked.

Tai shook his head. "I haven't spoken to them since they returned. Petra sent me a cryptic message but is lying low. Told me not to contact her. She doesn't want me involved."

Something tightened in Finn's gut. "What do you mean you haven't heard from them? What about Avery? Is she okay?"

"I think she's being held," Tai said slowly, his brows drawn. "I think they took her."

"Who?" Finn snapped.

Tai shrugged. "I don't know much of anything—just that Petra is back with the others and safe. And that Avery isn't with her. Command isn't revealing any of their cards to us lower ranks, but they've been rounding up humans for the past twenty-four hours. And even over the past week, things have been . . ." Tai trailed off, as though not wanting to voice his thoughts.

"Rounding up humans?" Finn took a step toward Tai, anxiety settling heavily in his chest.

Tai shifted on his feet. "Yeah. And your whole registration thing has made it pretty blazing easy to find them."

"Those records are sealed," Finn protested, his fists tightening. "Nobody should have access to them except government officials. They're meant to be used for coordinating relief efforts—exploiting that information could violate the treaty Avery negotiated, putting the entire thing at risk."

"I think that's the point," Tai said quietly. "For the past few days at least, things have been strange. Some of the commanders have been . . . more volatile toward the humans. Hateful, even. Like someone flipped a switch in them. Some of the soldiers, too. Even a few of my friends."

The first tendrils of real panic crawled their way up Finn's spine. Tai was scared. Finn cursed under his breath.

"But when I heard you were being held here, I figured I might be your best bet for getting information and getting out of here. Regardless of whatever Petra says, I still want to help."

Avery had said he was a decent kid—and it seemed she was right. He even went against his sister's direct orders. The trouble Tai would be in if someone found out he was there . . . Finn didn't want to think about it.

"So, your big plan was to, what, come talk to me, and we storm our way out of here together?" Finn asked with a grin, hoping to lighten the mood.

"Maybe," Tai acknowledged. "But I didn't realize how many guards they had stationed here, or how many humans they'd have in custody by now. The loading bay is filled with them, lined up on cots by the hundreds."

Finn ignored the pang of dread that tore through him.

How the blazar had the Elders organized this so quickly, and on such a large scale? If they were using the human registrations as a list, Finn had as good as handed over the humans on a silver platter. His blood froze. He was ashamed to have missed something like this building right under his nose.

He'd been back on Echo for a week, but he'd been so embroiled in the registration efforts that he wouldn't have noticed either way. It's not like he made a habit of visiting the Elders on a daily basis. That was Avery's domain.

The stupid communication blockade that prevented information from passing through the Gate was the worst idea they'd ever had. If the Elders were trying to undermine her efforts, it made sense for them to wait until she left the galaxy for her testimony. He never should have encouraged Avery to leave Echo.

"So they're holding all the humans here. Where are we, then?" Finn asked tightly.

"The sports arena—by the bay." Tai nodded to the small cement-walled room. "But you're being held on one of the lower levels. I think they use this for storm shelters or something."

"Okay," Finn said, his mind working. The bay. That was miles away from the city center, from the capitol building. If they had taken Avery, she would most likely be held there. He had no idea what they'd use to contain her—or how they'd even go about it in the first place. Her powers should have made her untouchable.

But if she was incapacitated, then he couldn't just sit around waiting for her to storm in and rescue him. He had to get his own ass out of this one.

"Here's what we're gonna do," Finn said, his voice low. "See what you can figure out from the soldiers here, but be discreet. The last thing I need is for you to get into trouble—Petra would shoot me outright."

"I was planning on it. I have some friends stationed here, so that at least gives me a valid excuse. I just have to—" Tai broke off with a gasp and brought his hand up to his temple as he winced.

"You okay?" Finn placed a hand on Tai's shoulder.

He pulled away violently, shooting a confused look at Finn.

"Easy." Finn lifted his hands, taking a step back. "What's wrong, kid?"

"I—I have to go," Tai replied stiffly, his breathing labored. When he turned to the doorway, his body was stiff. "I'll be back as soon as I can."

As Tai left, the same guard reappeared in the doorway, resuming his vigilant watch over Finn. In silence.

Finn rubbed a hand over the back of his neck.

What the blazar was wrong with that kid?

He knew Petra was a little sensitive, but Tai brought a whole new meaning to the word. Finn hoped he could count on him. Hoped he would be back. He couldn't see any other option for getting out, especially if the entire place was crawling with soldiers. Finn didn't even have so much as a toothpick to use as a weapon.

Markes and Linderly were still out there, though. They hadn't been taken into custody, he was sure of it. He grinned. Linderly had a hell of a mouth on her, cursing out those soldiers in the room as they handcuffed him and dragged him away. In the end, Markes was the one who had to hold her back. If anybody could organize a rescue, it would be those two.

Finn let out a hiss, realizing he should have mentioned them to Tai.

One thing was certain—he was stuck in that room for the time being. He would have to sit tight until he knew more or until Tai brought new information.

If Avery really was being held somewhere, he would have to figure out a way to get to her. Petra had to be doing something, presumably with Grigg, Nova, and Krez. Surely with all of them, they could find a way out of this mess.

The Reanges were rounding up humans—all of the humans left on Echo, from the sound of it. And it wouldn't be for humanitarian aid.

Finn sunk down to his cot, bracing his arms on his knees. Guilt twisted deep in his belly, tangling violently with his hunger until he felt nauseous.

As ambassador, Finn was responsible for every human on Echo. The faces of the people he met with over the past week, of the couples and families he had interviewed, flew through his mind. They had come to him for help and for safety, looking for a way to live in this new world or return to Earth. And all those efforts had blown up in his face.

Never once had he considered the Elders might use that information against them. And he *should* have considered it. Nick would have. He never missed an angle, not when it came to politics.

But Avery had been so confident, so certain about this path. Hell, even Finn had been fully on board with the idea. She had made so much progress with the Elders in the past months aiding the Council. What could have happened in so short a time to cause this change? She had only been on Earth for a blazing week. There was no way they could have coordinated this so quickly.

Tai mentioned the commanders in the military had seemed different. What if that meant they were being influenced? Could someone be controlling them?

Finn tangled his fingers together, tightening them to the point of pain.

Avery would need to be ready. If her position was being challenged, then she would have to fight for her place.

And when she needed him to act, he'd be ready.

Avery was falling.

Not through the air, but through some black void—some eternal stretch of nothingness.

Her body flew downward, swallowed whole by a shadowy weight. It fought her, holding fast to her limbs as she dropped.

She was choking. The thick darkness clogging her lungs until she could no longer breathe. The void pressed down on her chest, emptying her oxygen entirely, crushing her beneath its weight.

Avery clawed at the air around her, frantic, reaching out with her gift to try to harness something, anything, that would make it stop.

A voice filled her mind, both within and without her.

"I promise you, it's all right. I am not afraid."

A flash of red hair, the clear and present balm of a life fully lived, vibrant and alive and glowing with warmth.

And then it was gone—only the void remained, endless and dark and empty.

And then the nothing.

Always nothing.

Avery awoke on a strangled cry. She lurched up, gripping the sheets between her fingers, her ragged panting slashing through the quiet of the room.

Safe—she was safe.

The darkness didn't take her.

The adrenaline began to subside, leaving only agony in its wake. Tears brimmed, falling from the corners of her eyes as she gave into them, sobbing quietly, folding in on herself.

Fiora.

Avery let out a harsh breath, shoving the pain back down, locking it away in the darkness, where it couldn't touch her. Not when she was awake. Not when she was alive. She was safe.

Where had they taken her? She had been shot, by an electrodart no less. She had hated those damned things from the first moment she'd endured their effects nearly a year ago.

Avery growled, wiping away the remainder of her tears, and swung her legs over the side of the bed. She hissed at the cold stone floor under her bare feet. Someone had removed her boots. They sat neatly placed together by the door.

She had been left in a small room with no windows and a bed tucked in the corner. She moved to the wall, running her hand across the strange dark rock. It hummed beneath her fingers like it was alive, shimmering in the dim glow of the light affixed to the carved-out ceiling.

Where was she?

Avery opened her mind, searching for some hint of the outside world, for some glimpse of energy.

Nothing—she could feel nothing.

Panic crept through her veins, a cold poison that threatened to freeze her from within.

Nothing. Always nothing.

She tried again, straining her mind until it hurt. It was no use.

Avery backed toward the bed and sunk down to sit. She focused on her breathing, in and out, the slightly damp air filling her lungs in a cool refrain, bringing her back into herself.

What had Leviathan done?

The door beeped before opening, sliding into its pocket in the wall. Mylan stood at the threshold, two armed guards behind him, his graying hair almost black in the dim light. He met Avery's gaze with his calm assessment, hands clasped behind his back. When he stepped forward, the door slid shut behind him.

Avery's nails bit into her palms, her eyes narrowing. Power roiled in her veins, seeking an outlet, screaming beneath her skin. The light above them flickered, but Mylan didn't acknowledge it.

"How are you feeling?" he asked. He made a show of taking a seat at the small table by the bed.

"What has she done to me?"

"It's only temporary," he explained, before clearing his throat. "It is against our laws to maim a So', as I'm sure you know."

"And what about taking over our government?" Avery snapped. "Using our gifts to manipulate the Elders? Controlling Reanges beyond their free will? I seem to remember that being against our laws, too."

Mylan braced against the table. "Sometimes these things become . . . more complicated in practice than in theory."

Avery frowned. "What has she done, Mylan? In the Council chambers, I could feel it—they were different. The Elders' minds . . . They've been altered." He said nothing. Did nothing. "I thought she didn't have that kind of power any longer—isn't that why you needed me in the first place? Isn't that why you took me to the Origin?"

"You do not fully understand our situation," he replied calmly. Placatingly.

Avery's power rebelled against his tone, straining beneath her skin. The lights flickered once more as the air charged, growing heavy.

"This is our home, Avery. The planet is ours—*ours*. The humans have no right to it, nor will they ever. Which is why we must remove them entirely."

Avery sneered, turning away. "You sound just like her," she hissed.

"I know this may take some time to get used to—"

"Wait," Avery interrupted, whirling back around. Dread tore through her. "What did you say about the humans? What are you planning?"

Leviathan had led an extremist group for decades, one that had no qualms about disposing of human life. Avery had not forgotten her time in their camp and the sentiments she felt there. The anger. How it had frightened her.

"What is she going to do?" Avery breathed.

Mylan was quiet for a moment, as though choosing his next words carefully. "You don't know what we have been through—what she has lost. What we do, we do for the good of Reanges, and we hold no allegiance to anyone else. The things we've endured . . . the things I've seen . . . they cannot be undone nor forgiven. Our people have a right to survive."

"Survival does not mean kill or be killed. We must compromise— we must change." Avery's hands shook from the trapped energy vibrating throughout her system. Without an outlet, her power set the blood in her veins thrumming in an unfamiliar discord. She froze, her heart skipping a beat as she lost her breath. "Both of our worlds are evolving, and you cannot stop it. Not even *she* can stop it."

"Even if we could negotiate with the humans, Reanges would always suffer. They would always be at a disadvantage. The groundwork for suppression has already been laid. Leviathan is right in this at least: we are too different."

"And yet I'm still being held against my will in another cell. Only it's not the humans this time." Anger compressed in her stomach, turning rancid. "From where I stand, you're not unlike the Federation at all."

If she could keep him talking, maybe she could get a foothold on her power. Leviathan had done something to her telepathy, but Avery still retained her physical abilities. At least she had in the chambers above. Surely they were still there.

Avery tried again, harnessing the energy within her, trying to force it up from beneath her skin.

"That won't work. Not here." Mylan nodded to her clawed fingers. He ran a hand across the smooth wall, adding, "This rock is the rarest mineral on Echo. It emits a frequency that negates any powers a So' possesses. The original capitol building was made entirely of it."

"That would have been useful today," Avery muttered.

She hated the way he smiled at her words. Hated the way she still wanted to like him, despite his betrayal.

But her desire to fight was drained, her body close to collapsing. She felt weak—defeated. Avery hadn't been so depleted since the ordeal on the Port Station when she'd brought Finn back from death. Her powers had taken days to return.

Avery scanned the dark wall. Even now, she could sense its effects and feel that low humming, a gentle burning along the edges of her mind.

"There's very little of it left in Milderion. Yet another thing the humans took from us," Mylan lamented, pulling his hand away from the wall. He stood and headed to leave. A quick rapping on the door, and it opened.

"I'll let you rest." His words were clipped as he stepped over the threshold. He hesitated, before adding over a shoulder, "You *are* one of us, Avery. And no matter how difficult the choice, we must always choose our own. She will keep you in here until you agree to cooperate."

Avery turned away, staring at the black stone. "Get out," she spat. And he did.

CHAPTER FIVE

Two days.

Avery had been in that room for two days.

She had seen no one other than the guards that swapped out shifts at her door and Mylan. He came at each mealtime, doing his best to persuade her to join them. To get her to speak with Leviathan.

And each time, she refused.

Leviathan couldn't really think this ploy was going to work. Avery would rather be thrown into the nearest black hole than go along with their plans.

The longer she sat in that room, the more opportunity Leviathan had to wreak havoc on all Avery had built. The more opportunity the distorted Council had to infiltrate the minds of every citizen on Echo. Who knew how far Leviathan's reach had spread?

Avery never would have guessed the old woman had enough power to pull it off in the first place. In fact, she had gone out of her way to make Avery assume that. What an idiot she had been to believe her.

She should never have left Echo—should never have left it vulnerable. Had presenting her testimony in Klein's trial been important enough to trade the stability she had fostered in the last six months? The answer was a resounding no.

But then, Klein was just as bad as Leviathan. Maybe even worse. Condemning her was equally important for the future Avery envisioned.

If Klein walked free on Earth, if she regained her position as minister, the people of both worlds would still be at risk. The only avenue for change was in weeding out the leadership—rid the governments of those who had planted the initial seeds of distrust and dishonesty.

And if Avery didn't wield her power to help bring that about, in every capacity available to her, then she didn't deserve to have it at all.

No matter how many times she asked, Mylan refused to disclose what they had done with Finn. Only that he was being held somewhere. At least he was still alive. She would know if they had done something to him—Leviathan would make sure she knew. It was only a matter of time until the Elders used him as leverage against her. Until they dangled his life before her as incentive for her acquiescence to their new regime.

Moons help her, Avery wasn't sure she could resist something like that. If they hurt Finn . . . She couldn't bear to think of it. She wouldn't.

On the third night, Avery was drifting off to sleep when she felt it.

A tug—a gentle pull, somewhere deep within her body. It hummed, warm and bright, a direct line to her power.

She sat up in the small bed, listening. Something was calling to her.

No—it was yelling at her.

Something was coming.

She needed to move. It was now—she had to act now.

She pulled on her boots and was at the door in seconds, knocking with enough urgency that the guards opened it without question.

As soon as the hallway was revealed, the humming vibrated through her with greater intensity, warmth flooding into her body in a rush, releasing whatever had been trapped. Energy came alive under her skin, snapping and tingling down her limbs, straight into her fingertips. She took a deep breath, relishing in its rightness, in the relief of utter control.

She dipped her head to the two guards watching her.

"I'm truly sorry about this," Avery said quickly. She threw her hand out, sending a wave of energy that threw them both backward, slamming into the wall. They crumpled helplessly to the floor.

She paused, listening to the silence of the narrow hallways beyond. No one came. Frantically, she threw out her mind, searching for the presence of any Reange nearby. But again, she felt nothing.

Avery tensed. Somehow, she still remained blocked.

But at least she retained her physical powers. That was something—enough to get her out.

She moved quickly but took care to step quietly, following the corridors without any idea of who lay ahead or where she was going.

That hum continued to call to her—guiding her. It pulled her onward, connecting with that innermost part of herself, and she had no choice but to trust it.

Eventually, she came upon a locked door, which she picked easily with a simple touch of her hand and a snap of her power. It revealed a cramped stairwell that disappeared upward into darkness. Avery followed it.

She climbed into eternity as the stairway folded back and forth on each landing, until the muscles in her thighs were burning and her hair was plastered to her neck with sweat.

Finally, the stairs ended, bringing her to another door. She doubled over and clung to her knees, gasping for air as she tried to slow down her speeding heart. She could hear nothing but her own pulse flooding her ears with its steady throbbing.

The warm hum was gone now, having receded the higher Avery climbed. She was once again alone, left to her own devices to decide where to go next. She straightened up, pressing her ear to the door. She flinched as she heard the steady rush of cruiser traffic whizzing through the sky. It was an exit—direct access to the outside.

She glanced back down the stairs, the sounds of her panting echoing off the smooth walls and into the depths of shadow. What had that feeling been? What had guided her to freedom?

It didn't matter—she couldn't afford to go back and find out.

She pushed the door open and found herself in the alley that lay between the capitol building and the apartments beside it. The sun hung high and bright in the sky overhead. Avery squinted, placing a hand above her brow as she adjusted to the light. It hadn't been night at all.

Her absence wouldn't go unnoticed for long. The guards changed shifts every two hours, and she had no idea how long she'd been climbing those stairs. She had to get moving.

She tore through the busy city streets, oblivious to the presence of any Reanges she might have passed. It was alarming to be so disconnected. She didn't realize how much she had come to rely on her powers, even for something as simple as feeling those around her. It was like she had lost a part of herself.

She kept to the sides of the buildings as best she could, avoiding the open air and training her golden eyes on the ground. One look at them, and anyone passing by would recognize her.

After a few blocks, she turned a corner onto a side street, allowing herself to slow her pace. She needed to decide what to do next— where to go. There was no telling where would be safe, or where Leviathan wouldn't find her, but Gran's apartment had to be the best place to start.

A shadow passed overhead. Avery plastered herself along the wall and looked up. The street filled with a rushing wind, her hair whipping across her face as a silver cruiser descended on her, the circled emblem of the Elder Council embossed on its door.

Her throat dried. They had already found her. She pushed away from the wall, energy crackling at her fingers.

Fine—if they wanted to play rough, Avery was ready.

Planting her feet, she whirled around to face the cruiser, ready for battle. This time, she would go down swinging.

The door lifted open with a hiss to reveal a familiar face framed by dark blue hair.

"What are you waiting for?" Petra yelled, her voice carrying on the wind.

Krez's face flashed before Avery's eyes. The way he had been at war with himself before attacking her. The way his fingers had dug into her arm to drag her away.

Avery hesitated. What if Petra had been taken by Leviathan, too?

Shouts carried down the street from behind Avery, and she looked over her shoulder. A few soldiers had spotted her and were now fast approaching.

She had run out of time to debate loyalties.

Avery bounded toward the hovering cruiser at a full sprint, the craft already rising into the air. She leaped for it, pushing off the ground with enough energy to carry her body the rest of the way to the open hatch with her arm outstretched, reaching for Petra.

They locked arms, Petra's fingers cementing around Avery's wrist as she pulled with all her strength. Another hand grabbed her. Grigg. He hauled her inside, and Avery crashed to the cruiser floor at their feet.

The hatch closed behind them, and they lifted off into the rushing air traffic of the city. Avery peered out the window to the street below. The group of soldiers stared up at them, growing smaller as they took off into the skyway.

"Are you all right? Did they hurt you?"

Avery looked to the pilot's seat. "Lissande?" Avery gasped, her heart squeezing. "Where is Gran?"

"Waiting for you," Lissande replied over one shoulder. "She's been worried sick. I can't believe we found you."

"And the others?"

"They're fine," Petra replied.

Grigg helped Avery to her knees. "Lissande found us when we tried to head to your grandmother's—the place is being watched by the Elders. We've been at their safe house since then, trying to figure a way to get you out. But you came straight to us on our first scouting mission. Made our job a hell of a lot easier," he added with a laugh.

"Safe house?" Avery asked, still breathless. "What the blazar is going on? What has happened?"

"The Elder Council proposed and approved a new order while you were gone," Lissande replied, her cool voice steady. "They kept it quiet and didn't make any moves until the day you were due back. There was no way we could get word to you through the Gate."

"What order?" Avery asked, clawing her fingers into her thighs. *Finn.* If only Finn was okay, she could get through this.

Petra pulled up her wristport, casting a newsreel that floated in the air between them. The soft voice of the AI filled the bridge, a slight combatant of the eerie silence.

". . . their most recent move, the Elders have confirmed the arrest of Earth Ambassador Finn Lunitia. Seen here on holovid, Lunitia's arrest came after the recent approval of the Elder Order 456, which requires all registered humans still residing on Echo to be held in designated internment areas until further notice. This, of course, comes as a shock, as Lunitia has been leading the efforts to properly register any remaining humans on . . ."

Avery's blood ran cold, her pulse throbbing loud enough to overpower the commentary. She blinked slowly, trying to catch up with her own thoughts. In the holovid, Finn was being herded by two soldiers down the steps of an office building with his hands bound in front of him. Like he was some kind of criminal.

". . . will be kept at the arena camp, along with the other humans still residing in the city until the Elders deem the Federation threat to be . . ."

"Federation threat?" Avery bit out angrily, finding her voice. "Everything was fine when we left—the Elders were supposed to be on a hiatus until my return. I never would have agreed to leave otherwise. How did she manage to change so much in such a short amount of time?"

"Who?" Grigg asked, lowering his head.

"Leviathan," Avery spat, gritting her teeth at the name. "She's back. And fully in charge of the Elders."

Grigg ran a large hand over his mouth. "Shit," he murmured, eyes traveling back to the capitol building they had left behind.

Petra was silent.

Avery watched the tall buildings blur past them as they moved through the city, cruisers merging through the lanes of air traffic. Leviathan must have been planning this all along, from the moment Avery had freed Echo.

And Avery had as good as handed over the government by allowing Mylan to remain on the Elder Council. She had been a fool—an ignorant, naive fool. She wouldn't make that mistake again.

"Where are we headed?" Avery asked, her tone sharp.

"The safe house," Lissande replied. "Your gran and I were able to gather a few humans there, but it won't remain secure for long. Whatever's happening, whatever happened to the Elders—it's spreading."

"Spreading?" Avery asked, her stomach clenching. That off-kilter energy she had sensed when they entered the atmosphere, somehow it made sense now. Leviathan had bigger plans than just taking over the government, and dealing with the humans on Echo would be the first item on her agenda.

Avery looked to Grigg. "Where is Finn?"

He raised a brow and touched his temple. "Why all the questions? Can't you just read us?"

Avery choked on a reply. In her stilted silence, the cabin grew heavy, weighed down by her strangled emotion.

Petra tensed. When she spoke, her voice was rough. "Why can't we feel you?"

Avery shook her head, acid bubbling up her throat. "I can't," was all she could get out, tears blurring her vision. She dropped her gaze to the floor.

Grigg placed a hand on her arm, sinking to his haunches beside her. A tear slid down her cheek, and she wiped it away quickly.

Regret would do her no good now.

CHAPTER SIX

"How did you know they'd be coming for you?" Avery shifted in the wobbly chair, arms folded over the meager kitchen table in the tiny ground-level apartment.

The air was stifling, sticking to the walls of her lungs. The space had barely any airflow and certainly no windows to open. The entire suite of apartments consisted of a dingy living room with an adjacent kitchen, two bedrooms, and a barely functioning bathroom. During Federation rule over Milderion, the building had been used exclusively to house Reanges who acted as servants for vacationing humans. And "servants" was a generous description for what they endured.

There was no way Avery would have lasted longer than a week living there. She couldn't imagine entire families cramming into the tiny rooms, suffering through years of their lives.

But it functioned well enough for their needs, offering a space to hide. For now, at least.

Gran poured green tea into Avery's mug, steaming water nearly flowing over the brim. Despite the heat, the familiar habit soothed Avery's nerves. Her eyes followed Gran's movements as she repeated the ritual with the others around the table. Her hands were steady. Calm and capable.

"Lissande got word first," Gran answered her question, casting a soft look at the other woman across the table. She placed the teapot down before picking up her own mug. "We were lucky, really. Many of her patients are on the Elder Council. As soon as Leviathan reappeared, we knew they would move quickly. And I didn't want them to use me against you."

"We never dreamed they would go after Finn. Not this soon," Lissande added with a frown. "Otherwise, I would have done everything in my power to bring him with us."

Gran nodded. "I didn't even message him, worried it would expose us. The best choice seemed to be to wait it out until your return."

Avery rubbed a hand over her forehead. "Yeah, well, that didn't help us much, did it?"

Lissande explained tightly, "Whatever Leviathan did, it was imperceptible at first. I didn't think it would be difficult for you to root it out with your power. But it seems I was mistaken."

Nova leaned forward, asking, "You don't think she's controlling them outright?"

Lissande shook her head. "I think it's something more akin to perception manipulation. They're still themselves, just . . . altered. When I went back to my offices on that second day, it had amplified overnight. As though the Elders were ready to move on the humans already."

"There's no way she could directly control so many people at once," Gran confirmed. "Not at her age."

"Why didn't it affect you?" Petra asked, adjusting her shoulder against the cabinets behind her. "Or any of us, for that matter? We've been here for days, and I still feel fine."

"Perhaps proximity plays a factor? She's not controlling everyone," Lissande said.

"Just the major players," Gran supplied. "The ones with influence and power."

Lissande bit her lip, wheels turning behind intelligent eyes. "I wouldn't be able to draw any conclusions without proper testing. Unfortunately, my labs are all located on capitol grounds."

Avery tightened her grip around her mug, its warmth seeping into her fingers.

"Leviathan wouldn't do this," Petra said, so quietly that her voice barely carried. "It would break ancient law. To influence free will in a time of peace . . . It's blasphemy."

"Well, she *is* doing it, Petra," Avery snapped, ignoring the way Petra flinched. "The Elders have been changed. I felt it with my own power, felt the way they looked at me before she—" Avery lapsed into silence, strangled by her own anger.

Petra was a fool if she didn't realize what Leviathan was. After all they had seen. After all they had been through.

But Petra had been raised in the Origin. She had done Leviathan's bidding for years. Avery couldn't feel Petra from where she stood in the corner. Couldn't sense her emotions or read her thoughts. It was maddening to be so restricted.

Petra's jaw ticked, her eyes trained on the floor.

"You should know more than anyone how difficult it is to take away free will, Avery," Gran brought up firmly. "How much raw power it takes to accomplish it, and on a mass scale such as this?" She shook her head. "I can't see her having the strength to carry it out."

"Great," Grigg said with a loud sigh. "So, whatever she's doing, it's something new? Something we haven't seen before?"

It was Lissande who replied, "I've studied So' powers for decades, both on Earth and here with the Rebellion. Whatever is happening here is different. There's no live connection—no direct control."

"What are you saying?" Avery questioned, not following the insinuation.

Lissande didn't reply. She looked to Gran.

"Avie," Gran said delicately, "we think, on some level, at least, that the Elders wanted this."

Avery straightened in her chair until it dug into her back. "They wanted this?" she repeated, shaking her head. "No. No—you're wrong."

"But surely you must consider the possibility—"

"I said no!" Energy surged from her, and the lights above them dimmed, flickering violently.

The humans who were gathered in the living room quieted, looking warily toward the kitchen.

Gran held Avery's gaze, her cool gray eyes assessing, knowing too much, always seeing through her—even now.

Avery pressed a shaking hand to her forehead. "Look, I know she's responsible for all of this. And she did something to me. Something happened back there, and it wasn't just those blazing black rocks they locked me up in."

Lissande looked up. "What rocks?"

"How else do you think they kept me contained? They threw me in this room, somewhere deep beneath the surface, fully carved out of this dark stone. It was . . . strange. Shimmering and nearly black. Mylan said it was sacred. That it blocked my powers."

"And you think it did?" Lissande asked.

"As far as I could tell," Avery replied. She didn't mention anything of the warmth she had felt there—that deep hum that still resonated beneath her skin. That had led her out. It didn't feel safe to discuss it yet. Even with them.

"Avery," Gran said gently, placing a strong hand over hers on the table. "Even if we wanted to figure this out, we don't have any devices here for analysis. No tools beyond basic med kits. Not to mention an apartment full of scared humans whose lives are now our responsibility."

Avery looked to the living room. No fewer than ten people sat gathered on the couch and the floor. And another family of five in the extra bedroom. The youngest girl, no more than ten or eleven, had been staring at her since she arrived, peeking out from behind a curtain of curling dark hair. The rest kept looking her way, fully aware of who and what Avery was.

They were all hoping she'd do something. That she'd be able to get them out of there. And if she didn't, who else would?

"We can't just sit here and let Leviathan win. I won't let her," Avery countered. She looked to Petra. "You know her best of all of us here. What would she be planning to do with the humans?"

Petra glanced briefly at the humans, her body stiffening. She crossed her arms firmly over her chest, lowering her voice as she replied, "Nothing good. And if I had to guess, it won't take long for her to carry it out. She doesn't like waiting."

Avery's jaw tightened. All those innocent people had been rounded up because of her blazing registration plans. She and Finn had been the ones to spearhead it, had intended for it to make a difference, to do good for those humans left on Echo. And now it was their fault—this whole situation was their fault.

Petra was right. Leviathan would make those humans into a symbol. The Origin loved its symbols.

And they had Finn. They had taken him from her. Avery's heart lurched in her chest.

"I won't let her get away with this," Avery got out through clenched teeth.

"Even with your powers," Grigg said, shaking his head, "there's no way we can take on the whole militia. She's clearly got her claws in them, too."

"Avie," Gran said quietly. "Even Krez turned against you. We can't trust any of them right now, not with your powers so limited."

"So you're saying I don't have a choice," Avery replied, her throat catching. "That I can't fight."

"I'm saying you need help. Everything you know about your power comes from what Leviathan has taught you. From what she has shown you. Perhaps she has hidden things, too."

Avery stayed silent, frowning at her mug of tea. Steam curled up from the pale green water, twisting on the thick air.

Petra straightened, saying, "There were Reange factions on Earth. Refugees in practically every major city. It's why I was assigned to infiltrate the Federation—to look for So's there."

"You can't go back to Earth." Nova placed a strong hand on the table, her brows drawing down. "You'd be at the mercy of the Federation. Who's to say we could even find anyone willing to—"

"It might be the only way we can gather information outside of Leviathan's influence," Avery interrupted. "If I can get my full powers back, then we stand a chance at stopping this."

She wouldn't be able to take on Leviathan alone, maybe not even with her full powers. There was still so much she didn't know about what a So' could do. The best chance at regaining control on Echo was to try to find help that was just as powerful, or more so, than Leviathan.

"You think there are more So's on Earth?" Avery asked.

"Why do you think I forbade you from venturing to the Underground?" Gran pointed out with a tired smile. "I knew you'd get tangled up in this mess, one way or another. But I was hoping I could give you some semblance of a normal life for at least—" She cut herself off as her voice turned gravelly. Lissande took her hand, squeezing gently. Gran cleared her throat, continuing, "There was someone who controlled the Underground in New San Fran. I never knew for certain if he was a So', but there were rumors. No one could touch him—not even the Federation."

"Good." Avery nodded. "Then we have a place to start. If nothing else, at least this will get *you* off Echo and out of danger while I figure out how to fix things."

Gran's eyes flickered to Lissande and back.

Traveling back to Earth to search for some rumor of a Reange with powers sounded like an insane idea, even to Avery. But it was probably the only avenue she had at this point. She couldn't stay on Echo, not within Leviathan's grasp. If they caught Avery again, she doubted she'd be able to escape a second time. If there truly were So's on Earth, they could help her regain her powers and figure out what was happening to her. Maybe even return to Echo with her and help stop Leviathan. There was still a chance to reverse everything the Origin had done.

Avery would not let the Origin harm the humans. She was determined to usher in new peace for the two planets. And Leviathan had put that all at risk.

She had always suspected there would be others like her, more So's out there on Earth. She would just have to test that theory sooner than anticipated.

"Okay." Avery rubbed a hand across her forehead before tucking a loose strand of hair behind her ear. "But first things first—we're not leaving without Finn."

"They'll know you're coming for him." Petra stepped forward. "It will be ten times more difficult to—"

"Don't even try it, Petra," Avery snapped, grateful when she went silent on the command.

"Well, if we're going after him," Grigg said, raising a hand, his mouth pulling into a smirk. "I think I have an idea."

"I can't wait to hear this one," Nova groaned, a blonde brow rising.

Avery only grinned. "Then let's get started."

Later that night as the others slept, Avery was awake, full of nerves.

A thunderstorm had rolled in not long after they laid down to rest, and she had been unable to sleep through it. So, she had moved to the kitchen once more, sitting alone in the shadows of the night, hugging another warm mug to her lips for comfort.

She felt uneasy—incomplete and alone in her own head. The darkness sat at the edges of her thoughts, haunting her. The emptiness.

How quickly she had grown accustomed to being surrounded by thought and feeling, to losing herself in the emotions of others. The silence of her mind was louder than their presence had ever been.

She was letting them all down. All the promises she had made, all the ideas she had for a new world . . . They were falling apart, slipping through her fingers like crumbling lunar rocks.

Avery couldn't be sure what Leviathan and the Elders wanted with the humans they had captured. Maybe a new deal with the Federation, using the humans as a bargaining chip. Perhaps they would just deport them all back through the Gate entirely.

But Avery knew—that would be a best-case scenario. Wishful thinking.

Whatever Leviathan had planned would be worse. Much, much worse.

"Hot water and lemon." Gran's whisper chased away the shadows as she emerged from the dark hall, hugging a black sweater around her slight frame. Her hair trailed over her shoulder in a single gray braid, mussed from sleep. "You always loved that drink when you were little."

Avery smiled, her thumb playing with the handle. "You'd make it for me when I had nightmares."

Gran nodded and took a seat beside Avery, the chair creaking beneath her. When Gran spoke, her voice was frail. "You used to have them every night. After I got you out."

Avery looked up in surprise. Gran never spoke of that time—hadn't spoken of anything really since they'd settled on Echo. Not that Avery didn't have questions, but Gran had been so busy, it had never seemed like the right time. Gran's involvement in the Federation experiments wasn't exactly easy conversation.

"I used to worry they would never go away," Gran continued. "I can't imagine the things you saw. What you went through before they brought you into the labs." Her eyes drifted out of focus, her voice trailing to the barest hint of a whisper. "You were so small."

Avery reached out, covering Gran's hand on the table between them. Her fingers were cold, biting into the heat of Avery's palm.

Avery cleared her throat, willing away the prickling sensation in her nose. Gran never did well with displays of emotion. So instead of tears, she took a quiet, settling breath.

After some moments, Avery gathered the courage to ask, "Do you know where I came from? Who my family was . . . before?" As soon as the words left her lips, Avery wanted to take them back.

Gran was her family.

But still . . . there was a part of her that wanted to know, that wondered. . .

Gran's eyes were steely gray, softly melting, shifting into something like regret. "No, Avie." Her voice was hard. "I never asked about the patients they brought us—I didn't want to know. And after, when we left, I thought it best not to go digging. They would have found you sooner if I had."

Avery nodded, swallowing around the lump in her throat. She busied herself with the handle on her mug, her fingers running down its slope. Things were hard enough without her questions muddling them up further.

"I'm so sorry," Gran choked out. Avery couldn't bring herself to look up. "What I did, what I was a part of . . . I'll never be able to atone for it. And I never meant for you to have to deal with this—any of this."

"Gran." Avery laughed around her name, trying to lighten the mood. Like Finn would have done. "I've been through worse. Do you remember when Megan and I snuck out to that party our sophomore year? And we got stuck on ground level—"

"On the other side of the city," Gran finished, smiling and wiping her eyes. "I think I saw red when you comm'd me."

"I'd never seen you that angry before." Avery smiled, glad the memory had chased away the melancholy.

"That's because you girls could have been in serious danger. Ground level is no place for a fifteen-year-old." She shook her head, biting her lip as she remembered. "I never knew what kind of trouble you two would get into. Nearly drove me mad from fear some nights."

"Speaking of, I'll probably have you stay with her as soon as we get back to Earth. Her apartment—well, it's her brother's, but still—" Avery stopped herself, noticing the shift in Gran's expression. The walls that went up. "Why don't I like that look on your face?"

Gran straightened slowly, every line of her body turning to stone. "I'm staying here, Avery. I'm not going back to Earth with you."

Avery wavered. She would be unable to sway her—not with that tone of voice—not against that steely resolve.

Gran continued, "Besides the fact that I couldn't bring myself to leave Lissande again, we have the rest of the humans to think about." She peered over her shoulder, at the people they had rescued who were sleeping quietly in the living room behind them. "I will be of more help here. The need may soon come for a healer who cannot be controlled."

"But we can't get messages through the Gate." Avery braced her arms against the table, clinging to the stability. "If you need me, I will be out of reach." Just saying it aloud sent a shiver down her spine.

What good was all this power if she couldn't even protect the ones she loved?

"I'll be careful," Gran assured her. "And I'm strong—you'll need me here when you get back. I'm human, which means I'm the only one you can truly trust out of those who stay here. I'm the only one who can't be influenced by her."

Avery couldn't argue with the logic. But she couldn't bring herself to abandon Gran. Not after what it had nearly cost her before.

"I can't lose you," Avery whispered. "Not again."

They were silent for a few moments, listening to the quiet sounds of the apartment. The gentle snores from the living room, the rain pelting against the streets just outside the building, the muffled hum of cruisers making their way through the airways of the city.

Gran stood. She touched Avery's chin, tilting her face up. "I raised you to be strong, too. And you're brave—braver than me. If anyone can find a way through this . . ." She bent over, placing a gentle kiss on top of her head. Avery felt like a little girl again. "Get some rest. You'll need it tomorrow. All of you will."

And then she slipped into the midnight shadows of the apartment, heading to her warm bed and Lissande's side. Avery took the words Gran had offered, letting them fill her, until there was no room for doubt, no room for questions.

She *was* strong and brave—and there was no going back.

CHAPTER SEVEN

It took three days for Tai to return.

By the time he appeared, Finn had nearly gone mad from boredom and worry, certain that the kid had been caught sneaking in to see him. The day before, his guards had taken him on a walk around the arena, presumably to show him off to the other humans held there. They bound his hands, shoving him roughly through the hallways on the excuse of prisoner "exercise."

Hundreds, Tai had said. There were more than that—over a thousand.

Cots lined the hallways of the arena's interior, filling every available room, crowding them together without much space to do anything other than sit and sleep. And Tai had been right: the loading bay was even worse. The humans watched Finn as soldiers paraded him through, their eyes tracking his every movement. He met each scared face, doing his best to smile at the kids. But the adults knew the seriousness of the situation. Knew that if Finn had been taken, there would be little hope for them.

One family he recognized from the week before: he had registered them himself in that glass office in the city. Two mothers and their son. The boy hadn't been able to stop staring at Linderly's tattoos. Eventually she had sat down and let him run his fingers over her sleeves, keeping him occupied while Finn helped his parents with their documentation. He had promised them they'd have access to the first ship leaving back to Earth.

They saw him now, too, but neither of the parents said a word. Their eyes were trained on the heavy blasters strapped to his guards' backs.

That day, Finn had bitten his tongue until he tasted blood.

He'd essentially given up on Tai, deciding to find his own way out of this mess. Waiting around had never been one of his strong suits.

So when the door slid open and Tai stepped inside the room, Finn nearly fell off his cot in surprise.

"What happened to you?" Finn said curtly, jumping to his feet. "It's been days, kid."

Tai said nothing as he stepped into the room.

"Are you okay?" Finn asked, frowning. Still nothing. He rolled his eyes, muttering, "And here I thought your sister was tight-lipped."

"Don't talk about her," Tai growled.

Finn froze, his brows rising. "Did I miss something here? Come on, Tai. We don't have time to play around. What did you find out? I need to get the blazar out of here."

"If you think I'd help you escape, you're out of your mind," Tai replied savagely, his lip curling. "The Elders have assigned me to guard you, and I assure you, I take my duties very seriously."

Finn scratched his neck. What was going on here?

A few days ago, Tai had been ready to help, ready to figure out what was going on. Finn hadn't just imagined that. He studied Tai, those eyes that looked a bit too glassy, brows drawn down in anger, in fear. This wasn't the same kid.

"So just to clarify," Finn said slowly, "you're *not* here to get me out. Have I got that right?"

"Why would I ever help a human?" The question carried with it such hatred, such poison, that Tai nearly shook on the end of it.

Finn frowned. "I really thought we were over the whole 'humanity as an insult' thing. What is going on with you? What have they done to you?"

"They opened my eyes. We've dealt with the humans as a nuisance long enough. And on the next holy day, we'll be free of you—free of you all."

"First insults, and now riddles? Looks like my week just keeps getting better and better," Finn drawled. "Look, I don't want to hurt you, but I have no intention of staying here. The only reason I lingered this long was because I was waiting for you to come back. Now I see that was a blazing horrible mistake, so if you don't mind . . ." Finn took a step toward him.

Tai reached for the blaster on his hip. "Don't come any closer," he warned.

"What are you gonna do?" Finn said with a laugh. "Shoot me?"

The blaster was in Tai's hand before Finn could register. Damn, the kid was a fast draw.

Finn heard the shot before he felt any pain, the sensation both familiar and abstract. He staggered backward from the impact, falling against the cot as fire tore up the length of his arm.

"You shot me!" Finn yelped, clutching at his bicep.

"I only grazed your arm. Run your mouth again, and I'll aim for something less likely to clot."

"Moons above, you two really are siblings," Finn hissed through clenched teeth. He forced air in through his nostrils, staving off the queasiness that always came with a wound of this kind. He hazarded a peek beneath his fingers, blood oozing out between them, warm and wet.

Tai was right—he had just grazed him. Finn supposed it wasn't bleeding too horribly, wasn't even that deep. Not only was Tai quick, but he was a blazing good shot.

It still hurt like hell, though. Finn groaned, getting the pain under control and pushing it to the back of his mind.

"Let's cut the bullshit," he spat at Tai. "What the blazar is going on here? I deserve answers. Where is Avery?"

"You deserve nothing, human," Tai replied disdainfully.

"Didn't I just say I wasn't a fan of the whole 'human insult' thing?" Finn got out. "You're putting everything at risk by holding me—by imprisoning all those people out there. Avery isn't going to approve of whatever they're making you do," he tried to reason. He didn't let himself consider the alternative—that she might not be able to do anything about it. "As a matter of fact, she's going to be pretty pissed off about this whole blazing thing."

A loud explosion rang out from the hallway, followed by the sounds of cement walls crumbling. Tai whirled. Finn dragged himself to his feet, adrenaline spiking and mingling with the ache in his arm. The charged crackle of electrodarts echoed up the walls, followed by a few grunts of pain. There was shouting, the heavy reverberation of bodies slamming to the floor.

Tai knelt in the doorway, blaster at his shoulder, ready to fire. Whatever he saw down the hall made him pause. His eyes widened, his weapon lowering slightly, hesitation rippling through his body.

The blaster flew out of his hands, slamming into the wall beside him with a metallic clang and dropping loudly to the floor, leaving Tai utterly vulnerable.

Finn didn't waste the opportunity.

He pulled Tai to his feet, landing a solid blow to the jaw that laid him out flat. Pain radiated up his shoulder on the impact, the wound on his arm quivering from the muscle use. Finn couldn't bring himself to feel bad about knocking him out. At least Tai was short—he didn't have far to fall.

"Finn!"

He would recognize that voice anywhere.

Finn spun to face the door. He caught Avery in his arms as she vaulted across the threshold, the exaggerated momentum from her powers making them stumble backward in a tangle of limbs.

"Thank the galaxy," she whispered, her words a balm in his ear. She tucked her chin snugly into the crook of his neck.

Finn ran his hands down her spine, alarmed by the shock of pure warmth that coursed through him at the feeling of her body beneath his fingertips.

"It's about blazing time." He was surprised to hear his voice graveled. He cleared his throat, fingers gripping her waist.

"You're hurt," she said, pulling away.

It took everything in him not to pull her back.

"It's not that bad," Finn replied, clearing his throat again. "You never told me Tai was such a good shot."

Avery's heart leaped to her throat. "What is he doing here?" she breathed, looking over Tai's body on the floor.

Even Tai was on Leviathan's leash? It wasn't like him. In the months she had gotten to know him, she'd realized Tai didn't have the same fighting spirit as Petra. He was gentle—kind. He had been fully in support of the human integration, eager for change. She frowned, dropping Finn's arm.

"Petra is going to be—"

"What's taking so long?" an angry voice shouted from down the hall. "We need to move!"

"Does she follow you everywhere?" Finn mumbled, mostly to himself.

"The others won't be able to keep them distracted for long." Petra was winded as she entered the room. "Grab your human, and let's get the blazar out of here."

"Petra." Avery did her best to keep her tone level. She had no way to temper Petra's reaction—no powers to influence her, no way to even gauge her emotions. It was like flying without a nav system. "There's a bit of a complication. I'm gonna need you to keep yourself in check and—"

"Tai?" His name was a gasp on her lips as she dropped to the floor beside him. "What happened? Why is he here?" She looked angrily at Finn.

"Hey, don't blame me," Finn defended himself, bringing a hand to his chest. "He showed up on his own. And then he came back and was—well, it's a long story, actually, and as you've already pointed out so eloquently, we don't have time for it. He was sent to guard me. Direct orders, apparently."

Avery locked eyes with Petra. Even without the merge, she knew her thoughts.

"They knew we were coming," Avery stated.

"I don't like the sound of that," Finn said, his voice tightening. "What the blazar is going on?"

"We have to go," Avery replied, picking up Tai's discarded blaster. She grabbed Finn's hand, pulling him behind her.

"Avery." Petra's voice was a plea, strangled and nearly broken.

Avery halted. Her blood was frozen. But she couldn't look back— she knew Petra would still be there, kneeling beside her brother.

They had enough to deal with just trying to get Finn out. Dragging an unconscious body along would only slow them down. Not to mention the fact that when he woke up, he'd most likely be a problem.

"We can't leave him here." Petra was immovable.

Finn's hand tightened around hers, and she looked up at him. He gave her the barest hint of a nod. Why did he always seem to know her decisions before she did? One corner of his mouth tilted upward.

"I'll carry him," Finn said flatly, walking back to them. Petra helped hoist Tai up to a seated position.

"Don't be ridiculous," Avery interjected, following him. "My power can hold most of his weight."

"Or it can help us fight," Finn retorted, wincing as Petra maneuvered Tai onto his back. "Given the two options, I'd rather have you clearing a path than hefting a kid through the halls."

"What makes you think I can't do both?"

Finn winked at her. "I have every faith in you, sweetheart, but I get the impression we're trying to not kill anybody. That means a little finesse is in order." He bent forward, draping Tai over his shoulders. "Let's go," he added with a grunt and stood.

Avery nodded. They would lose more time debating it anyway.

Avery took off down the hallway toward the service entrance where they'd find stairs to the open-air arena. They were lucky Finn had been kept near the back of the structure in solitary confinement. They'd been able to avoid most people on their way to him.

And the fields in the center of the facility were the best place to land a ship, the quickest avenue for escape. The guards would be expecting them to try to head out the front, not go deeper into the building.

After a few minutes, they reached the stairwell and started climbing. By the time they cleared the top floor, Finn's panting was a loud interruption of the otherwise quiet surroundings. Avery leaned against the wall, her palm settling on the handle of the door.

"What are we waiting for?" Finn wheezed. He shifted Tai on his shoulders, wincing again.

Avery brought a finger to her lips. "The signal," she whispered.

"As though we could hear anything over his mouth-breathing." Petra moved to the other side of the door, watching the stairs behind them, searching for any signs of pursuit.

"I don't know if you've noticed, but I just carried your dead weight of a brother up five flights of stairs," Finn snapped between pants. "Would it hurt you to throw a little 'thank you' my way?"

Petra leveled him with a look. "Yes."

"Would both of you shut up?" Avery leaned farther into the door. "I can't hear anything." At least they both had the decency to look embarrassed. "What is taking him so long? Grigg knew the timeline— they should be here by now."

"Wait, *Grigg* was in charge of the signal?" Finn asked.

Avery nodded.

"Whose idea was that?" He shook his head, a low chuckle bubbling up from his lips.

"Is something about that funny? Nova is the better pilot. It only made sense to—"

A loud boom sounded, rocking the building. The walls shuddered violently, tremors reverberating through the floor, turning it to near-liquid. Avery shot out her hands, encircling them in a bubble of energy and neutralizing the vibrations that threatened to knock them all off their feet.

A second later, the lights flickered, and they were plunged into total darkness.

CHAPTER EIGHT

"What was that?" Avery asked slowly, adrenaline surging through her.

Finn moved closer to her in the dark. "*That* was Grigg's signal."

Petra let out a strangled sound, suspiciously close to laughter.

"What?" Avery's question echoed harshly down the stairs. "I told him to cause a diversion, not blow the building apart!"

"Yeah, he's never been good at the whole stealth thing," Finn replied. "You should have left that to Nova."

The emergency lighting flickered on, illuminating them in a soft blue glow. Finn was grinning at her. She rolled her eyes.

"Then let's move." Avery opened the door, and bright sunlight poured over them, blinding her momentarily.

"We've got company," Petra warned, just before the shouts of pursuing soldiers floated up the stairwell.

"Don't shoot anyone—we don't know who Leviathan is controlling," Avery reminded her. The last thing she needed was more Reange blood on her hands. Avery squinted at the open arena beyond. There was no ship. Only open acres of dirt marking the playing field, surrounded by the oval of empty seating and a startlingly blue sky above it all. She shifted on her feet. "Where the blazar are they?"

Blastfire ricocheted up the walls behind them, and Avery hazarded a look over her shoulder. The hallway lit up with flashes of blue and white, dark burn marks scarring the cement in long smearing streaks of black.

Petra pulled an electrogrenade from her belt, tossing it down the stairs. Its rhythmic beeping mingled with metallic clangs as it tumbled toward their pursuers. The crackling sound of electric netting reached them, followed by the painful cries of those unlucky enough to have been caught in its range.

Avery grimaced. "Do you have to use those?" They weren't lethal, but the pain was unbearable. She'd had enough experience with electro weaponry to last her five lifetimes.

"They're effective" was all Petra said. She tucked her blaster against her shoulder and aimed down the stairs, ready for anyone who had made it through.

"Is that *my* ship?" Finn asked, confused.

Avery whipped around. The large gray vessel circled the sky, dropping onto the center of the arena. Finally.

"Let's go!" Avery tore through the doorway, running at full speed across the packed dirt toward their single avenue of escape.

She could only pray that Nova and Grigg were piloting it—Avery couldn't exactly reach out with her mind to verify who was onboard. If she had full use of her powers, she would have known for certain how many were on the ship, and who they were. She could have done so for the entire city block, for that matter.

For now, she was forced to rely on faith.

She threw a glance behind her. Finn lumbered after her, but Tai's weight slowed him down significantly. Petra trailed them both, half running backward to keep an eye on the doorway to the stairs.

Avery pushed forward, calling on her power to drive her feet faster. She had a good lead on the others, reaching the ship almost exactly as it touched down. The hatch was open, the ramp fully extended as it slammed into the ground. The impact shook the field beneath their feet.

"Avery!" Finn yelled in alarm.

She slowed, whirling to face him just in time to see Finn drop a squirming Tai to the ground. He was awake.

Tai jumped to his feet, struggling against Finn who was trying his best to subdue him and drag him to the ship. They grappled, falling to the dirt in a tangle of limbs. Finn's injury put him at a disadvantage.

Petra reached the two, pulling Tai off Finn. But he got a solid kick to her chest that sent her sprawling.

"Get inside!" Grigg bellowed, suddenly beside Avery, shoving her at the ship. He didn't stop to see if she obliged, passing her down the ramp at a dead run, headed straight for the others.

Avery had to think quickly. She no longer had anyone in her head to guide her—no longer had their shared experiences to inform her choices. She didn't even have time to properly weigh the options.

Movement caught her eye. She looked past Finn and Petra, back to the doorway they had left. Soldiers filed out, taking formation on the field in a line of gray uniforms, blasters ready and aimed—straight for them. A few shots rang out, but they missed, clanging harmlessly against the hull of the ship.

Avery gaped at the burn marks on the hull, and her breath caught. They weren't electrodarts—the soldiers were actually shooting to kill.

She turned to the soldiers pursuing them, trying again to reach them telepathically. But there was nothing. No sign she had ever even had the ability to begin with.

Avery had no choice.

She launched herself into a sprint back to the field, using her power to take each stride farther, covering more ground than should have been possible. She passed the others in seconds. She heard them call her name. Heard Finn tell her to stop.

In moments she was in front of the soldiers, halting a few feet before their line. Dirt swirled up and around her, clouding the air between them. They stared at her, uncertainty—perhaps fear—staying their actions. At least she still could inspire awe. Maybe it would allow her to reason with—

A shot blasted, heading straight for her.

Avery raised a hand, spreading energy from her core, bracing for the impact.

The blastfire halted against her palm, warm and tingling and harmless. She blinked. She had caught the blast entirely.

She turned her hand over, clawing the little ball of shimmering yellow light. It vibrated against her skin, a tingling burn that tickled her fingers, running up the length of her arm.

She frowned. They had tried to shoot her—*her*.

With a growl, she threw the blast up into the stands of the arena. It blew apart a few seats, which started a small fire that sizzled in the silence.

The soldiers paused, terror plainly written on their faces. Avery didn't like it—being feared. This wasn't what her power was meant for.

But she couldn't hesitate now.

She rushed forward, relying on her training to guide her.

Avery leaped at the nearest soldier, coming down to chop his neck in a move that rendered him instantly unconscious. Still floating in the air, she whipped around to slice a dropkick on the woman beside the first soldier. The woman fell to the ground, clawing at the dirt as Avery flattened her with a fist of energy. She stilled, passing out from the crushing weight.

The two remaining soldiers lunged at Avery, and she leaped up, carrying her body higher than before, above their heads. She twisted, a spinning kick catching both soldiers in the temple with her booted feet. They both fell to the ground, motionless. Avery landed in the dust, catching herself with one knee on the field.

"Behind you!" Petra shouted.

More soldiers had reached the top of the stairs, now using the door as shelter. They fired. Avery threw up a hand, deflecting the blasts into the stands as more seats blew apart in their wake. She stepped forward, sweeping an arm across her chest, pulling the door shut with her power. It slammed against the frame with a loud metallic clang.

Avery twisted her wrist, and the door crunched inward, crumbling into a mangled mess of metal. They wouldn't be opening it anytime soon. She turned on her heel, running for the others.

Finn and Grigg pinned Tai to the ground, his legs flailing in the dirt, struggling to free himself. Petra stood over him screaming, her face furious.

"We don't have time for this." Avery jogged over to them.

"I am so glad you said that." Finn followed his comment with a hard jab to Tai's face.

He went limp.

"Did you have to do that?" Petra scolded, helping Grigg lift Tai to his back.

"Yeah, I really did," Finn replied. He grabbed Avery's hand and took off in the direction of the ship, dragging her with him.

Their feet hit the ramp as it lifted from the ground, clunking up the metal grates and into the belly of the ship. Grigg dropped Tai's weight, and Petra sunk with him to the floor. She cradled his head in her lap, smoothing a long lock of blue hair from his forehead.

Avery was suddenly in Finn's arms, surprise melting away from the pleasure in her belly. She tangled her arms around his waist, closing her eyes, leaning into him.

"Don't ever do that to me again," Finn whispered into her hair.

"Worried about me, Lunitia?" she asked, grinning. She indulged herself in his warmth for a few more seconds before pulling away. Her body felt cold. "Grigg, help Petra secure Tai." She inspected Finn's wounded arm, wincing. "I need to get to the bridge with Nova. Do you need help patching that up?"

"I can do it."

Markes's voice drew Avery's eyes upward. He was already vaulting down the stairs from the curved upper deck.

"Where did you come from?" Avery almost laughed.

"You didn't think Linderly and I would just leave Finn to rot, did you?" Markes joked, his wide smile filling his face. "You told us to watch out for him, remember? Besides—I kind of like having him around. Even if he is a human."

"Kid, you are absolute shit at compliments," Finn said caustically. But he reached out to shove Markes's shoulder playfully, and they both laughed.

Avery bit her lip on a smile. "Is Linderly with Nova?"

Markes nodded, pushing Finn off him. "Hacking the surveillance feeds so we can get out of here undetected. Let me see that." He reached for Finn's arm.

"It can wait," Finn said. He turned to Avery, his head dipping.

"Those soldiers tried to shoot you—why did you only use your physical powers back there?"

"I'll explain later," she promised, backing away for the stairs. "We're not out of danger yet."

CHAPTER NINE

"You're telling me the Origin has control of Echo now?" Finn couldn't keep his voice from rising. His fingers tightened on top of the dining table. "Didn't we already do the whole 'overthrow a sadistic tyrannical government' thing once? In case you guys don't remember, that didn't go so well for me the first time around."

Avery's eyes met his, their golden depths dimmed, uncertain. It rankled him, made him want to protect her from whatever—or who-ever—had done this to her. And he wasn't used to that feeling any-more. It had been a long time since she needed saving.

And he couldn't shield her from this, even if he tried.

"Well, we've still got your secret weapon, so you should rest easy," Grigg commented dryly.

"Some secret weapon I'll make now," Avery said, too softly. "I don't even have full use of my powers."

"I think those soldiers whose asses you kicked would disagree—you looked pretty blazing powerful to me," Finn joked, trying to in-ject some lightness back into her. She was too hard on herself. He couldn't bear it.

Ever since she had taken the new position on the Elder Council, she had struggled with the weight of that responsibility. It was like the more time she spent on Echo, the worse she treated herself.

And Finn had no idea how to help.

He definitely understood the urge to take things too seriously. His own position as ambassador came with a heavy dose of burden.

Especially as he tried to aid peace negotiations with Earth. Especially now that it had all gone to shit.

Images of those humans back in the arena flashed through his mind. That family and the promise he had made to them. The way they had watched him being shoved through the halls, fear and uncertainty shining in their eyes.

His jaw clenched. His father would be ashamed of him. Nick would be ashamed.

No—Nick was gone.

Another memory surged through him—Nick's battered face covered in his own blood; Finn's knuckles covered in it, too. Something sharp slashed across his chest, robbing him of breath, and he suppressed it, locking it away before it could take root. He ignored the way Nova watched him, tensing across the table.

They had always known the Origin would resurface. He and Avery had discussed at length Mylan's participation in the newly formed government. Ultimately, they had assumed it would be a way to demonstrate cooperation with all parties. Finn should have advised against it.

But he never thought it was too great a risk—her powers made it nearly impossible to hide anything from her. None of them could have predicted that they would strip a part of her gifts away. They never even knew it could happen at all.

Avery may not admit it to herself, but she had come to rely heavily on her abilities. They allowed her to immediately understand everyone around her. She could meet someone and within seconds know how to reach them, how to sway them.

And she had built her new reality around that gift. She was building the new government around it. She facilitated the Elder meetings by opening the channels between them, letting empathy drive the conversations, letting connection dictate their votes.

This could break her.

She would be more fragile than even she realized. He wasn't sure she could handle any more stress.

Finn placed a hand on the table, saying delicately, "I don't think going to Earth is necessarily the best step forward. We should stay here—try to find help in one of the outer cities. We can't just leave the humans to the Origin's devices."

"If there was help on Echo, if there were other So's here, we would have found them a long time ago," Petra argued. "There is no other option but to leave."

"Of course you'd say that," Finn sneered, his temper rising with each word she spoke. "You've never given a shit about the humans, and now you're—"

Avery stopped him. "Finn, I've already decided." She pressed a hand to her forehead, leaning against the surface of the metal table. "I don't want to leave them vulnerable either, but Petra is right. There is no other choice right now. The only conversation I want to hear moving forward is about logistics."

Finn lapsed into silence, his jaw tightening. She had even less power on Earth than she did on Echo. Just going back for their testimonies had been dangerous enough. And the planet was in transition, with unrest and conflict in every major city.

But Avery was clearly not up for a conversation about it.

Finn leaned back in his chair, crossing his arms over his chest.

Nova cleared her throat. "I received word from the Federation. They've approved your request for entry."

Finn's head snapped to Avery. "You already contacted them?"

The others went quiet at his outburst. Except for Markes, who whispered loudly in the corner with Linderly as though nobody else could hear it. Finn shot a glare at both of them, and Linderly kicked her brother's leg before distancing herself from him.

"I told you, I've already made my decision." Avery's tone was clipped, hard like glass, but just as breakable. "How long before the jump?"

Nova tilted up her wristport. "A little over an hour. But this docking station should be safe until then, thanks to Finn's cloaking code. It's the reason we risked our necks to steal this ship back in the first place."

"Risked *our* necks?" Grigg asked indignantly. "I'm pretty sure I'm the one who got beaten nearly to death trying to access the hangar."

Nova leveled him with a cool look. "You survived, didn't you?"

Markes snickered into his hand. Grigg bristled.

"Actually, we're lucky you're so bad at stealth," Linderly pointed out brightly. "While I did have to cover your tracks breaking in—really, you should do a better job checking the security layout next time—at least it alerted Markes and me to your location."

"Was that an insult?" Grigg asked, genuinely confused.

Finn and Nova shared a look before bursting into laughter. Linderly grinned sweetly, merely shrugging her shoulders.

Grigg sulked, sinking farther into his chair. "I don't see what's so blazing funny."

"That's what makes it so good," Finn got out between chuckles. He gestured to Linderly. "Looks like all that time with me is really paying off. She's one of us now."

He caught Avery's gaze. She smiled, shaking her head at him, her eyes lighter than before. The small gesture sent Finn's stomach somewhere down to the floor.

But within moments her smile was gone, and she turned to Petra, sobering. "Is Tai awake yet?"

"I gave him a sedative," Petra replied, stiffening. "Until we can decide what approach to take with him."

"You drugged your own brother?" Finn muttered. "Why am I not surprised?"

"It could be valuable to speak with him," Avery said, ignoring Finn's comments. "He might have more insight as to what happened."

Finn leaned forward. "Something was definitely up with him. He came to my cell the day after they took me and seemed like himself. He was going to find a way to get me out." Petra's eyes widened as he spoke. She looked almost . . . vulnerable. "He didn't come back again until this morning, and he was entirely different. He couldn't even remember our conversation. Like he became a human-hating extremist overnight."

"Just like the others," Markes murmured. Linderly leaned against his shoulder.

"That's not Tai," Petra added bitterly. "He's different. Gentle."

Finn cleared his throat. "He also went out of his way to let me know he'd been assigned to me. *Specifically* to me."

Avery looked to Petra. "You were right—they knew we'd be coming."

"Sounds like they were counting on it," Nova said.

"There's more." Finn frowned. "He said something about the humans they were holding—how they'd be rid of them for good. By the next holy day."

Avery's breath caught, the lights briefly dimming in the wake of her emotion before she reined herself in.

"What does that mean?" Grigg asked, looking to Nova.

"The next holy day—that would have to be the full moon alignment."

"Su'elben," Petra confirmed, her mouth a thin line.

Avery's eyes flickered around the room. "Remind me again which one that is."

"It's a sacred holiday, intended to celebrate the ritual of renewal. It's not observed so much anymore in the old ways, but we took it very seriously in the Origin," Linderly explained softly. "Generally ritual sacrifices are made."

"You can't be serious," Avery scoffed.

Markes was quick to clarify, "She means offerings. But the more you give up for the offering, the better, so we often refer to it as a sacrifice."

Nova shifted forward. "If that's our timeline, then we've only got—"

"Ten days," Petra bit out.

"Shit." Finn ran a tense hand through his hair.

Avery leaned heavily against the table, rubbing her temples. "We've got to figure this out," she said quietly. "I don't understand how Leviathan could have that much power. She wasn't supposed to have anything left." Her shoulders slumped, and Finn's heart lurched.

He bumped her knee with his. She looked up at him, eyes weary. "We'll find the answers we need, sweetheart. We'll get through this.

Just like we always do." He smiled at her, and she gave him a shaky smile of her own in return. At least it was something.

Petra stood. "I'll go check in on Tai." Her words were as clipped as the sound of her boots on the floor as she stalked out of the room.

Nova rose, too. "I'll head back to the bridge—make sure the drives are all checking out for the jump. Linderly, I could use your help if you're up for it?"

"Absolutely." Linderly bounced into the hall.

Nova stopped short on the threshold, looking back at the others. "Grigg, you coming?"

"Nah, I'm kind of hungry." Grigg pointed at the food stores. "I'll probably whip up something to—"

Nova cleared her throat, jerking her head suggestively.

Finn rolled his eyes. *Subtle. Real subtle.*

"Why are you grunting at me?" Grigg asked, confused.

Finn couldn't prevent the chortle that escaped from his mouth.

"Oh. Right." Grigg stood too quickly, his chair scraping against the metal floor. "I think I'll go help Nova with . . . something."

"I guess that's my cue." Markes stood awkwardly, waggling an eyebrow at Finn. He gave Avery a little mock salute and went to follow the others.

And then Avery and Finn were alone together.

The air tensed. Silence stretched.

He pushed back his seat, walking around the table to stop in front of Avery. She didn't look up.

He took her hand and pulled her to her feet. Her fingers were cold as always. Her eyes flickered to his, a flash of pure gold, bright and glowing. Finn's heart tripped over itself.

He took her other hand, holding them both at his sides. She was shorter than him—he had forgotten how much.

"Hey," he breathed.

She rolled her eyes with a laugh. "You're ridiculous."

"Since when?"

"Since always." She still wouldn't look at him. "It's really becoming—"

He cut her off as his lips found hers, silencing her with a kiss.

Her mouth was soft, slow to respond as he deepened the caress, searching her, exploring everything he had missed. He kissed her for all those nights they had spent apart, for the way she called him ridiculous, for the startling beauty of her eyes.

Her fingers tightened in his hands, tangling with his, and she pressed closer, coming up on her toes to meet him. His gut flipped over, and he angled his head, the kiss changing, evolving into something deeper. Something primal.

And she met him for all of it, wanted all of it.

Finn was the one to pull away before it went too far, resting his forehead against hers, their bodies flush, their rough breathing mingling together. His hands had found her hips somewhere along the way, and they tightened into her clothes. Her fingers were threaded through his hair. She tickled the skin on his neck, the feeling distractingly delicious, running straight through him.

"You were saying?" Finn said breathlessly.

"I was?" Avery asked, tilting her head back.

"Something about how romantic I am, I think."

"Must not have been very important," she drawled, a smile blossoming on her face. She paused before saying, the words quiet and soft, "I missed you."

He pulled her to him, wrapping his arms around her, rubbing his chin on the silk of her hair. "I missed you, too, sweetheart." They stood that way for a while. Finn would have been content to do so for millennia. But his thoughts were racing, no matter how fervently his body ached to hold her. "Are you sure we should do this? Go back to Earth?"

She stiffened, separating herself from him. He balled his hands into fists rather than reaching for her again.

"I told you, I've already decided." She crossed her arms over her chest. Her lips were red, swollen from his kisses. "Don't make me say it again."

He bit his tongue. It wasn't like her to run from a confrontation. She hadn't done that for a long time. "This feels like a shot in the dark," he said softly. "Kind of like you charging into the middle of that arena and rescuing my sorry ass. We barely got out of that one."

"And who taught me to act first and think later?" she pointed out harshly, her tone raw. "You've never been one to second-guess your split-second decisions. It usually pays off for you. Why can't I give it a try?"

"That's not exactly the same thing."

"Why not?"

"Because I'm not you." He should probably stop talking. But silence had never been one of his strengths. "You're too important, Avery. I take risks because I'm the only one *at* risk."

"You have responsibilities now, too," she reasoned, her face flushing. "You have a position, as much as me."

"True," he acknowledged, trying to keep his voice level. "But an entire world depends on you and your gifts. If something were to happen—"

"What was I supposed to do?" she said forcefully, choking on her words. "I couldn't just leave you there. We have no way of knowing what she has planned or what she would have done to you. I couldn't just leave you," she repeated.

"Avie," Finn said gently, taking her hand again. "We've been through this before. When the time comes, you choose them. It always has to be them."

Her eyes shimmered, molten gold and angry. Clearly, she didn't agree.

"I shouldn't have to choose." Her voice was immovable. "And it will be fine—after this meeting with Klein, we'll have a free pass on Earth."

"Meeting? What meeting?" Finn frowned. "Avery, tell me you didn't agree to sit down with that woman."

She didn't answer, instead biting her lip. And that was answer enough.

Finn groaned, running a hand through his hair. "Whose idea was this? No, don't answer that. I know nobody in our crew would agree to it—this was all you."

"And it's a blazing good idea," she said defensively. "The Federation won't be able to touch us as long as all eyes are watching. And Klein can't do anything, with the vote so close. She wouldn't dare rock the boat now."

"And you think that will stop them?" Finn let out a sharp laugh. "You don't walk straight into a Dectarian lair and expect them to come out with all your flecks intact."

Avery blinked. "I don't know what that means, but yeah, I'm pretty sure I can."

"And why is that?"

"Um, what part of the 'I can stop blastfire with my mind' thing have you forgotten?"

Finn rolled his eyes. "That doesn't mean you're invincible."

"It has so far," she countered. He couldn't tell if it was a joke.

He sputtered, looking for words, but he couldn't seem to make his brain function cohesively enough to form any.

"Look, just . . . just trust me, okay?" she pleaded. "I've gotten us this far, haven't I? The added publicity will only help sway the popular opinion against her. It will give us a chance to really impact the vote—beyond our testimonies and your interviews."

"I thought the whole point of this thing was to get your powers back."

"It is. But if putting myself in front of the media is what it takes to keep us safe, then I'm going to milk it for all it's worth."

Finn stared at her, mulling over her words.

Of course he would trust her. He would follow her anywhere—across the universe, if she asked him to. They were bound together, in a way that couldn't be undone.

If they were going back into the public eye, then he'd have to deal with questions about Nick and his disappearance. Again.

When in reality his brother was probably dead—by Finn's own hands. Shrugging off his absence in every interview over the past month had been a living hell. Every time he stepped in front of a camera, his soul screamed.

But he would do whatever it took to stay with her, just like the rest of their crew spread throughout the ship. They were family now, every one of them.

And it was all the family he had left.

CHAPTER TEN

Petra stared at Tai. He was unconscious, lying on the cot in the small room that served as a makeshift brig. She'd been the last person locked up in that very room. It seemed like a lifetime ago. She had been a different person then, with different beliefs and different goals. And that had all changed.

Because of Avery.

Petra made a fist against her leg. There was still a breach between them, leftover from Petra's betrayal so many months ago. She was furious with herself, with her own actions. They still haunted her, the wound as fresh as the day she had hurt Avery.

She should have been honest about her involvement with the Origin from the start. Avery would never be able to entirely look past that association. She was too good of a person—truly honest and decent. She would not tolerate extremist antihuman views. Not from anyone.

Even though Petra had shifted allegiances and chosen to follow Avery completely, there would always be this thing between them. Uncrossable. It was excruciating.

And Petra hated herself for it.

Tai groaned, his head rolling from side to side on the pillow.

She moved closer to him, touching his arm. He was good, too, even if he tried to hide it behind bravado. Petra knew he was different than her—kinder.

And that was what Petra had always wanted. For him to live a normal life, to keep him shielded from the realities of the war. She had done her best to protect him their whole lives, even when they were kids. It was what drove her to enlist in the Origin's ranks in the first place.

While Petra had found a home among the extremists, she knew it was no place for Tai. So she made a deal—one that would keep him safe. But the Origin never forgot a debt. Never forgot to mark your weaknesses.

If the Elders had sent Tai to guard Finn, if he had changed into this violent person overnight, it was intentional. Leviathan wanted her to know she still held power—that she was still in control. She was sending Petra a message.

Tai was within her reach, and she wanted Petra to know it.

Petra stood, pacing across the room. When she came up on the port window, she braced against it, her fingers pressing into the cold glass. Leviathan had done something to him.

The way Finn described Tai, the very idea that someone had meddled with his mind, made Petra want to rip Leviathan apart. Yes, she believed in the So's' authority. In their right to command the Reanges. But not like this.

Avery had shown her a different reality.

The So's could lead instead of command. It was unlike anything Leviathan had ever taught any of them, and Petra valued it more than her own life. If this was the path forward into their future, then she would follow it, and gladly. Even if it meant living alongside humans.

A vision of blonde hair and blue eyes flashed through her mind, making her stomach drop. Petra's grip on the window frame tightened.

Megan.

Petra kept thinking about her. Couldn't get the human woman out of her blazing head. Petra and Megan had grown close during Avery's recovery, bonding over their love for her following their confrontation with the Federation. Despite Petra's misgivings, Megan had come through for them. A human had helped them take down Minister Klein. When their friendship began to shift, Petra was helpless to stop it. Attraction had blossomed between them before Petra even realized it was happening. And she had done everything she could to avoid Megan once that started.

Megan was everything Petra hated in a woman: feminine, vain, and hot-tempered—stubborn, to a fault.

But Megan fought for the ones she loved. She had fought for Avery.

And she was human. *Human.*

As though that mattered now. Not in Avery's new world.

But if Megan ever found out what she was—what she had been. The things she had done . . .

It was probably just as well that Megan had returned to Earth. Petra certainly hadn't tried to stop her, and she had avoided her while Avery was there for the trial. She would be safer there anyway, far from the uncertain fate of the humans on Echo. Far from Petra.

"How is he?"

Petra jumped, whirling around as Avery entered the room. Her heart ached, guilt swirling in her belly as she tried to shut down her thoughts.

But Avery couldn't read her mind anymore.

Relief surged through her then, loosening her limbs at once. Petra had forgotten what it was like to not have to hide her feelings.

"He's fine." Petra smoothed down her shirt with her hand. "Still out."

"That's probably best for now," Avery said gently from beside the bed. She was worried. Petra could see it in the stiff lines of her face. "What do you think we should do with him?"

"Whatever you think is best." Petra's voice came out strangled.

Avery cast an amused smile at her. "Really? So if I wanted to turn him over to the Feds as a known associate of a terrorist organization, you'd be okay with that?"

Petra's eyes widened briefly before she released a breath of relief. "You're joking," she confirmed, laughing softly.

"Of course I am." Avery leaned over and bumped Petra with a shoulder. "You know we'd never do that. He's family."

Petra didn't reply. She couldn't. She didn't deserve the kindness—

any of it.

"Thank you," she managed, her words stilted. She didn't like feeling this way. Was desperate for it to end. Perhaps the loss of Avery's telepathy, the forced separation of their connection, would dull her feelings.

Avery was silent, but the air in the room changed, charging with some kind of electricity, turning heavy. Her physical powers had become more potent since losing her telepathy. Petra wondered if she had noticed.

"Let's hope it will wear off," Avery said at last. "Whatever Leviathan has done to him . . . maybe distance and time will help."

"I can't believe he shot Finn." Petra couldn't keep the grin from spreading across her face. Maybe Tai was tougher than he looked.

"You don't have to sound so amused," Avery chastised.

"I can't help it." Petra laughed. For some reason, she wished Finn were there to make fun of. "He probably deserved it."

Now Avery smiled too. "I don't think I've heard you laugh in a long time."

Suddenly Petra couldn't breathe. Avery's words had knocked the oxygen right out of her.

"You haven't been yourself in a while." Avery sighed, rubbing a hand across her forehead. "But then, I guess none of us have. All the stress of Earth and the trial, and then to have this . . ."

There wasn't anything Petra could think of to say. So she remained silent.

Avery was one of the few people in the world who was fine with Petra's propensity for silence. She didn't pester her to talk. For all the changes in their relationship, at least they still had this.

After some time, Avery spoke. "You know it's just going to get harder. This plan. And what I have to do."

Petra frowned. "We," she amended.

"What?"

"What *we* have to do," Petra said slowly. "We're still in this together. All of us."

Avery grinned, and it lit up her whole face. The gold of her eyes shimmered. "Thanks for the reminder."

They stood there together, watching Tai's breathing in companionable quiet.

Avery finally stood, heading for the door. "Keep him sedated. I don't want him waking up until we're through the Gate."

When she was gone, Petra brushed a lock of hair from her brother's face. He looked pale.

She had never thought her choices would affect him negatively. She'd only ever wanted to give him safety, to give him a home again. Surely they deserved that much.

And now she was dragging him along with her into the middle of the fray. Some older sister she'd turned out to be. Her mother would never forgive her. She had broken her promise.

But Petra was lost to the Origin forever now. While it had given her purpose for so many years, she could never go back to them, to that life.

Still, the rejection left her feeling empty. Without that burning hatred, she didn't even know who she was.

She sniffed, clearing her throat and reaching for the box of supplies on the table beside the bed. She pulled out a sedative patch and secured it to the softest part of Tai's forearm, rubbing her fingers over his skin to ensure full contact.

It would keep him out for as long as Avery needed.

The crew gathered in the bridge an hour later, anxious to move. Avery glanced nervously at Finn as he entered the room. His hair was mussed, as though he had just woken from sleep.

He had taken her advice to rest—that had to be a first.

Avery was irritable, her temper laser thin. She hated that Leviathan could do this to her. That even after everything, she was still at someone else's mercy.

Finn was right about one thing: going to Earth was a risk. Of course it was. Avery would be stupid not to realize that. But it was the only way forward. There was so much she still didn't know about her own powers. And if there were others on Earth who could help her realize the true extent of what she was still capable of, then she would gladly embrace the danger of finding that out.

But she wouldn't gamble with Finn's life, and she didn't regret getting him out of there, no matter what he said about the choice. She didn't need Petra to tell her Leviathan would have made quick work of him. He would have been killed. Of that she was certain.

And Avery loved him.

She loved him so much that it scared her. She would never be able to choose anything over him, not even her life—not even her duty to her people.

And he wouldn't want that. He would never understand it if she made that choice.

No one would.

We must always choose our own. Mylan's words haunted her.

Her eyes tripped over Finn's, and he grinned, that dimple deepening. With a quick wink, he brought a flush to her cheeks.

"Are we all set?" His voice was confident, any indication of exhaustion gone. "Ready to pass through the sphincter of the universe?"

"You have the humor of a five-year-old," Grigg chastised from his seat against the wall.

"I've seen you both fall into fits of hilarity over a joke about space-rat excrement," Nova stated in a low voice. "I don't think either of you have room to judge the other's humor."

"I resent that," Finn protested.

"So do I," she countered, pressing a hand to her chest. "Who do you think has had to listen to it for the past ten years?"

Avery grinned, moving to Petra at the controls. At least those three had fallen back into their normal routine with ease.

"Are you ready?"

Avery jumped and peeked over her shoulder to find Finn close behind her. His blue-gray eyes were vibrant and endless, like the watercolor fabric of the darkening sky outside the window.

She nodded, turning her attention back to the nose of the ship.

His hand brushed against hers, their fingers entwining. He squeezed gently, grounding her.

Her face flamed. The others were definitely watching them. But she didn't pull away.

When Finn was with her, she didn't have to go through things alone. She had forgotten. The knot in her chest eased.

"Let's go," Avery said calmly, nodding to Petra. "We've only got one shot at this, so let's make it a good one."

"Got it." Petra initiated the sequence, her hands slipping into the vibrant blue holocontrols that wrapped around her fingers. "You guys might want to sit down."

They strapped in quickly as the ship pulled out of the hangar, merging seamlessly with the traffic of the city.

Finn's ship was too large to mingle with the other city cruisers for long without notice, so Petra took them higher immediately. They pushed through the lanes layered on top of one another as they flew up, away from the rising towers of Milderion, until the only thing ahead was graying sky. It quickly melted away into the blackness of space, stars winking into existence ahead, the three moons standing out in stark relief against the black backdrop of space. The Gate loomed in the distance, the huge ring isolated, waiting for them to sail through.

"Almost in the clear," Petra said. It would take a few minutes to reach it, and then they'd have to hail the regulator from the Port Station on the other side to open the connection.

Just then, something crashed into them with a loud blast, rocking the ship. Avery gripped her seat, the Gate slipping out of view as they careened off course.

"You just had to say something, didn't you, blueberry?" Finn ground out.

"That was a fighter blast," Markes said.

"Whose?" Grigg gripped his seat, angling for a better view. "Echo doesn't have any space units."

"Whoever it is, they're on our tail." Petra twisted her hands to bring the ship around. "We might be able to make it to the Gate in time, but—"

"It's a Federation fighter class," Linderly supplied, typing furiously at the controls in front of her monitor to bring up the sensors so she could survey the damage. "Approaching from the rear."

"But how?" Nova asked. "All the Federation troops pulled out months ago."

"But they didn't take all their weapons," Finn said ominously.

Avery shivered at the implication. The Origin must have taken control of the leftover Federation tech. They were now equipped for a war of their own.

"Damn it," Grigg muttered under his breath.

"The blast hit the loading deck," Linderly said warily. "It took out the warp drive."

"We can't make the jump without it being operational." Petra was focused on evasions, her voice strained.

"No shit," Finn confirmed, already unbuckling himself.

"Where are you going?" Avery demanded, watching his movements.

He struggled to stay on his feet as another blast hit them, rocking him to the side. "To fix it." He tore off down the hall, pushing away from the wall as momentum carried him into it.

"Get back here! Finn!" she called after him, but he was gone, already out of sight.

"I'll go," Nova said, unbuckling to follow.

"No." Avery held out a hand to stay her. "You're the next best pilot after Petra; I want you here. Call ahead to the Gate and get them to open the portal. We'll need them to be ready for us. I'm going to get that idiot."

"You can't—"

"Markes, Grigg, you're both on guns," Avery said, ignoring Nova. "But only if absolutely necessary. We will not kill anyone unless *absolutely necessary*. Is that clear?"

"No murdering. Got it." Grigg nodded sharply, pulling out the side panel that controlled the artillery functions. Markes was at his side in a moment to man the secondary controls.

Avery took off down the hallway, following its curve around the centered living quarters. Her boots clanged heavily on the metal floor, the motion of the ship threatening to throw her off her feet. She countered the momentum with her power, steadying herself into some semblance of a run. Reaching the rear stairs that led to the cargo bay, she vaulted off the platform, easily lowering to the floor with a cushion of energy.

"Finn!" She raced to the large cylinder that served as the ship's engine. It was hot there, so close to the pulsing heart of the ship, and a fine sheen of sweat broke out across her forehead. "Finn, dammit, where are you?"

Metal clanged from below her feet, a grunt of pain following.

She fell to her knees and poked her head inside one of the open grates in the floor panels. He was tucked within, his large frame barely fitting in the hole he'd revealed.

"Are you a blazing idiot? I told you to stay on the bridge!" she bellowed. She scanned him for injuries, which was difficult considering she could only see the top of his head. His arm was shoved into the wall of wires, buried up to his shoulder.

His head turned up to her, eyes widening. "Why did you follow me? I told you I was going to fix it!" he yelled.

"You're going to get yourself killed!" she yelled right back. "Get out of there right now."

"I've almost got it," he grunted, his face contorting. He struggled to squeeze his hand farther into the wires, but his broad frame barely fit in the cavity below. He'd never be able to get to the drive.

"I'm serious, Finn, get the blazar out of—"

Another blast rocked the ship. Avery slid across the floor, slamming into the steel cage that protected the engine's core and knocking the air from her lungs. Finn cursed loudly from his hole just as smoke began to billow from it.

Avery scrambled on all fours back to him, leaning over the edge to grab the collar of his jacket. With a solid heft and a good bit of her power, she lifted him up in a single motion. He fell on top of her, his weight pinning her to the floor.

He didn't move.

CHAPTER ELEVEN

"Finn?" Avery ran her hands over his arms, fear strangling her throat at his silence.

His head cocked to the side as he leaned up on his forearms, lifting most of his weight from her. "If you wanted to get me horizontal, all you had to do was ask."

She rolled her eyes, pushing him roughly away with enough energy to slam him into the panels behind.

"Ow," he said dryly, rubbing his head. "I don't know what's more hurt, my pride or my back."

Avery was already back to the floor panel, choking in the smoke from the electrical fire. She closed her eyes, focusing on the molecules circulating in and around the wires below. Reaching out a hand, she swept it backward, pulling the air out entirely with her power. The fire extinguished immediately.

"Forgetting something?" Finn said caustically. Avery looked at him. He held up the drive, one dark eyebrow raised in question.

"Why didn't you say you got it out?" she snapped as he knelt beside her.

"I can't help it if I like watching you work." The ship shifted violently, sending them crashing together again. Finn grabbed her shoulders, steadying them both.

"Can you repair it?" she asked quickly.

"The wiring melted straight through," Finn replied. He bent his head over the fist-sized metal piece. Sweat dripped down his temples, turning his hair black at the nape. The engines were working overtime to keep up with Petra's maneuvers. "If I can just . . ." He concentrated on the small opening in its side, his large fingers surprisingly adept. He began to pull the blackened bit of yellow wire apart, cut it away with his teeth, and tossed the ruined section to the floor. He stripped the coating off with his nail, rejoining the raw wires with a deft twist.

"We need to solder them," he said, holding them out to her. "Do you mind?"

Avery held her hand over the wires, envisioning the molecules that connected them, drawing heat together and weaving them until the binding was secure.

"That'll have to do." Finn lowered himself to the ledge of the opening.

"No." Avery stopped him, a hand on his arm. "I can reattach it without even touching the component. They need you back to the bridge."

"No chance, sweetheart." He shook his head. "I'm not leaving you here alone."

"They need proof that Ambassador Lunitia is with us—that was part of the deal I made with the High Council for passage. And the last time I checked, that was you."

"What?" he snapped, frowning. "Why didn't you tell me that before?"

"It didn't seem relevant until now." She snatched the drive out of his hand, a rush of power sending him sliding across the floor to the stairs. "Go!"

She didn't wait for his response, jumping into the hole herself, her boots landing with a hard thud. It was cramped inside, considering she was shoving her body into a cylinder of wires beneath the floor. She didn't know how Finn's large frame had fit at all.

She looked around, found the hole Finn had been digging in, and shoved her own hand in amid the components. Why did they put one of the most integral pieces of the ship behind all this blazing wiring? Her arm was fully extended, but it didn't reach the hook up. She was short by mere inches.

Avery closed her eyes, inhaling deeply. She grasped the drive in her mind, focusing on the wiring around her, ushering the ball of metal through the air. It brushed against the components, knocking clumsily without connecting. She cursed. Trying again, she twisted it, and at last it clicked into place.

The drive surged to life with a gentle hum, the ball shimmering with green light from within.

"Thank the moons," she whispered. She tugged her arm out, debating how to let Petra know they were ready to jump.

But Linderly must have seen the drive was back online and operational.

Before Avery could even pull herself out of the floor, gravity surged around her as the ship shot forward. Her body slammed against the wires at her back, the journey through the Gate ripping her apart at the seams. It was much more violent than passing through on a huge cargo transfer, the folds of space roughening their passage through the controlled wormhole, shaking the small vessel until Avery worried it would break into pieces.

And as soon as it had begun, it ended.

Everything went quiet, still. Avery panted heavily, leaning a sweaty forehead against the warm metal beside her.

They had made it through.

"Avery, you better get up here." Petra's voice ricocheted off the ship walls, breaking the silence. A broadcast from the bridge. "We've got trouble."

Avery stared wide-eyed at the fighter ships that surrounded them. There had to be at least a dozen of them in formation, blocking the path to Earth. Her breath came in heavy gusts, still winded from running across the ship.

"Those are Federation ships," Finn said tensely. It set her on edge.

"Can't we catch a break?" Grigg slammed a hand on the paneling beside him.

"What do they want?" Avery asked Petra.

"They sent a comm as soon as we came through," she replied and played the generic holovid recording. "It's an official escort into atmo."

"And presumably all the way to Alexandria," Nova added.

"Klein." The name was a curse on Finn's lips.

Avery whirled. "But she couldn't. The inquiry—"

"Is a formality at this point," Finn finished. "We may have blocked her from any legitimate government action, but nothing prevents her from welcoming foreign dignitaries."

"Is that what you call this?" Avery gestured back to the window. "A welcome party?"

No one replied.

"What do you want to do, Avery?" Petra asked.

Avery's mind raced.

If they allowed themselves to be taken to Earth by the Federation, they could be signing up for extended custody. She'd never be able to find a So' after that. She would never make it back to Echo—even if Klein was voted out.

But wasn't a very public arrival exactly what Avery had wanted? Making a scene in front of the media would ensure their safety. She just hadn't considered that Klein would want the same thing. There's no way this could serve any benefit to Klein.

Of course, the ships outside could be there for the opposite reason, sent to escort them to the surface in secret. And if Finn was right—if the inquiry hadn't made her entirely powerless—then they were still at risk.

Regardless, they didn't have a choice. If they tried to escape, Avery couldn't guarantee they'd make it. Her powers were stronger, yes, but could she block fire from a fighter ship? She didn't want to have to find out.

"Avery?" Finn had moved closer—so close she could feel the heat emanating from his body.

Finn. He was the best card in their hand right now. Avery had nearly forgotten. She turned to him, a smile playing on her lips.

He tilted his head, a lock of hair falling over his brow. "I'm not sure I like that look you've got."

"Are you ready to prove your worth?"

His eyes traveled her up and down. "Always."

Somewhere behind them, Markes made gagging noises. Nova and Grigg laughed. Linderly sighed.

Avery's face filled with heat.

She pushed his shoulder, shaking her head to dispel the warmth he had made her feel. "You're hopeless," she muttered weakly. "Put your game face on. We'll need the ambassador for this one."

She saw something passing over Finn's eyes, but it vanished before she could identify it, replaced by an easy grin. "Anything my So' commands," he replied, a hand over his chest.

"I'll keep that in mind." To Nova, she said, "Contact all the major media outlets. Those vid bots need to be on us the moment we enter atmosphere. I want them to know we're coming."

"I hate to burst your bubble, sweetheart," Finn drawled, "but I just got done with a media tour on Earth. I think they're a little sick of me by now. Could be difficult to drum up much enthusiasm for my face as a selling point."

Avery grinned. "Then we'll just have to give them something extra to talk about."

"Finn, darling, when I heard you wanted to speak with me, you know I just *had* to drop everything! I was crushed—absolutely crushed—when your publicist told me I couldn't have more than five minutes with you last month. Imagine my surprise when you messaged *me* for a change!"

"You know me, Mixtie," Finn said, laying it on as thick as possible. "I'm always full of surprises."

He couldn't believe this was Avery's brilliant idea. To call up the biggest celebrity media reporter and offer an exclusive interview on the fly. Finn knew it would be hell for her.

"Speaking of . . ." Mixtie's eyes lit up as he motioned to Avery, the pink lace cuffs of his shirt fluttering with the gesture. The camera zoomed in on her, showcasing Earth floating peacefully behind her and Finn, clearly visible through the wide observation window. They were still off planet, hoping to draw attention before even entering the atmosphere. "Do tell me about this delightful little turn of events that has the galaxy's most eligible bachelor sitting next to its most eligible bachelorette. I need to know *all* the details."

Finn casually slung an arm over Avery's shoulders, replying easily, "After everything we've been through, we thought we'd take a small break." Avery leaned into him, nestling perfectly into his side. Finn didn't have to fake the flush that warmed his face. "Get away from the pressures of our new positions for a while."

"Oh, I can only imagine. I haven't gone so long without a trip to our little vacation planet in ages! I have to say, I am missing those Echo beaches right about now. But it must be an absolute nightmare dealing with all those responsibilities—how are things settling over there, Avery?"

"It's definitely a challenge," Avery agreed with a nervous laugh, her tone stiff and awkward. She'd have to do better than that if she wanted sensationalism. Finn stroked a thumb across the exposed skin of her neck. Her eyes widened, and she tensed.

Not that Finn could blame her. He'd always hated doing these damn interviews—hated playing this game. Even though he was good at it, Finn had never wanted the role. It was Nick who had insisted on him mastering the rules in the first place.

Finn had wanted to make a real difference; to play a substantial part in the revolution that Echo had needed to survive. And ultimately that desire had led him straight to Avery. She had accomplished more in the twelve months or so he'd known her than Finn had been able to in his twenty-three years.

But even if he didn't want that role, Finn had learned to work the press to suit his own needs. And right now, Avery needed him to show off what he'd learned.

"She's being modest," Finn added, tossing an adoring look at Avery. "You have no idea, Mixtie. Juggling the politics and the pressure, not to mention the outrageous expectations. She's phenomenal." Avery looked up at him, her luminous golden eyes boring straight into him, pulling him down into their molten depths.

For a moment, Finn forgot where he was. Forgot that they were being watched by millions of viewers. He forgot everything but the familiar lines of her face, the patterns of freckles across her nose, and the way the fire in her eyes stirred up every quiet corner of his soul.

"Is it just my imagination, or do I feel sparks through this vid screen?"

Mixtie's joking voice brought Finn's head swinging back around to the host, vision clearing.

He covered the sincerity of the moment with a laugh, running his free hand through his hair. "You're not far off," Finn confirmed, with a wink at Avery for good measure. She bit her lip, a wry grin tugging at her mouth.

"Does this mean we can finally discuss this little piece of gold I've been sitting on since last year's Petralias?" Mixtie asked, just seconds before a vid popped up on the screen, eclipsing their faces.

Finn knew it was coming—dangling the vid as bait was how they got Mixtie online with such short notice.

Broadcasting live, to a viewership of millions, was footage from last year. Finn saw himself with Avery and Petra, dressed in evening finery amid a crowd of similarly glamorous partygoers. Even now, the sight of her in that green dress made his breath hitch. And in the next moment, Finn watched as he pulled Avery into his arms to kiss her.

The kiss went on. And on.

A grin tugged his lips. Had they really gone at it that long?

The Avery who sat by him now stiffened. He brushed his knee against hers; the best comfort he could offer.

"Can I finally confirm that this was you with our lady Avery after all?" Mixtie asked slyly, digging for dirt. "You firmly denied anything other than professional association with each other during your interviews last month. As a matter of fact, your people did everything they could to suppress this footage."

"We just wanted a little space. You know how things are," Finn replied, shrugging off the question.

"Oh, of course," Mixite said, adding a solemn nod of his head, black curls falling over his smooth face and too-high cheekbones. "I can imagine things are especially tense with the racial conflicts here on Earth. Have either of you considered speaking on the subject?"

Finn paused. He couldn't believe Mixtie would bring up politics in a social interview. He certainly never had before, not in the decade Finn had known him.

"What do you mean?" Avery replied before Finn could stop her.

"Only that with the demonstrations and unrest across the globe, even the bombings, it could be good for your fans to see you standing strong together—human and Reange. Uniting the species, as it were." He delivered the hard-hitting implication effortlessly, a bright smile spreading across his face. As though they were discussing what designer had styled them or what model of ship they were flying.

Finn locked his arm around Avery, a signal for her to stay silent. He grinned at the camera. "We don't have any such plans at the moment. Our priorities lie with Echo. We are just here on Earth for some much-earned relaxation time."

"Goodness, traveling to Earth for a vacation." Mixtie laughed loudly, a high-pitched guffaw that grated on Finn's nerves. His teeth were blindingly white. "I've never heard anything so absurd! You live on the most beautiful planet in the universe, darling!" After more laughter, he sobered, leveling Avery and Finn with a mock-serious face. "Come now, surely you have an opinion on the Citizens Liberation Front. Do you support them and their efforts? Do you think they're behind the bombings?"

"Mixtie," Finn warned.

"Oh, come on, Finn. I'm merely looking for a story—you can't very well blame me for doing my job."

"The only thing you're digging for is sensationalism."

"Oh, Finn, I'm hurt!" Mixtie exclaimed, clutching a hand to his chest, long black nails pressing into his vermilion jacket. He followed with a cackle and waved. "Who am I kidding? I love sensation and so do my viewers!" He swiftly turned to face his camera, his audience. "But let's set the record straight once and for all: Are you two an item?"

Avery leaned forward. Her voice was full of teasing mirth as she said, "If he plays his cards right."

It surprised Finn enough that he looked down at her, one eyebrow raised. She raised her own back at him, throwing in a bubbly tilt of her head. She was playing the game. Beautifully.

Finn's stomach flipped, his lips twitching.

But some of his anxiety melted away. Even if Mixtie asked about Nick, Finn suddenly knew he could handle it. He could handle anything with her by his side. He wasn't alone in this anymore.

Another flush crept up his neck.

"Moon above, is that a blush, Finn Lunitia?" Mixtie screeched, making Avery wince.

Finn's face flamed.

Mixtie had caught a rare moment of authenticity from Finn, and he knew it. "Why, Avery, you are going to be good for business." His excitement was palpable, even through the vid screen.

Finn leaned into Avery, attempting to hide his embarrassment from the cam with a nonplussed smile. "Go easy on her, Mixtie. The whole reason we're doing this interview is to satisfy your voracious appetite for gossip."

"Oh, but this is barely an appetizer, and you know it, you little tease," Mixtie purred. "I want to know all the dirty details about your romance. Falling for each other in between the intrigue and politics on a foreign planet? I can't imagine!" He let out a gasp of delight. "Go on, tell us: Did you sizzle from the moment you met?"

"As a matter of fact, I couldn't stand him," Avery said plainly, and Finn let out a bark of laughter at her candor. Finn's mind strayed to the first time they had really met. She'd threatened to shoot him.

Even then, he had known that she'd be important. And not on a "save the worlds" scale. But important to him. Essential.

"But that's the thing with Finn," she continued, nudging him with a playful shoulder. "He grows on you."

Finn didn't have to force the adoration that colored his face, gazing down at her head tucked neatly into his shoulder. He knew Mixtie would eat it up.

Nova caught Finn's eye from behind the cam, where she had been focused on the tablet in her hands. Linderly perched on the table beside her, smiling like some besotted teenager. Which Finn supposed she was. They had long ago kicked out Grigg and Markes, who couldn't stop laughing as they went over talking points.

Nova gave him a small smile and nodded.

Their plan was working. The Federation ships were pulling away, making room for the news bots that were headed for them, eager to record their descent to Earth. With any luck, they'd be tailed all the way into the city. They'd be able to get ahead of whatever Klein had been planning.

Finn had to take control of the interview. "As much as we'd love to get into the details, we have a few other interviews to get through, so I'm afraid we'll have to cut this short." If he didn't watch it, Avery would learn how to work the press better than him. And then what would she need him for?

"Oh, Finn, you can't be serious!" Mixie complained. "This was barely even a chat!"

"I know, I know." Finn grinned. "We'll set something up for an in-person sit-down, I promise. No rest for the beautiful."

Mixtie's pout turned to a sardonic smile as he thanked them, and Nova cut the feed before the intrepid gossipmonger could ask anything else.

"How was that?" Avery sat up to face him.

Finn grinned, cupping her cheek. "Not too shabby, sweetheart. We'll make a celebrity out of you yet. You handled that subject change beautifully."

She frowned, her eyes darkening. "Do you think we should be worried? About the bombings, I mean. What if our presence does more harm than good—stirs up more violence? Klein could use that to her advantage."

"What's the alternative? To hide?" Finn countered, his temper flaring. "Change doesn't come quietly—we have to rip it from their hands by force. I won't be cowed into submission by fear or any other means, and neither should you. I'll never hide what I feel for you."

She flushed, dipping her chin.

Finn suddenly felt awkward, embarrassed by his passion. But it was true. He would fight for Avery. Fight for their future. Some speciesist bigots weren't going to stop them. Even if they had to change the whole world in the process.

Avery asked Nova, "And the coverage? Is it working?"

"Top trending story," Nova confirmed, pulling up the feeds on her tablet and casting them to a hologram in the center of the table.

Linderly read out excitedly, "'Echo Ruler and Playboy Ambassador Officially an Item, Return to Earth for Love Nest Getaway.'"

Finn grimaced. "'Love nest getaway'? They really couldn't come up with something better?"

"Oh, that's not even the best one," Linderly replied excitedly, scrolling through the incoming coverage. "'Native and Human: Star-Crossed Lovers,' 'Finn Lunitia Finally Commits!'"

Finn groaned in disgust. "Do *not* let Grigg see these," he warned.

As if in response, raucous laughter echoed from the hallway. Markes and Grigg were suddenly having a hell of a time.

"Too late," Avery said, giggling as she stood. She saw Finn's face and laughed harder, dragging him up to his feet. "Don't worry, I'm sure they'll let it go. We've all got bigger things to worry about." She leaned in close, whispering in his ear words that stole his breath: "And I love you, too."

When they reached the bridge, Grigg was giddy, riding high on Finn's embarrassment.

He read the headlines aloud the whole way down to the surface.

CHAPTER TWELVE

F inn was reeling.

"You didn't even give yourself time to acclimate? Moons above, Avie, we just got off a major broadcast an hour ago. You were shaking from that adrenaline alone." Finn tried to keep his voice as calm as possible.

"This was the deal—I have to meet with her on arrival. I didn't exactly have room for concessions," Avery said, her voice muffled from the bathroom. She had taken a quick shower and was changing before they made their way to Klein's offices.

"You're exhausted." Finn leaned against the wall of his quarters. It was a small space, but the largest on his ship. It had everything he needed in a pinch. He looked over to the bed. "You just used an incredible amount of energy saving our asses from the Origin, not to mention that performance for Mixtie. I know you haven't rested more than five minutes."

Her head popped out of the door. "Don't you think I know that?" she chastised before disappearing again.

"Weren't you the one who yelled at me to rest? You can't push yourself like this."

"It's unavoidable."

"It's not unavoidable—you're just being stubborn," he reasoned.

"It's not like time is on our side. What's your suggestion for what I should be doing?" she drawled, finally emerging. She wore a deep blue tunic over form-hugging black trousers. Her warm brown hair hung in loose waves over her shoulders. The deep colors of the outfit made her eyes burn so brightly that they glowed.

Finn's mouth went dry.

He moved closer, needing to be nearer to her. "I can't exactly . . ." He cleared his throat, pulling her into him. ". . . think of anything right at this particular moment."

"Finn," she chided, rolling her eyes.

He grinned, threading his fingers into her hair.

"What?" he asked innocently, loving the way she admonished him. But now wasn't the time to tease her. She was hanging by a thread.

Sobering, he brought his head down, resting his forehead against hers. Her breath brushed his lips, a welcome torment. He spoke softly. "I know you're strong. We all do. Just . . . be careful, all right? You don't have anything to prove."

"You're telling me to be careful?" She smiled, placing her hands on his waist. "Coming from you, that request loses a bit of its potency."

"Since when am I not careful?"

Avery laughed.

"I always manage to get out of my scrapes," he argued, hands tightening around her hips.

"Mainly because I'm the one who keeps—what did you call it? Saving your ass."

"Oh, so you want to play rough today?" he asked, closing the distance between their lips with a fierce kiss. It was meant to diffuse her tension but quickly turned, veering off course and out of his control. Finn struggled to keep up with her.

She pushed him backward, and he stumbled, his calves meeting the bed. She didn't stop, carrying them both down to the soft surface, crawling over him. Desire pooled deep, a rush of pleasure making his fingers claw into her hips. She pressed against him, and he groaned.

Her hands ran up his sides, pulling his shirt along with them, her fingertips grazing the skin underneath. And then the shirt was gone entirely, and she flattened her palms against his bare chest, fire traveling down his torso beneath her touch. She kept kissing him, growing desperate, her teeth clanging against his in her haste.

Avery made a sound, so small that it could have been mistaken for pleasure.

But something sliced through Finn when he heard it, and he froze, like raging fire doused in cold water. He broke away, even as she tried to keep going, as she tried to pull his mouth back to hers.

"Avery," he breathed against her cheek, feeling wetness there. Tears.

Something was wrong. She moved to his neck, her mouth opening on his skin, hot and wet against his jaw. Her hands were at his pants, fumbling with the buttons, shaking. He stopped her, moving her wrists away.

"Avery, not like this." Not desperate and quick—not as an attempt to distract herself from feeling.

They hadn't slept together. They had come close, so close, too many times to count. But as she found her footing with her new life, Finn hadn't wanted to rush her. He had moved too quickly before, made too many mistakes. And he wouldn't do that with her.

She tried to kiss him again, but he shifted away. He brushed the hair from her eyes, holding her face in his hands. There were tears on her cheeks, soaking her freckles, turning her nose red. His heart squeezed.

He brought her to his chest, enveloping her in his embrace, shielding her the only way he knew how. Her arms wrapped around his waist, fingers digging into his back, gripping on to him with an intensity that frightened Finn. Like he was the only thing keeping her from disappearing—from floating away into the vast expanse of space.

"You're all right," he reassured her. She sobbed, her back jerking against him as she gave in to the tears. "You're all right," he said again, whispering into her ear.

It broke him to see her so defeated. So lost.

She had been carrying around the stress of it all, refusing to acknowledge what had happened to her. What Leviathan had taken from her. Even now, as he waited for her sobs to run dry, for her to speak, Finn knew she wouldn't break completely. She would hold something back.

But he wished she would let go.

Ever since she had accepted her position of So', Avery had held a piece of herself in check. There was something guarded about her. Something she couldn't share—even with him. The weight of her position, of the power she wielded, was beginning to drag her beneath the surface.

And the worst of it was that Finn wasn't sure he could keep her from drowning.

Nick had clearly caved under that same pressure. And his brother hadn't even endured a fraction of the expectations placed on Avery in so short a time.

There was still a part of Finn that blamed himself for Nick's betrayal.

If he had just seen the signs. If he had just paid closer attention. If he had realized that underneath all that political prowess and seemingly infallible sense of duty was a real person. Maybe he could have done something to change Nick's mind. Maybe things could have been different.

Maybe Finn would still have a brother.

His arms closed tighter around her.

He may have failed Nick, but Finn wouldn't make the same mistake with Avery. He would find a way to help her get through this. He would be what she needed—whatever she needed.

After several long minutes, Avery sniffled, rubbing her cheek over Finn's chest. His skin was wet from her tears. He felt bereft without her against him. Empty.

"We have to get going," she said, wiping her eyes with the back of her hand.

"Avery, are you—"

"Just let me get through this, okay?" Her voice was thin—brittle and ready to shatter.

Finn nodded, sitting up without a word.

She sniffed again before commenting, "You should probably take a shower."

Finn couldn't keep the laugh from spilling out of him. "If you wanted to see me naked, all you had to do was say so."

"I'm saying you stink, Finnegan." Her explanation was deadpan.

He laughed louder, clutching his chest. "Ouch, sweetheart." He grabbed his discarded shirt and threw it at her as she left.

The sound of her laughter followed him down the hallway and sank into his heart, the familiar melody already an immovable part of his soul.

Whatever she needed.

CHAPTER THIRTEEN

"Miss Vey." Klein's voice was low and pleasantly rough with a lilting cadence. The kind that would do well as an actress or newscaster. "I've heard so much about you. It seems almost strange that we've never actually met."

"Likewise," Avery replied, unsure how to respond. She took Klein's outreached hand, a dozen media bots capturing the moment, crowding around them. The lights they cast made everything overly bright and artificial. Klein's grip was strong, and Avery met her pressure with a false smile plastered to her face. Her cheeks hurt. "Thank you for agreeing to sit down with me."

"The pleasure is wholly mine." Klein nodded gracefully to Finn. "And it's lovely to see you again, Finn. Congratulations to you both—I saw your interview with Mixtie just this morning. It was a lovely surprise."

Although Avery knew that Klein found absolutely nothing lovely about the interview, there wasn't a line on her face that would give it away. Klein was an absolute master of her craft, ideally suited to the intrigue of politics. It was as much awe-inspiring as it was frightening.

"We always aim to please," Finn replied smoothly, dipping his chin. Avery resisted the urge to grab his hand.

Klein merely gave him a soft smile that warmed her eyes. She turned to Avery, gesturing toward the doors beyond the entry rooms. "Let's continue to my office, shall we?"

Finn made to follow them, but Klein's guard detail stepped forward to stop him. He didn't like it, that nonchalant mask of his almost slipping.

"It's fine," Avery said quietly, telling herself it was true. "I won't be long."

Finn's eyes flickered to Klein before he backed away with a nod. He whirled to the cams, aiming to distract them with gossip.

She followed Klein into her office, unsurprised by the wide expanse of windows that made up the length of the outer wall and offered a beautiful, unobstructed view of the Alexandria skyline. The sun made its way down the tips of the towers, and a flash of light bounced off one of the tall buildings, making Avery blink.

The door slid shut behind them. They were alone.

Klein's heels were the only sound, clicking on the marble floor as she maneuvered around her large glass desk. "Now that we've dispensed with the pleasantries—and our guard dogs—perhaps we can be honest with one another. Would you care for a drink, Miss Vey?" She didn't wait for an answer and poured the amber liquid into two small glasses from the recessed bar behind her. She looked up as she lowered herself into an ornate silver hover chair. "Please, sit," she added, sliding the drink to the edge of the desk.

Avery hesitated only a moment before grabbing the glass. She sat slowly into one of the chairs facing Klein. Swirling the drink in her glass, Avery watched as the alcohol beaded along the rim and slid down the sides in a leisurely path.

"It's not poisoned, if that's what you're thinking," Klein commented, clearly amused.

"The thought hadn't crossed my mind," Avery replied. It had. But she took a long swig anyway. The burn within her throat steadied her nerves.

Klein smiled, the expression genuine enough to make Avery uneasy. "You are fascinating, Avery—may I call you Avery? Even if this is our first meeting, I do feel like we've become close. Our roles are so . . . inextricably entangled with one another."

"Really? I don't see how your impeachment has anything to do with me."

Klein took a sip of her drink, allowing the silence to stretch. There was no noise beyond their own breathing, not even the commotion beyond the doors. The office must have been soundproofed.

"This vintage really is quite something, isn't it?" Klein said, studying her glass. "This bottle has been in my family for generations—unopened since before the Final World War. I never could understand why my father kept it locked up. It was too important to lose, he used to say. A link to our past." Her eyes clouded before downing the rest in one long swallow. She poured another.

Avery leaned forward, placing her glass on the desk. "I'm not sure I understand you."

"We both believe in the future, you and I," Klein replied calmly. "And we believe that future lies on Echo."

"What?" Avery frowned, her question cutting.

Klein's posture hardened. "I was under the impression you came here to speak with me to negotiate your position following the banishment from your planet. Was I mistaken?"

Avery's blood ran cold.

Klein knew. She knew what was happening on Echo, and why they were there.

Avery took a shallow breath. "No." It was all she could get out.

Klein smiled again. "It seems we are both in similar positions, ideally situated to help one another through this difficult time."

"Similar?" Avery's power flared from the anger that rose to the surface. Her fingers tingled. "Let's get one thing straight. I asked for this meeting only so I could get through the Gate, and I asked for it to be public so that you wouldn't be able to touch me while I was here. I don't know what you're proposing to me, and in all honesty, I don't care. I have no intention, nor will I ever, of helping you. And as soon as the vote of confidence takes place, you will be finished—done."

The lights flickered ominously on the end of her words, and Klein glanced to the ceiling. Avery clenched her jaw. She couldn't afford to lose control. Not here, with a hundred media bots sitting just outside those doors.

"Such a temper." Klein seemed unfazed by the attempted display of power. "You haven't even heard my proposal."

"Why would you ever think I would help the person who's been the cause of so much pain for my own people? You've killed thousands of—"

"I forget sometimes that you're still a child." Klein stopped her. "You have a lot to learn about politics if you hope to stay in them. There is never one person behind any agenda, Avery. The government is a machine, working to protect the populace by any means necessary. Even if it means doing things the average citizen could not."

"Like genocide?" Avery spat. "War? Torture? Unregulated inhumane experimentation?"

Klein tilted her head quizzically. "I am but a line of code in a much larger program. If you truly want to learn the truth about that experimentation, perhaps you should ask your grandmother." Avery's mouth dried. "Or maybe your Ambassador Lunitia. His family's hands are stained much redder than mine, I assure you. His father was instrumental in our program, not to mention a close personal friend."

Avery's heart stopped. Finn's father? Gran had never mentioned anything about that, nor Finn. And if he had known anything, he would have told her. She would stake her life on it.

Either Klein was lying, or even Finn didn't know the truth.

And Avery couldn't deny that she still didn't know much about Gran's past. That conversation in their safe house kitchen had been the closest Gran had ever come to revealing anything about that period in her life. Avery had wanted to give her space and time to heal first.

Maybe Avery had made a mistake in not insisting they discuss it. Was Gran still hiding things? Even now?

"And then there's that face," Klein drawled and chuckled. "You'll need to get much better at concealing your emotions, Avery. You cannot control minds here, you know. What a gift that would be—the things we could accomplish," she pondered aloud. Her gaze drifted to the windows, out at the city. "Democracy . . . choice . . . personal agency . . . These elements of government are parts of a wonderful dream, but the people themselves can't be trusted to choose the right path. They must be led to it. Left to their own devices, they can't even handle reality without destroying themselves in their futile attempts to understand it."

There was a kernel of truth in her words that kept Avery from speaking.

Look at what had happened on Echo. If she had been allowed to use her gift—to influence the government—she could have prevented the situation they were in now. It would be easier, so much easier.

"It must be so much easier for you." Avery's chin jerked up at the words that had just flown from her own mind. "To lead," Klein clarified.

Avery couldn't breathe.

"You have used that power before, to make decisions that you never had to answer for. I can only assume you use it in your own government," Klein goaded, her tone darkening. "You've used it to kill. Poor Harding. He was only following orders, really. But then, I suppose he deserved it. He did shoot your friend in cold—"

"Enough." Avery stood up, slamming her hand on the desk, her fury carrying an excess of power along with it. The glass fractured beneath her fingers with a loud crack, a long fissure spreading out from her palm in the direction of Klein, like ice fragmenting in two. "I didn't come here to play your games."

"I am merely offering an olive branch."

"Which I would be stupid to take."

Klein didn't respond, the only sign of emotion in the faint spasm on her cheek. "Only a fool refuses to hear the terms before considering negotiation. Even from their enemy. I am trying to help us help each other," she bit out tersely. "Situations are developing that will require concessions from both sides to save lives, and I am willing to discuss—"

"I have no interest in discussing anything with you," Avery spat, her entire body stiff, tense. "You are grasping for power even as the people take it away from you. You are scared and desperate, and I'm done with this sham of a meeting. Enjoy prison."

A frown creased Klein's face, hardening her peaceful features to a mask of stone. Her perfectly manicured nails—a pale, natural pink filed to points—clawed at the cracked glass beneath her fingers. "You'll regret this," she said ominously.

"Not likely." Avery was already walking to the door. "But thanks for the drink."

CHAPTER FOURTEEN

"Found him!" Megan exclaimed, smiling brightly over her wrist-port.

Petra pretended to focus on the screen in the living room. She had been steadily avoiding eye contact since they had arrived. Had been avoiding speaking altogether.

"You got in?" Nova twisted toward them from her spot on the couch. "Do you have a lead?"

"Damn, Megan," Grigg drawled, leaning back in a large pink chair that made even his broad frame look small. "I didn't know you had such shady connections."

Megan winked. "There are a lot of things you don't know about me."

Nausea rose up Petra's throat.

"Looks like they have a name for him . . ." Megan scrolled through the message boards. "The Acquirer."

Grigg laughed. "The Acquirer? What kind of name is that?"

"I guess he acquires stuff for people." Megan shrugged a pale shoulder. Her bare skin was accentuated by the soft pink of her shirt, the wide neckline showing off a considerable amount of her chest.

As though sensing her, Megan looked up, spearing Petra with her pale blue eyes, sparkling with something like a challenge. Petra turned away, focusing on the screen again. The newsreel started, and a vid appeared of Avery and Finn shaking hands with Klein. They were smiling. Petra froze.

She should be there with them, by Avery's side at that meeting. Petra wasn't content to sit there and do research, especially not if it meant relying on Megan for the help. She didn't care how many connections she had.

But Avery didn't want Tai anywhere near the capital or Klein's forces, insisting they drop him here and bring Megan up to speed. And where Tai went, Petra would go, too. She wouldn't leave him alone when he was so vulnerable.

Petra glanced to the hallway, at the vibrant green rug lining the floor. Grigg had carried him to one of the bedrooms only hours earlier. And Tai had still been asleep. She hoped when he woke they would have more answers.

"This thread says he owns a club," Megan said, reading more. "Apparently it's Reange only, but humans can get in if they—oh my God, I've heard of this place!" Her eyes widened, and she rose to her knees on the couch. "They broadcast a live feed of the entry line, and viewers get to vote you in."

"And that passes for entertainment?" Nova laughed, shaking her head. "It sounds ridiculous."

"Welcome to Earth. We're pretty starved for entertainment here."

"No wonder humanity is trying to steal our planet," Petra muttered beneath her breath, unable to stop the comment from surfacing.

"Are you going to sulk over there forever, or would you like to join us?" Megan's voice danced across the room.

"This is a new level of rude, even for you," Grigg added sourly.

Petra ignored them. She clasped her hands behind her back, something catching in her chest. She would rather be anywhere else.

"What's your problem?" Megan's voice was beside her, low and tense.

Petra jerked, as though burned. She took a step to the side, putting space between them.

"Seriously?" Megan questioned tightly.

Petra refused to respond. If this was what she had to do to get space, then so be it.

"Excuse me," Megan ground out harshly. She grabbed Petra's arm, phantom vibrations ringing beneath the surface where Megan's skin met hers.

Petra drew her eyes slowly to Megan's. "What?" she snapped.

"I know you didn't just say that to me." Megan was incredulous, voice lowered. "I'm trying to blazing talk to you, Petra."

"I can see that," Petra replied lazily, taking her arm back. "What I don't understand is why."

Megan flinched.

A low whistle sounded across the room. "That was harsh."

Petra heard the sound of Nova punching Grigg solidly in the arm and his ensuing whine.

"Well, it was," he added sullenly.

Something twisted in her belly, but Petra ignored the sensation. The atmosphere in the room shifted, growing heavy.

"I think we'll go down to the docking bay," Nova said tactfully, rising from her seat. "The others should be back soon." She grabbed Grigg's collar as she went, dragging him with her to the door.

"Why do I always have to go with you? It was just getting good," Grigg mumbled. The door slid shut behind them.

Not that privacy would change anything.

Still, Petra's palms grew sweaty.

She looked back to the interview once more, willing Megan to leave her alone.

"I don't know what she's thinking," Megan murmured, playing with the curled ends of her hair. She stared at the screen, too. "This meeting will only help Klein in the long run. It makes her look reasonable, like Avery wanted to sit down with her. It will seriously impact the vote."

"And what would you know?" Petra scoffed, her defenses rising. "It's not like she had a choice. She's doing what's necessary."

"What *she* thinks is necessary. Did she even ask you guys before diving into this?"

Petra scowled but said nothing. She couldn't.

"I didn't think so. If she's going to learn how to use her power, she needs to start listening to other people."

Petra sneered. "If I grew up surrounded by humans, I don't think I'd listen to other people either."

Megan frowned at the sting but thankfully stayed quiet. They lapsed into silence, the voice of the newscaster the only sound in the room.

After what felt like an age, Megan awkwardly asked, "Do you think Tai will be okay?"

Petra shook her head, pushing hair behind her ear. It was genuine concern. Megan and Tai had bonded from the first moment they met on Echo. He had certainly never held her humanity against her.

But then, he was better than Petra.

"I hope so." Her voice came out steadier than she thought it would.

"He really went after Finn?"

Petra let a grin tug at her mouth. "Shot him, actually."

"You're horrible." Megan shook her head, pink lips forming a pretty smile. "I'm sure he'll be fine, Petra. He's stronger than you give him credit for."

Petra covered the sudden dryness in her throat with a cough. She didn't trust herself to speak, worried that any words would betray her emotions.

"Maybe this guy, the Acquirer, can do something for him?" Megan suggested, shrugging. "Anybody that can help Avery regain her powers should be able to fix Tai, right?" Petra didn't reply, so Megan continued, unwilling or unable to sit in silence. "I've never actually been to this club, but I've heard it's absolutely insane if you can get in. I know somebody I can contact that's been there before, so maybe they can help us find him. You know how I—"

"You're not coming with us." Petra refused to consider it.

Megan raised a fair brow, crossing her arms over her chest. Her nails were filed into such sharp points that Petra didn't know how she kept from stabbing herself. "I didn't know I answered to you."

"It's too dangerous," Petra reasoned. "You just said humans aren't allowed. It will be swarming with Reanges."

"I said they're not commonplace. But they *can* get in. And if you think I've ever been denied entry to a club, you're out of your mind."

Petra snorted at the vanity.

"And besides, Finn is going," Megan added, bouncing on her feet. "The whole crew, in fact, so I'm definitely on board."

"When have you ever been a part of the crew?"

Megan flinched, her smile gone in an instant. "I'm going to ask you this again, Petra," she said slowly. "What is going on with you?"

Petra met those blue eyes without wavering. "Nothing," she lied.

"Nothing?" Megan scoffed. "I thought we were friends, Petra. At least we were when I was on Echo. And then I come back to Earth, and you freeze me out. I know we haven't known each other that long, but I thought—"

"You thought wrong." Petra grit her teeth, forcing her mind elsewhere, forcing control.

Megan grabbed Petra's arm, her grip strong as she forced Petra to face her. Her perfect features scrunched together, anger morphing her beauty into something fierce.

"Moon above, you're actually serious right now," Megan breathed.

Petra remained silent.

"Coward."

Petra's eyes narrowed, her anger flaring brightly in her chest, burning against her ribs. What did this spoiled human girl know about cowardice?

But Megan didn't stop. "You want to push me away? I feel it, too, Petra. Whatever this thing is between us. But if you want to ignore it, that's fine with me. I'm not the one who's letting my prejudice get in the way of living my life."

Something wrenched in Petra's chest. When she spoke, her words were acid. "If you ever thought I could actually be friends with a human, then that's your mistake, not mine. Stop trying to drag me back into your life. In fact, if you could leave me alone entirely, that would be great."

"Leave *you* alone?" Megan balked. "In case you've forgotten, you're the one who showed up on *my* doorstep unannounced asking for help."

"It was Avery's—"

"It's always Avery, isn't it?" Megan said.

Petra couldn't respond. She was treading too close to disaster.

Megan pushed further. "You think you hide it, but everyone knows. Your aversion to humanity is rather ironic, considering your obsession with her. This may have escaped your notice, but she's in love with Finn. And nothing—nothing—is going to tear her away from him."

Petra's eyes dropped to the floor. For the past year, Avery had been the only thing Petra had wanted. She had needed her, for the cause and for their people.

But Megan was telling the truth. Avery had chosen Finn, despite him being human. Petra couldn't fathom it. She would never choose humanity over her own people.

"I love her, too, you know."

Petra startled. It was as though Megan had read her thoughts.

"You can love her and still want things for yourself," Megan added, her tone softening.

"It's not about that," Petra grit out. She nearly choked on the words.

"Then tell me."

"You want me to tell you?" Petra stepped closer, until they were nearly toe to toe. She could feel the warmth radiating from Megan, could smell her perfume wafting around her like a cloud of wildflowers. "I watched humans slaughter my parents in front of me. Slaughter our whole village."

Megan was silent, those large eyes even wider now, glistening. Her back stiffened.

And then suddenly, words poured out of Petra like they had a will of their own. "Tai was there. I had to hold my hand over his mouth to keep him quiet. Afterward, we ran to the beach. We hid in the caves beneath the cliffs. But I was too scared to move us. For days." Petra laughed acerbically, horrified at the words still tumbling out of her mouth. "We ate nothing but seaweed because I was too frightened to light a fire. It was three days before the Origin found us. Before we finally felt safe." Her voice was shaking now, and she hated it. Hated the way Megan was looking at her. The pity in those eyes.

Petra dug her fingernails into her palms, the pain grounding her as she turned away.

"The Origin gave me a purpose," Petra said harshly. "A way to keep the fear at bay. So don't talk to me about how I should feel about humans. You have *no idea* what I've seen. What I've been through. The things I've done."

Megan was quiet. For one wild moment, Petra wished Megan would touch her. She wanted her to. But if Megan touched her now—

Megan cried out, the pained sound mingling with a roar of anger.

Petra whirled, heart in her throat, as her hand went straight for the blaster on her hip.

Tai was awake.

CHAPTER FIFTEEN

Tai wrapped his hand around Megan's hair and dragged her from Petra, a ragged snarl rending the air as he commanded, "Don't touch my sister."

Petra lurched forward with raised hands. "Tai," she said delicately.

His other hand wrapped around Megan's throat. She whimpered. Petra's pulse skipped at the sound, her stomach turning to rock.

She looked at him, meeting his eyes, the same shade of green as her own. They were wide, pupils dilated as they shifted around the room. "Where are we? Petra, where are we?" he asked, sounding small.

She took a steadying breath. "I'm right here, Tai." She inched closer.

His hand clamped down, fingers digging into Megan's neck.

Petra froze. "Let her go, Taisto. You don't want to hurt her—this isn't you."

He grimaced, as though in pain, shaking his head. His eyes squeezed shut.

She took the opening.

Petra moved forward in a flash, wrenching his hand from Megan. He dropped her hair, eyes opening in surprise as Petra grabbed his arm and swiftly vaulted him over her shoulder. He came down hard, slamming into the floor, and started wheezing as he lost his breath from the impact.

Petra stood over him, shaking. She didn't look at Megan—couldn't.

He crawled to all fours, confusion on his face. "Petra?" he asked, as though he barely recognized her. She struggled to breathe, frozen under his stare.

He was on his feet, focused on Megan again. Anger brewed in the green depths of his eyes. He launched himself at her.

But his body caught in the air. He hovered above the floor as he fought against whatever held him, limbs flailing.

"I guess he woke up." Avery stood in the doorway, a hand held out at Tai. Finn stood beside her, wide-eyed and silent, the rest of their crew behind him.

Grigg was already helping Megan to her feet.

Petra nearly collapsed, relief making her knees weak. She didn't think she could hurt him again. She didn't have that in her.

Avery took control, strong-arming Tai back to the bedroom and locking him inside. He didn't seem to want to harm anyone other than Megan and Finn—the only humans among them. Once he was alone, he calmed down considerably. But they couldn't afford to keep him sedated. His system couldn't handle any more drugs. They would just have to keep him separated.

"He's getting worse," Avery said when she returned to the living room, Grigg on her heels.

Megan rubbed her throat, the skin pink and mottled where Tai had grabbed her. Petra let out a low exhale, still trying to calm her pulse.

When Megan spoke, her voice was raw. "You're saying everyone on Echo is like that now?" She sunk into the couch, seeking comfort from its plush gray cushions. Linderly brought her a glass of water, curling up beside her.

"Not everyone," Avery replied, "but enough to matter."

Time wasn't making Tai any better. Whatever Leviathan had done to him, it wasn't going away.

Petra clung to Megan's idea. Maybe this So'—the Acquirer—would be able to do something for him. It would be the only option now. The only way to get her brother back.

She shifted on her feet, restless.

"Did you pick that outfit out, Avie?" Megan's shallow question had Petra scowling. She was pretending already, like she hadn't just been attacked minutes ago. "It looked great on camera. Maybe I'm rubbing off on you." And she kept going, the fear seeming to leave her body as she told Avery and the others about what she had found. About the Acquirer. "I already messaged my friend—she said she'd meet us there tomorrow night. Before you guys got here, Petra and I were just discussing our next moves."

Petra stiffened.

Megan lied so easily, slipping back into a facade of stability. When they both knew her emotions were anything but.

Finn caught Petra's gaze, his face contemplative, but she ignored him. Let him think what he wanted.

"Megan." Avery's voice was forcibly casual. "You know I can't let you come with us."

Finn laughed. "Good luck with that one."

Megan sighed dramatically. "You know better than anyone that nobody *lets* me do anything. I'm going."

"I agree with Megan," Linderly chirped, and Megan gave her a conspiratorial grin.

"You'd agree to anything she said." Markes took up a seat on the arm of the couch beside her.

Linderly stuck out her tongue. She pushed him off the couch and onto his ass. Megan giggled.

"Better watch it, little man," Grigg warned Markes after reclaiming his seat in the pink monstrosity of a chair. "Beneath that bubbly tattoo-covered package, your sister has teeth."

Markes rolled his eyes as the others laughed, leaning back on his forearms on the floor.

"Besides," Megan continued, "your powers are seriously limited. You're as good as human again." She stole the briefest look at Petra from beneath her lashes. "You need me."

"She's got a point," Finn said. Avery glared at him. "Come on, Avery. It'll be fun. Like the good ole days before I flew you off to fame and fortune."

"Is that what we're calling it now?" Avery asked.

Megan leaned forward and made an exaggerated pout. She clasped her hands together in a plea.

Avery burst out laughing, throwing her hands up. "Fine, but don't say I didn't warn you."

"Excellent." Megan stood, smoothing the pink fabric of her shirt down her torso. Her eyes were bright, vibrant again, no trace of fear left, although a high blush still stained her smooth cheeks. "Now, first things first, my beautiful Reanges—wardrobe."

Petra tuned out the conversation, instead heading to the kitchen for water. She was desperate to busy her hands.

Linderly's giggles mingled with Avery's laughter, and Petra's jaw locked.

Megan always had this way with people. She could put them at ease in an instant. Even Tai had immediately taken to her.

Something stirred in her chest, flipping her stomach in a strange combination of pleasure and discomfort. But Petra refused to name it.

If she acknowledged it, if she accepted it, she wouldn't be able to go back. So she locked it away with the others that hid in the shadows, willing it down into the depths of her soul.

And focused on the anger instead.

"Who puts a club entrance at the end of some ancient sewer system?" Finn asked, hovering close to Avery in the darkness. His face was illuminated by the glow of his wristport as he directed them through the tunnels beneath the city.

"Well, nobody's likely to come snooping around here. How deep below the surface are we?" Avery asked, hopping over a dark puddle. The shoes Megan had chosen for her hadn't exactly been practical.

But apparently practicality wasn't likely to get you entry into an exclusive Reange club.

"If you'd just get a new wristport, you wouldn't have to ask," Finn replied.

Avery shrugged. "I like not having one. It's freeing."

After her wristport tech had been fried by Gran's malware, Avery had decided to leave it broken. She rarely missed the connectivity, and the added privacy had been wonderful. Of course, that was before she had lost her telepathy.

Finn shook his head at the map projected from his arm. "Just nearing nine hundred feet. That's about twice as deep as the markets, and these tunnels are still descending." He threw a look behind them before adding, "I can't imagine this is the only way in. There's no chance people climb through this muck on a regular basis."

"I hope the others are okay," Avery said, fear worming its way through her stomach.

They had been forced to separate when Megan's friend mentioned the club limited groups to no more than three in a party. Avery and Finn were alone together.

She scanned the rock above their heads, uncertain if the pressure she felt was real or imagined. The air was damp and cool, reminding her of the caverns on Echo, of her time spent with the Origin and her training. Of Fiora.

Avery shivered, rubbing her hands over her exposed arms. She cursed Megan for the dress she wore. The silver slip of fabric provided little cover. It wasn't much more than sparkling sequins held together by neon-pink string. The halter glowed in the darkness, staining a fuchsia line across her neck.

Finn pulled her to a stop, replacing her hands with his. His fingers were hot on her chilled skin, warmth infusing straight into her blood. "This blazing dress," Finn cursed, a quiet murmur that wrapped around her, turning her feverish from within.

His hands slowed their journey up her shoulders, fingers trailing beneath the pink-corded halter, up the side of her neck. Waves of pleasure traveled through her body, making her toes curl, banishing any memories threatening to surface.

"Then again," Finn added suggestively, leaning forward, "maybe it has its advantages."

His breath was fire on her neck, and she arched into him. She didn't have time to think about the way she threw herself at him the day before, and while she was glad he had stopped her, Avery was tired of waiting. If anything, going through this kind of danger again had reminded her of the fragility of peace—of life.

His lips touched her skin, grinning against her as his arms snaked around her waist. She gasped. His hands splayed across the small of her fully exposed back, burning straight through and up her spine.

Laughter echoed down the tunnel, bouncing off the walls around them.

Avery pulled back sharply. They both turned their heads to find the source.

Finn let out some combination of a groan and a growl as he pulled away. But his fingers lingered on her skin before grabbing her hand. "That must mean we're close."

"I should have paired you up with Grigg," Avery lamented, trying to cool the lust that still clouded her vision.

"Absolutely not," Finn replied over his shoulder. "He never lets me get past first base."

Avery laughed loudly at his joke. She adored him. She adored the way he could always bring her out of her head. "You should save that for this entry line," she reminded him. "If we're going to have to perform for a virtual audience, they'll want to see something good."

"Damn." Finn's mouth twisted. "You're saying I wasted all my best moves with nobody to witness it?"

"You call those your best moves?"

Finn glowered at her with a look that promised retribution.

"Look," Finn said, slowing.

She stopped beside him as they came to the end of the tunnel, opening into a wide domed cavern that reached a few stories tall. There were other tunnel entrances lining its edge, suggesting more than one way to enter the galleried space. A red glow drew their attention to the far end of the room, running up the curved wall, bathing a long line of partygoers in its light and casting arching maroon-tinged shadows. Voices stretched up and over them, bouncing off the ceiling, filling the room with a low hum.

Finn's hand tugged hers, and he nodded to the line. Grigg, Nova, and Markes stood together near the middle. Nova caught their eye, dipping her head almost imperceptibly. At least Avery didn't have to worry about Linderly, who had elected to stay on the ship with Tai. She had been pretty eager to offer, actually. Avery searched the faces, freezing as she found Petra and Megan near the front of the line.

"I wouldn't want to be that bouncer with those two around," Finn said dryly as they took their place at the back.

"They did seem pretty angry about being thrown together. I thought Petra was past her whole human thing," Avery said, frowning. "But she's the most capable of protecting Megan. She'll keep her safe."

"Avery," Finn laughed softly, drawing her eyes to him. His hair was a dark red in the glow of the light, falling over his forehead. "There's something going on between them."

"What?" Avery scoffed, rolling her eyes. "You're crazy."

"Didn't you catch on when we came back to the apartment yesterday? Why do you think Grigg and Nova were hiding out in the docking bay?"

"They were waiting for us to get back!" Avery reasoned, hackles rising. But Finn's point nagged at her, like she had missed something. Something big. Had she been relying on her gift so much that she couldn't even pick up on regular cues anymore?

No. Megan would have told her if there were something between them. She wouldn't have hidden it. She never hid her flings. In fact, she went out of her way to throw them in Avery's face. There was no way that Megan and Petra could be—

"Shit," Finn let out. The crowd around them lit up with excited energy, the conversation growing louder.

She tore her eyes to the front of the line. Megan and Petra were being led to the platform, ready to be judged.

CHAPTER SIXTEEN

Avery held her breath as Megan climbed the stairs to the viewing platform, her shimmering purple mini dress barely covering her ass. Petra followed, sporting a pair of black slacks and a matching blazer that closed with a single diamond button in front, exposing her chest and midriff. She was wearing a very practical pair of chunky black boots. She had refused to let Megan dress her. Avery should have been as stubborn.

They approached the vid bot hovering above the platform, its small spotlight encircling them in a halo of white. Megan smiled seductively at the camera, giving it a little wave. They must have known she was human somehow. It must have been why the bouncer had chosen them to prove their worth to an audience.

Petra looked like she was in pain as she approached Megan. The bouncer said something to them, and Megan giggled, plastering herself to Petra's side before she winked at the crowd. A few of them laughed at whatever she had said.

A hologram popped up above their heads, two progress bars projected from the vid bot itself. One green, one red. Yes and no.

Megan whispered something in Petra's ear, resulting in a fierce scowl.

The bars started moving. The red bar filled rapidly. The green struggled to keep up.

"Damn it, Petra, don't just stand there," Finn muttered beside Avery, shifting on his feet. They needed Megan in the club to find her friend who would help them. And they couldn't very well leave Petra outside. But at this rate, they'd be thrown out for certain.

Avery leaned over to Finn. "Maybe putting them together wasn't a—"

Avery stopped as Megan plucked the diamond button of Petra's blazer open. Megan stepped between Petra and the camera to slip her bare arms into the garment. Rising on her toes, she nuzzled into Petra's neck. Petra's eyes widened, shock blooming across her face.

The green bar started gaining speed.

Megan tilted her head, whispering something only for Petra. Whatever it was spurred her into motion.

Petra grabbed a fistful of Megan's loose blonde curls and tugged her head back, exposing her neck to the camera. In one long movement, she ran her tongue up the expanse of Megan's bare chest and all the way up to her chin. She exposed her teeth, hesitating a millisecond before biting down on the pale flesh of Megan's throat.

The people around them went wild, cheers and shouts filling up the cavern. Beside Avery, Finn was laughing.

The green bar above the platform surged forward, passing the red one until a golden check mark appeared, heralding approval.

Petra jerked away from Megan, as though scalded. She dipped her head, fastening the button on her blazer as she hurried down the steps. Petra didn't wait for Megan to follow.

"What the blazar was that?" Avery hissed.

"I told you," Finn replied with a shrug. "Chemistry."

Something coiled in her belly, making her feel sick. If she had missed this, it was because they didn't want her to know. Megan was her closest friend, and Petra was—complicated.

But she loved them both. Like sisters. Why hadn't they trusted her with this?

"But Petra doesn't even like her," Avery reasoned, stepping forward as the line moved. They would be stuck there for at least another half hour. "When I visited Megan last week during the indictment, she didn't even come with me that day."

"Exactly," Finn said simply.

"You think she was avoiding Megan?"

"Or maybe this is all some long-game foreplay."

"Finn," Avery warned.

He laughed, tugging her to his side. "Don't give me that look. You know, for someone who can read peoples' minds, you're awfully clueless sometimes."

The stab of pain from his words was fleeting, and Avery lapsed into silence. Even Finn seemed to know them better than she did.

The rest of their wait was uneventful, and the others were let in without incident. Every few minutes heads would turn Finn and Avery's way, recognition making whispers rise. Apparently they weren't just famous among the humans on the surface levels. At least no wrist-ports raised to capture vids, which would have revealed their location, and possibly their intentions, to the Federation. The exclusivity of this club relied on secrecy, a concept that even the patrons chose to respect.

But when they approached the bouncer, there was no indication that he knew them. Avery had partly worried their celebrity status would single them out, forcing them to the stage. Finn's disappointment at not being chosen was palpable. No doubt he had quite the performance planned.

They passed through the large red door protecting the entrance and stepped into another world.

First, the thrumming music enveloped them into a protective sound bubble, drawing them farther into the crush of people that filled the space. Neon lights and strobes caught on the holosmoke that billowed over the dance floor, curling around bodies, swirling between feet, flashing to the beat of the bass. Like people were dancing in the clouds, amid lightning and thunder raging in a synchronized rhythm.

"Do you see them?" Avery yelled into Finn's ear.

"No!" he replied, pulling her closer behind him.

They spent a few minutes searching, getting a good layout of the place as they worked their way through the crowd. The entire club was a circle that surrounded a large monstrosity of a bar, a column housing liquor, mirrors, and vid screens that reached up to the ceiling.

A chill touched the back of Avery's neck, and she shivered.

Nearly everyone were Reanges. Avery didn't need her gifts to know that. There were gen mods everywhere they looked. Neon hair, patterned skin, glowing eyes . . . features that Avery had never seen anyone bold enough to try before, even on Echo. Desperately, she reached out to that part of her, hoping she could feel their presence. Their energies should have been as easy to grasp as breathing.

Nothing. Still nothing.

Someone bumped into her, and she lost her grip on Finn. Large hands grabbed her hips, twisting her around and drawing her into a dance. Avery reacted on instinct, pushing the tall figure away with a heavy shove of her palms on his chest and a bit of added energy. He stumbled back and shrugged, twisting from her to the beat of the music, gone in a flash of white hair and glittering skin.

Finn found her hand then. He mouthed a worried "Are you okay?" and she nodded. In response, he led her forward, and she let him. She relished in the stability that flowed between their palms, pushing down the tickling unease that teased her chest.

She felt wounded—clumsy. She reached for her power, letting energy move through her veins and fill her body with strength, and her breathing finally steadied. At least she still had this.

They made their way to the bar, passing through another sound buffer as the music quieted, presumably to allow for alcohol orders and conversation. Finally, they caught sight of the others. Grigg and Markes were already holding drinks, while Nova leaned over the counter to talk with a bartender, her long blonde pony trailing down her back contrasting with the dark blue silk of her jumpsuit. Petra stood slightly apart from the others, staring grimly at the dance floor. Megan was nowhere in sight.

"There you are!" Grigg exclaimed loudly as Finn and Avery approached.

"You don't have to yell." Markes frowned at him, leaning away.

Grigg ignored him, leaning forward, his eyes wide. "You've got to try these drinks. They have actual bartenders here—not just bar bots."

Finn rolled his eyes, but he grabbed the offered glass and took a swig. "Actually, it's not bad." He tried handing it to Avery, but she shook her head. He shrugged, then downed the rest of it.

"Hey!" Grigg looked dejectedly at the empty glass Finn handed back to him.

"Where is Megan? Did she find who she was looking for?" Avery asked, hoping they had gotten somewhere.

"I don't know how we're going to find anyone in here," Markes confessed. He held up his wrist before adding, "They have a block on all comms. Even Linderly's patches can't get past it."

"Well, at least that means the Federation can't find us, right?" Finn pointed out.

"I guess they take the whole secret club thing pretty seriously," Grigg said, taking a sip from the glowing blue straw in Markes's glass. Markes frowned and quickly took back his drink.

Nova approached them after finishing her conversation with the bartender, looking solemn. "We're shit out of luck. The Acquirer isn't here."

"You got him to talk?" Grigg commented sullenly. "That bastard gave me the cold shoulder. I thought real bartenders were supposed to be good at conversation."

Nova shrugged, grinning. "I guess you've lost your touch."

"Maybe you need to take lessons on how to hit on Earth-bounders." Finn slapped him on the back, smirking.

"So this has all been a giant waste of time?" Petra asked sharply over their banter.

"There's a VIP area," Nova replied, glancing toward the back of the club, around the central column of the bar. "I guess our best chance at finding somebody who has a connection to him is there. He's got white hair, apparently. That's all the bartender would say."

"Great, another Elder. Just what we need," Finn said darkly.

"Did somebody say VIP?" Megan popped her head into their circle, curls falling over her bare shoulders, a smile on her lips. "I've got good news and bad news. I can't find my friend anywhere—this place is a circus."

"I thought you went to the bathroom." Petra sounded harsh,

turning the comment into an accusation.

"I did" was all Megan said before turning her back on Petra. "And then I met this guy standing in line who had the most fabulous hair, striped blue-and-pink, so I stopped to let him know how gorgeous it was. He was drunk off his ass, apparently drowning his sorrows over the fact that he shelled out big credits to be here on a night when the Acquirer isn't even attending. Only it took me a minute to figure out who he was talking about—he kept calling him 'tsek.'"

"Tsek?" Markes asked in a low voice, his features drawn.

Nova took a step closer to Megan. "He used that word?"

Megan nodded. The others exchanged worried looks.

Avery reached out to their minds for an explanation before remembering she couldn't. So instead, she asked, "What does it mean?"

Petra spoke first. "The tsek is an animal that is revered on Echo. In the ancient myths, they were the moon guardians that bestowed the first powers to the So'."

"They're crafty and have a mean bite if you come across one, not that they're easy to find," Grigg explained. He nudged Nova before adding, "Nova and I used to hunt them in the mountains when we were kids. They say if you capture one, it will grant you a wish."

"Sort of like a sacred fox," Finn explained, conjuring up a mental picture of a cute furry creature with large ears and a fluffy tail. Well, that couldn't be so bad.

Megan giggled. "So, what, he'll grant us a wish when we meet him?"

"Sounds like we need to figure out how to get into that VIP area first," Avery said.

"I thought you'd never ask." Megan pulled out a wristband from somewhere in the bodice of her violet dress.

"Do I want to know how you got this?" Avery asked skeptically.

Megan grinned. "Striped Hair wasn't exactly paying attention to my hands when he was busy sticking his tongue down my throat." She made a show of daintily wiping the corner of her mouth.

Grigg burst out laughing, and Markes choked on his drink. Petra turned toward the bar. Finn elbowed Avery, nudging her to acknowledge Petra's reaction, but she ignored him.

"You only have one?" Avery asked, plucking the clear band from Megan's palm. It was heavy and warm against her skin, as though it were made of solid glass. Strange, to use a physical object instead of just digital access via wristport. This place really was offline.

If you wanted one, all you had to do was ask.

Avery tensed instantly. Every muscle in her body was on alert at the intrusion in her mind. She turned to scan the dance floor.

"What's wrong?" Finn was beside her in a moment, his hand on her elbow.

A face flashed through her mind, unbidden. Avery brought two fingers to her temple, focusing.

A woman, tall and muscular, with hair in such a vibrant combination of orange and pink that it glowed in the dim light of the club, reflecting against her dark skin. And there was a presence that hovered nearby, testing the edges of Avery's consciousness. It was cold, unfamiliar.

"Avery?" Finn asked again.

"What's wrong?" Petra inspected the space as though she sensed something, too.

The presence laughed softly, amusement curling in and around Avery like a seductive, frozen mist. She fought to keep it from fully filling her mind, drawing up whatever barriers she could summon.

And as quickly as it had appeared, the coolness swept away, dissolving into the clouds of the dance floor and leaving Avery alone in her head.

"He's here."

CHAPTER SEVENTEEN

"Do you see her anywhere?" Finn yelled to Grigg and Nova as they circled the dance floor.

"Negative!" Nova replied, turning to sneer and push off an overeager dancer who had grabbed her and tried to pull her into the crowd.

Frustration burned through Avery's chest. For the thousandth time, she reached out, fumbling for a hint of the presence she had felt moments before. And again, nothing.

Was this some sort of test? Why would this So' play these kinds of games with her? If he could access her mind, he certainly could read the others'. He would already know the situation on Echo and how many lives were at stake. How much his aide meant to her. Avery didn't even know if Gran was safe, or Lissande. Or Krez.

There were so many people who needed her. She didn't have time to waste on some egotistical idiot who partied in clubs and got off on toying with her.

Who the blazar would call themselves the Acquirer? It was ridiculous.

I didn't pick the name, darling.

She whirled, catching sight of orange and pink from across the floor. The woman stared at her, bodies threading between them, smoke curling up around her waist. She smiled. And disappeared into the throng.

"There!" Avery gasped, taking off after her.

She barely heard Finn yelling in her wake. Avery couldn't miss the chance to follow her, even if it meant leaving her friends behind.

She struggled against the crowd, her small frame making it difficult to get very far. She threw out a wave of energy, pushing the bodies farther, carving a path by force. A few shocked glances flew to her, backing away in fear. Others barely even noticed she had done anything, resuming their gyrations to the changing beat.

She caught another glimpse of that pink hair, following it deeper into the club. The dancers pulsed around her, thickening as she moved forward until she couldn't push them away any longer without inflicting harm. So she danced with them, moving her body to the rhythm to make progress.

Until she met a wall.

Avery frowned. She ran her hand up the empty air, pressing against the barrier. It was cold to the touch and smooth. Curiously, the others dancing around her seemed oblivious to the field preventing them from going farther. She pushed on the invisible wall once more, the surface giving slightly, bouncing back against her hand.

So the Acquirer wanted to play games. Avery could oblige him.

In one swift move, she infused her arm with the energy that pulsated around her and struck, driving her hand into the wall. It resisted for a half second before bursting beneath her fist, sending her stumbling forward.

The scenery around her changed, unveiling a hidden room. Avery recovered her balance and glanced behind her. A shimmering opening revealed the dance floor where the ear-splitting music trickled in after her, like a ripped hole in a heavy fabric curtain. As quickly as she had broken it, the field healed itself, blocking out the sounds of the club. She could still see the dance floor, but it was dim.

When she turned back around, she gasped.

She stood in the center of the galaxy, soft stars dancing on pillows of galactic dust, spreading up and around her, expanding into infinity. Her feet were supported by nothing but the empty void of space. Avery stepped forward, and her stomach dropped, her heels finding purchase on some invisible surface.

A soft breeze cooled her skin, drying the sweat at her nape, and she closed her eyes, just briefly, enjoying the sensation. The music was different there, softer. A gentle techno beat that soothed instead of the harsh thrumming of the main club.

She finally realized there were dark couches spread among the stars, where various Reanges perched in quiet conversation, lounging in repose and drinking champagne. This had to be the VIP area they'd been looking for. Avery couldn't imagine how much it would cost to install tech like this. She hadn't seen its equal since Petra had shown her the viewing room in Nos Valuta, where you could go anywhere in any time on Echo through virtual reproduction.

Avery scanned the room, finding the woman easily. Her orange-pink hair lay in heavy braids down her shoulders, vibrant even in the low light and striking against her dark skin. She stood at the base of a dais, waiting, as though she hadn't just led Avery on a chase for no damn reason.

Anger churned in Avery's veins, her blood crackling at the promise of confrontation. She gathered her power, siphoning energy from the room, and let her fury clash against the molecules in an attempt at dominance. The galaxy around them glitched, flickering in and out of complete darkness.

The woman grinned.

"I assume there was a reason for all that?" Avery asked as she strode forward, wishing more than ever that she had her full power. She'd wipe that grin right off her face.

The woman raised a pink brow, glancing up to the dais.

Silver eyes flashed from the shadows of a large winged chair, where a man sat leisurely, one long leg crossed over the other, the picture of languid tranquility.

Avery frowned. Why hadn't she noticed him when she got here?

He rested his chin on his hand, an elbow leaning heavily on the arm of the purple velvet.

His attention slid to Avery, and her breath caught. He was the most beautiful man she had ever seen. He had smooth, perfectly sculpted features, with a lush mouth and seductive eyes that tapered to gorgeous tips beneath dark brows. His hair fell down his shoulders, long and straight, in a silky, pristine white. She wondered if it felt as soft as it looked.

So not an Elder, then. He was young. Her age—maybe a bit older.

He grinned under her perusal, as though he knew the direction of her thoughts, his skin shimmering in the light of the stars.

Recognition hit her, and she froze.

White hair . . . shimmering skin . . . The dancer from earlier.

His smile grew, until she could see the glint of his teeth from the shadows. He had been playing with her from the moment they stepped into the club.

Avery curled her lip in disgust. She jerked up her chin, sending a snap of energy at him. It threw his crossed leg off the other. He lurched forward, catching himself before he fell off the chair completely.

In a flash, the woman was on Avery, a hand at her throat that threw her off balance enough to need her powers to counter. Avery regained her center, driving the woman off her and landing a vicious uppercut to her face.

Before she could advance, hands grabbed her from behind, twisting her arm painfully into her back. Avery went with the movement, using energy to flip her body and drag the unknown assailant with her. She slammed them down into the ground, pressing her knee against their neck. She stared into the surprised face of another woman, her hair buzzed close to the scalp, making her large gray eyes feature prominently on her pale face as they widened. Her hands clawed at Avery's thigh as she tried to relieve the pressure against her throat.

"Impressive."

The word was loud in the room that had gone dead silent. Avery's inhalations pounded in her ears, at war with her racing pulse. The orange-pink woman now stood beside the Acquirer, working her jaw slowly, teasing the injury.

Avery knew how much force she had put behind that blow. It would hurt for a good while longer. She hoped it would bruise.

But they seemed to be backing down, at least.

Avery lifted her knee from the second attacker's throat, getting up with as much grace as she could muster in the silver mini dress. She was going to kill Megan.

"And here I was, thinking you looked absolutely delicious," the Acquirer purred.

"Get out of my head," Avery hissed, energy sizzling from her fingertips. She put up her mental defenses, but her gift had been so damaged that she worried if her attempts to keep him out would amount to anything.

If this was the kind of person they had to deal with, she didn't want anything to do with him. Maybe Finn had been right. Maybe they shouldn't have come at all.

The Acquirer's grin returned, his silver eyes flashing. They were unnerving, glowing in the darkness of his domain. The unnatural light was a unique result of their use of power, and one that couldn't be replicated, even by gen mods.

For the first time, Avery worried that her own eyes set others on edge. Did they bother Finn?

"Such a temper on this one," the Acquirer said, rising from his chair and lengthening to an impressive height. His body was lithe, clothed in a black shirt with a deep-cut neckline topped by a velvet suit tailored close to his lean frame. Everything about him suggested wealth, even the way he moved, sauntering down the steps with a languid grace. "Don't you know how to have any fun?" His gaze traveled down her body and back to her face. *My poor little revolutionary. Blocked, are we?*

She resisted the instinct to step back. "If you know why I'm here, then stop playing games with me," she replied vocally, hoping it would keep him out of her mind. "I came for help. Not to amuse you."

"Avery Vey," he said her name slowly, as though exploring its sound on his lips. His hand lifted, carefully brushing a lock of her hair over her shoulder. The look in his eyes was unreadable—dangerous. "You've been under my nose in my city for years, and I never knew you existed. Rem?" he called out behind him. He didn't move. He didn't even look away from Avery.

"Yes, Qav?" a man answered from the dais, rising from his seat on the couch. *Qav?* Was that his name, or another alias? Avery hadn't noticed the man called Rem before. A surprise, really, as he was clothed in a bright pink floral suit, a pair of wiry yellow-lensed coding glasses perched on his nose.

"Remind me again why we didn't know she was in our city," Qav pressed.

"Well, that would be a complicated answer, not to mention the fact that we don't make it a habit of keeping tabs on lower-level dwellers," Rem answered, with a toss of his head to shrug shaggy dark bangs out of his eyes.

"Don't I pay you good money to keep tabs on everything and everyone?" Qav turned to face Rem now, tilting his head. His stance was almost playful. "And that goes for you, too." He leveled the comment at the woman with the buzz cut.

She merely grinned, sharing an amused glance with the orange-and-pink-haired fighter.

Avery snuck a look from the corner of her eye at the people in the room who had been talking when she'd arrived. None of them were moving: still as stone, silent as death, oblivious to anything around them. Qav must have been controlling them. All of them. Just how powerful was he?

She knew then—it was a mistake to have come here. She shouldn't have brought the others. Should have come alone.

Avery took a few steps backward, eager to put distance between herself and them. She could be better prepared if she had space to work with. She began gathering power, letting it pool in her palms, weaving it around herself for defense.

Qav turned back to her, noting the increased space between them before his gaze drifted to her hands. "You are a feral little thing, aren't you?" His hand lifted toward her, a casual flick of his wrist the only warning of what was to come.

Energy crashed into her, an icy stab against her shield, making her gasp. She nearly pushed it away but realized that would mean releasing her only defense. She brought her hands up, braced against his power, and was shocked to see actual sparks flying from her fingers, carving an electric mark through the air from her body to his.

His energy shifted, wrapping around hers, freezing her solid. Something locked into place, their powers linking together, opening a channel directly from her consciousness into his. She felt him, cold and effervescent, like a mist made of pure ice. Whatever he had done had left him vulnerable. Her breath caught. She could walk straight into his mind if she wanted.

Avery took her chance. She found his mind was a shimmering world of silver, cold and overwhelming. Quickly, she reached out to his thoughts, grasping clumsily before the connection abruptly severed.

She was thrown out, stumbling on her heels as she slammed back into her own head.

"Shit," Qav gasped, his breathing labored, taking a small step back himself.

"You okay, boss?" the orange-and-pink-haired fighter asked. She planted her feet near Qav, ready to face off with Avery if needed.

"She's gonna be worth it." Qav laughed dryly.

Avery frowned. Her mind raced, turning over the thoughts she had stolen from him. Nothing concrete, but a distinct feeling all the same, singular and absolute.

He needed her.

For what, she hadn't been able to glean, but she knew he wanted her for something. Maybe it would give her an opening to negotiate.

Qav's eyes swept beyond her to the club still full of dancers. "I see you surround yourself with hotheads."

Avery whirled. Past the dim veil of the barrier, Finn, Grigg, and Petra were shoving people out of the way, tearing violently through the crowd. She'd never seen Finn so worried, his eyes moving frantically from face to face as he yelled something to Grigg over his shoulder. Nova and Markes worked through the dancers, interrogating whomever they came across, while Megan teetered behind them, uncertain.

"Do you know how much money I'm going to lose on free liquor after this little performance?" Qav sounded bored. "Syla. Ennis. Bring them." The two women nodded. They walked past Avery and effortlessly through the barrier.

"All you needed was the key," Qav whispered in her ear.

She swung back around, nearly losing her balance. He reached out to steady her, a wide hand wrapping around her arm, bringing her flush against his body.

Avery craned her head back, meeting his eyes. "What?" she snapped, still off-kilter.

"The bracelet. You didn't need that fancy show of force. Although I have to say I'm impressed you were able to break through it. I was told that energy field would be impenetrable."

"Well, then, I guess you wasted your money," she commented dryly.

"Wasting money is one of my favorite hobbies." He smiled, dimples deepening his cheeks, giving his sharp features an almost boyish quality.

It reminded her of Finn.

"You seem preoccupied with that human. I guess your performance for the media wasn't just a ruse after all."

Avery's blood curdled. He had been watching her.

"Be careful, gnima. I tried the human thing once, too. It didn't end so well."

She frowned, both at the comment and the endearment she didn't recognize. "You should let me go," she said ominously, but his grip only tightened.

Not a chance, he answered. He took a piece of her hair between his fingers, rubbing its texture. He clearly wasn't going to cooperate with her anytime soon.

And she was done trying.

"I said let me go," she bit out, lurching backward and shoving him away with a surge of force that sent him flying clear across the room. Any other person would have slammed into the dais. But he caught the energy and twirled his body in the air with momentum before landing on a knee, white hair flying around him like some kind of mythical creature.

"Avery!"

CHAPTER EIGHTEEN

Finn yelled her name, fear slicing through him as the rest of their group entered the room just in time to see Avery shove the Acquirer away.

Avery twisted to face Finn, eyes wild. Finn slowed as the two women continued on toward the center.

"Perfect timing," the Acquirer said in an even, controlled tone. He stood in a fluid motion, straightening his jacket, then running fingers through the white hair Avery had ruined. Finn thought he saw his skin glisten, shimmering in the light of the holostars.

Finn started as the room then came alive, igniting with conversation that nearly drowned out the soft music. He realized there were people there, sprawled out, sitting on couches and chatting, as if nothing were amiss. If any of them thought their group looked out of place, they didn't seem to care.

Avery stepped carefully out of the way as the two women, they'd introduced themselves as Ennis and Syla, passed her. The latter glared at Avery shrewdly beneath hot pink brows. Finn came up to Avery, pressing his arm against hers to let her know he was there. Petra and Nova stepped in front of her while Grigg kept to the back with Markes, Megan tucked behind them.

"It's Qav, right?" Avery said, doing her best to sound unfazed. "If you're not going to help me, then we'll be happy to get out of your hair."

"It seems like you're awfully attached to it," Finn remarked tensely, ready to fight. So things hadn't gone well. This was bad.

Qav's silver eyes cut to Finn, assessing him, before returning to Avery. "You've got good taste, I'll give you that. Your ambassador is even more handsome in person than on his vid feeds," he said suggestively. Then he gestured to the others. "Are you sure bringing them here was a good idea?"

Megan yipped, and Finn whirled, reaching for his blaster, but his fingers grasped only air. Right—they hadn't been allowed to bring weapons.

Finn's stomach dropped as he tried to make sense of what he saw. Markes held Megan close, a gun pressed to her temple. Where had he even gotten a blaster? Markes would never attack Megan—the Acquirer had to be controlling him.

Nearby, Grigg spread his hands out, moving slowly, weighing his options.

But it was Petra who stepped closer first. Markes activated the gun. The piercing beeping of its charger struck loudly in Finn's ears.

Megan whimpered. Petra's eyes were wide now—fearful.

The Acquirer—Qav—could control any Reange. It had been foolish to bring them here. Avery had been worried the So's would be difficult to convince, but even Finn had never anticipated outright conflict.

Before any of them could act, Avery threw a hand out toward Markes. Energy hit his body, swiping him away from Megan, like a powerless doll, and he slid straight into one of the couches. The people sitting there jumped up, shrieking in surprise. Markes didn't get up.

Finn turned to Qav. "It takes a real classy guy to hijack a kid." His words were slow, anger lacing up through his throat and into his voice. Avery placed a hand on his arm. He understood what she didn't say aloud.

This guy was out of their league.

Qav sighed loudly, then murmured, "I detest scenes," almost too quiet to hear. He turned on his heel, toward the back of the room. Syla trailed closely behind, her pink braids swaying against her back.

Ennis lingered. She dipped her smooth head to Avery before joining the other two. And then they were gone, enveloped by darkness, disappearing into the infinity of the surrounding stars.

A man descended the dais, garbed in the loudest floral suit Finn had ever seen. He offered a placating smile as he approached. When he spoke, his voice was musically formal. "I'd like to extend an official welcome to you, Avery Very, and your companions. And I feel I must add that Qav is excited to get to know you as well. He couldn't be more thrilled you've come to us."

Finn sneered, "He needs to work on his communication skills."

"Unfortunately, he's not always the best at hospitality."

"You think?" Petra spat, tearing her gaze from Megan. Her hands shook.

He didn't reply, giving them a quick bow of his head. "Remmington Lancel. I'll be helping you settle in as we decide how to approach your issue, Avery."

"Settle in? He expects me to stay here after that stunt he just pulled?" Avery replied angrily. "I'd rather dive straight into a black hole."

"You're not the only one," Grigg added from beside Markes, who leaned on Grigg's arm as he struggled to get to his feet. Markes cradled his head, casting an apologetic glance at Megan. At least he was back to normal.

"Yes, well," Remmington shifted awkwardly before continuing, "I'm afraid the choice has already been made."

"Like hell we're staying here," Petra hissed.

"I really would appreciate it if we didn't cause any more friction here at the club," Remmington said delicately, grimacing as he looked around. The patrons in the lounge were staring. His next words were casual. "After all, your other friends are already settled and waiting for you."

Avery tensed, stealing a nervous look at Petra.

Linderly and Tai.

"You have Lind?" Markes's voice was a scratchy mess, his face pale, contrasting sharply with his neon hair.

Finn's stomach clenched. He had spent weeks with them, long

enough to know how close the siblings were. How frightened he must be for her.

Avery was a live wire, her anger visible along the rigid lines of her body. He touched her arm, wrapping his fingers around her gently, before she did something she'd regret. Something they'd all regret.

Remmington noticed, stepping back deliberately and clearing his throat. "Now that we understand each other, if you'd follow me, please. We have a strict schedule to keep." He swiveled on his toes, heading off in the direction where the others had disappeared, evidently expecting them to follow.

Avery looked over the others, her face drawn in thought. She lingered on Megan who was now closely shadowed by Petra. Avery noted the barely perceptible tension between the two that had her fingers clenching.

"What do you want to do?" Finn asked, keeping his voice quiet. She needed him to be steady now more than ever.

Her gaze met his. Her eyes were glassy, uncertain. Finn could nearly read her thoughts through those golden pools of emotion.

She had given up her power the moment she'd stepped into this place.

But Avery gathered herself, straightening to her full height and looking over her shoulder, where Remmington had left them. Where they would have to follow.

When she finally spoke, her voice was calm—collected. "What I want doesn't matter anymore. We don't have a choice."

CHAPTER NINETEEN

They followed Remmington deeper into the lounge until the stars around them morphed into complete darkness, removing any sense of place. Finn brushed Avery's hand, reassuring himself she was still there. A gentle blue glow appeared ahead as they entered a small antechamber, where a door slid open to a narrow corridor.

They continued on, the hallways weaving into one another until any hope of finding their way back to the club was gone. If they were being led into a trap, they'd be screwed. Not that it could get much worse than the mess they were already rolling around in.

Finn had assumed the worst, but he had secretly hoped to be proved wrong. That they'd find the So's and get the help they needed with enough time to return to Echo before Su'elben and sort everything out.

He should have known it would all go to shit.

Avery walked just ahead of him, her pace steady. He studied the gentle curves of her profile. Her features were drawn, almost pained. She would be blaming herself for this.

He prayed to whoever was listening that Linderly and Tai were okay, for their sake and hers.

Fiora's death weighed on her. Not that she discussed it. Ever.

But he knew how she felt. Finn remembered each soldier who had served under his command, especially the ones who were lost. If only he could figure out how to tell her that he understood that pain. That responsibility.

It was a difficult aspect of leadership that he wasn't even sure he had accepted. Perhaps they weren't meant to accept it. But certainly Avery, who felt emotion so deeply, would never be able to come to terms with that burden.

She wouldn't be able to bear losing anyone else.

Remmington slowed as they approached a set of elevator doors, offering a polite smile over his shoulder, then touching his wrist to the control panel. "I'll need you all to sign nondisclosures before we head any farther. Seeing as you're public figures, we require your discretion concerning anything you observe from this point forward."

"Is this guy for real?" Grigg muttered, his anger palpable.

"You can take your nondisclosure and shove it up your ass," Petra sneered.

When Avery's eyes shifted to Finn, he nodded. He'd sign whatever they needed to keep moving. It wasn't as though they weren't already used to keeping secrets.

"Finn and I will sign it," Avery agreed. "And since we're the only public figures here, the others shouldn't need to."

Remmington was still, as though weighing their energy. The elevator arrived behind him, the doors opening with a soft whoosh of sound. He clasped his hands behind his back. "That is acceptable." He gestured behind him, stepping to the side and adding, "After you."

There was plenty of room in the considerable size of the elevator pod. They were either accustomed to large groups or they used it for something other than transporting passengers.

Finn bumped into Petra and their eyes locked, something unspoken passing between them. At some point in the past few months, they'd become allies. They would both put Avery first, and that common ground was a foundation of trust upon which they had built some kind of awkward friendship. Damn if he didn't like her now. Most of the time.

Remmington typed something into his wristport and the doors closed, the pod beginning a steady descent. He turned to Avery and Finn, projecting a data document from his wrist. "You're welcome to read it in full, but I assure you, it's your standard NDA. I drafted it myself."

"And we're supposed to trust your word?" Finn replied acerbically.

"Of course, Ambassador. I take my job very seriously," he countered, pushing his glasses farther up the bridge of his angular nose.

"And what job is that? The Acquirer's errand boy?" Finn muttered as he scrolled through the holodocs. He had no blazing clue what he was reading, but he wasn't about to show it. Avery brushed up beside him to also run through the pages.

"Your frustration is understandable," Remmington said, either refusing to answer or ignoring the insult. "If you'll stand still, please." He leaned closer to Finn in a cloud of floral-scented perfume that rivaled his suit for ostentation. A deft touch to his glasses completed a retinal scan authentication before he moved to Avery, repeating the gesture.

The pod picked up speed, although they could see nothing but the dimly lit interior, illuminated by purple lighting set into the floor panels. The club itself was situated at eight hundred feet below surface, yet they continued to drop. It was deeper than he had ever been, on either planet. Despite his time in the void of space, and in the mountains of Nos Valuta, Finn suddenly felt a twinge of claustrophobia. His palms grew clammy.

"So this is like, what? A secret society?" Megan piped up, finding her voice again. She stood beside Grigg, who let out a chuff of laughter. Avery's shoulders relaxed. Megan had lightened the mood significantly, and Finn had a feeling it was deliberate.

He grinned. Megan was made of steel underneath all that delicacy. She would assimilate with them easily. Finn had met enough soldiers to identify the ones that could handle pressure. It was easy to see why Avery loved her so much.

"Where are you taking us?" Avery asked.

"Apparently to the center of the Earth," Nova replied dryly. Evidently, Finn wasn't the only one affected by their continued plunge.

Before Remmington could answer, the pod slowed. As they kept moving, the walls changed, revealing they were actually made of glass. The entire pod was.

Megan gasped and clutched Grigg's sleeve. Markes let out a whispered expletive.

"Holy shit," Finn uttered.

There, spread out beneath the curved glass of the elevator, lay a city.

An entire city, hidden beneath the surface of the Earth.

CHAPTER TWENTY

They had an unobstructed view as the pod continued downward from the domed ceiling. The cavern reached up at least two hundred feet, spreading wide to cradle the city beneath which fanned out in a wide, flat circle. Lights twinkled from above, simulating the effervescent glow of a night sky full of stars, echoing the lights from the structures on the ground.

Between the buildings that rose up to meet them, a large canal carved a twisted line through the city center. Towers layered along the waterway, some as tall as ten stories, reducing in size as they spread toward the edges of the dome. There were no roads, only smaller canals that veined out to access the grid-ways of the city. Finn could make out small boats traversing the waters, white plumes of waves spreading behind them, glistening in the lights.

"What is this place?" Avery moved closer to the glass and pressed a hand on the surface.

"There's no official name," Remmington acknowledged, his voice quiet—reverent. "But the residents have taken to calling it Sanctum."

"How the blazar have you kept this place a secret?" Finn asked, unable to tear his eyes away. They all stood just above the tallest of the buildings, following the line of a skyway that wound into the heart of the city. Faces looked up curiously from below, as though the inhabitants weren't used to seeing the pod in use.

"Are they all Reange?" Petra was still, her voice careful.

"No humans are allowed in the city," Remmington confirmed.

Finn did look at him then, raising a brow. "Usually," he amended.

They slowed further as the skyway wove between the towers, tall fingers of sleek metal and glass rising from the dark waters below.

Remmington continued, "Refugees must apply for residency, but generally any Reange is welcome. A place is offered to those who have nowhere else to go, or to anyone who cannot adjust."

"Adjust to what?" Grigg asked.

Remmington looked at him, confused. "To life above."

"Is Tai here?" Petra asked.

"What about Linderly?" Markes's voice was unusually timid.

"They're both already waiting for your arrival in your quarters. I assure you, they're quite safe."

"What about my ship?" Finn muttered, loud enough for only Avery to hear. He got an elbow to the side for the comment and suppressed a smile. He was only joking. Mostly.

They came to a stop on the roof of the tallest building, the pod doors opening to a receiving platform. The sticky, hot air hit Finn in the face, making him pause. But they followed Remmington onto the roof, where a gentle breeze teased them, its coolness betraying its synthetic nature.

Avery walked over to the edge of the building, her silver dress shimmering in the light of the artificial stars, the fabric swaying with the movement of her determined strides. She hesitated, looking out over the city. The others followed suit. Finn stood close to her side, their fingers barely touching.

The sounds of the city beneath floated up to them. The whirring of a motorized boat . . . the gentle rhythm of the water . . . an occasional laugh from passersby.

The city must have held thousands of refugees. Tens of thousands.

To keep something like this hidden would take tremendous coordination. More than a few NDAs could ever guarantee.

"If you would follow me please," Remmington called from across the rooftop. He waited for them near the wide glass doors that led into the building, his sharp chin raised expectantly, his face pinched. He seemed like the kind of person who would be annoyed by any kind of delay, no matter how small.

They lingered for a moment more, the magnitude of this place sinking in.

Finn couldn't imagine what this would mean to them, but he could feel it: the energy coursing through Avery, bleeding into the others, mingling with their own. There were more survivors than they had ever imagined. And now that Echo was reclaimed, there was hope for them.

They could go home.

Finn watched their faces, a familiar otherness settling into his heart, carving a chasm between his ribs.

He had been raised among Reanges, but he would never be one of them. He was both a part of their world and entirely separate from it. This place was not meant for him.

Megan's eyes caught his and held as though she knew his thoughts. He plastered a smirk on his face, winking at her before looking away.

Staring out at the lights of the city from her top-level apartments, Rebecca could almost forget the precarious situation she found herself in and the stakes that rested on her success. She could even forget the reason she had trouble sleeping these days.

She had fought her whole life for the role in which she now sat. For the title she now held. Minister Klein, leader of the High Council and Commander of the Federation. She had always wanted it. Always.

It was only at this level that she could finally make a difference. She could impact real change. And she had been doing a stellar job of it until that girl had been dumped into her lap.

She had thought Avery Vey was a blessing, gifted to her after all these years of searching for more Elites. Just as their time was running out. They would finally be able to secure a solution that would bring some degree of cooperation. Some degree of peace.

Instead, Avery had turned out to be more of a danger to the cause than Rebecca could have ever imagined. The physical damage she inflicted was nothing compared to what she had done to the people's faith in their government. It had the potential to bring it all down. To ruin everything she had built.

Her fingers clenched the glass in her hand, perfectly manicured nails scraping the cool edges. The High Council had turned on her. Had given in to the demands of an outraged public and initiated this sham of an indictment. That ridiculous excuse for an incriminating vid capture was barely enough evidence to convict anyone, but her rivals had seized any chance to smear her good name.

Avery had merely provided the perfect opportunity they had been waiting for. Like sharks in the water, always circling, always waiting.

But they didn't know. They would never understand what it took to truly lead. To make the best choices for those in your charge, whether they agreed with those decisions or not. That was the sacrifice Rebecca was willing to make, to ensure the continuation of something far more precious than ideals.

Thankfully, that fool Harding had served one purpose at least. He'd been a casualty of the entire mess and could serve her better in death, if nothing else. In truth, he was the reason things hadn't been handled properly the first time around. Rebecca blamed herself for that misstep. She should have handled things herself instead of passing it off to some incapable man with anger issues. But he made an easy scapegoat, which she had utilized to the fullest.

It had allowed her to keep what allies she currently still retained in the Council. They would be essential to her now.

That damned vote of confidence.

The fact that her power rested entirely in the hands of the public was grating, eating away at her insides. Hadn't she proven herself enough time and time again in the past decades? She was no green politician, straight out of university with useless dreams and outrageous policies. She had made things better for the citizens of Earth. A humans-first approach was the only way to ensure the continuation of the species.

"Why didn't you tell me you were meeting with Finn?"

Rebecca didn't turn at the question, keeping her vigilant watch over the city. She took a slow sip from her glass, relishing in the familiar burn down her throat. Large hands encircled her waist, a scruffy jaw nestling in the elegant curve of her throat.

"You know I want to be informed of these things," Nick crooned, his voice scratchy with desire.

"I couldn't have you storming down there to confront him," she replied, letting his hands continue their perusal of her body, his warmth penetrating the silk fabric of her nightgown. The loungewear had cost more than the average Earth family's yearly income. But she'd always had a taste for expensive things and made no qualms about spending good credits on herself. "And we both know that's what would have happened had I told you he was here."

"I'm not some rage-fueled idiot." He pulled away, moving in front of her, his body a shadowed outline against the sparkling city lights. He was shirtless, his pants made of the same silks as her gown. A gift. "You're not the only politician in this room, Rebecca."

"Yes, but, darling, I'm the only one who's supposed to be alive, remember?" She regulated her voice to a low, seductive timbre. It was important to keep him level.

Nick often couldn't control his temper when his brother was the topic of conversation. Since their confrontation, Nick had been unable to concentrate on anything else during his recovery. And Rebecca couldn't afford him being distracted by that family nonsense. Not now that he was an integral part of their success.

He didn't reply for several silent moments, leaning into thought. At least he was improving. A few weeks ago, this amount of discussion on the topic would have set him off.

"My brother is important to me. I know I can bring him to our side if you just give me more time. Allow me to speak with him."

"I believe I've already given you plenty of time. And you've tried to sway him before, without success. It might be an indication you should move on from the idea."

"I won't abandon him again."

"He nearly killed you, Nick. Sometimes we have to cut our losses—"

"You don't understand," Nick said tightly, his shoulders stiffening. "He was just hurt and confused. Once I explain—"

"Enough," she said firmly. "Let's not ruin a perfectly good evening with family drama. We can discuss it later." She had no intention to do so. Only time would help him move on.

He was silent for a few moments, as though weighing her words. He wouldn't press it more that evening, she knew. But his mind wasn't settled on the subject. She would need to rectify that.

"Your meeting with Avery was well received by the public," Nick finally said. "At least that element is going according to your plans."

"And how do you know what my plans are, Nicky?" she asked, laughing quietly.

"Because we're the same, you and I."

He wasn't wrong, she supposed. They were both experts at manipulation, had both mastered their positions. But she had clawed her way to power from the very bottom. He had been born into his. Nick would never understand.

However, he was as smart as he was handsome. Both of the Lunitia boys had the looks of their father, along with his intelligence. They boasted luscious dark hair, chiseled faces, and sharp minds. And some twenty-five years earlier, their father's good looks had landed Rebecca in a precarious situation. At least she was the one in control this time.

Perhaps she was being hard on Nick. He had sacrificed more than she gave him credit for. His humanity, for one. Although she doubted he would have ever recovered without the drastic measures they took. She wasn't lying when she said Finn had nearly killed him.

She took another sip from her glass. "What's most important now is that I retain power. And the more progress we can make with our research in that time, the better. Should things go sideways—"

"They won't," Nick interrupted, taking her hand in his. She felt the warmth of his fingers but nothing else. "I've been making strides each day. I'm certain we'll have the results you need shortly."

"Good," she replied, offering him a smile. "No more episodes, I take it?"

"Not for days," he confirmed with a shake of his head. He paused, as though considering his next words carefully. "If they've disappeared again—Finn and Avery, I mean—I could help you find them. It's about time I tested myself."

She pulled her hand away, gaze sharpening. "How would you know that they're missing? Unless you've been listening to conversations you know you're not meant to hear."

He shrugged, proffering his hands out. Playing the innocent. "If this is going to work, Rebecca, you'll need to trust me in some capacity."

"You are not to go after them, do you understand me? I don't want you exposed. You're too valuable to us now."

He tore away, shoulders drawing up. When he spoke, his voice was ragged, teetering on the edge of control. "I have to see him. I have to explain. Once he realizes what we're—"

"Oh, darling, it's not that I don't trust you," she said, rushing forward, suppressing the fresh tide of frustration, reaching out to cup his cheek. "You'll be ready soon. And once you are, you'll be able to make him listen—he won't have a choice. But not until the time is right."

His breathing steadied as he leaned into her hand. "You said yourself we don't have time. The vote of confidence is around the corner. If they do something in that time to jeopardize your image further, you may not recover from it."

She smiled in earnest, downing the rest of her glass before sliding up against him. His entire body was hot under her fingers, even stronger now than it had been before.

"That's the beauty of the project, darling." She drew him down for a long kiss, her fingers tightening forcefully around the hair on his nape. He groaned, a twisted sound between pleasure and pain, and she felt the first stirrings of desire. He was panting by the time she pulled away. "If your progress goes well, then the vote won't matter."

CHAPTER TWENTY-ONE

The building was an immaculate structure, as pristine on the inside as its architecture suggested. They had been shown to a suite of apartments that took up an entire three stories, the middle of which housed common areas layered by two floors of living quarters. Remmington suggested the place was used for high-ranking visitors, special guests of Qav. But if they valued secrecy, Avery couldn't imagine it was used often.

As soon as they stepped into the entryway, a dark-haired head popped up from the couch in the living room, wide violet eyes on alert. Linderly squealed, vaulting up and over the furniture, charging toward them.

"Lind!" Markes broke away from the others, meeting her halfway and catching her in a fast hug, his voice a near sob. "Are you okay? Did they hurt you?"

"I'm fine," she got out a smothered response, her arms latched around his waist. "I'm so glad you guys are all right. They wouldn't really tell me anything except that you'd be here soon."

Petra rounded on Remmington. "Where is my brother?" she asked harshly, advancing. To his credit, he held his ground, even as she made a move to grab him.

Avery latched on to Petra's arm, and she halted, their eyes clashing. Qav wouldn't look the other way if they harmed one of his people. They couldn't afford to make any stupid mistakes.

Petra wrenched out of Avery's grasp, crossing her arms. She settled for leveling Remmington with a cold stare.

He cleared his throat, lightly adjusting his glasses. "Given his recent affliction, your brother will be contained within his room on the lower floor. Until Qav has time to address the situation, I recommend the humans seek accommodation within the upper suites so as to avoid any further confrontation."

"And here I thought you didn't care," Finn commented dryly.

"His door is activated by retinal key, so those in your party who are not human will be allowed to enter and exit. Excepting Taisto, of course. You all are welcome to go anywhere in Sanctum during your stay, so please feel free to explore." He looked up the spiraling staircase that coiled through the levels as a tall woman descended hurriedly toward them. "Ah," he said, as though surprised to see her. "This is Brehna. She'll be assisting you during your stay with us. If you should need anything, just let her know, and she'll acquire it."

"Isn't that the Acquirer's job?" Finn muttered, but Remmington seemed to ignore the comment.

Brehna said nothing but smiled warmly and nodded, wrinkles crinkling the corners of her eyes, as though she laughed often. She lingered on Avery. Her dark eyes and twisting brown hair belied little to no gen mods. She could have easily passed as human.

"Don't worry about Tai, Petra," Linderly said with a little smile. "He was a bit of a grump about being locked in that room, but what else is new? Other than that, he's fine. But I didn't really want to stay down there with him."

Petra was already making her way to the staircase, not waiting for permission. Megan shifted as though to follow her, but Nova cut her off.

"I'll go with her," Nova said gently, disappearing after Petra down the stairs in a flash of blue silk. It wasn't like Megan could go near Tai anyway.

"Now that you're in good hands, I'll see myself out." Remmington was already at the door.

"What about Qav? When can I speak with him again?" Avery asked.

"He has business aboveground. We'll be in touch as soon as he returns." And then he was gone, the scent of flowers lingering in the air around them.

"Business aboveground?" Finn bit out angrily. "We came *below*-ground to find his fancy ass in the first place."

Avery's hands turned to fists at her sides. Frustration boiled within her, seeking an outlet until her skin was vibrating. She stared at their reflection in the ornate mirror that lined the foyer. They looked ridiculous, dressed and ready for a party that had turned into disaster. And it was her fault.

She threw her hand out, letting go of the energy, relishing in the satisfying crack of the glass, their image in the mirror splintering apart. The others said nothing.

Avery inhaled slowly, turning to Brehna again. She was watching her, a strange look on her face. "Do you have any idea how long we're expected to wait here?" Avery asked.

Brehna shook her head apologetically.

"She doesn't speak," Linderly explained, stepping forward. "But we've been getting by on miming well enough."

Brehna touched Linderly's shoulder in a motherly gesture, smiling again. She brought a hand to her mouth in a repetitive motion before heading off down the hallway in long strides.

Linderly watched her go. "I'm pretty sure she's going to bring us food. She's already fed me five times in the past four hours."

"This place is insane!" Grigg called out from across the room. He had found his way to an expansive terrace that sat beyond the wall of floor-to-ceiling sliding glass doors. Markes and Linderly grinned at each other and hurried off to join him.

The living area itself was bigger than Avery's entire suite of apartments back on Echo, with a gargantuan gray couch in the shape of a half circle that dominated the space. The terrace lay just beyond that, offering a view of Sanctum. An ostentatious chandelier made of braided glass floated above them, casting long golden streaks along the ceiling.

Avery watched them go, letting out a long sigh as she followed. Finn fell into step beside her, lacing his fingers through hers. She leaned into his side.

"Ugh, you two are so gross," Megan said, swooping over to Avery's other side, looping their arms together. Avery laughed, the weight on her chest lightening. She couldn't imagine being able to handle this without them both. She wouldn't want to.

Finn nudged her before moving ahead, leaving her alone with Megan. She nearly kicked him as he left, he was so obvious about it. But she was grateful for the privacy. They sauntered slowly together toward the doors.

"How are you holding up?" Megan asked quietly, the question for Avery's ears alone.

Avery shrugged, suddenly unable to speak, her nose prickling.

"I thought so." Megan nodded to Finn, who headed for the others, a grin spreading across his face as he said something to Grigg. "Please tell me you've locked that in by now."

Avery flushed, shooting her a look. "Megan," she chastised, laughing awkwardly.

"What? Just look at that ass—he always wears the most deliciously tight pants. You can't just let something like that go to waste."

Avery laughed for what felt like the first time in days. Finn's gaze drifted over to them, his expression softening. Her cheeks heated.

"I'll take that blush as a no."

Avery tilted her head, heart in her throat as she asked, "What about you? That performance with Petra didn't look like just an act. Anything you want to share with the audience?"

"You saw that?" Her eyes turned vulnerable before she laughed, the sound gilded, carrying across the terrace. "Oh, you know me . . . I just wanted to rile her up. Worked pretty well, don't you think?"

Avery layered a smile on her face, doing her best to hide the disappointment that deflated her. She avoided looking at Finn. They walked to the railing, then leaned against it, looking out over the city below.

"Is this your life now?" Megan whispered cryptically. "Danger around every corner?"

Avery studied Megan's face, reading the remnants of fear that lingered there. The way she tried to hide it.

"I told you not to come," Avery pointed out in a stilted voice. She forgot that Megan wasn't used to this. Wasn't used to the way adrenaline soaked into your veins like poison, diluting your blood, coiling you tight.

"I'm not going to let you go through this alone."

"I have before," Avery breathed.

"But you don't have to now." Megan turned to her. "You have me and Finn and the others. I know it's hard, but—"

"Do you?" Avery laughed.

Megan looked away, her gaze hard.

A pang of guilt sliced through Avery's chest. Megan was just trying to help in the way she knew how. "Sorry," Avery apologized awkwardly. "I think I'm just tired."

Megan shrugged. "Well, it looks like we'll be here for a while. We should make the most of it," she said. She moved away, returning to the others. And Avery let her go.

They all spent an hour or so on the terrace, viewing the city beneath them from cushioned seating that had been arranged for just that purpose. They made plans to explore the next day, deciding it could be a good way to gather intel on Qav.

Later, Brehna brought out a veritable buffet of foods, presented with the finesse of the worlds' finest chefs. To Finn's and Grigg's audible delight, it tasted even better than it looked.

Linderly took them on a little tour, bouncing excitedly at being the one with information to share. On the central floor, there was a large gym, a fully immersive theater, and even a full-size swimming pool to keep them occupied. Although how they were going to enjoy them without proper clothing, Avery had no idea.

By the time Nova joined them, they had gone back to the terrace to relax. Grigg and Megan found the fully stocked bar in record time and were well into a bottle with Linderly's help. But Avery was too alert to enjoy any amount of drinking, and Finn took his cue from her. Markes passed out on the couch soon after eating.

Petra never returned from downstairs, and Avery told herself she'd check on Tai in the morning.

She stayed up as long as she could manage, her eyelids eventually drooping amid the sound of everyone's laughter. Finn's rumbling chuckles resonated through her body where she lay against him, cradled in his arms, sharing a settee.

Her mind drifted, conjuring images of some mystical moon fox that lived in the caves of Nos Valuta. The tsek. It darted in and out of the shadows of her imagination, glimpses of white fur and pointed, furry ears. From the darkness its silver eyes glowed. Watching.

Su'elben was just around the corner. If that was their deadline to get back to Echo, they had very little time to spare. She needed Qav's cooperation—needed her powers restored.

Even now, the worst could be happening to the humans on Echo, and she was an entire galaxy away. Powerless. At least in the ways that could help stop the Origin.

Qav's power made Leviathan look like the old woman she truly was. And yet she had so easily stripped Avery of her power. What was Qav capable of? What could he do to her if he chose to?

It didn't matter. Avery would get them out of this. Even if she had to become a mythical creature herself.

The hour grew later, and eventually Finn dragged her to her feet, stumbling through the apartments to the upper-level rooms. She awoke long enough to wash her face before falling into the alluring comfort of the plush bed that took up nearly half the room. Finn's weight sunk into the mattress beside her, and she curled up along his side. His hand drifted lazily across the bare skin of her back. She still wore her dress, uncomfortable with nudity, even with him. Finn retained no such modesty.

She let her thoughts float away into nothingness, whisps of smoke in the darkness of her mind, and in moments, she was asleep.

Avery was somewhere in between.

She was caught—trapped, stuck in that familiar place of heaviness and terror. She had no body and yet could not move. Forced to observe, to react. To feel the darkness that coursed over and through her, wave after wave, until she drowned.

But she had been there before. Countless times before.

A glimpse of movement, red hair, laughing green eyes.

Avery tried to turn away but couldn't. She was anchored to the dark. Movement returned, taking shape before her, a woman full of life and vibrance and light. Icy guilt drove through her soul.

"You killed me," Fiora said flatly.

There were no more smiles, no laughter. Only anger. Confusion. Accusation.

No! Avery longed to cry out to her, to fall at her feet and beg her forgiveness. But still, she could not move. She looked down at her body and saw none, panic surging through her veins, her brain struggling to reason.

She looked up. But Fiora was no longer alone. Krez stood beside her, sobs racking his body, broad shoulders shaking as he leaned over his wife, gathering her desperately in his arms.

Fiora paid him no heed, her eyes on Avery.

"You did this," she said. She turned to Krez, her pale fingers stroking his dark cheek. "Always remember this was the price you paid. The sacrifice you made—the offering."

Avery choked on tears that would not come, gasping on emptiness. Fiora began to dissolve, her body wasting away into plumes of smoke. And Avery felt it, as though she was taking her life along with her, a part of her passing with Fiora to where she couldn't follow. Not yet.

"No!" Krez cried, his voice a torturous howl soon swallowed by silence.

And then Fiora was gone, Krez's arms now clutching air.

Avery's soul split in two, pain rushing through her as she slammed back into her body, forcing that excruciating agony upon her that she tried so hard to forget. Fiora's life ripped away from her, tearing from the merge and taking something down with it. It was excruciating—unbearable. It *nearly killed Avery, too.*

She looked down at her hands, given form once more, her fingers stained red with blood and glistening through the blurred vision of her tears.

Something hammered into her—Krez—his broad fingers wrapping around her neck as he squeezed, bearing down with all that strength. All that grief. Tears leaked from the corners of her eyes, pain searing through her closing windpipes and spreading throughout her body. Spots blackened her vision.

Leviathan's laugh echoed through the darkness beyond.

And Avery did nothing to stop it. It would be easier this way. Better.

She fell backward, slipping through the veil into another reality, leaving the pain and darkness and heaviness behind.

Avery panted, eyes wild as she looked everywhere at once, her surroundings unfamiliar.

She was outdoors, beneath a clear night sky, bathed in the vibrant light of three full moons. She stood on a grassy hill, dotted with flowers that smelled like—lavender. It was tranquil there, a soothing relief to the emptiness she had just left, a balm against her subconscious that assuaged any hint of anxiety or fear or pain.

She took a deep breath, letting the scent of the flowers flow up and through her, steadying her racing pulse as she released it on a long sigh. She had never been freed from the nightmares before. Was she still dreaming?

A warm breeze pulled at her loose hair, obstructing her vision in a tangle before she pushed it behind her ears.

And then he was there.

A man stood across the field, his face in shadow. He stared at her, his body still, silver eyes glowing in the dark nearly as vibrantly as the moons themselves.

"Avery!"

She frowned. His mouth was still. Unmoving.

"Avery!"

It wasn't him shouting at all.

"Avery, wake up, sweetheart."

Finn was shaking her shoulder, his touch gentle as she woke. The barest hint of morning light brightened the windows of their room. He stood beside her, his face level with hers. His voice was delicate, as though he was scared she would break.

Dreaming. She had been dreaming.

She dropped, her stomach lurching as gravity pulled her down quickly.

Finn's arms were around her in an instant, hardening as he caught her, bringing her full weight against his chest and falling to the bed. He said nothing, anchoring her to him, their breath mingling.

She had been floating in her sleep.

Sweat trickled down her chest. Her entire body was clammy, her hair plastered to her neck. Finn was hot in comparison to her chilled skin, his naked chest branding her. Avery concentrated on the tenor of her breath to try to match his, to ground her into reality, bringing her down from the adrenaline.

"You're still having the nightmares?" he asked, voice brittle.

Avery's looked into his eyes, their gray-blue depths glassy with concern and something like fear. She nearly broke down from that look alone.

It had become so easy, hiding this side of herself. No one could truly understand what that pain had felt like. What she had been through. And Finn . . . he would only try to make it better.

She didn't want to feel better.

"I didn't want to worry you." Her voice was a hoarse scratch in the shadows.

His arms cinched around her a fraction, but he said nothing.

Once she had calmed, he released her, moving off the bed to pad to the bathroom. He returned with an armful of towels and a glass of water.

"Drink." He handed her the glass. When she had taken a few sips, he took it from her and handed her a towel. "That dress is soaked. As much as I'd love to lie by your naked body for the rest of the morning, you'll be more comfortable in this." His grin was back as he turned away, adding, "I won't even peek."

Avery let out a huff of laughter. He always handled things this way—with humor as his sword and shield. But she was grateful he didn't press it at least.

So she slipped from the dress, wrapping the plush towel around her, curling up beneath the sheets. The large cloth probably covered more than the dress had anyway.

He slipped quietly back into the bed beside her. His fingers laced through hers. They lay on their backs, staring at floral etchings on the ceiling.

After a while, Finn's breath evened out into the soft rhythms of sleep.

But Avery was still wide awake, unable to stop her racing pulse.

Her mind was filled with rolling hills beneath moonlit skies, the smell of lavender, and a pair of silver eyes in the dark.

CHAPTER
TWENTY-TWO

Avery slid from the bed before Finn awoke, using her powers to soften the impact of her steps and tiptoeing across the floor. She grabbed her dress and left the room quietly, nearly stumbling over the stack of clothes left at their door, a pair of shoes resting on top. She sent Brehna a silent thank-you for the thoughtful gesture. The practical garments, loose green pants and a flowing white shirt, fit perfectly as she pulled them on in the central-level bathroom. Even the black boots were her size.

She ventured to the spiraling staircase in the foyer, placing her dress and the towel on the stairs to carry up later. Avery surveyed the mirror she had cracked the night before. She blinked. It was smooth and clear of fissures, as though she had never broken it in the first place. Had Brehna replaced it in the middle of the night?

As though hearing her thoughts, Brehna appeared, rounding the corner from the kitchen, looking fresh despite the early hour and the work she had evidently been doing all night.

"Good morning." Avery smiled, tilting her head as Brehna approached, meeting those kind brown eyes.

Brehna returned her smile, bowing her head over clasped palms, then pointing inquisitively at Avery. That one was easy—she was asking how Avery slept.

"*Me?* Did you sleep at all?" Avery asked, avoiding the question. "And how the blazar did you fix that mirror so quickly?"

A mysterious smile played on Brehna's mouth as she shook her head, bringing a finger to her lips. She seemed determined to keep her secrets.

It might have been ludicrous, but something told Avery she could trust this woman. Her eyes conveyed a certain depth, a sadness beneath her compassion that contrasted with the laugh lines on her face. Avery suspected Brehna had seen tragedy in her life, and it gave her a convincing authenticity.

"I thought I'd check on Tai before the others woke." Avery looked past Brehna to the stairs winding downward.

Brehna frowned, pointing to her temple, eyes questioning again.

Avery understood immediately. She wanted to know why Avery didn't speak in mind. Embarrassment flooded through her, and she shifted on her feet, staring down at her boots. They squeaked on the marble floor.

"I can't," Avery got out pathetically. She didn't know how to explain that she was broken. So she just said, "That's why we're here. So he—Qav—can fix it."

Brehna's hands settled over hers, and Avery glanced up, startled as Brehna lifted Avery's fingers to her lips, placing a kiss on them. She cupped Avery's cheek before pulling away. And then she was gone, a blur of mauve skirts disappearing down the hallway.

Avery didn't linger, taking the steps down to the lower floor. It was identical to the upper level, a long hallway branching down either side of the stairs, floors and walls built from veiny gray marble. She saw a black cam bot outside the closest door on the left and walked up to it, letting it scan her retina. The door beeped twice before sliding open.

Inside, Petra looked up from her seat on a large chair by the windows. Tai stood nearby, watching the city. The room was a copy of Avery and Finn's, from the unobstructed view of Sanctum to the white flowers carved into the ceiling.

"Nice of you to join us," Tai fumed over his shoulder. "Am I going to be a prisoner here forever?"

Avery's stomach twisted. It didn't sound like him at all. He was bitter. Angry.

She cleared her throat and ventured farther into the room. "We're all prisoners here until I get my powers back."

He laughed, whirling on her. "Oh, really? I didn't know you had a lock on your door, too."

Petra rubbed a tired hand over her forehead. "We've been over this, Tai. It's for your own good."

"My own good?" he sneered, green eyes alive with hatred. He focused on Avery, sauntering toward her. "Is that what your humans are for? Is that what you tell yourself when Finn is between your—"

"Tai!" Petra was on her feet, enraged.

He laughed again. "What? Don't tell me you're not thinking it. I've seen the way you—"

"That is enough," Petra thundered. She grabbed his arm and threw him at the bed, her teeth bared.

"Petra," Avery cautioned, reaching out to Tai as though she might catch him. But she pulled back at the last moment.

Tai stumbled and fell onto the mattress. He stared up at them. "You both are pathetic," he breathed. "You and your humans. We'll be rid of them all soon enough."

The air left Avery's lungs. The Tai she knew—the Tai Petra loved—was gone. And it was her fault. All her fault.

She ached for her powers, her need for them burning a hole in her chest. If only she hadn't been weak, she could have prevented this. She could have stopped it from happening in the first place.

Panic clawed up her throat, and her vision blurred until she could barely see either of the siblings through the tears that threatened to spill over onto her flushed cheeks. There was nothing she could do for him now. Nothing she could even say.

So she left.

In the hallway, she leaned against the wall, savoring the coolness of its surface. The door beeped again, and Petra emerged. Avery realized for the first time that Petra was dressed in something other than her sleek black suit, now sporting a casual outfit similar to her own. Brehna must have made the rounds with everyone.

"Sorry," Petra said, sidling up beside Avery. She took a breath. "About what he said—"

"Don't worry about it." Avery forced a smile. "We both know that's not him."

Petra nodded. "Yeah."

And they didn't say anything else on the subject, both ignoring the wounds Tai had opened. Ignoring the truths they didn't say to each other.

Avery straightened, infusing her voice with as much normalcy as she could muster as she said, "I was heading to the gym. Care to join me?" The one place she could think of where no one would expect or want her to talk. Petra nodded gratefully.

In silence, they walked to the central level and down the main hallway, stopping short once they crossed the threshold to the gym. They weren't alone.

A heavy set of weights clanged to the floor as Nova dropped them on a grunt, sweat dripping from her brow. Her honey-blonde hair was pulled into a pony atop her head, perfectly coiffed as ever. She was wearing the outfit Brehna had given her, too.

"I guess I'm not the only one who couldn't sleep." Nova grabbed a towel, wiping her face.

"Judging by the amount the others drank last night, I doubt they can even get out of bed this morning," Avery said wryly, and Nova let out a full belly laugh.

Petra said nothing, already on her way to the circle of treadmills in the middle of the room.

Nova raised a light brow. "You'd be surprised at what Grigg can handle and still be ready for duty the next day. Finn too, for that matter. Where is he, by the way?"

"I wanted to let him sleep." Avery made a show of observing the equipment. She had come here to avoid questions, not answer more.

The room spanned half the floor, its longest wall covered in vid mirrors ready for casting. It boasted every type of machine imaginable in duplicate, the cardio equipment arranged in a circle that spread outward from the center. A ringed light embedded in the ceiling mimicked the pattern above. There was even a mat for sparring and ground work in the far corner from the entrance.

Nova utilized the antigravity-weight area. Avery had exercised with her enough over the past few weeks to know she preferred anaerobic gains for stress relief. Grigg liked to say it was because she was trying to keep up with him in the ring.

Not that Nova needed brute strength to beat him. She was the most skilled fighter of all of them. Her flexibility and swift instincts made her a force to be reckoned with. And Grigg knew it.

"Are you okay?" Nova asked, always too observant. "If you ever need to talk . . ."

"I know," Avery replied, plastering a smile on her face that didn't reach her eyes. "But I'll be fine. I just need to work it out."

Nova nodded, picking up her weight again and launching into more reps. "I guess I'm glad Grigg's not up yet. He's way too competitive. It takes the fun out of it."

Avery laughed. "You can say that again."

"Believe it or not," Nova continued between curls, "*he's* the one who says I used to be the real asshole on that front."

"What? You, competitive? I don't believe that for a second." Avery started her warm-up series, limbering her body for the run she had planned.

"He's right," Nova explained. "When I was a kid, I was obsessed with being the best at everything. If somebody offered me help, I took it as an insult. So I pushed people away—isolated myself. I thought it was the only way to focus on my goals."

Avery gave her a look. There was no way Nova had ever been anything but calm and caring. On the other side of the room, Petra was already sprinting on a treadmill, her pace savage and demanding, as though she was trying to outrun something. If her fierce scowl was any indication, she wasn't having much success.

Avery crossed an arm over her chest, stretching out her back. "So, what happened?" If it made Nova feel better, she would let her talk.

"Grigg happened." Nova laughed, her face warming. "He was an orphan from the cities, sent to the mountains for sanctuary from the war. He blew my little bubble of isolation to hell—wouldn't leave me alone."

"Well, that certainly sounds like him."

"And before I knew it, I had changed. I opened up a little, and it was the best thing that's ever happened to me. It brought me to Finn—and you." She looked to Petra and smiled. "And the others."

Avery tried to smile back, unable to find words.

If they had had this conversation a week ago, she might have agreed. She might have said yes, it was best to lean on others and open yourself up to them. It was a nice sentiment. And for any other person, it made complete sense.

But Nova didn't understand what Avery carried, the weight she bore. Where one wrong move could undo everything and send a whole world into chaos.

Where one wrong move could extinguish someone's existence, leaving nothing but a shadowed, empty void where the fire of their soul once burned.

And so Avery said nothing at all.

Finn woke alone, a stab of fear ripping through his gut as he reached for Avery and found her side of the bed cold. He had enough presence of mind to throw on pants before bolting out the door and down to the main level.

"Avery?"

There was no answer.

He scanned the living room, giving the terrace a once-over before continuing down the central hallway. The floor was freezing beneath his bare feet.

Just ahead, Petra emerged from the gym. As soon as she saw his naked chest, her face scrunched into a glare.

"Where's Avery?" He tried to keep the panic out of his voice.

That garnered him an amused huff and a quick roll of Petra's eyes. "Calm down. She's in there with Nova." Petra jerked her head in the direction behind her, wet hair falling over her forehead. She was soaked in sweat.

He hid the relief that flooded his body, lacing his voice with a flippancy he didn't feel, determined to remove that pity he saw on her face. "Did you just run a marathon, or have you been with Megan this morning?"

It was a low blow. But it worked.

Petra's eyes widened for a millisecond before she caught herself. She lowered her chin. "You're disgusting," she bit out, stalking past him. Her hand connected with his shoulder, shoving him roughly out of her way.

He stumbled into the wall but then found his balance and grinned. She was pissed as hell, but thankfully she seemed to forget about the desperation in his voice.

"And put on a shirt," she snapped without breaking her stride.

"I've never had any complaints before." Her shoulders stiffened, but she ignored him and disappeared down the stairs to her lower-level chambers.

Finn exhaled loudly, running a hand through his hair.

Avery was safe. Of course she was. He was overreacting.

But regardless of Remmington's assurances, there was no way Finn was going to trust these people. Especially not where Avery was concerned.

She was pulling away. From him. From them all. They were together again, but she couldn't have been farther from their reach.

Losing her power—her connection to the Reanges—was poisoning her from the inside.

Moons above, he would do anything to save her the pain of being alone. He knew, better than anyone, the agony of solitude. He fit in nowhere. Belonged to no species.

But even his position placed burdens on him, in a different way. Finn was responsible for the humans who resided on Echo. The ones who were currently at risk, their lives a ticking time bomb, dependent entirely on their success for survival. And it had been his blazing plan to register them, to offer them help in their time of need, that had been exploited to arrest them in the first place. He'd spent the past week practically drawing up a list for the Origin to check off, one by one.

If they couldn't make this work—if Qav didn't fix Avery so they could get back to Echo . . .

Avery would talk to him when she was ready. And until then, he would be whatever she needed.

Besides, they were finally in a situation where his humanity was an asset. That white-haired bastard couldn't influence or control him. Thank the moons for small mercies.

"You working out in that?"

Grigg sauntered toward him from the stairs, his barely red eyes offering the only betrayal that he had imbibed too much the night before.

"I forgot how hilarious you are before sunrise," Finn replied dryly.

Grigg smirked, clapping a hand on his shoulder and pushing him to the stairs. "I saw the pile of clothes still sitting in front of your door. Go change, and then get back here. Kicking your ass is always the best cure for my hangovers."

"I have doubts that you even know what a hangover is," Finn muttered on his way back up the steps.

By the time Finn returned to the gym, Grigg had already tried to challenge both Nova and Avery to a sparring match. They declined by reason of his insanity. They both could best him easily anyway. Finn, however, was happy to oblige him.

Markes showed up later, opting for a swim when he saw how Finn and Grigg were grappling. Like they both had something to prove.

After, everyone showered and changed into the new clothes that had been waiting for them in their rooms. Everyone gathered on the terrace, ready for the day.

Finn was ravenous, his stomach growling as he surveyed the impressive spread of Echo delicacies that lined the long table bordering the edge of the living area. He may have had qualms about why they were there, but Finn could appreciate the food. Brehna had really outdone herself. Grigg wasted no time before diving face-first into his plate, not waiting for the others to serve themselves.

Linderly finally appeared, her skin pale from dehydration. Her tattoo sleeves stood out harshly in the morning light. "Moons above, tell me there is coffee." Her voice was flat, devoid of its usual bubbles.

Finn grinned, pouring her a steaming cup from the kettle. She snatched the mug from him like a feral animal. Finn laughed. "Whoa, remind me not to get on your bad side."

"You have no idea," Markes said around a mouthful of fruit. "You should see her when she's sick. It's frightening."

Linderly snarled at him, grabbing a piece of grilled meat and walking to the edge of the terrace. She nibbled on it, her face pulled into a scowl.

"And *that* isn't frightening?" Finn asked, eyes wide.

"Just wait until Megan gets up," Avery warned. She sipped from a steaming cup of tea. "She's gonna be a real treat."

"Are you talking shit about me, Vey?"

Avery froze in her chair. Her eyes locked with Finn's, and she winced comically. His grin widened.

"Megan!" Avery's voice was forcibly bright as she turned around in her seat. "You're up already? I thought you'd sleep in later."

"Clearly," Megan said, squinting as she approached the table. "Aren't we underground? Why the blazar is it so bright out here?"

"Artificial sunlight," Nova explained, pointing up to Sanctum's cavernous ceiling. "They're casting it from the panels in the dome. We had something similar in Nos Valuta."

"That's the base under the mountains on Echo," Avery elaborated.

"I'm well aware what Valuta is, Avery, thank you," Megan stated tartly. She pulled out a chair for herself and plopped down unceremoniously, then grabbed the nearest glass of water and downed it in one long pull.

Petra rose from the table to join Linderly against the railing.

"You know, this place isn't all that different from home," Markes pointed out. "Hidden stronghold beneath the surface? It feels just like—"

"The Origin," Linderly finished, not moving from her stance against the barrier. Petra stiffened.

Even Finn's blood ran cold at the comparison, the energy of the group turning solemn. He looked to Avery. Her entire body seemed to shudder, like she was locking herself away.

Their time in the Origin had been tenuous at best, and she had endured the most there. He had been in a blazing coma for half of it. If this place was anything like that, then they'd do well to get what they needed and get out.

Avery's eyes clashed with his. Something flipped over in his heart.

This time, he would be there for her. She wouldn't have to go through it alone.

She held his gaze, as though unable to look away. There it was again, that feeling surfacing somewhere within his chest. Like the gentle fluttering of a flame wanting to ignite. It grew, lengthening between them and reaching out across the table, a line of electricity trying to make contact.

Avery shifted, glancing down, and whatever it was dissipated.

"Anybody up for a movie?" Grigg asked in a pathetic attempt to change the subject. Finn snorted.

"How long are we planning to sit on our asses doing nothing?" Petra was at the table again, her palm flat on the surface as she leaned on it menacingly. "We came here for a reason, but all we've done so far is play house. They've been getting drunk, your gifts are still limited, and Tai is . . ." She stared at her hands. Her jaw set. "Tai is getting worse. We can't just sit here and do nothing. *I* can't just sit here."

Grigg took a sudden and passionate interest in his mug, swirling around a mouthful of coffee.

"We're at his mercy, Petra," Avery said wearily. "Even if we wanted to try another city—to try and find another So'—it would be too late. Our days are running out."

"Then let's go home. We can stop Leviathan there. Use our time there."

"The smartest course of action now is to see this thing through."

Avery's voice was low—final.

Finn frowned, not sure that he agreed. If it came down to it, they would have to leave Earth and return to Echo anyway. Petra might be right. Perhaps it would be best to cut their losses now. To return and stop the Origin, even with Avery's powers as they were.

Was it their choice to gamble with so many innocent lives at stake? Lives that would be on Finn's head, should they fail.

"He's playing with us," Petra replied through clenched teeth, her fingers clawing the table. "Like he did in the club. This is all part of his game."

"Then I suppose we had better learn the rules." Avery stood, draining the rest of her coffee. "We're free to explore the city. I'm going to see what I can learn from the people here. Maybe I can glean some information on how to handle Qav the next time we see him."

"I'm coming, too." Megan popped up from her chair, all surliness forgotten. She wouldn't look at Petra. "All of you may be used to underground cities, but this is kind of a new thing for me. I'm not gonna sit here and miss out again."

Petra stared at Avery for a moment longer before breaking away. Her gaze landed on Megan before whirling around to resume her post at the terrace railing. Her shoulders were locked, and her head was pointed down, blue hair curtained over her face.

And for the first time, Finn understood her.

No, more than that.

He felt the exact same way.

CHAPTER TWENTY-THREE

In the end, everyone went with Avery to the city.

Built atop the water, there were no roads of any kind, nor air lanes for cruisers. Instead, the people traversed the canals and waterways on boats of all shapes and sizes. A few were sleek and modern, almost silent as they drifted by. But most were built from scraps, welded together in a patchwork of metal and showcasing enough rust that Avery was surprised they could stay afloat.

The largest canal snaked through the city center, wide enough for at least four boats to operate side by side. On its bank stood the building where the group had been staying, their apartments on the top floors. An arched pedestrian bridge bowed over the water, leading them to the other side and deeper into the heart of Sanctum. From there, they could walk along the paths that lined the smaller canals that spread out into the city, twisting between buildings and homes.

While some of the boats may have been ramshackle, the walkways and the city itself were immaculate. There wasn't a hint of dirt or trash, even in the darker alleys between structures, as though the citizens routinely cleaned their shared spaces. It was nothing like the Earth's surface.

In fact, Milderion was just as pristine and well-kept by its citizens. That part of the Echo culture had survived, even here.

Although the waterlogged city was unlike anything Avery had ever seen, Nova was quick to point out there was a similar place on Echo.

"It's called Dru-hali. Located on the outer peninsula, near the eastern continent," Nova explained as they walked. "The weather isn't great, and it can be quite cold for our standards, but the type of fish they sell there is renowned for its flavor."

"There's nothing like it," Petra contributed, her first words uttered since they left the building. When she spoke again, her voice was stilted. "We used to sail there for the summer festivals. My mother always loved the drumming performances."

At that, Avery nearly stumbled. It was the most she had heard Petra talk of her family or her past in front of others. Ever.

"I'd love to see what you consider bad weather," Megan interjected drolly, not missing a beat. "Echo is known for its mild temperatures. We can barely even see the sun here on Earth, and that's considered a good day."

Avery gave her a thankful look. Megan smiled, linking arms with her as they approached the central market. Brehna had been able to give them rudimentary directions and a general idea of where they should explore first. It had led them down the edge of the main canal until the buildings thinned out at the edge of a dark lake.

The water spread outward, reaching all the way to the walls of the dome. The only break in its smooth surface was a small island in its center where a massive building was perched, easily a mansion, the sides of its three stories shimmering white against the shadowy waters beneath. There was no bridge to access it: the grounds were completely surrounded by water.

Their group attracted a few sly looks as they passed pedestrians, but it was nothing compared to the open gawking they received once they entered the market proper. As they continued along the water's edge, they found themselves encompassed by a crowd of vendors and patrons. Avery felt out of place and awkward, much like she had in her first days on Echo.

But this was still different in many ways. She was stronger now, even if she wasn't at her full power. And she had people to protect, friends as dear as family who counted on her. Who stood by her.

The air was laden with delicious smells, promising fried foods and sweet pastries as the walkway widened into a large open area on the water. It was filled with stalls of all sorts tucked next to the tall buildings, offering anything one could need, from foods and produce to scrap electronics, even pottery and other forms of art. Somewhere in the distance a band was playing some kind of jaunty electronic melody.

"Look at those dresses!" Megan's voice was shrill and excited as she tore away from Avery's arm. "No offense to Brehna, I mean, I just adore combat boots, but moon above, I hope they take standard credits." And she was off, disappearing into the crowd.

Before Avery could call out to her, Petra took off, hot on Megan's heels. Avery felt a twinge of something like jealousy. But she didn't follow them.

"Damn," Grigg said, laughing. "Color me shocked on that one."

Finn elbowed him, throwing a quick glance at Avery that she tried to ignore.

"What?" Grigg shrugged.

"Nova's right." Markes tilted his head quizzically. "You really are dense sometimes." He grinned mischievously before Grigg lunged for him. But Markes jumped swiftly out of reach and made a break for it. His freedom was not long-lived. Grigg had him in a chokehold a moment later, demanding an apology.

The thickening crush of people made it difficult to stay together, and soon the group parted to explore on their own after agreeing to meet up for lunch by the waterfront later.

Finn and Nova stuck with Avery, and they walked quietly together toward the vendors lining the edge of the markets where there were fewer people. They would have the leisure to talk longer with the vendors if there were less patrons. It also meant there weren't as many stares, for which Avery was grateful. Or, at least, the people out there were more discreet about it. Either way, she felt calmer.

But they didn't find much luck with their inquiries. Every time she brought up Qav, she was met with the same responses. He was a "blessing from the moons" sent to offer them relief. His "benevolence was unmatched" in the two galaxies. One woman even claimed they were graced just to be able to look upon his beauty. And after each person finished waxing lyrical about their tsek, they'd move straight on to selling their wares. Like the conversation had never happened.

By the fifth fruitless interview, Avery could feel the energy sparking along her skin, her frustration seeking an outlet.

They had started for the next stall when Finn halted, his stare locked on the side of the building ahead. Avery swiveled around to follow his gaze. And her pulse jumped.

Painted on the wall was a mural spanning the length of the building. It was Qav, his face exactly as Avery remembered it. He was garbed in black so that his white hair stood out against the darkness, his eyes piercing and gray as they watched over the city. Avery shivered.

"That's . . ." she sputtered, trying to find the words.

"Unnerving," Nova said.

"Creepy as hell," Finn uttered.

Nova let out a terse sigh. "They're not going to say anything about him. At least not to us."

"If I have to listen to somebody else tell me how blessed they are to have *that* as the protector of their realm, I'm going to shoot them," Finn added miserably, running a hand through his dark hair.

"Do you think he's controlling them?"

"How?" Avery reasoned. A little girl suddenly ran past them, her eyes bright and happy. She was laughing, red sweets from the market clutched in her hands. "He's not even here right now. He would need to be at least in the vicinity. We're miles beneath the surface."

But then, Tai was still impacted by whatever Leviathan had done to him. And she was an entire galaxy away. If Qav could control these people from such a distance and on such a grand scale, then what hope did she have against him? Ice grazed her mind, sending a chill up her back. She brushed it away.

"Let's try one more," Avery said, heading for the last stall in the row. Unlike the others, made of plain cloth and scraps, this one was draped in purple fabrics, rich and luxurious and layered. No visitors loitered nearby. Avery pushed through gauzy lilac curtains and entered, greeted by the smell of incense. Behind her, Finn coughed.

The smell was strong, but Avery felt comforted by the strange scent. A floral sweetness that mingled with smoke and something richly spiced.

A large table featured prominently within the tent, an ancient wooden piece with the phases of the moon carved down each leg. Avery's eyes widened, not at the surface, which was piled high with charms, candles, and herbs, but at the sheer value of the table itself. No one had made furniture from trees in hundreds of years, maybe more.

"I was wondering when you'd come." A woman approached from the shadowed recesses of the tent, the ends of her long black robes trailing on the ground.

Shock jump-started Avery's pulse as the woman spoke. Her face was instantly familiar.

"Brehna?"

Finn and Nova flanked Avery, ready.

But no, not Brehna. The hair was all wrong. This woman's was longer, cascading over her shoulders in ringlets against the dark fabric.

As the woman walked forward, another face appeared behind her. Identical.

"Brehna is my sister," the woman explained, nodding to Brehna, who now stood beside her. Her tapered fingers clasped in front of her as she added, "Forgive her for not telling you. She had hoped she would be able to speak with you in mind, but it seems that's not possible."

Brehna gave Avery a reassuring smile, placing a hand on her sister's shoulder.

"Then who are you?" Finn asked, his body tense.

She looked directly at Avery before answering. "My name is Bedria Clythe." A mischievous grin spread across her face. And when she spoke next, she did so silently. *And I'm here to answer your questions.*

CHAPTER TWENTY-FOUR

Avery stepped back on a gasp, shock rippling through her as Bedria's words entered her mind.

"What is it?" Finn asked sharply, rigidly holding his ground. His body was angled, preparing to fight.

"She spoke to me," Avery said softly, her eyes not leaving Bedria's.

"And, what, you've got a problem with her name?"

"Not out loud, you idiot," Nova muttered, calling him on his poorly timed humor.

"Are you a So'?" Avery asked, ignoring the exchange, hope blooming. "Can you help me?"

"Do you honestly think if I were a So' I'd be selling mystical trinkets? That I'd be living here in this half-assed attempt to recreate our home world?" She gestured at the curtains fluttering in the breeze.

Brehna moved her hand to Bedria's elbow, drawing her sister's eyes to her.

Bedria drew in a slow breath. "No, I'm not a So'; nothing so grand as that. There isn't really a word for what I am. I make things . . . inconvenient. I am immune to the So's' influence."

Avery tilted her head. "But you can speak telepathically?"

"Only to So's, unfortunately. And I've had the pleasure of knowing just one since arriving on Earth. That was years ago, after the initial Fleeing." She didn't have to explain about whom she spoke. He was the reason they all were there. "Don't worry; I can't delve into your mind or read you. I can only communicate. The bond is one-way."

Avery faltered, making a connection. Mylan. He had spoken to her in the same fashion as this when they had first met. Avery had never thought to dwell on it. He must have had the same gift.

No wonder he could stand up to Leviathan.

The incense in the air suddenly turned overwhelming, making her feel ill. Every time she caught up on her knowledge about her culture, something new surfaced. It was maddening.

"What is *that*?" Finn's voice cracked.

Avery's eyes flew to Bedria.

There on her shoulder, peeking out from behind her neck, sat a small creature, its tiny clawed fingers clinging to the dark fabric of Bedria's robes. Its ears were sharply pointed upward, and it had rich brown fur and a bushy tail nearly the size of its body that curled behind its head. It wore a perfectly miniature purple vest, a matching shade to Bedria's clothing.

"Is that a rat?" Nova asked cautiously.

Bedria scratched a finger beneath its chin, cooing, "Don't listen to them, Raki. They've just never seen the likes of you."

Avery bounced on a sharp intake of breath. "That's—that's a squir, isn't it? I've only ever seen one in old vid movies. Aren't they supposed to be extinct?"

Bedria laughed, a boisterous sound that cracked on the ends, as though she hadn't allowed herself the indulgence in a long while. "A squirrel," she corrected. "They are extinct in the wild, like most animals on Earth. But you'd be surprised how many trained professionals live in Sanctum—even our own Cloneist. Not that he can do much these days. But if you find the right genomes, he'll cook up whatever you pay the right price for."

"No shit," Finn said, his voice reverent as he reached a hand out to the animal. It snarled at him and ran over to Bedria's other shoulder.

"He doesn't like strangers," Bedria explained with a shrug.

"It looks like any other rodent to me," Nova said caustically.

Bedria narrowed her eyes. "Are you just here to insult my pet? I was under the impression you needed information."

"She's right," Avery said, frowning at the other two. "Then what can you tell us about Qav? Is he controlling the people here?"

Brehna only watched the exchange quietly. Observing.

"Where Qav is concerned, things are always . . . complicated." Bedria sighed and walked around the table to stand before them. Finn eyed the squirrel skeptically. "He was born here on Earth and found his powers early. Even for a So', he's remarkably skilled with his control. He built an empire in the world above before he ever crafted this one in the deep. And Sanctum does offer protection for us. It's home, of a sort." Her hand fiddled with a locket that hung low on her chest. "Or as close as we'll ever get to it again."

Brehna joined her sister at her side. She gripped Bedria's hand tightly and then let go. She approached Avery, placing that same hand over her own heart, her dark eyes glassy.

Brehna was asking her to trust them.

Finn arched a brow at Avery. This would be her choice. But she had to rely on instincts she had never honed. If only she had her power, she could know in seconds the absolute truth.

Avery hated the fear that haunted her every thought, her every decision. Hated what Leviathan had taken from her.

"Does he control the people? Not exactly." Bedria found her voice again. "But he influences them. Keeps them calm. Placated with this place."

"But not you?" Nova angled her head at the question.

Bedria did grin at that, letting out a soft chuckle. "No, not me. I'm a bit of a black sheep, you know. But they tolerate me since I'm old as dirt and thus remember the old ways. I keep traditions alive." She gestured around the shop, to the religious and mystical paraphernalia littered throughout it. "But I'm not exactly quiet about my skepticism where the great tsek is concerned. It doesn't go over too well."

"Then why does Qav tolerate you?" Avery asked.

"That, I'm afraid, is anyone's best guess. Brehna has a few whimsical notions about it." She gave her sister a look. Brehna merely smiled, tilting her head. "But I fancy he just likes the challenge. You should be careful with him. All of you should," she warned, her tone lowering. "He's cunning and selfish, and his skill with his gift is unmatched by anything I've heard of. Even during my days on our world."

An image frosted Avery's mind: silver eyes, watching from the darkness.

"But you, Avery Vey," Bedria went on, reaching out to take Avery's hand, "you have restored balance. You have given us hope; something we haven't felt in decades. They see you in the media feeds, they see what you have done, and they hope for a better world. For our world."

Avery's chin dipped, realization dawning. "You want to leave. To return home."

She gestured to Brehna. "Before we fled Echo, my sister lost her family in the attacks on our city. And I almost lost her," Bedria said brokenly, the first sign of real emotion. The squirrel—Raki—curled into her neck, as though he sensed the shift in her mood. "We'll never find peace here. We'll never heal here. None of us will."

Her words lingered in the air, mingling with the thick scent of the incense, the weight of their meaning settling heavily on Avery's shoulders. She had essentially handed Echo over to Leviathan. Had put even more people at risk in the process. And she had fled. Powerless.

They wanted to return to Echo. Of course they did. Now that the war with Earth was over, they should have been free to do so. But just contemplating the logistics of such a maneuver was overwhelming. They'd never be able to sneak thousands of Reanges through the Gate unnoticed. And that was assuming Avery would be able to defeat Leviathan and restore balance there. She would just bring more people to be controlled home with her.

"I can't," Avery said tightly. "I don't even have full command of my powers right now. The entire reason I'm here is for Qav to fix me."

Bedria nodded. The information wasn't new to her. "In regard to that, I think I've found a—"

"What did Qav tell you about interfering in his business, Bedria?"

They all turned to the entrance, where Syla dipped beneath the lilac strips of fabric, peering inside. Avery held out a hand, staying Nova and Finn. But she gathered energy to her palms, preparing for a fight.

"I'm just having a conversation with some shoppers," Bedria said innocently, shoving items into a bag that she pulled out from seemingly nowhere. Brehna had disappeared, like a ghost, a figment of their imagination. "Some of us have to make a living, you know."

"Right," Syla replied succinctly. To Avery and the others: "Get your shit, and let's go."

"I don't think we were done talking." Finn's comment was casually rebellious.

"I don't think I remember asking if you were."

"I preferred it when you didn't talk at all," Avery said, warning in her words as she stepped over to Syla.

Syla didn't back down, squaring off in front of her. "You're lucky I have orders to not touch you."

Finn laughed. "Why, because she'd beat your ass again?"

Somewhere behind them, Bedria snickered.

But Avery didn't want to cause a scene. As far as they knew, she still needed Qav, and he had as good as said that he knew how to fix her. If he was back in Sanctum, then her cure could be as simple as finally sitting down to talk.

"Let's go," she said, following Syla out of the tent, but not before turning to Bedria and grabbing the bag with a muttered "thank you." Her eyes darted through the shadows, searching for Brehna. But she was gone.

Back outside, they walked toward water, away from the thickest parts of the market crowds.

Syla said abruptly, "Bedria is a crazy old witch. You shouldn't listen to a word she says."

"This coming from an incredibly reliable source," Finn muttered, and she rounded on them, stopping short.

"Anything we do is for the good of the whole. It's people like Bedria who complicate matters. If it were my decision, that old bat would be thrown out on her ass."

"Then why does he let her stay?" Avery was genuinely curious.

Syla's face shuttered, going quiet as her eyes shifted away. "I'm not here to discuss her. Where is the rest of your circle?" She frowned in a way that accentuated the unevenness of her nose, as though she had broken it more than once in her life. "Never mind." She continued marching, not waiting for an answer, her long strides forcing Avery into a brisk pace to keep up. "I assume they'll find you soon enough."

"Where are we going?"

"As if she knows," Finn said dryly. "Qav's probably got her on a leash, too. Like the rest of this cursed hellhole."

Syla halted and spun around to face him. "If his name passes your lips again, I'll—"

"You'll what?" he taunted, raising his eyebrows and stepping closer.

"Finn," Avery cautioned.

He ignored her. "As far as I can tell, you're just as powerless as the rest of us. And if I want to call your boss a selfish, controlling son of a bitch, then I think that's my prerogative."

Syla's lip curled into a silent growl before she launched herself at him, a lightning-fast jab headed straight for his face.

But Avery was faster.

She threw her hand out, catching Syla's fist inches before it connected with Finn's nose.

Avery gripped her wrist, enhanced strength bearing down on the bone, knowing it would bruise. Syla's gaze jerked to Avery, the brown depths turning molten with surprise and anger.

"Don't," Avery warned, reading her will to fight, but it was too late.

Syla wrenched free and brought her other hand up in a swift uppercut. Avery dodged it, jumping backward, pulling her away from the others.

And yet Syla advanced, throwing jab after jab that Avery blocked with raised arms, protecting her face, blunting the blows with a cushion of air against the attacks. But she missed one, and it connected with her side, knocking the breath right out of her.

"Is somebody gonna do something?" Suddenly Megan was there, her voice panicked. Avery glanced her way for no more than a second. The others were all there, too.

"Leg!" Petra yelled, too late.

Syla took advantage of the distraction, swinging her body around to deliver a full kick to Avery's torso.

Avery took the hit, air whooshing out of her again. But she caught Syla's leg, using the momentum to pull her off her feet and slam her into the ground.

Syla caught herself, rolling away in a deft tumble, and twisted on her back, sweeping a leg beneath Avery that knocked her feet out from under her. Avery landed hard on the ground, her breath fully gone until she rolled over, coughing, trying to regain her oxygen.

"Stay back," she wheezed at the others moving to intervene.

Syla was on her feet, grinning.

Avery pulled herself up, willing air in and out of her lungs. She faced Syla, eyes narrowing. The woman was well-trained, better than anyone Avery had fought for certain. Even Finn and Nova.

But she was quick to anger, eager to use her fists, and worked for a pseudo-criminal who toyed with the fate of a desperate people. And that, Avery realized, made her mad. Anger, she could work with.

Avery let the rage fill her veins, welcoming it, gathering the energy around her until her skin crackled and sparked.

She raised a brow, a silent invitation.

Syla charged forward, trying her jabs again, but Avery dodged each of them, too fast to touch. Syla moved in closer, wrapping her arms around Avery, flipping her body over, heading straight for the ground again.

But Avery was ready this time, rolling with the movement, catching herself on her toes. In a flash, Avery maneuvered beneath Syla's arms until she became the aggressor, holding the woman's neck in a firm lock.

But Syla wouldn't submit.

Her long, muscular legs pumped away, scrambling at the ground, trying to use her height to dislodge Avery. She landed a solid elbow into Avery's ribs, the pain resonating through her back, traveling up her spine.

"That hurt," Avery sneered into her ear.

She called on the energy around them, tightening her grip and lifting them both into the air. Avery embraced the weightlessness while Syla frantically held onto her, choking from the pressure on her neck.

"Do you yield?" Avery bit out between clenched teeth.

"Eat shit." Syla's voice was a gargled mess but loud enough that Finn let out a bark of laughter beneath them.

"Syla!"

The low voice was sharp and clear, ringing through the square and straight for them. Syla stilled.

A rush of coldness cut into Avery, startling her enough that she dropped the woman. Syla fell the five feet to the ground, managing to break her fall, wheezing as she rolled to her back.

Qav had emerged from nowhere. He strolled along the waterway, hands in his pockets. Ennis and Remmington trailed behind him, their eyes wide as Syla struggled to her feet.

Their fight had drawn quite the crowd.

Nearly the entire market surrounded them, gaping. Bedria was in the back, a wide grin on her face. She nodded slowly at Avery.

Shit. This was not the plan she had envisioned of lying low and gathering intel.

Avery lowered herself to the ground in degrees, her feet touching the cement just as Qav reached them. He bent to help Syla stand, and she looked like she'd rather push him into the lagoon than take it. But she did, letting him pull her up.

"I sent you here to issue an invitation, not to start a new spectator sport." His voice was silk, winding its way in and around the crowd. Even Avery felt it despite her barriers: the way he wove serenity and distraction through them, an expert with his gift. "I'm certain you didn't mean to derail everyone from their routines."

Syla held Qav's gaze, her features drawn. "No," she said simply, throwing a deadly glare at Avery before stalking off and out of sight.

In moments, the crowd was gone, milling about the square, returning to their business. As though nothing had happened.

Amusement played across Qav's face, gone in an instant. "Apologies for her behavior," he said, rubbing his hands together slowly. "She can be a little overprotective. But then again, I guess you're used to that." A little smile tugged at the corner of his mouth.

"An invitation to what?" Avery snapped.

"Sorry?" He frowned.

"You said you sent Syla to issue an—"

"Oh, right." He smiled, those eyes drifting over her lazily. Like they had all the time in the world.

Avery nearly growled. "I hope you're here now to deliver on your promise to help me."

"I didn't promise you anything, gnima," he clarified, lifting a finger. "But seeing as you've come all the way here to find me, I'm willing to indulge you in a conversation. However, I don't do business in the middle of the street." His gaze traveled across the market to the viewers who hadn't quite forgotten they were there. He stepped closer to Avery, until she could feel the ice radiating from him, his power a tangible layer atop his skin. "It was an invitation to dinner. Where we can discuss it further." His eyes flickered to Finn and back, his next word a low promise: "Alone."

"In your fucking dreams," Finn snarled.

Avery didn't look Finn's way, scared of what she would see on his face.

Qav didn't spare him a glance. "Do you always let your pet speak for you?"

"Where I go, they all go."

His chin tilted, and it was there on his face again, that amusement. He seemed to consider arguing. But at last, he conceded. "Very well. We'll make a party of it, then. Syla was meant to be your escort, but I suppose Ennis will have to do now. Unfortunately, Rem can't drive a boat to save his damn life."

"It wasn't in my job description." Remmington's offended mutter was barely audible but rehearsed. Like they'd had the argument before. "And this little jaunt has already made us fall behind schedule. I told you sending her was a bad idea—"

"But he's great with time management and offering opinions that I never asked for." Qav was already turning away. "Bring the boy," he called over his shoulder. It took a moment for Avery to realize he was referring to Tai. As though he was an afterthought. And then Qav disappeared from sight, blending into the crowds.

"What the blazar was that?" Finn was still fuming.

Ennis drew closer to them, her chin dipping. "He meant no disrespect."

"And I suppose you're gonna say *she* didn't either?" Finn asked, referring to Syla.

"Oh, Syla always means to offend." Ennis grinned, stretching a scar that splintered down the side of her face. She looked up at Finn as she neared him, the difference in their height comical. "But I wouldn't worry about it. Qav has a thing for pretty faces, even if they are human. You'll be safe from her."

She walked on, headed back toward the main canal, knowing they had no choice but to follow her.

"Did she just call me pretty?" Finn pointed a finger to his chest.

Avery rolled her eyes. "We'll never hear the end of it now," she said, her mouth twisting.

"So we're going, then? To this dinner?" Petra asked.

"I don't think he left her much of a choice," Megan said softly.

"There's no way Tai can handle being around them," Linderly added, gesturing to Megan and Finn. "How the blazar are we going to get him to sit in a boat with the lot of us?"

"He'll have to," Avery replied, starting off after Ennis, who had stopped ahead to wait for them, as though she had intentionally given them privacy. "We're not missing this chance."

CHAPTER TWENTY-FIVE

Tai couldn't handle it.

Finn volunteered to be his tester, but the kid had gone after him the moment he stepped into the room. Whatever the blazar was going on with him was getting worse.

Petra's mood darkened after the incident, and it rattled Avery further. Her anxiety was palpable, and even without her gifts, the others could feel it. Hell, Finn could feel it.

It was Ennis who offered to transport them in two separate trips, allowing them to avoid throwing Tai in with the humans. As far as Finn could tell, she was a pretty decent person. She had kept mainly to the terrace as they changed over and dressed for dinner, doing her best to offer them privacy among themselves. It was thoughtful enough to be suspicious.

Unsurprisingly, Qav liked to play dress-up for his dinners. More clothes had been laid out for them when they arrived: a satin black suit for Finn and a plunging red dress for Avery. He assumed the others had been given something similar. Their closets had also been filled to the brim with all manner of outfits for any need that could arise.

But Brehna was nowhere to be seen, despite the luncheon that had been set on the long stone dining table for their return. Finn hoped her disappearing act in the markets allowed her to escape unnoticed by Syla. Strange that someone connected so closely to Bedria would be allowed to manage such high-profile apartments.

By the time they were done testing Tai, the sky was already darkening into the artificial nighttime of the dome. The days were passing quickly. Finn turned queasy thinking of the way time was slipping through their fingers. Who knew what the Origin was doing to the humans back on Echo? And they were here, dressing up like idiots to pacify some egotistical maniac.

But after tonight, if all went well, Avery would be back to normal. And they could finally leave.

Finn waited on the terrace with Avery, Megan, Grigg, and Nova. Ennis escorted the rest of their group to the canal, where they'd take a boat out to the lake mansion. They watched until the small craft took off from the dock. The night sky was out, stars winking on the surface of the lake around them. Linderly waved wildly from below, and Avery smiled, the gesture making Finn's throat constrict.

Avery was hurting—suffering—and yet she still smiled.

For a wild moment, he let himself imagine they were alone. He would take her into his arms, spread his hands over the red silk of her dress, and kiss her until they were both mad from wanting. A grin tugged at his lips. What would she do if he did it anyway, with the others still standing there?

She caught him staring as they made their way inside to get to the street. "Why don't I like that face?"

Grigg slapped him on the back of the neck, pushing Finn away roughly. "Because he's about to do something we'll all have to kick his ass for."

"I think Avery can take care of herself," Nova said dryly, heading after them.

Megan looped her arm around Avery's, sighing. "It seems pretty blazing romantic, from where I'm standing."

Finn didn't have to look back to know Avery was blushing.

They made their way down to the canal's edge, walking along the waterway as they waited for Ennis to return. The streetlights cast a soft glow that illuminated their path, reflecting off the water. A boat passed by, its wake sloshing against the edge, distorting the light into wavy ripples of gold.

This place existed apart from the rest of the world, isolated and safe. And Reanges lived happily there. They had seen and heard as much from the residents they spoke to that morning.

But what price did they pay for that safety?

Qav wouldn't build a place like this without exacting a fee—he was a dealer. The Acquirer. The only person he thought about, the only person he sacrificed for, was himself. Finn had met enough people like that to last him more than one lifetime.

"I don't like that we had to split up," Megan said, her voice soft. "Should Finn and I have stayed back?"

"I need you with me. Both of you." Avery's arm tightened on Megan's, drawing her closer. "And I may not trust Qav, but I trust what I saw in his head. He wants me for something. Which means technically we have the upper hand."

"Something tells me he doesn't see it that way," Nova said. "Unchecked power working on vulnerable minds is a heady veil through which to see the world."

Avery stared out across the water, her face stern. "We'll be careful."

"Sounds like he needs a good kick in the ass, if you ask me," Grigg commented under his breath.

"No arguments here." Finn crossed his arms over his chest, his black jacket stretching against his shoulder blades. "That is, assuming Petra hasn't already tried it by now." They all laughed at the thought.

A silver boat sidled up to the dock, Ennis manning the controls, and they lapsed into silence. She said little as they maneuvered out into the canal and took off across the water.

The wind pulled at Avery's hair, casting it out into chestnut ribbons that danced on the warm night. A heaviness layered over her, as though she was gathering armor for the battle she would face. A battle Finn would have no hope of ever helping her with. None of them could.

There were some things that she would have to conquer alone.

The island ahead was fast approaching from its isolated perch in the center of the lake. Finn could only support her so far. There would always be limits.

Maybe Qav was right—he was little better than a pet. Finn's position by her side held barely any true worth.

But then, he and Megan were the only ones Avery could trust to see things clearly. The only ones that bastard couldn't manipulate. And there was value in that.

The mansion was larger up close than it had seemed from across the water, sprouting from the dark atop a mound of carved rock. They docked, then went up the chiseled-out stairs illuminated by the soft golden glow of embedded lights, eventually reaching a wide court-yard.

"What the blazar are they doing here?"

Tai's voice was a boom that echoed off the rocks, bouncing onto the water and fading into the night.

"I told you to go inside," Ennis reprimanded, moving forward on swift feet. She placed herself between the two groups.

"And let you separate us entirely? Not likely," Petra sneered, hold-ing Tai's arm, her fingers white from the grip. He struggled against her violently.

"Let me go, Petra!" Tai ground out forcefully, his jolting move-ments turning frantic. "They're a plague on us; don't you see? Don't you remember—what they did that day on the docks?" His voice changed, a panicked plea. Petra stared down at him, surprise widen-ing her eyes. "The way they died—the smell of all that blood. It was *them.*"

She faltered.

In the next breath, Tai was free from her grasp and tearing off across the footstones to the new arrivals. His eyes were wild white orbs that shone in the dark. They zeroed in on Finn and Megan. Ready to kill.

CHAPTER TWENTY-SIX

"Tai, stop!" Petra screeched, her voice breaking among the low-hanging trees that shrouded the group.

Ennis braced herself, ready to lay him flat as he full-on sprinted at them.

Avery raised her hand, hesitating. She had never used her powers against someone she loved.

But before she could reach him, Tai slowed. He frowned, as though confused, until his movement was no more than a sluggish walk. And then he stopped, his body motionless, eyes vacant.

"Haven't I made myself clear about making a scene?"

Qav stood at the entrance to the house. The light from inside cast a delicate halo around his white suit, spilling out into the darkness of the garden.

"What did you do to him?" Petra's voice shook almost as much as her fingers did as she reached up to touch Tai's cheek. If he could see her, he gave no indication. He was no more than a hollow shell.

"I stopped him from trying to kill your humans." Qav danced casually down the small set of steps to meet them. "I'm sorry; did you want me to let him go, Petra? I know you bear no love for humans, but I thought you were rather attached to the blonde one."

"Do you know what's wrong with him?" Avery asked, plowing past his insinuation.

Qav approached Tai, silver gaze roving over him, seemingly fascinated by what he found. He jerked his head at Petra. She stepped back immediately, giving him room.

Qav circled Tai, a finger slowly tracing his own lips. "Interesting," Qav said simply, leaning forward to examine Tai's eyes.

"What is?" Avery stepped toward him.

"His mind is a mess," Qav replied without moving. His eyelids fluttered closed, long dark lashes settling against his cheeks. "Memories are scattered, intertwining with reality and fear." He frowned. "No wonder the poor kid is manic." His voice was so low that only Avery could hear.

"Can you fix him?" Petra's words were vulnerable—raw.

"There's only one way to find out." Qav lifted his hand.

Avery acted on instinct, grabbing his wrist to stop him.

He opened his eyes and peered down at her. "Cold feet?"

Here in this city, he was in total control. And he knew it. They were defenseless against Qav's influence, should he wish it. He didn't need to stop unless he chose to do so.

This was another game. And he was waiting for her next move.

"What will she choose?" he mocked in a whisper.

What would he expect?

Trust was a tentative, delicate thing, so difficult to earn yet so easy to lose. How could she even begin to trust someone who had the ability to manipulate everything and everyone around them?

But she wielded the same power. She was just as capable of abusing it in the same way. Maybe they weren't so different.

She lowered her hand.

Someone would have to take the first step, and Avery was willing to try. If she had already labeled him a villain, then he would have no chance to prove himself otherwise.

A smile teased a corner of his mouth.

Qav returned his attention to Tai, placing a hand against the side of his head. All traces of humor were gone, his face now focused. The others fell silent, waiting agonizingly long moments as his eyes closed and his breathing steadied.

A breeze rustled through the courtyard, trees swaying in a chorus of hushed sighs. A lock of hair dislodged from the half bun Qav wore, falling in front of his face and brushing the sharp line of his jaw. Its silvery color was stained a soft gold in the light that poured from the house.

The minutes dragged on; the only sounds were that of their breathing and the rustling garden.

"Is it working?" The question burst from Petra, her voice steadier than before.

"Let him concentrate." A quick whisper. Syla had joined them at some point, arriving unnoticed from somewhere on the grounds. A ring of dark purple had already blossomed on her chin and another by her left eye. Avery couldn't bring herself to feel sorry about the bruises.

At last, Qav pulled away from Tai, the barest hint of strain in his movements. Whatever he had done, it hadn't been easy.

He opened his eyes, refusing to take them off Tai. "I think that should have . . ."

Tai came back to himself slowly, taking in his surroundings as though awakening from a dream. He stared at Qav for a moment before looking to Avery, then Petra. He teetered forward, wobbly on his feet, arms reaching out. Qav backed away, avoiding the touch, but Petra was swift and caught Tai in her arms as he collapsed.

"Tai?" Her voice was controlled. She let him sink to the ground, gently slapping the side of his face to bring him back.

"What did you do to him?" Avery rounded on Qav, energy crackling.

His attention went to her hands for the briefest moment. "I had to weed out the terror from the reality. Help him sift through the memories and untangle the mess in there. Who did this to him?" He waited a second before gleaning the knowledge on his own. "Leviathan—she's also responsible for your issues. Who is this woman?"

Avery went quiet, so Finn stepped forward to answer. "Another So'Reange with too much power and not enough conscience."

Qav fixated on Avery while digesting Finn's words. *She did this to you as well?* he asked voicelessly. *Your power far eclipses hers. Why did you let her?*

"Let her?" Avery replied for them all to hear, refusing to speak privately, to allow his presence in her mind. "You think I *let* her do this to me?"

He didn't respond but merely stroked his lip, watching her. Those silver eyes might as well have pierced clear through her. He looked at Petra, hunched on the ground beside her brother. Megan was at their side.

"He'll be fine," Qav said, replying to an unspoken question. "His mind has been through a nuclear explosion. It will take time for his body to get rid of the radiation."

"Do you always talk in metaphor?" Avery snapped, her chin tilting up. "What does that mean?"

"Sleep," he clarified, turning away to head back into the house. "He needs to sleep. Now, let's eat. I'm famished, and dinner is getting cold." When none of them moved, he added over his shoulder, "Syla will take the boy where he can rest. You are welcome to join him, Petra."

Avery knelt beside the siblings, brushing a hand across Tai's forehead. She met Petra's gaze.

Qav had helped them, at least with this one thing. Maybe this meant the next step wouldn't be so hard. After all, what could he truly want from her? She would pay any price to help her people.

Avery glanced at the rest of her ensemble. They needed her to push forward. They were ready to make the tough choices, confident in her path. Hesitation meant more time lost, more opportunity for those being exploited and abused on Echo to suffer. At least the humans on Earth had a choice in their leadership. Even if that choice had once been Klein.

If she allowed Leviathan to continue unchecked, the Reanges on Echo would be nothing more than puppets. And the humans . . . The humans would be dead.

Avery needed her powers back.

She gazed out at Sanctum, a vision of glowing light in this chasm beneath the surface, a beacon in the darkness. There were many Reanges who called this place home. But even they deserved to be the ones who made that choice for themselves.

She let out a terse breath, trying to ignore the way Finn watched her. He held no powers of telepathy, but he still saw too much. He still knew her, sometimes better than she knew herself.

She rose to her feet, following the evening's host inside.

CHAPTER
TWENTY-SEVEN

"We have these imported daily through the Gate," Qav said, picking up an oyster from the platter of ice in front of him. "Of course, it's been a while since we've had them on such a regular basis, thanks to your efforts. That embargo really has been lovely." He threw the shell back, devouring its contents with more grace than Avery could hope to manage. She didn't touch them, knowing she'd make a fool of herself.

"It's such a shame the seafood on Earth is inedible," Megan lamented, reaching for an oyster and following his lead. She was doing her best to make the situation less awkward for them all. In fact, she fit into the surroundings quiet well, elegant and perfect in her gray gown that tapered over one smooth shoulder. Of all of them, Megan was likely the only one who could.

The inside of Qav's home was even more ostentatious than its exterior. The dining room featured an imposing chandelier situated in the eaves of the high ceiling, a riotous twisting of purple glass the size of a small cruiser bike. It probably weighed just as much. And beneath it, a banquet table carved from solid wood that could easily seat fifty people. It felt wrong, sacrilegious even, to eat off the piece. It was probably worth more than Finn's ship. Surely an item like that should be in a museum. At least the tall chairs, which boasted ornately curling backs, were metal: a much more reasonable material for daily use.

Syla had returned soon after settling Petra and Tai in some other area of the house. Avery hadn't asked where, opting to display some amount of trust in the situation. Never mind that Qav had done so little to reciprocate, but they had to start somewhere.

By the time they had all taken their seats, fresh drinks appeared in their hands, delivered by a quiet servant with purple hair. The first courses were already laid out and waiting. The middle of the table was piled full of delicacies, some Avery was familiar with, others not. There was some kind of sea creature with four eyes and innumerable tentacles arranged in the center, various fruits arranged artfully around it. Qav's taste for the eccentric went beyond his clothing.

"If you're going to insult my style, at least do it so the rest of the table can hear you." Qav took a long swig of the sparkling wine in his glass.

Beside Avery, Finn straightened.

She needed to keep things light. "It's not my fault you have an issue with eavesdropping," she replied casually. "You must really have a thing for velvet."

Grigg choked on his wine, sputtering into a coughing fit. Markes patted his back, trying to help the situation, but probably made it worse. Grigg swatted his hand away.

Qav watched them curiously as though weighing her words and the energy around them. "I suppose I have Rem to thank for it," he said, gaze shifting to the end of the table where the man in question was picking at a plate of fruit. "You told me velvet was de rigueur."

Rem's dark brows drew down behind the yellow lenses of his glasses. "Three years ago. I haven't been able to get you to move on from it."

"Fashion is all about confidence. You can get away with pretty much anything with the right attitude. And you pull it off beautifully," Megan said, glancing up at him from beneath long, fair eyelashes. She was flirting.

Avery had never seen Megan scared a day in her life. Or, at least, she was an expert at pushing the fear beneath the surface. Once she decided on a course of action, she ran straight ahead, full force and without apology. Avery adored her for it. She wished she could be more like that herself.

"At least one of you has taste," Qav replied, his voice smooth and shadowed. "I don't often open up my home to strangers. And humans, at that. But you two certainly complement my aesthetic."

"Personally, I favored the sparkling skin," Grigg said slyly.

"A temporary gen mod," Qav explained. "It helps with some degree of anonymity when I want to go dancing."

Avery nearly flushed at the memory of his hands on her waist pulling her to him in the club. The way he had smiled at her before turning away. So he hadn't just been there to toy with her, to find her. It was strange to think that Qav enjoyed something as common as dancing in a club.

"Can we cut the shit?" Finn interjected acerbically. His fingers were white where they clutched his glass. "What do you want from her? And spare us the riddles; they're getting old."

"Finn," Avery chided. He tore his eyes away from Qav to focus on her. He was angry. Furious. Regardless, they still had to play by Qav's rules.

"Are we really sitting here eating fucking shellfish and talking about fashion? Am I the only one who remembers what's happening back on Echo? People could be dying, and this asshole is—"

"Enough." Avery regretted the force in her response as soon as it left her mouth. But Finn hushed, his lips forming a thin line, eyes churning. He was always calm under pressure. Always smooth with his words and the way he used them against others. She didn't understand why this was any different. He knew the stakes. They all did.

Qav laughed. "No, he's right." He leaned back in his chair. "Besides, you're all thinking it. He's the only one who's really being honest here. And that, I can respect."

Finn's jaw tensed, and he looked down at his plate. Avery would try to talk to him later. She didn't like this barrier that was rising between them.

"Then what *do* you want from Avery?" Nova was the one to ask this time, her face blank, the image of calm blending with the soothing pale green of her dress. "We know you brought her here for a reason."

"Blackmailed us, you mean," Markes added, raising his chin. Like the brief comment had taken more courage than he thought.

Ennis shifted in her seat, clearing her throat, but Qav seemed to ignore her. He took a sip of his drink again before saying delicately, "There's something I need to procure–for a client. And so far, my contacts have been unsuccessful in acquiring this item. The job calls for special skills, and unfortunately mine alone will not be enough."

"What a surprise," Finn muttered.

"What kind of item?" Avery asked. It had to be important, extremely so. Whatever she had glimpsed in his mind had been significant to him.

"Classified, I'm afraid." Qav smiled, waving at their surroundings, to the arched stone ceiling and lines of windows offering a view of the Sanctum skyline. The city looked beautiful at night, nestled in its dome of stars. "I didn't build all of this by betraying confidence."

"Convenient." Avery swirled her own glass of wine, refusing to acknowledge his artful attempts at boasting.

"How are we supposed to help you steal an item if we don't even know what that item is?" Grigg leaned forward, waving a fork full of sliced meat in the air. Unlike Finn, the tense situation hadn't prevented him from appeasing his appetite.

"Thankfully for you, I don't require the assistance of anyone besides Avery."

"I told you already, they go where I go." Avery gripped the napkin in her lap. Finn was a statue beside her.

Ennis cleared her throat. "Perhaps we can compromise. It's clear we both need each other, as Qav is well aware." She held his silver stare longer than Avery thought possible. She didn't fear him.

"Very well," Qav agreed, sighing. "Grigg, Nova, and Linderly, then."

Finn nearly came out of his char. "So you can corner her by controlling them? Like hell is that happening—I'm going."

Even Avery would admit that she'd prefer to have Finn with them. He was a phenomenal fighter, but he was also immune to Qav's influence. It would give her invaluable peace of mind.

"I don't work with humans," Qav said simply. "Nothing against you, but I don't trust what I can't control."

"Did you just hear yourself?" Avery scoffed. "That's not trust at all." Anger surged through her, curling into a dense ball in her stomach.

"Can you honestly tell me you don't feel the same way? You know, without a doubt, that you can rely on people who have the ability to lie to you—hide things from you? That's no way to live."

"Of course I can rely on them. They are my family. I would trust them with my life."

"Family." Qav's smile was serpentine. "Is that what you said about your grandmother, too? What else has *she* been hiding?"

Avery blanched at his words, the lights of the chandelier above them flickering as her energy flared, casting stuttering shadows across the food. Her conversation with Klein. Qav must have seen it somehow. He must have known the doubt it had planted deep within her.

"I've felt it in you, Avery. The uncertainty. The fear. Why do you think you want your power back so badly?"

Avery stood, screeching her chair back violently. It clanged against the wall, metal snapping. "I am nothing like you," she spat. "What you're saying, the way you control people, it makes them no better than slaves."

"I look out for myself and take advantage of my skills. I won't apologize for existing. You shouldn't, either." He lifted his glass to his lips.

Avery flung a wave of energy at him, knocking the glass from his hand. It shattered on the stone floor, the sound echoing in the silence that fell over the room.

"That was *vintage*." Qav's eyes were on fire, lit from within by rage. Avery had never seen true emotion from him, and it tempted her to do more, to make him feel more.

She flung out her arm, sending his other guests flying back from the table on sliding chairs. There was a shriek from Megan and various curses from the rest. Avery glanced up at the ridiculously ornate chandelier hanging above the table, the purple glass offering a shimmering temptation.

Don't even think about it. Qav was on his feet now, his chin drawn as he glared at her, reading her thoughts. He looked sharply to his people, a slight shake of his head the only indication to stay back.

"I told you before," Avery hissed. "Stay out of my head!"

She brought her hand above her head, aiming directly at the chandelier, and then pulled, tugging on the energy around it until it gave way, loosening from its cables in a satisfying pop and tearing toward the table.

But it didn't land on its target. The spiky orb bounced in the air just above the dishes still piled high with food, floating with mere inches to spare. Qav held out both hands at the chandelier, feet planted and brows furrowed. His breathing was labored, his face pale.

He was struggling.

Avery grinned. He wasn't as powerful as he wanted her to believe.

She raised her other hand now, then brought both arms down together in a sweeping arc, pulling as much energy as she dared to use. The chandelier sputtered for a moment before succumbing to the pressure and slamming first into the table and then through it. Dishes shattered, food and debris flying as Avery pressed further. The table let out a loud crack, a fissure snapping up its length as the glass spikes of the chandelier pierced its wood. She twisted her right hand, and the glass exploded, splitting the table in half. It folded in on itself, absolutely ruined.

"Watch it, Avery!" Finn called out, and she jerked sharply, ready for the attack a moment too late.

Qav was on her, long fingers curled around her throat, energy pressing in on her windpipe. But he hadn't locked the movement properly, leaving her open to counter.

She didn't resist the grip, instead leaning into him, pulling his hands toward her and dislodging him at his weakest point. As he lurched forward, she lifted a knee to land a solid blow to his abdomen, almost sending him to the floor.

Avery braced her feet, landing a forward kick directly into his chest with a boost of energy that had him soaring backward through the air, away from the table. He crashed into the wall, barely missing the window behind him, then fell to a knee, his face obstructed by a curtain of silver hair that had come loose.

"Qav?"

A voice from behind them. Syla.

"Stay out of it," he ordered, sounding strained.

He was on his feet in a flash, raw energy hurtling at Avery with a gleam of silver eyes. She barely had enough time to create a physical barrier of her own before his struck, pure ice knocking her back on her feet. Electricity lit up the room, strobing flashes of silver and blue, the air compressing with the charge.

He tried the same move as before in the club, wrapping his energy around hers, trying to control her. But this time, she was ready.

Avery bent the energy to her will, twisting the very atoms in the air, pressing down on him. She forced the power into his energy field, regaining control of any molecules he claimed until there were none left for him to command.

She slashed a hand through the air, sending Qav stumbling back against the wall, immobilized. Her energy locked around him, tangling with his in an attempt to find purchase. Something shifted, clicking between them, but she ignored the sensation. It didn't matter. She was stronger. She had won.

His eyes were wide, his face illuminated in the rhythm of the sparks that still danced through the air around her. But in his next breath, the shock on his face melted away.

"My turn." His voice was calm, his mouth curved.

And that was the last thing she heard before the world disappeared around her.

CHAPTER
TWENTY-EIGHT

"Where the blazar are we?" Avery hated the way her voice swayed. Hated the fear that churned in her stomach, the helplessness.

The world had gone dark, any semblance of the dining room fading away on a shadowed mist.

Brightness flashed, blinding her, and Avery shielded her eyes. When she looked again, she was in another world entirely.

She stood beneath the open sky, atop a hill in an ocean of grass that stretched out as far as she could see. The sky above was a perfect azure, vast and unending on the horizon, marred only by the occasional puff of white clouds that sailed lazily on the wind. The breeze carried a scent, heady and familiar. Lavender.

Qav. He stood a few paces away, watching her. He was no longer disheveled, his hair fell in a perfect waterfall down his shoulders, blending in with the white of his form-fitting jacket.

"It was you. In my dream." Avery turned in a quick circle, looking for any vulnerability, any exit. She swung back around, flinging power toward him.

"That won't work in here." He was apologetic, his voice on the edge of pity. She hated him all the more for it.

"What do you *want* from me?" she screamed at him, her voice carrying on the wind.

He held her gaze, his face at last serious. "I told you. I need you for a job."

"That's not what I mean, and you know it," she bit out. "Why are we here?" She splayed her arms wide, desperate. Helpless.

Qav slid his hands in his pockets, tilting his head. "I've never been that great at the physical aspects of my gifts. But you . . ." He dipped his head, eyes turning to dark storm clouds. "Your power, the raw energy you can not only summon, but command . . . it far exceeds anything I've even imagined possible. And I want it."

Avery let out a short laugh. "You think I know how I do it? That I can train you? In case you haven't noticed, I've got my hands full at the moment. And even if I knew how to teach you, I would refuse. I can't think of anything more dangerous than a narcissist like you imbued with even more power than you already have."

"Always so quick to judge," he scolded. "Don't you even want to hear my terms? Unless things have changed, I'm not the only one who needs something here."

"I thought you wanted help with your heist. Wasn't that the deal?"

He rolled his eyes, laughing. "'Heist.' I promise it's nothing so dramatic. What we're looking for, no one will even miss. And no, that wasn't the deal. You help me retrieve this item, and then, once we are back here and the item is safely in the hands of my client, we will negotiate terms. A trade in services, of a sort."

She frowned. "So you do know how to fix me, then?"

A grin spread slowly across his face. "In many ways, gnima."

She grimaced. "You are abhorrent." That nickname again. It made her blood curdle, even if she didn't know its meaning. "I don't have time to play your ridiculous games. There are people on Echo being forced into committing genocide. Thousands of humans are going to die because of me if—"

"I know what's happening there. Your friends' minds are full of it. Taisto was . . ." He paused, brows furrowing as he drew in a quick breath. "I don't need to be told your stakes. But they are not mine. In any business dealing, the first step is to understand that your goals are not shared by everyone at the table."

"But you're a So'Reange. Echo is your home—your responsibility."

"Earth is my home," he clarified, irritation grating against his normally casual tone. "And the only responsibility I have is to myself. I learned that a long time ago."

Avery said nothing. She wouldn't even know where to begin, and she would get nowhere if she tried to talk him through it. The very heart of their power centered around empathy and shared experience. But he had perverted it, twisted his gift into something selfish and unnatural.

If only she had access to his emotion, she could share her experiences. Surely if he could feel that, then he would be able to understand. Their gifts were a conduit for hope. Hadn't Bedria reminded her of that? The So's power offered a way for their people to feel one another and connect across divides. They were meant to prevent conflict, to cultivate understanding.

It was not just an avenue to create your own world. Like Sanctum. Qav was a god there, as much as he was in this place within her head.

"Why did you bring me here?" She gestured to the world around them. "Why not just lay out your requirements in front of the others?"

"You didn't really give me much choice with that little display of violence. If I let you continue, I wouldn't have had a single piece of furniture left in the whole place. Do you have any idea how long it took me to find that table?"

"I thought wasting money was one of your favorite hobbies."

His eyes flared, alight with mischief. "Did I say that? That will teach me to spew words haphazardly at you. Who knows what you'll take literally next." He stalked through the grasses, stopping just before her. She looked up at him, resisting the urge to back away. "So, what do you think? Do we have a deal?"

She glanced at his outstretched hand. It would be pure lunacy to enter into a bargain with him. She barely even had any details on where they were going or how long it would take.

"A day at most," he replied to her thoughts. "And I'll get you up to speed as soon as you acquiesce—or Rem will. I don't concern myself with details."

"Of course, you don't." Avery shook her head, weighing her options. "How can I even begin to trust you?"

"Didn't we cover this already? You can't." He smiled, exploring her features. "Don't worry, I may be able to read you, but I still can't control you. That's where things get fun."

She held his gaze, trying to glean what she could from instinct. He was selfish, yes, but she doubted he would harm her outright. He had an inner circle. Syla. Ennis. Remmington. They followed his lead and seemed to trust him despite his power over them. That had to count for something.

She took his arm, hands clasping wrists in the traditional Reange hold.

"Excellent." His smiled deepened, reaching his eyes. He really was incredibly beautiful. And she would bet her life that he knew it. Reveled in it.

Avery blinked. She was standing in the dining room, Finn and Nova at her side, a hand on each arm. There was no trace of the bright skies, the sun-kissed grasses or dots of purple flowers. As though she had never been there at all.

"Ennis will see you back to your apartments," Qav drawled, sauntering past the others as though nothing had happened. "I'll be by to collect you first thing. Dress comfortably."

Remmington gave them a curt nod before following him out of the room, Syla on their heels.

"What was that?" Finn asked, tightening his grip on her arm. She could feel the fear coursing through him, as though it ran straight from his veins into hers.

Avery shivered. The smell of lavender lingered in the air. "Things just got more complicated."

"I told you, you need to train more."

Qav ignored Syla. The comment was undoubtedly the beginning of an oncoming lecture. Maybe she would keep it to herself if he didn't acknowledge it.

"You were right about her," Rem observed, falling into step beside him. "She is incredibly strong, given what we know from Ennis's research on the history of your gifts."

Syla snorted. "Even without the power, she could have kicked his ass. She's had training. Honestly, it's embarrassing more than anything else."

Shut your mouth before I shut it for you. Qav sliced his eyes to her in warning.

"I'd like to see you try. You're barely on your feet now after all of that."

Qav bit the inside of his cheek, his strides lengthening. "She may be blocked from using her telepathy, but her mind is still a fortress. Just trying to breech her consciousness while she's awake is . . . difficult." That was an understatement. Qav struggled to even read her thoughts when her shields were up.

He had met only two other So' in his life, both underwhelming. Avery made them look like children in comparison.

And to think, she had been raised her entire life as a human. It was baffling.

He had been honing his skills since he discovered them. He was only five when he first compelled his mother to buy him red sugar candies at the markets. To this day, it was still his favorite. He kept jars of it around the house, a wrapped piece always in his pocket.

Avery had no idea the extent of her power, how rare she was. That old woman in their memories—Leviathan—had certainly done her best to keep that a secret. And she had done a number on Avery.

Not to mention the kid. Tai.

It was no wonder Qav was exhausted. Syla was right about that. He was about to collapse on his feet after untangling the mess inside that boy's head. If they had an entire planet full of people that had been corrupted to that level . . . Avery had no chance in the galaxy at fixing them all.

What had Leviathan used to poison so many minds from such a distance? Qav would pay a high price indeed to gain that knowledge. It would be invaluable. His plans for his empire depended on continued control of the Reanges left. It was already difficult enough to keep them happy, even when he provided everything they could need.

Echo. He hated the very word. The way it bounced around his own head, a mockery of double meaning. There was nothing for them there. It was their past. His own parents had been obsessed with returning. They still were. If it hadn't been for Qav and his ambition, his willingness to adapt and carve out a place for them here, then they'd still be living in the gutters. Begging for blazing scraps.

"What did Avery agree to?" Rem asked, his voice cautious. "Cora has been inquiring about our delivery. Pretty insistently, I might add."

"Cora can wait," Qav replied sharply. "And that goes for the others too, if they ask. We'll get it to them by the deadline, as agreed."

"They must be scrambling with the vote looming." Syla snuck a look at Qav, assessing. "Are we worried about it?"

"Why should we be?" He shrugged a shoulder. "It won't make a difference to our operations either way." Qav didn't miss the look Syla and Rem shared, diving into their minds for context. They were worried about the future. Worried that things were different now. "Those in positions of power are just cogs in the same wheel. It doesn't matter to me if they're replaced. And if it doesn't matter to me, then it shouldn't matter to you."

He was done with the subject and sluggish, ready to sleep off the evening that had stretched him to his limits. They had reached his wing of the house, and he sent a mental command for solitude. He continued on along the hallway, Syla and Rem leaving him in peace.

Qav drew a slow hand over his face, letting out a rush of breath in the silence, the sound of his shoes on the stone the only other break. He ascended the stairs leading to the veranda hallway that opened up, looking out over the lake. Slowing to a stop, he braced his hands on the ledge, looking to the bright lights of Sanctum, its near-mirror reflection winking back in the still waters at its edge.

He had built this place from virtually nothing. Less than nothing.

When they first arrived on Earth, his parents had been sick with grief over losing their home, even as they welcomed their only child into the world. They chose to give in to that emotion rather than pick themselves up and move forward. If he had followed that path, if he had lamented over the loss he never truly felt, he never would have reached his full potential.

Sanctum would have never been born.

Responsibility to Echo? He laughed at Avery's words circling in his head. He claimed no responsibility to anyone except himself. Not anymore. Anyone that did otherwise was signing themselves up for disappointment.

Movement caught his eye, and he slid his gaze to the courtyard below. Ennis led Avery's little crew down the front path to the dock. Her family.

Laughter floated up on the air, mingling with the sounds of the lapping water and rustling trees. Any one of them would lay down their life for her. But that didn't mean she owed them anything. That didn't mean she needed to destroy herself fighting for them.

Deep down, Avery knew that. Knew that she was different. That she was more.

And he would prove it.

Golden eyes looked upward at him, cleaving the darkness with their soft glow. Qav paused, his grip on the stone hardening, not daring to breathe. If he had strength left, he might have reached out to her—no, he would have—eager to feel her power brushing against his own.

But she turned away, and the moment went with her, flying across the star-soaked water along with his fanciful thoughts. He watched her go, welcoming the silence that was left.

CHAPTER TWENTY-NINE

Finn didn't talk the entire ride back to the apartments. Avery would barely look at him. He was grateful for Nova, who kept up some semblance of conversation. But Finn couldn't trust himself to speak. Not yet.

Fear still coursed through him, mingling with adrenaline and rage until he could barely think straight. Seeing Avery standing there, helpless and vacant, her eyes empty while Qav rummaged around in her mind . . . Finn could have killed him for that alone.

He barely felt the wind on his face as they soared across the water, nor heard what the others were saying to one another. The most he could do was smile blandly as they laughed at some joke Grigg made.

Whatever Qav had said to Avery in her head, it had convinced her to agree to his one-sided terms. She would leave Finn behind, twirling his thumbs on the sidelines when she needed him with her. Against Qav, he was one of the best assets they had available. It made no sense.

By the time Ennis left them, apologizing for Qav's shortness and the quick ending of their meal, the others had gathered on the terrace, finding their seats among the cushioned furniture there. Petra fairly carried a barely awake Tai downstairs to his room, and Megan disappeared with them.

"What I don't get is why he wants *me* to go along, of all people,"

Linderly said, her voice hushed. "Grigg and Nova make sense, but me?"

"Don't sell yourself short," Nova said with a soft smile. "Your coding skills are no joke."

"If Remmington is all he has in that department, it's no wonder he wants you." Markes spread his legs out on the chaise he had claimed. "That guy has a real stick up his ass."

Nova rolled her eyes. "Moons help us, you're starting to sound like Grigg."

"He should be so lucky," Grigg added, chuckling as he swiped Markes's feet away to settle down beside him.

Avery stood apart from them by the railing, looking out over the city, her bare shoulders stiff beneath her crimson gown. Finn wanted to go to her. To take her hand in his and tell her it would be okay, that whatever she was thinking, she was wrong.

She wasn't alone. She didn't have to carry the burden by herself.

But his feet were locked in place, cemented to the floor.

If she felt alone, it was because she went out of her way to isolate herself. Even from him.

This path would only hurt her—weaken her. Why couldn't she see that? If she would only open up to them, lean on them . . . they wouldn't judge her for it. Finn would never judge her.

But in this, she was being an idiot. And it would cost them thousands of lives. Human lives. If they didn't make it back to Echo in time, if they didn't find a way to stop the Origin, then all those people would die. Because of him.

Nova's eyes caught his, her head angling in question.

Finn turned away, heading back inside to the dimly lit living area. Nova had always been so in tune with the energies around her. He wondered if maybe she had a So' in her lineage.

But he couldn't sit there with them all, pretending everything was fine, that Avery wasn't walking them all straight into a trap.

"Finn?"

He stopped. Avery had followed him after all.

He ran a hand through his hair, releasing a fractured breath. He didn't want to talk, didn't know if he even could.

"Where are you going?" Avery's voice was uneven. He swore he could feel a physical thread of uncertainty in the air between them, piercing him somewhere near his back. He stiffened.

When he turned to her, he kept his face controlled, bracing himself. Of course. She only noticed him when he tried to leave.

Her eyes widened as though she heard his thoughts. "What's wrong?" she breathed.

He let out a short laugh. "What's *wrong*? Are you really asking me that?"

She frowned, that little line he loved appearing between her brows, the freckles across her nose scrunching together in a beautiful mess. "Is this about tomorrow?"

He gritted his teeth, looking away, clinging to composure. It took effort to keep his voice lowered when he said, "You should never have agreed to his terms."

"What?"

"I don't know what the blazar he said to you, but we can't trust him. Megan and I are the only safeguard we have in this place, and you willingly gave that up. Said you didn't need me with you."

"Is that what this is about?" Avery asked again. "You think I don't need you?"

"No." *Yes.* Finn lapsed into silence.

But he knew the truth. Avery was brave and strong and glorious in her own right, more powerful than he would ever be. She *didn't* need him. No more than a planet needed a satellite trapped in its orbit.

She kept talking. "He can't control me, if that's what you're worried about. He told me so himself."

"Oh, and he's been a paragon of honesty?" Finn mocked, shaking his head. "And what about Grigg or Nova? Did you stop to think about how they would feel—if he used them to hurt you? Or Linderly? She's barely more than a child. Markes is still shaken up over what he did to Megan under Qav's influence. We can't afford to be naive."

"I'm not naive," she said forcefully. The dining table vibrated in the wake of her words, her power churning before it settled. "You saw what happened back there. I can hold my own against him in a fight."

"Until he gets inside your head, too!"

Silence wrapped thickly around the ends of his words, and Finn realized he had shouted them.

Avery was stone before him.

His gaze flickered to the terrace. The others looked away too quickly to be natural. Nova launched into some discussion about the squid that had been sitting on the table during dinner.

Finn let out a puff of air, turning on his heel toward the stairs. He never meant to have this conversation. He just needed space. Once he had a handle on the thoughts rushing through his head, he would be able to see things clearly. He always found a way out of a mess—always.

"Don't walk away." Avery's words were a hushed plea as she followed, the heat of her body singeing his back. She stayed close to him, up the spiraling stairs and to the dimly lit privacy of their room. She tried again. "Talk to me. I *do* need you, Finn. You're the only one who knows what I— Who knows how much I—"

"I told you that wasn't the issue. You acted without thinking of anyone but yourself tonight," Finn snapped, rounding on her. He ignored the way she flinched. "We're a team. You, me, the others. It doesn't work when we cut each other off. We are weaker apart."

"Who do you think I'm doing this for? You're the one who always shoves the responsibilities of my position down my throat. 'Choose them. It always has to be them.' Do you think I'm doing this for my own amusement? None of this is easy, Finn—none of it."

"You think I don't know that? I've spent half my life playing a very public role in the name of responsibility. I've never been in charge of my own destiny, not in any way that matters. Until I met you, Avery. Yes, you have to choose the greater good. But not like this. Not by yourself." He stepped closer to her, the heat of his anger dissipating into something softer, gone in an instant.

A lock of hair had fallen across her face, and he reached out, brushing it behind her ear. His fingers lingered there, grazing the skin on her neck. "You gave me a place to belong. And when I tried to go it alone, you're the one who told me it didn't work that way. So don't shut yourself off from me now."

"I'm not," she said, in barely a whisper. She stepped even closer, pressing her hands to his chest. "I don't mean to." Her eyes were gilded pools, shimmering and bright. A single tear fell, trailing across freckles and down the curve of her cheek, taking the last of his anger with it.

His fingers drifted to cup her face, wiping the wet streak away with the pad of his thumb. Her face was illuminated only by the soft glow of the under lighting, fanning trails of muted blue up the walls and throughout the room. Her eyes were drowning in the wetness of more tears, their golden depths swirling with unvoiced emotion. Thoughts she was leaving unsaid.

"Let's leave this place." He kept his tone delicate. Careful. "We can find another way. And then we can come back and save these people—take them home."

Her eyelids fluttered, her head shaking. "It's too late for that. And Qav is a solid option. He *is*," she clarified, seeing the doubt on his face. "I've been inside his head, Finn. I don't think he's as callous as he pretends to be." She paused, pressing her hand to his jaw, her fingers cold on his skin. "Everyone has a mask."

Finn covered her fingers with his own as words tumbled out. "Back there . . . when he— When we couldn't reach you . . ." He stopped on a shuddering exhale, his words shaking. "It scared the shit out of me. Where you went, I couldn't follow. And you were gone. For a solid minute, you were gone." He pulled her close to him, their bodies flush, her arms wrapping around his waist.

"I'm right here." She tucked her chin into his chest. He felt the tears that bled through his shirt, burning his skin.

"If I lost you . . . that would be it for me," he got out, the words breaking over one another in the quiet.

They stood like that, tangled in each other's arms, their embrace lengthening into a moment of infinity in the dark. Finn rubbed his chin over the top of her hair, relishing the smooth texture, breathing in the familiar scent of her. He would have stayed that way for a millennium.

But time wasn't on their side. It never had been.

Time folded in on itself, and Avery wanted nothing more than to stay tucked in the safety of Finn's arms forever. When they were together, everything else seemed to melt away. Even when they were fighting, she still felt more aligned, more connected to him than any other person she'd ever met. He was a part of her, had carved out a space within her soul, and a piece of him would always be there.

She knew this wasn't easy for him. If their roles were reversed, she'd probably be acting the same way—worse, even.

But things were different for her. It wasn't fair of him to compare them.

When Finn had tried to go it alone before, he had nearly died. If Avery hadn't forced her way in to help him, then he would have. He needed to learn that she could take care of herself. The others did, too.

Qav wouldn't hurt her, she was mostly certain of it. He was just misguided. Hadn't she also been that way once? She had been ready to turn her back on it all before. He would help them; she had to believe that. She just needed to show Qav what they were fighting for and how things could be different.

And that started with earning his trust.

At last, Avery straightened, tilting her head to meet Finn's eyes. They were calm, a hypnotic shade of blue that always soothed her. She was grateful for his energy, steady and strong and always rooting her to reality.

"Trust me, Finn. Can you just try?" she asked, hopeful.

"I do trust you. Always." He leaned forward to rest his forehead against hers, their breath mingling. "It's that white-haired bastard I have more trouble with," he added from the corner of his mouth.

She nearly laughed, a grin pulling at her lips.

"He's testing us—testing me," she explained, leaning back to examine the rough angles of his face. "That's what this whole thing is about. He wants to see what else I can do."

"And you think it's a good idea to play into his hand?" Finn was skeptical, his head tilting.

"He fixed Tai, didn't he? What was that if not an offering of good will?"

"He likes games, Avery. It could be a long play."

"Then I'll study the rules until I play it better than him," she reasoned. "And until then, I'm starting with trust, which means a few concessions. I won you over, didn't I? Another arrogant male enamored with his own good looks can't be that much different."

"You think he's good-looking?" Finn growled, throwing her off balance until she was clinging to him.

"It's an objective observation," she said, laughing. "But I believe you missed the part where I called you gorgeous."

"I believe what you *actually* called me was narcissistic," he clarified, leaning down to nuzzle her neck.

"If the shoe fits." Her giggles dissolved into gasps as pleasure fizzed through her body, straight down her spine and into her stomach. Finn nipped her neck, hard enough to leave a mark before covering the area with an open-mouthed kiss. His tongue ran delicate circles over her, and she arched her neck toward him.

Finn took the invitation, gathering her to him as his mouth moved downward, taking advantage of the thin red straps of her dress. He left a trail of fire in his wake, each new inch of skin he claimed only stoking Avery to higher flames of desire.

In this world of mouths and tongue and skin and pleasure, there was no thought, no doubt. She wanted him, and that was enough.

Her fingers dug into his shirt, the fabric bunching beneath her hands. She needed it off him—needed his skin against hers. Their harsh panting echoed around them, and Avery delighted in it, bathing in the hot feel of his breath against her neck.

Frantically, her mouth sought his, pulling his head to her as she brought him into another deep kiss. His hands were at her hips, pressing her against him. She nearly groaned from wanting.

A deep burn ignited somewhere within her chest, carving its way from beneath her ribs directly into him. Whatever that feeling was, she wanted to follow it. Wanted more, needed the connection it teased, the bond it promised, fierce and immovable.

Avery pushed him toward the bed, legs tangling as he shrugged out of his jacket, stripping the shirt from his body. Her hands were on Finn in an instant, all hard muscles and strength, his skin hot against her fingers. She straddled him, lost in his kisses and not caring—or caring too much—that the taste of him was driving out all thought.

Her dress rode up her thighs. She pressed closer. And then his hands were there, wide and broad against her legs, moving in a slow caress that drove her mad. She bit his lip, drawing a groan from him, low and strangled. It echoed deliciously through her body.

Finn pulled away, and she nearly wept.

His chest rose and fell to the sharp sounds of his breath, matching her own. Strong fingers bore into the sides of her hips, his dark brows rising, his eyes hooded. His voice was desperately soft as he asked, "Are you sure?"

The tenderness in his gaze nearly broke her.

The burning beneath her ribs, that tendril of electricity between them, widened, growing stronger. Her heart ached—nearly as much as her body—and it was unbearable.

Avery nodded. Her fingers curled in the edges of his hair. "Yes."

Finn's eyes flared, exploring her face in silence.

Avery would have given all her powers away to know what was going through his head in that one moment.

Still. She knew. Even without them.

She leaned into him, slowly, until their lips were barely touching. "I love you." Her words were barely there, shadows dancing on the air.

She felt him smile, moving his mouth against hers in a delicate brush of lips. He teased her, moving back and forth, his breath hot, not saying it back. She clawed her nails at his neck, and he laughed, crushing their mouths together, teeth clanging.

Avery pressed against him, her fingers exploring his hair and down his firm back, muscles rippling beneath her. Pleasure cut her deep, and she ground her hips against his, a groan slipping from her lips.

Finn was no longer laughing, his face intent in the moments she glanced from beneath her eyelashes. At some point, her dress pooled on the floor. Finn's hot hands were on her naked back, their bodies pressed against one another.

And he returned the words to her a thousand different ways before they were done.

Later, as Finn lay beside her, lazily stroking the curve of her hip, he asked quietly, "Why didn't you tell me about the nightmares?"

Avery couldn't respond at first, unsure herself of her answer.

Losing Fiora in the way it happened . . . no one would ever truly understand that. Even if she could put it into words, there would be no point.

Fiora was dead. And it was Avery's fault.

That was something she would have to live with. If the occasional nightmare was the punishment for it, then it was the least she deserved.

But instead of all that, she merely said, "You've had enough to deal with. Your new position, and Nick, and . . ." She shrugged, not mentioning what Klein had told her about his family. About his father. He was more sensitive about the subject now than ever before. She would tell him when she knew more.

"I didn't want to bother you," she finished on a whisper, tracing patterns over his chest.

"I *want* you to bother me, Avie." He pulled her chin up with a finger, forcing her to meet his eyes. "That's the deal with this thing between us. I bother you, and you bother me, and we figure it out together."

Tears prickled her nose, her eyes welling. She nodded mutely, curling back into his side. If she held his gaze, she knew she would cry again.

Finn pulled her closer to him, tucking her beneath his chin. His fingers played with the ends of her hair, sending sparkles of pleasure down her scalp, skittering across her skin.

They could have laid there for minutes or hours. Avery wouldn't have noticed either way. Eventually Finn's breathing evened out, softening into the gentle rhythm of sleep.

Avery stared in wonder at the firm lines of his face. A hint of stubble along the line of his chin. Dark eyelashes that feathered against his cheeks. Sinfully curved lips that only ever stilled during sleep.

And he was hers alone.

Her skin vibrated, the energy within her veins turning effervescent in the shadow of what they had just shared. That bond between them, their connection, had expanded into something tangible and real. Even now, she could feel it, running a warm line between their energies as real as her bond with any Reange.

But Finn was human. It would be impossible for her to use her gifts with him. Maybe it was her imagination, or some lingering effect of the best sex she'd ever had in her life—not that she was an expert on that front.

But she had known it would be like this with him.

This chasm that had opened within her soul after their lovemaking was raw, like a newborn star, burning blue-hot and fast, even with millions of years ahead. Avery was completely at his mercy, in a way that scared her. She couldn't fight that kind of power and didn't have any desire to try. What she felt for Finn was not small—it never had been. Their love would forge galaxies.

She would move forward with that newfound strength, carry its power within her soul.

Finn was right. She had started to close herself off to the others and to him. It was difficult to keep herself open when her powers had done that by default. She had been relying on them too much.

Once she got back from this mission with Qav, she'd approach things differently. She said they were her family, and she meant it. It was time to start treating them like it.

A pang surged through her, guilt striking her gut. She needed to tell Finn about his father and what Klein had told her. If the Lunitias had been involved in the Reange experimentation, then Finn deserved to know. They would need to figure that out together.

But he worshipped the memory of his father. And after Nick, it would wound him deeply, maybe beyond repair.

Still, she didn't want any secrets between them.

Avery ran a finger down the line of his nose, a centimeter above touching, tracing his profile. Would he ever know how much he truly meant to her?

She would never be able to choose anything other than him. As much as she wanted to, as much as she knew he would never make the same choice, Finn would always come first for her.

He thought she didn't need him. She nearly laughed aloud. She only pushed as hard as she did because of his ideals. Hadn't he been the one driving her from the start? She could do so much with her power, be so much as a So', but beneath it all she was still alone.

But not with him—never with him. His was the hand that held hers in the dark.

And this moment with him, when their souls had melted and fused together, would live on forever, infinite within the chasm of her heart.

CHAPTER THIRTY

If anyone noticed the difference between them at breakfast, they didn't say anything. Although Grigg kept giving Finn looks, widening his eyes, waggling his brows. Avery glowered at him, which only seemed to make it worse. After a few minutes, she flung energy across the table at him, snapping a hefty serving of porridge directly into his face.

Nova choked on her coffee, dissolving into a fit of laughter that had Markes and Linderly giggling into their plates. Megan had the good grace to try to hide her amusement behind a napkin. But even she had given Avery a knowing smile when she sat down, proving there was no such thing as privacy among them.

"I don't know what you're all laughing at." Petra stabbed at a cut of sliced meat. "We're sending Avery off with some criminal psychopath who could easily kill her today."

"Lighten up, Petra. It's not like she's going alone," Grigg pointed out, still wiping food from his face.

Petra shot him a look that would have frozen a star. "Why doesn't that make me feel any better?"

"We'll be back by tomorrow," Avery said calmly. "And once I help Qav, he'll show me how to regain my full powers. I thought you'd be happy about it—he did heal Tai last night."

Petra's mouth twisted. "Tai's barely been able to keep his eyes open. Who knows what he did?"

Finn raised his glass, saying, "Well, the kid didn't try to strangle me with his bare hands on the way home, so I call that a win." Avery's eyes collided with his, his mouth twitching into a grin.

She looked away, cursing the blush that flooded her cheeks.

"Besides, you didn't see Avery kick Qav's ass last night," Markes added, smirking around a mouthful of food. "If anybody should be scared about today, it's him."

"Who knew my bestie was a certifiable badass," Megan said cheerfully, her hands curling around a steaming mug. "I'll never forget the way he went flying across the room like that. Or the look on his face when that table cracked. How much do you think that thing was worth?"

"Priceless," Linderly got out between giggles, her joke sending Markes into fits.

"I'll cheers to that." Finn clinked his mug against Megan's as they shared conspiratorial grins.

Avery shook her head, unable to prevent the smile that crept up on her. "You two are dangerous together," she muttered, earning a wink from Finn. Her face ignited again.

Rem arrived a few minutes later, his movements awkward as he approached the table of laughter. Avery couldn't see Qav and the others sharing much revelry between the four of them. How strange they must have appeared to him. And stranger still, when they all insisted on accompanying them to their send-off.

Rem escorted them to the rooftop where a sleek ship awaited them, entirely matte black and curved lines, clearly a custom design.

Markes whistled low. "Now *that's* a ship."

"I'll try not to take that comment personally," Finn replied. But even he couldn't conceal his appreciation as they approached the vessel.

The breeze was colder atop the building than Avery remembered, tugging at the hair she had wound tightly into a braid down her back. She shivered, pulling her black jacket closer around her.

Rem proceeded to the ramp that disappeared into the hull of the ship, leaving her to say goodbye. And somewhere inside there, Qav watched them. Avery could feel the barest touch of icy tendrils against her, like grazing fingers across a fresh cryotube. She scanned the lines of the ship, searching for a viewport. There were none.

When she turned to the others, Finn was clasping Nova's arm, speaking to her in hushed words. Grigg stood with them, his face serious for once, nodding. Markes was hugging Linderly, his bony arms surprisingly fierce in their embrace.

Megan bounced forward on light feet, despite the chunky green heels she wore, courtesy of her market excursion. She threw her arms around Avery in a cloud of curls and a softly floral perfume. "Be careful, Avie." Her words were a quick whisper on the edge of tears. But before Avery could reassure her, Megan tore away, fleeing for the doors that led back inside.

Petra closed her eyes briefly as Megan passed, her face pained. And when she met Avery's gaze, her eyes were fiercely green in the pale light of the dawning dome above. Finn was probably right about them; their attraction was palpable. Avery didn't understand why they were hiding it from her, though. It was like things were changing, the pathways of their futures balancing on the edge of a knife.

Petra raised her voice, her flat words cutting across the roof. "Don't trust him. Not any of them." And then she was gone, following Megan back into the apartments below. She didn't look back.

Finally, Finn approached her, the others developing a sudden interest in the skyline beyond. Grigg said something that earned him an elbow to the ribs from Nova. Finn's lips twitched.

"They really are horrible," he said.

"Oh, the absolute worst."

He pulled her to him, the heat from his body seeping through her clothes. He was always warm, like he functioned entirely on sarcasm and sunlight. Desire rushed through her, searing her veins in a way that had nothing to do with the transfer of heat. That burn tugged at her chest, electricity running between them. His eyes widened a fraction of an inch, his hands tightening around her waist.

Avery realized with sudden clarity that she didn't want to leave. The thought sent a rush of pain stabbing through her rib cage. But it was too late now. There was no choice but to go forward alone.

And then he was kissing her, pulling her closer, angling his head to delve deeper into her, dragging her very soul through her lips. She clung to his arms, meeting his fervor, dying to be closer to him.

Someone coughed.

Finn pulled away. Slowly.

Avery was shaking, unsteady on her feet. His eyes were an unnerving shade of blue as they took in every inch of her face, his brows drawn. She could feel it, the nerves rioting through his chest. Finn was scared. His arms were taut beneath her fingers.

"Get your ass back here," he said gently, leaning his forehead against hers.

She smiled, nodding once before pulling away. She didn't trust herself to say anything, worried she'd change her mind and insist he come along, which would set them back. So instead she devoured one last look at him and turned away.

And she wasn't alone, entirely.

She had Nova, Grigg, and Linderly. If she couldn't trust Qav, she could at least trust them. He said he wanted to learn more about her power—then she would give him a show. If it meant getting her powers back so she could fix what had gone wrong on Echo, then she would perform, and gladly.

Avery ascended the ramp, the other three close behind her, dissolving into the darkness of the ship's shadowy core.

Qav turned toward them as they entered the bridge, a secretive smile softening the angular lines of his face. He leaned back on a low couch, one arm stretched out, a leg crossed leisurely over the other. His presence crept up to her, teasing the edges of her mind. *And here I thought you'd be out there all day*, he said silently.

"Keep your thoughts to yourself," she snapped. "First rule of this little excursion: if you're going to talk to me, then talk to me. That goes for them, too." She nodded to Grigg, Nova, and Linderly, who had taken up places close by her side.

Qav laughed, showing a good deal of his perfectly white teeth. "The first rule?" He pushed his mind directly into hers, an unwelcome and chilling invasion. *The first rule is that I make the rules.*

Avery stiffened. Nova and Grigg both felt it, their heads jerking up. They braced their feet, ready.

Ennis rose from her seat at the controls. Qav's eyes rolled to her, expectant.

He sighed, the gesture elongated and dramatic. "But I'm willing to make concessions for the sake of collaboration." As swiftly as he had forced his way into her head, he pulled away, a bitter breeze receding into the night.

Avery slammed her defenses back up, determined to keep it that way. Leviathan had taught her well, despite ulterior motives. Avery wouldn't forget again.

Rem stepped forward. "Please, take a seat wherever you're most comfortable. We do have a schedule to keep."

Avery lowered herself to the sofa facing Qav, Grigg and Nova settling down on either side of her. Linderly perched on the end, her hands clasped together tightly, knuckles white.

The bridge was, like the rest of the ship they had seen so far, outfitted fully in black. Dim lighting ran in thin strips down the walkways and floors, casting an ethereal purple glaze that barely combatted the darkness. The instruments at the controls were slightly brighter, the entire console underlit in a vibrant glow of blue. Ennis was bathed in it as she typed in commands, her pale face stained cobalt.

"Then let's go." Syla's impatient voice startled Avery. She was seated near the back on one of the only single chairs. They must have passed by her without noticing. But she had been there the whole time. Lurking.

The darkness of the room faded away into light as a wide window revealed itself at the front. Of course. The ship wasn't windowless; it merely had full privacy shields. Another cost that would have been astronomical to install. Avery had little time to dwell on it before they were up, flying away from the tower, away from Finn and Megan and the others.

Avery longed to crane her neck, hungry for another glance before they were out of view. But she stayed where she was, feet rooted to the floor. Composed and in control.

Grigg leaned forward, bracing an arm on his knee. "Call me crazy, but I don't think there's a sky for this thing to take off in. Where are we going?"

Ennis grinned, bringing them around to hover over the lake until they had a full view of the city. "When you can't go up," she said, excitement lighting her eyes as she twisted her hands on the holocontrols, pointing them toward the water, "you go down."

They shot toward the lake at full speed.

Linderly gasped, grabbing on to Nova's leg in a panic. The surface of the water gave way to the sleek nose of the ship, encompassing them within the depths below. They plunged into darkness again, the water around them flying by on smears of purple light that emanated from the command windows.

"Neat trick." Even Grigg was impressed, giving into a reluctant grin.

Beneath the surface, the edges of the lake opened up into a wide tunnel that fit the ship perfectly, as though it was designed for that purpose alone. And it probably had been.

Qav had built himself more than just a mansion in Sanctum. He had his own private entrances and exits. Avery wondered if the people within it had the same privileges. Could they come and go as they pleased? She was angry with herself for not asking before.

"Are you going to tell us where we're going?" Avery asked Qav. "I believe you promised me details at this point."

Qav studied her a moment before nodding. "True enough. Rem?" He swiped a finger forward, gesturing to the front of the bridge.

Rem rose from his seat behind Qav, tapping something into his wristport as he moved before them. He flipped his hand over, palm up, where a hologram appeared. It was Earth, floating in suspension, outlined in blue light. "We're headed to the center of the Asian continent." As he spoke, the hologram zoomed in, revealing the land mass in question, and then closer, to its heart, far away from any ocean.

"There is a hidden facility there which contains within it specific documents requested for retrieval by our client."

"Documents? As in physical copies?" Nova asked, leaning forward.

"At this point, we're uncertain," Rem confirmed.

"Uncertain?" Grigg nearly laughed. "This is gonna go real well."

Rem touched the edge of his glasses. "The documents have been marked with specific code tracers linked to atomic signatures. Once we get inside, we'll be able to run a program that will tell us specifically where they're located, at which point we'll discover what exactly we're looking for."

"Which is where you come in, my little tattooed pixie," Qav purred, his fingers dancing at Linderly. "You see, what Rem here fails to add is that he's been unable to run the code quickly enough in any of our sims."

Linderly blanched, her eyes darting to Avery and back again. "What?" Her voice was little more than a squeak.

"You hacked into the Port Station, didn't you?" he asked. "A little secret facility should be no problem."

"But I haven't even seen the code streams," she protested, shaking her head. "You want me to jump into this without any prep? Are you insane?"

Rem continued, ignoring her protests, "This place is fully off grid, and we can only access the network from within the building itself. But it only opens its servers for external capabilities once every twenty-four hours. The timeframe is determined by an internal algorithm that randomizes the time slot. Ideally, that's where we'll need to start."

"So we don't even know our window for this?" Avery balked, the likelihood of success dwindling in her mind. "Who owns the facility? What happens if we get caught?"

Qav hissed on a grimace. "Best not to ask that one. I don't get caught. Ever."

Avery frowned. "Right," she scoffed.

He definitely knew who they were stealing from. Qav wasn't the kind of person to go into anything without being fully informed.

More likely, he didn't want them to know.

"If hacking was essential to this plan, we should have brought Megan," Linderly said, her hands clasped in her lap again.

"She's right," Avery confirmed. "Megan is the most gifted coder I know, besides Linderly."

"Interesting," Qav said, a finger passing over his lips in thought. "So there is something going on inside that pretty head. Unfortunately—"

"Let me guess," Grigg interrupted him. "She's human."

"Give the kid a gold star," Syla replied sarcastically, clapping her hands together in a soft staccato. Qav's mouth twisted to the side, preventing a laugh.

Nova pointed to the facility schematics now floating in front of Rem. "What about security? I assume that's why you needed me and Grigg. And Avery's muscle."

"You're correct," Rem said succinctly. "The window for the servers is also the only time the facility opens for entry or exit. During that time, armed guards patrol both sides of the entrance, and the main hallways within. There are simply too many for us to take down *and* complete the coding needed to access the network inside."

"Why not use more Reanges, then?" Avery looked pointedly at Qav. He had no qualms messing with people's minds. "Wouldn't that be a viable option?"

Ennis angled her head toward them, a slight movement that was barely noticeable. Qav glanced in her direction before saying, "Normally, yes. But the ladies here have particular rules about these sort of things when the stakes are high."

"I thought you made the rules."

His eyes sliced to her, molten silver in the dark. They narrowed. The air turned heavy. Cold. Avery didn't look away.

Rem cleared his throat, shifting on his feet. "We have a few hours yet to go over a plan of action and your roles," he said. "Syla is our combat expert, so she'll walk you through the approaches there."

"Great. We get the cranky one," Grigg muttered too loudly. Avery bumped his knee. Regardless of their situation, they still needed to cooperate.

Rem continued, "Linderly, if you would accompany me to the conference room, we'll patch in and find the approximate time for landing. I assume you have your own bots you'll want to work with?"

Linderly looked to Avery hesitantly.

"We'll be right here if you need us," Avery said, trying to keep her voice comforting. Linderly was little more than a kid—maybe Finn had been right about that. Avery should have insisted she stay back.

But Linderly just smiled, dimples deepening focal points into her cheeks, and rose to follow Rem from the room.

"I guess that means it's my turn." Syla stood, stomping her way to the center of the room. She pulled up a holo from her own wristport, the schematics identical to the ones Rem had shown them before.

As Syla spoke, Avery cautioned a glance at Qav. His long legs stretched out before him, an expensive black boot that was more fashion than function crossed over the other. His head rested against the back of the sofa. Those eyes were closed for once, dark lashes fanning out over his cheeks, his breathing concentrated and rhythmic.

He had fallen asleep.

CHAPTER THIRTY-ONE

Petra knew Finn had a plan as soon as he appeared in the foyer with Markes glued to his side. His face was set, a mask of stone that had chiseled away his annoyingly upbeat humor.

She stood immediately, startling Megan, who nearly spilled her mug of tea. Whatever he was thinking—whatever he had planned—she wanted in on it.

Finn strode purposefully to the long dining table where they sat, scanning the room. "Where is Brehna?" he asked sharply.

Megan cocked her head, a blonde curl falling over the perfect curves of her face. "Why? Is something wrong?"

"I'm going after them."

Silence met his words. Petra relished the strike of adrenaline that hit her veins, the promise of action. She resisted the ludicrous urge to grin. "Finally, someone is talking some sense."

"Count me in," Markes added. "I don't trust him, whether he's a So' or not. He'll use us at the drop of a hat." His eyes flickered to Megan.

"Agreed," Petra said shortly.

"Wait just a second here." Megan placed her fingers pointedly on the table before her. "We promised Avery that we'd go along with her plan. Do you know how pissed she's gonna be if we disobey her?"

"Less pissed than if she's dead," Finn quipped. Markes let out an amused grunt. "We're not going to sit here and let that asshole take advantage of her. She's our responsibility, and if it's in our power to help her, then I'm damn well going to do it."

Megan stood, placing a soft hand on Petra's arm. Her skin burned beneath the light touch. She met Megan's eyes, perfect and blue and endless, like cloudless sky over open water, like the eternal horizon of an azure sea. Like home. Petra's throat tightened.

So much had changed in so little time. She struggled to make sense of anything. Like she had been pulled into an undertow and couldn't find the surface, drowning on the tangled mess that was left of her feelings.

The worst of it was that others seemed to see her so clearly. Megan could see her so clearly—better than anyone else. Even Avery.

But they were from different worlds, in the most literal sense. Petra had been raised to believe the worst of humans—had seen the worst of them. It had been hard enough to reconcile her feelings for Avery and the complexity of her relationship with the human world.

Megan was entirely of Earth. A human. She should have been the last thing Petra wanted.

But Petra wanted her all the same. Desperately.

For as long as she could remember, Petra had seen the world and known her place in it easily. She had known the right choice immediately. Had known her side of things and where she stood. She had known herself.

But Megan . . . Megan flipped all of that assuredness upside down, switching off the gravity and throwing Petra's life into weightless chaos. And Petra wasn't sure she even cared.

"Are you sure about this?" Megan breathed.

"Is she sure about what?"

Petra looked sharply to the stairs. Tai stood in the foyer, his hair a disheveled mess.

For a moment, she would have believed he was still a child. Still a sticky-fingered mess following her around the harbor, begging to go with her, to be included. A pang struck her chest, her nose prickling.

"You're awake," Petra said dumbly, already halfway to him. She pulled him into an embrace, pressing his head against her shoulder, relishing in his familiar scent.

"Yeah, sorry," he murmured against her jacket, his words muffled. He extricated himself from her arms, bringing a hand to the back of his head, scratching it lightly. "I know this is gonna sound weird," he started, looking around the room and out toward the windows at the city beyond, "but where are we?"

Finn let out a bark of laughter.

Petra frowned. "You don't remember anything?"

He shook his head, eyebrows high.

"Nothing?"

A whoosh of breath left his lips. "It's weird. I have . . . I dunno . . . flashes? Brief images, but just a few here and there. A conversation with the Elders. The ship. Some guy with silver eyes." He stared at Finn in surprise. "Did I—did I shoot you?"

"Barely." Finn shrugged. Petra was thankful for the way he played it down. "Trust me, kid, I've had much worse."

"That's not what you were saying when we patched you up," Markes added wryly. Finn glared at him, and he shut his mouth, taking a sudden interest in the chandelier above the table.

Tai winced. "Sorry," he apologized lamely. "The last thing I remember was leaving the arena to try and find a way to get you out, but then I . . ."

"What is it?" Petra asked.

"I—I was summoned to the Elders." Tai frowned, shaking his head. "Things get fuzzy after I entered the capitol building."

Finn took a step forward. "You don't remember what they did to you? Who you spoke with?"

Tai shook his head again. "It's a total blank. But whatever it was, they must have done it to the commanders, too. There was an assembly after you guys left for Earth—that's when the changes started. And that day they arrested Finn, that was when they started rounding up the humans, sending units into the city to bring them in."

"And everyone just went along with it?" Finn snapped.

"Finn," Petra warned.

"They strategically targeted leaders," Tai explained, leveling Finn with a stare. "You know better than anyone we can't go against orders.

And with Avery off planet . . . it happened too quickly."

"It wasn't your fault," Megan said gently, her words sending pleasure curling down Petra's spine. "We're just glad you're safe and back in the land of the conscious."

Tai's mouth twisted in an embarrassed smile. "Can you catch me up? Why do I get the feeling we're not on Echo anymore?"

Before Petra could answer, Finn said, "As much as I'd love to sit here recapping, we've got someplace to be." He looked to Megan, a dark brow rising. "So what do you think, beautiful? Are you in or out?"

She stared at Petra for a long moment before something shifted in her eyes. Subtle but resolute, those soft blue seas hardened to chiseled sapphire. As though she had decided something monumental.

Her face melted into a dazzling smile that she cast to Finn. "Flattery will get you everywhere, Ambassador. Let's go get our girl."

Finn laughed. In truth, they both were alike in many ways. Quick to smile, quick to lighten the mood of those around them. But Megan was significantly—*significantly*—less annoying than Finn. Petra nearly smiled herself.

What the blazar was wrong with her? She made a point to frown.

"Now, where is Brehna?" Finn took off down the hall, calling over his shoulder, "I need to see a woman and a squirrel about a ship."

Tai's brows drew together. "What's a squirrel?"

Petra just shook her head. Far be it from her to interpret what went on in Finn's brain. She had given that up a long time ago.

But when it came to Avery, they saw things similarly. He had been right about one thing: she was their responsibility. Avery was the future of their people—the future of Echo itself—a beacon of hope that would lead the Reanges out of the darkness toward lasting peace.

And Leviathan had betrayed her. There was a time when the old woman had been the epitome of everything Petra aspired to be. She had grown up in the Origin, still working for them even after she and Tai were placed in Nos Valuta. Everything Petra had been, everything she had become, was because of the Origin. Because of Leviathan.

But it had all been a lie. Even the purists within the Origin had ultimately gone back on their word and violated sacred law. What Leviathan was doing to the people of Echo—what she had done to Tai—was unforgivable. An utter disgrace to the traditions that had guided their people for centuries.

Avery would never turn her back on her people that way. She was everything Petra had been taught a So' should be. It hadn't come easily to her, but she had embraced it in the end.

Maybe that was what Petra had fallen in love with. Not Avery herself but the idea of her. The promise of what a future with her leadership, her light, would bring.

And Petra would never turn her back on that.

It was raining by the time they surfaced from beneath the water. The sun was low on the horizon, casting a sickly rust to the enveloping clouds as they crossed the Pacific Indian. It was illegal to venture beyond any global city borders, but Ennis explained the ship was equipped with advanced stealth barriers. As long as they kept below regulated speeds for registered space vessels, they would easily go undetected by scanner bots all the way to Asia.

Avery hadn't seen much of the Earth—or any of it, really—beyond New San Fran, Alexandria, and a few other major cities she had visited during her tour. Not that there was much to see outside of the metropolitan areas. The majority of the planet was submerged, consumed by the exponentially rising water levels of the past century. Whatever was left consisted mostly of wastelands, scorched by pollution or radiation, unusable in every sense of the word, even for the hardiest crops. At least the Hydroponics Initiative had counteracted the need to grow foods within soil. Earth could still supply its own food, but barely. They had been exploiting Echo for crop importations for decades.

Earth was no comparison to the lush greenery and vibrant landscapes found across Echo. The Reange home planet was a living, breathing world, full of potential and uncorrupted resources. It was no wonder the Federation had sought to take it by force and manipulation. A government in greed would grasp at any avenue to secure power, even genocide.

That was the entire reason Avery was there in the first place. She couldn't stand by and watch her people, human or Reange, repeat their history. She hadn't pulled the Reanges out of oppression only to be forced into one of a different kind.

But perhaps all government was a kind of oppression, regardless of its intentions or methods. A way for those to cling to power—to control.

The only true path toward progress was agency of self. The people deserved the right to make their own choices. To decide their own fates. And she would be the one to give that to them.

A pang of guilt sliced through her chest. They were running short on time; they had lost so much of it already. Once they returned from this mission, it would be imperative she convinced Qav to help her. And then she would have to hope that the restoration of her powers would be enough to change what was happening on Echo.

Unless Qav came with her.

Leviathan wouldn't stand a chance against both of them. And with another So' on her side, she could share the burdens of her position. They could make real, lasting change.

But could she ever trust Qav enough for that? He had crafted his entire life around the fundamental theory that his gifts were meant for himself alone. He held no allegiances. Honored no duty.

Avery stole a covert glance at him from beneath her eyelashes. He stood by Ennis near the front of the bridge, watching the dark surface of the ocean pass by beneath them. At least he had changed into more practical attire.

Qav's casual clothing was tailored closely to his frame, just like his suits, hugging the long lines of his body. A pair of matching silver blasters were holstered to each of his thighs, glistening against the dark fabric of his pants. His hair was gathered into a bun atop his head and a few locks of silver framed his face, the layers too short to restrain.

There was something in the way he carried himself, the way his body exuded his power, even during sleep. Avery couldn't tell if it was vanity or ego, or some combination therein. Like self-assurance was the steel from which he crafted his armor, not a chink to be found. And that armor was as cold as the power he wielded.

Her mind traveled to that field in his mind, with its soft grasses and warm lavender-scented winds. The peace there—the serenity. Surely someone who envisioned that world couldn't be unreachable. Avery had felt the goodness within him, within that place, even if it was just a faint trace.

If she were at full capacity, she would dive headfirst into the places he tried to keep hidden. She would have forced that goodness to the surface, forced him to acknowledge it.

Before she knew it, Avery pushed her energy outward, seeking the tether of his thoughts, blindly grasping for the icy tendrils of his consciousness.

He whipped his head to her sharply, silver eyes flaring.

Avery withdrew quickly, blood thrumming through her veins. She had connected with him! Even if she hadn't felt anything on her end, he certainly had. That, at least, was something. Maybe her powers were closer than she thought.

What happened to your rules? he asked, a brow lifting. He wasn't angry. Intrigued, perhaps.

Avery glanced to Grigg and Nova, who were playing a game on their wristports. If the sour look on Grigg's face was any indication, Nova was winning.

She looked back to Qav. He gave her a deliberate smile.

Worried what they might think of you? he jeered. *Their perfect So', paragon of light and virtue, savior of their revolution. Stooping to consort with a selfish—albeit beautiful and alluring—bastard like me?*

She rolled her eyes. *Please. You think too much of yourself, oh mighty tsek.*

For once, his smile reached his eyes, warming them. He turned back to the window. She thought he was done with the conversation, but he continued, *I never asked for them to call me that. It's about as flattering as the Acquirer. But it serves its purpose.*

Oh, and I suppose you didn't commission that mural of yourself in the markets either?

No, that I most certainly did. There's only so much mental manipulation you can do to a group of people that large. It helps to have conventional methods of control, too. He glanced at her over his shoulder, adding, *Something I learned well from your friends in the Federation, as well as the High Council.*

She supposed he meant Klein. Propaganda was a favored technique of politicians around the globe, and the Federation paid no expense on their campaigns. It was an underhanded technique to influence the opinions of average citizens. And yet . . . *effective.* And yet effective.

Avery frowned. Had she said that to herself twice?

I hope you're ready for what this will be once we arrive, Qav's voice intruded on her thoughts once again. *We'll need to be in sync.*

I'm fairly certain I've already illustrated the fact that I know what I'm doing far better than you do, she countered, letting him see the mental image she conjured of him flying across the room the night before.

As much as I hate to admit it, you're right on that front. Syla has been harping at me for years to train more. Or at all. In my defense, I've never had to worry about fighting anyone with abilities like mine. He turned around, leaning against one of the viewing chairs to face the room. He took his time crossing his arms over his chest. *But I meant truly in sync. I'll need to connect us via the merge. That means your friends. And you.*

The merge. It required absolute trust. Opening your mind entirely, allowing the So' free rein within . . . . It wasn't to be taken lightly. Anyone within the merge was fully connected in thought and experience. It was the ultimate avenue to act and fight as one, and essential in combat.

Avery hadn't used it wholly, hadn't been able to bring herself to use it since—no. She wouldn't think of what happened. She couldn't.

Who is Fiora? Qav's simple question burned through her mind, searing a hole straight through to her chest.

Avery flinched, sucking in a hiss of breath. Nova looked up at her sharply, her eyes jumping to Qav and back again. Grigg stood, his face uncertain.

Qav didn't look away from Avery as he drawled, "Sit down."

Grigg complied, his face slackening into acquiescence. Nova didn't move. Her eyes were still fixed on Avery, blonde brows drawn. Waiting.

Heat filled Avery's veins, rushing up to her face, the sound of her blood drowning out anything else. A vision of red hair, a laughing face. And then nothing—always nothing. Pain scalded her again, white-hot in her chest. The lights around them flickered dangerously. Ennis looked to Qav.

"Sensitive, are we?" Qav mused.

Avery shot to her feet, hands shaking at her sides. She couldn't move beyond that. Had no words. Her mind was blank. There was nothing—nothing.

Breathe. Breathe. She focused, moving the air in and out of her lungs at a regular pace. Finn would make her laugh. Distract her. He should be there with them.

But he wasn't. She had left him behind.

She just needed space from Qav, needed room to think, needed space in her head.

"I'm going to check on Linderly," she said numbly. She forced herself into motion, dragging heavy legs toward the door.

Grigg and Nova rose to follow her, and she didn't object.

CHAPTER THIRTY-TWO

"Got it," Linderly chirped from across the table. She held up her tablet confidently, her eyes jumping to Rem. A small pair of circular coding glasses perched on her nose, identical to Rem's except that they were tinted pink, not yellow. A gift. From Rem or Qav, Avery wasn't sure.

For the better part of the past hour, they sat around the long oval table in the conference room. The far wall was composed of tall windows, giving a wide view of the scenery outside, not that there was much to see. It was fully dark on this side of the world. After a brief trip over barren mountains, Ennis set the ship down in the middle of a vast desert. Rippling sands stretched out toward the night horizon, an endless ocean of arid blues and shadow in the cold moonlight. Avery had never seen anything like it.

Linderly worked diligently, coding her way into the algorithm that would reveal their window. The music from her ear pods was loud enough to cast a tinny beat in the quiet room. Every once in a while, she would mumble to herself, a soft voice barely audible under her breath.

But when she made the exclamation and pulled out her ear pods, Rem was at her side in a moment, leaning over her shoulder to view the code himself. She had actually beaten him to it. Even Syla turned from her spot at the window, curious and surprised.

"I thought we'd be at it for another couple hours at least," he murmured and laughed. "Where in the galaxies did you learn skills like this?"

Linderly shrugged. "When you grow up in a hidden extremist camp, there's not much else to do. Besides, they valued certain— skills."

Avery frowned at her description of the Origin. What had Linderly's life been like there? Growing up there? Both she and Markes were incredibly adept in their fields to be so young. What had Leviathan done to ensure their proficiency? What price had they paid for their skills?

When Avery was fifteen, she had just gone to her first rave with Megan. She had kissed her first boy the year before. They had been more concerned about passing exams and getting caught out past curfew than anything else.

But Linderly had been fighting. She had always been fighting— and still was. Avery shifted in her seat.

"When?" Syla's sole word was as much a command as a question.

Rem quickly reviewed the information on the tablet. He froze, a rare curse tumbling from his lips. Syla frowned, at his side in a moment. He touched his wristport before speaking into the embedded mic. "Ennis. We've got to move, and fast."

"Is it that close?" Avery asked.

Rem didn't answer, filtering through the messages for more intel.

Linderly replied for him, "The window opens in eighteen minutes." Her eyes darted to Avery, uncertain.

"But we're at least a half hour away from the drop point." Nova was already on her feet.

"Precisely," Rem said curtly. And he jogged out of the room, heeled boots silent on the soft floors beneath them.

"Are you serious—is he serious?" Grigg asked, his head tracking Rem as he left without another word.

Syla didn't acknowledge the question. "Come with me." She didn't wait to see if they followed her from the room.

The ship lifted up and away from the dunes beyond the window, rising into the night sky. They were already in flight.

"I guess this is happening now," Avery said to them, energy crackling along her veins in anticipation. Linderly rose from her chair, clutching the tablet to her chest. Avery gave her a reassuring smile. "We'll be fine. We just need to stay together and keep clear heads."

Grigg let out a short laugh. "Like that's a possibility with him rummaging around in our brains." He was rolling his shoulders, already warming up his muscles for the fight ahead.

"Are you sure about this, Avery?" Nova asked, her voice calm. "If you feel it's too much, then just say the word."

"Ten to one we can take those guards out without ever needing the merge," Grigg chimed in. He had moved on to squats, limbering up his quads after sitting for so long.

Avery paused before replying, "I'm willing to take the risk of letting him in if it means getting this done safely. If he was going to take advantage us, he would have already." She prayed he wouldn't prove her wrong.

For better or worse, there was nowhere to go but straight ahead, following Qav's lead into the moonlit skies.

The facility was a low structure with six sides, nestled deeply in the sands of the desert. The smooth edges of its organic design and dark walls blended in seamlessly with the shadowy landscape around it, making it nearly impossible to see from above.

The single entrance was in the center of the roof, where a landing platform was revealed only at the start of the hour-long window. All connectivity, communications, and physical entries had to be performed during these sixty minutes. The entrance was the only way in or out, a single point of access.

And they couldn't just land on the platform either. Any unscheduled vessel approach would activate the security systems, sending the entire facility into an immediate lockdown.

Ennis landed half a mile away, tucked under the cover of a massive sand dune. The ship's advanced cloaks would take care of any radars or bot patrols, and for added protection, Ennis would remain behind on the ship along with Rem to monitor. They would stay on the periphery of the merge, assisting if and as needed.

And the ground unit would be forced to go in on foot.

Which was why they were now trudging through sand under the cover of darkness, each step sinking deeper into the sliding ground. Progress was slow. Avery's calves burned, the arches of her feet screaming despite the sturdy soles of her boots. A fine sheen of sweat gathered along her skin, turning her neck clammy in the chilly desert wind.

Along with weapons, Syla had outfitted them all with black shemaghs, long wraps of cloth meant to keep out the sand and sun. Although the sun wasn't much of an issue, they had the added benefit of providing some measure of stealth. Particularly for Qav. Without it, his hair would have glistened in the moonlight like a silver beacon.

Linderly stumbled, falling to her knees in the sand.

Grigg grabbed her arms, helping her to her feet. She looked to Avery, her eyes tired, skin sweaty beneath the fabric covering her face. If Avery was hurting, she imagined Linderly was truly struggling. The girl barely trained at all. She was much more accustomed to relying on her coding skills than any kind of physical prowess.

"How much farther?" Avery's voice was eerily loud in the stillness of the dry air.

He paused, turning back to them, his eyes bright in the shadows of the shemagh. A chill slithered down Avery's spine. They shifted to Linderly. "Not much farther. Are you ready?"

Avery knew that he didn't mean for the mission ahead. He was asking if she was ready to trust him. To open herself fully, laying herself and her crew at his feet.

This was no time to be squeamish about risk. There were others counting on her, both Reanges and humans that needed her help. This was a necessary step to achieving that goal.

Avery clenched her fists at her sides, nodding silently. "Do it."

And she let down her shields.

At first, she thought he didn't hear her. Qav just stared down at her from the dune where he stood, the fabric of his coat snapping on the wind. The moonlight caught the glint of the blaster strapped to his thigh, winking silver through the night.

A chill sidled up against her mind, stroking the length of her, seeping in on the back of a cold mist until it filled her completely. But it was familiar now, and she didn't fight it. The mist teased her, seeking purchase as it turned into icy fingers, wrapping around her every thought.

Something shifted, settling against itself, locking into place.

Avery took a sharp breath, her eyes widening.

She could see from her own eyes and those of the others. Saw herself standing there, looking up at Qav. The eerie glow of her golden eyes, lit from behind the shadows of her own headdress. So like his. *The same as his.* The same as his.

They were within the merge, connected by Qav's tether on their minds. They shared the same experiences, the same perceptions, and were able to draw on one another's knowledge. Whatever they did from here on out would be entirely in tune. Entirely as one.

Avery waited for the panic to hit her, the anxiety that was sure to come from the connection. She had been avoiding this for so long, surely an attack was inevitable. But if the terror tried to rise up from that dark place within, she didn't feel a twinge of it. There was only a frigid assuredness, freezing out anything that threatened her focus.

Time is ticking. Syla gestured for them to keep moving.

They picked up the pace this time, pushing harder. Linderly struggled but did her best to keep up with the group. Avery reached out with her power to carry some of her weight, giving her the boost that she needed to stay apace. The sand didn't seem so deep anymore, nor the distance so far. They pressed on.

Qav was right—they were close after all. Once they crested the final dune, the facility was practically directly upon them. *Hunch down.* They leaned low to the ground, concealing their bodies against the sands. Syla pulled out a scope, viewing the landing platform through the digital magnification. Directional lights strobed red across the now exposed panel. It was empty.

Weren't there supposed to be guards? Grigg asked, his stare not wavering from the building ahead.

There. Linderly pointed. An opening appeared in the floor of the platform where four guards now rose from below, lifted by some kind of riser.

There were four, just as planned. Easy enough to take down, even if Avery was alone.

Let's move. Qav launched to his feet, breaking into a steady run down the side of the dune. They followed his lead, barreling down in a synchronized group, half sliding their way to the bottom of the slope. The sand leveled out and hardened, becoming much easier to traverse as they neared the building.

They reached the outer edge of the fifth wall, where Rem coded a blind spot into the sensors. Barely noticeable to anyone watching the vid feeds, it would provide them with the space needed to scale the side.

Avery looked up the sheer face of the building. About twenty feet. Not so bad, considering. The entire facility had been constructed using anti-tamper tech, so physical tools were out of the question. The only way to get up there was to fly.

Which is where you come in. Qav curved his fingers to Avery, telling her to join him in position.

Excellent. All her power boiled down to a glorified springboard. Avery clasped her hands together, squatting to offer a foothold, while Qav took up an identical position across from her. The others lined up a few feet away.

Syla ran at them full speed, her booted foot connecting with Avery's hands as she vaulted upward. Avery grasped to the molecules around her, calling on more energy to compound the natural movement. Syla soared upward, her arms outstretched for balance as she cleared the roof, disappearing over the edge.

They saw from her perspective where she landed gracefully, rolling to the ground and into the shadows, out of sight. None of the guards noticed. She was in the clear.

It worked. Grigg's surprise shimmered down their connection, his laughter nearly audible.

Nova, Grigg, now you. Qav jerked his head toward them.

Just as with Syla, they took their turns, both flying up and over the edge on the enhanced power of their velocity.

Linderly was next. She hesitated. Panic trickled down to them, sharp and alarming. Heights. She hated heights. But as soon as the feeling touched them, it was gone, floating away on an icy fog, easily forgotten.

No need for that, Qav calmed her. *A quick jump, and it's over.* His confidence filled them, rushing down the bond like a river of freezing waters, fresh and cool and . . . invigorating. Avery opened herself, letting it wash over and in and through her. Nothing could touch them—nothing.

Was this what it felt like to be in his head? *More.* She wanted more.

Linderly ran at them, a sprite in the dark, her slight weight lifting against Avery's hands until she bounded up and over, after the others.

Qav turned slowly to Avery, silent for a moment. Still. The wind blew against them, rustling the fabric still covering their heads, obscuring most of their faces. He opened his mind to her, a small window that allowed her to see through his eyes.

And she saw herself. Those strange golden eyes looking back from the dark.

Not strange. No—not strange. *Powerful.* Her eyes looked powerful. Bright and shining and powerful in the shadows. They were her birthright. This power was hers and hers alone. She answered to no one.

Qav gestured to her hands. *Be gentle with me.*

Avery shook her head, clearing it before clasping her hands together again. He didn't need a running start, using his own power to launch his body into the air from the added energy of her hands. He cleared the roof above her, leaving Avery alone on the ground.

She wasted no time, backing up even farther than the others had before. When the base of the closest dune still wasn't enough distance, she crawled up it a ways before turning to survey the length. Well— there was only one way to find out if it would be enough.

She took off down the sands, adding power to each pull of her thighs, increasing the speed in each stride until she was flying across the sands. The wind snatched at her shemagh, stripping it from her in a sting of flapping fabric. Avery braced herself, drawing energy from the atoms around her, charging her muscles until they felt as though they would burst.

And she leaped.

She launched upward toward the building ahead, her body soaring in an arching path over the sands.

But the path she carved through the air was wide—too wide.

No, no, no!

Avery kept moving through the night sky, an unstoppable force, her legs swinging to keep her balance in the air around her. She sailed over the others near the edge, who watched her with equal expressions of horror and awe. Finally, she came down to the surface, breaking her fall in a compacted roll. She used the momentum to right herself, one knee on the ground, bracing her hand to the floor. The concrete was cold under her fingers.

Lights flashed around her, turning the floor a strobing red in the dark. *Damn.* She had fallen directly in the center of the landing platform.

She looked up.

The four guards surrounded her.

Avery was frozen. Identical looks of shock were plastered to the faces of the guards above her. They surrounded her—she had essentially landed in the center of their patrol—but none of them spoke.

They just stared at her, slack-jawed and immobile. Finn would have laughed.

Move, dammit! Grigg shouted through the merge, sending a rush of adrenaline straight to her limbs along with the message. He was right. She should already have been in motion.

Avery was on her feet in an instant, running toward a guard, sliding to the ground before him. She grabbed a leg, flipping him up and over to slam into the surface. Another reacted quickly enough to grab her blaster and aim, but Avery was already on her.

She leaped through the air in a twist, bringing her leg down in a fierce drop. Her foot connected with bone, the guard's hand crunching as the gun dropped to the ground. Avery finished with a swift jab to the face and a chop to the back of the neck. The guard fell unconscious, as useless as her discarded blaster.

Behind.

She heard the shot before she turned. Avery acted on instinct, sending out a wave of energy beyond her that shuddered with the impact of the blastfire. But she was unscathed.

The two men paused, eyes wide and white in the night. Avery raised a hand, flinging the power outward in a wall that threw the two remaining guards backward into the shadows.

She ran at them but knew what she would find. Grigg had disabled one, dragging them farther to the edge of the roof with Nova's help. Syla had the second guard in a chokehold, sliding to the ground as he fell unconscious.

Qav pulled down the fabric covering his face, revealing an impressed smile. *You can stop blastfire? How did you learn that trick?*

Painfully. Avery couldn't prevent the flash of memory from surfacing. She ran with Finn through the white halls of the Station, barefoot and bleeding. Fed soldiers had been chasing them then. Her power had just barely awoken, and yet . . . it had come to her when she needed it most. *Instinct.* It was instinct.

Avery moved past Qav to take care of the two guards she had subdued. She grabbed an arm of each, using her power to help move them across the platform to the edge where they'd stay hidden until they were gone.

Avery felt Syla's intentions as she strode purposefully toward the guards. She would throw them over the edge, straight to the ground. A fall from that height would do serious damage, if not kill them. Avery reached out to grab onto Syla, to control her—to stop her. But there was nothing, no tether she could grasp. Too late, Avery remembered she had no power here. Qav was in control.

Stop! Avery commanded, but still, it was too late.

Syla pushed the first guard off with her boot.

Avery flew to the edge, sending out a rush of power beneath the falling body, cushioning the guard before he landed softly on the sand. Unharmed.

Irritation bristled against her, prickling and sharp within her skull. Qav stepped forward, his head tilted. *This isn't some friendly game, Avery. These guards shoot to kill.*

No, Avery countered, anger simmering through her limbs, energy crackling at her fingertips. *We did not agree to murder.*

Qav stared at her, his eyes narrowing on the word. He sighed, long and slow.

Fine. Then catch them.

And he swept his arm, a wave of energy surging toward the remaining three, brushing them off the side of the roof.

CHAPTER THIRTY-THREE

Avery's stomach dropped with them.

She held out both arms, calling on the air around the guards to manifest and hold. She pulled against it, slowing their bodies just in time for them to tumble in a loud heap to the ground. But not a crushing blow.

Damn it, Qav. She whirled on him, eyes ablaze.

He was grinning. *I just wanted to see if you could do it.* He turned to the others, issuing a direct command down the merge. *Let's go.*

And they all went. Even Avery.

They stepped onto the elevator near the edge of the landing platform, a touch pad rising from the floor as they approached. Linderly kneeled before it, concentrating on the tablet she now held in her hands. Her coding glasses glowed nearly purple against the blue light of the screen.

It took her a few seconds before the elevator began its descent, pulling them deeper, past the point of no return. The night sky disappeared above them, and they braced for what lay ahead.

Nova and Grigg were vigilant at Avery's sides. Whatever Finn had said to them in those moments before they left had set them on high alert. That idiot thought she still needed protection. Avery couldn't decide if it was sweet or just annoying. *Maybe he didn't trust her.* Maybe he didn't.

The light from below chased away any shadows as they descended, illuminating them fully as the elevator came to the floor in a clash of metal locking into place. They were in an antechamber, empty except for the heavy steel door ahead.

Keep going. Qav moved forward on lithe feet, pausing at the entrance. He looked to Syla, who monitored her wristport. From back on the ship, Rem patched in to the security feeds, updating them on the guards' movements.

Linderly was already at the access panel, unlocking the door in seconds. It flashed green on two long beeps, opening with a hiss, a cloud of vapor billowing up around them. They pushed forward.

It was freezing. Avery's muscles protested the drop in temperature, even colder than the arid desert night outside.

She ran through the layout of the building from shared memory, visualizing their route. The large hallway they entered ran along the outer edge of the hexagonal building. At each of its six corners, hallways dissected the structure moving toward its center to a control room.

As far as Avery knew, or as far as Rem had told them, the facility housed a vast array of quantum computers. Each of the rooms held hundreds of components and circuit boards kept at near-freezing temperatures. But she hadn't expected even the hallways to be so cold.

There was a total of fifteen guards, along with four systems engineers whose sole job was to monitor the computers and run operations. By heading straight for the control room, they hoped to avoid the other guards altogether.

Pick up the pace. Qav jogged forward on light feet, Syla at his side.

Two guards ahead. Rem's voice came through their connection, his first intrusion into the merge since they left the ship. *Wait thirty seconds and continue.*

They did as he said, rounding the corner just as the guards disappeared beyond the angled wall ahead. Without hesitating, they pushed forward into the corridor leading toward the control room, reaching the final door. But even with Rem on the security feeds, they couldn't see what awaited them; there were no feeds inside the hub itself.

Linderly moved to the access panel as Syla sidled up to her, clutching a blaster, ready for whatever, or whoever, lay beyond. Another sixty seconds before the next patrol would round the corner and see them—they were fully exposed. If they didn't get into the room, there would be no hope after that. The guards would lock the place down entirely.

That won't happen; we don't get caught. Qav drew Avery's eyes to him with a single thought.

She resisted giving him a rude gesture. His faint grin said he saw it in her head anyway.

Hurry. Rem's anxiety trickled to them, a spark of adrenaline surging through the group as the seconds sauntered past.

Linderly didn't so much as lift her head. Despite her nerves, she was trained for this; she had been raised to do her job and do it well under pressure.

Grigg turned, dropping to a knee, his blaster raised at the main hallway entrance. Nova moved in front of Avery, her own weapon up by her ear. It wouldn't come down to that.

And if it did, Avery wasn't about to let either of them get hurt. No matter what Finn had told them.

Brace yourselves. Two guards approaching from the south side.

Avery held her breath, gathering energy at her wrists. She was ready, too.

The door behind them beeped twice. Avery whirled around, the panel flashing green before it slid open with a soft whoosh. They acted as a single unit, in the room within seconds, the door already closed behind them.

Their eyes adjusted to the dim interior in degrees. Syla and Grigg fanned out to secure the room. Nova didn't leave Avery's side.

Rem. Qav was stone-faced, waiting for an update.

A rush of relief fell over them, Rem's answer pouring through the connection. *You're clear. They saw nothing.*

Avery uncoiled at last, letting herself look around. The room featured a circular glass table in its center, surrounded by no fewer than ten chairs. A large circled light mimicked the table's design, casting a dim blue glow throughout the space. But it was empty—entirely empty.

Another jolt of alarm surged through her. Where was the engineer?

Keep moving, Qav said to them, that icy calm threading through his thoughts.

Rem did a quick scan of all the feeds, finding the missing operator quickly. She was in one of the computer rooms, speaking with another worker.

Stick to the plan. We get in; we get out.

Syla nodded, moving to one of the three doors, standing guard. Grigg and Nova followed suit with the other two. Linderly went straight for the table, knowing instinctively the glass would open up a holo-interface. She took a seat, ready to work.

Linderly touched the side of her glasses, and a small cable emerged from the frame, which she connected directly to the device. The coding glasses would enable her to make changes with her eye movements along with her hands, so she could work on separate strings simultaneously. She would need every bit of speed she could get.

It was quiet. None of them spoke, even in mind.

Linderly's eyes moved quickly behind the lenses of her glasses, shifting like lightning over the unending lines of code. They could do nothing but wait.

Something tugged at Avery's stomach, and she turned a tight circle. Her eyes shifted to Grigg's door. Something was coming—someone.

Engineer headed your way. Wait, no—It's two of them. They're coming together. Approximatively forty-five seconds. East door.

Grigg's door. Avery froze. Nova was already there with him, and they pressed against the wall on opposite sides. Grigg grinned, white teeth shining in the darkness. The seconds dragged.

The door slid open, white light carving through the dark as two women walked across the threshold, murmuring to one another before they lurched into silence. The taller one let out a gasp. The door slid closed.

Grigg and Nova moved as one, maneuvering behind them and dealing an expertly executed hold to their necks. Their eyes rolled back, one after the other, slipping into unconsciousness. Grigg and Nova caught their targets and guided them gently to the ground.

It would have been better if they hadn't seen us. Qav barely glanced up from Linderly's work.

Always a critic. Grigg threw Avery a sardonic smile. Nova bore no such humor, returning to her post.

You won't be laughing when they recognize Avery from the news feeds.

Even Grigg went silent. Avery hadn't thought of that. Moons above, if they linked her to something like this, who knew the repercussions it would have on Echo's reputation? On the vote of confidence next week? On Klein's final grab for power?

As a matter of fact, the facility reminded her of the Port Station—of Klein. The tech was similar enough and—

Avery braced a hand on the table, fingers curling on the cold glass. *Who the blazar are we stealing from, Qav? This isn't just some rich citizen, is it?*

He brought a long finger to his lips, the edges curving upward. He was enjoying this, holding something just outside the bounds of her knowledge. Another game.

I'm in. Linderly suffused the connection with a deep pulse of satisfaction. Her eyes were bright behind her pink lenses, as alive as the smile on her face. *Now I just have to input this line of—got it. Pulling up the location now.*

Qav was more intent than ever, leaning close to her shoulder, watching the files zoom past as Linderly's bots swept the system for the matching tracer code. Something leaked through their link, teasing the edges of Avery's mind. It was almost like . . . curiosity. Anticipation.

Avery started. So Qav *didn't* know what they were taking. That didn't bode well.

The screen flashed, opening a window of code that was illegible to Avery.

It's a digital file, after all. I just have to hack into this drive, and we'll have what we came for. Linderly dug into her tablet, working through the system's defenses faster than they could follow. In what seemed like mere seconds, she let out a small cry of triumph. The file opened. *They're video files.* She selected one, casting the holovid to the center of the table.

It was a capture of this very room, only the lights were up, each corner in full view. And it wasn't empty. People filled the chairs surrounding the table, deep in discussion. But Avery zeroed in on one member in particular. She stood while the others sat, not a wrinkle in her perfect white suit nor a hair out of place on her blonde head.

Klein? This is her facility? Avery slammed her hand on the table, the glass shuddering beneath the force.

Qav had tricked them.

She never would have agreed to this if she had known, never would have brought the others. Klein was too unpredictable—too dangerous.

And if Avery were found tampering with the trial, it could hinder everything she had worked toward. Everything she had built. Everything Leviathan hadn't already stripped from her.

Rage surged through Avery's veins, igniting her blood with pure fire. She curled her lip at Qav, at his revolting self-satisfaction. He didn't look away. *You knew—you knew this whole time I would never have agreed to this.* The screen dimmed for a fraction of a second.

But that was all it took.

Qav glanced at Linderly, alarm sneaking its way through his filter. Something was wrong. Linderly was beginning to panic in earnest.

The system detected that surge—its bots are coming after my hack, patching me out.

Copy those files—we need every single one of them. Qav braced a hand on the table beside her, watching her operate, infusing control into every move Linderly made.

It's not working. There's extra encryption on the files. I need time to break it. But they all knew from her own mind that they didn't have time to spare. The bots would lock her out before she could ever get through.

There's no way she'll get in before it locks down. Once it's on alert, no one can break that system. Rem broke his silence on the merge. *You need to leave. Qav, get them out of there. You have seconds before those alarms sound.*

Qav ignored him, fixated on the screen as Linderly typed into the tablet, her fingers a padded staccato on its surface. Inspiration struck her, a pierce of light blinding the group, her mind too quick to follow, those fingers even faster.

"There!" Linderly shouted the word, her voice swallowed by shadows. She looked up at Avery, a little smile of disbelief in her eyes.

Even she was surprised she had done it.

Guys. Grigg's warning pulled their attention to the corner where the two engineers lay slumped against the wall. Their wristports were flashing, a bright red strobe in a synchronized rhythm. *That can't be good.*

Linderly returned to her screen, eyes turning panicked. *Shit.* Her single word carried a weight of anxiety as she tapped furiously into her tablet once more. The holoscreen froze, flashing a solid block of blue before disappearing entirely.

Linderly looked up to Qav, then Avery. A second passed in silence. None of them so much as breathed.

A moment of peace before everything exploded into sound.

CHAPTER THIRTY-FOUR

The alarms grated in a discordant cacophony of sound, piercing the inside of Avery's brain. The lights cut out, leaving them in total blackness. Linderly activated her tablet, the blue glow that illuminated her face offering the only light in the room.

Damn it, the feeds are down. Rem's mind was a blur of anxiety and images, moving too quickly to sift through. *Get out of there. Now.*

This way. Syla beckoned. They followed Linderly's light as they moved toward her door. Syla's soft curse was barely audible. *It won't open.*

Linderly was at the front again, typing furiously on her tablet. *I can't get into the system either. They've completely blocked us out of the grid.*

Avery slowed her breathing to keep from shaking. Grigg and Nova were heavy presences at her back. If they were caught, they'd fall right into Klein's hands—she wouldn't hesitate to use this against them. This entire facility could be Federation property.

Qav? What do you want to do? Syla was a shadow by the door.

Avery didn't so much as look his way. He was the one who had dragged them into this mess. And for what? Some vid footage for his "client"? There were bigger things at play in the universe than his petty grasping at money and power.

Avery stoked her fury, igniting the air around her until it was alive and crackling with energy. She wouldn't just let this happen.

"Move," she bit out, her voice steel.

As soon as it was clear, Avery braced herself, pulling back an arm, drawing in power as she inhaled deeply. Her exhale was quick as she drove her fist forward in a single strike. The door crumpled beneath the sheer force of the blow, like a sheet of glass melting in on itself.

She looked back at the team, now bathed in the light of the hallway.

Damn, Avery. Grigg's was the only reply.

Let's go.

They wasted no time, filing out ahead of her into the hall. Her eyes flickered to movement behind them, where one of the other doors opened across the control room. Avery stepped forward, raising a hand to fling energy toward the circular table. It slid across the room, legs screeching on the floor, landing solidly against the opening.

Avery, move! Qav's hand was a vise on her arm, swinging her around and against the wall behind Syla and Nova. A shot of blastfire landed where she had been standing, the surface dark and sizzling beside her.

Four guards had taken up positions at the far end of the corridor, blocking any exit. Syla and Nova defended them against a barrage of blastfire with nothing but their own shots. Linderly crouched behind Grigg on the other side, wincing with each fire. They were fully exposed.

Avery stepped into the center of the hall, jumping away from Qav's grasp as he reached for her. She threw up her arms, casting a field of energy that spanned the length of the hallway. Blastfire bounced harmlessly off it, the effects rippling through to her body as nothing more than a gentle tingle.

Avery tossed the word over her shoulder: "Now!"

Grigg and Nova pressed forward at a run, Avery following them with her shield. The guards ahead paused, one lowering their blaster entirely, eyes fearful. Avery didn't let it impact her as she lifted a hand to throw the two on the left against the wall. Grigg and Nova took care of the other two.

Damn, you really are worth it. A wry grin pulled at Syla's face as she jogged toward them, Qav and Linderly on her heels.

Keep moving. Qav didn't pause, running past them to the antechamber that they knew would be around the next corner. They all fell into step behind him, blocking out the screeching alarm that threatened to drown all thought. Qav didn't break pace as they tore around the final bend.

They met three guards, ready and waiting for them, who fired on sight.

Avery reacted on instinct, sending a surge out from her body. Energy radiated through the air, encompassing Qav and rendering the blastfire useless. But she didn't stop there. The wave continued on, hitting the guards a millisecond afterward, knocking all three into the wall behind them.

They struggled to their feet, but not quickly enough.

Qav leaped through the air on the energy of his own power, flying overhead in a twist of silver hair and black clothes. The guards tracked him with disbelieving eyes while Syla took advantage of the distraction, jumping atop one, locking her legs around his neck. She used the momentum to bring him crashing down into another, slamming them both against the floor and rolling to sweep the feet out from under the third.

They lay motionless, defeated.

Grigg and Nova shared a look of surprise. Grigg shrugged. *Not bad.*

Linderly hacked the lock without issue, and it opened with a hiss. They piled onto the elevator platform, lifting in seconds. Avery looked up, the night sky opening above them, the crisp air beckoning them to safety just within reach.

Which was why she didn't see—none of them saw—the guards enter the room below them.

Pain ripped through Avery's side, and she gasped, clutching at her abdomen. Another strike ripped through her arm, jerking her entire body, the air leaving her lungs. She had been shot.

Adrenaline spiked, and Avery clung to it, threading power through her hands in a strong surge that launched at the guards in the room. Through the sliver of visibility left as the elevator lifted away, Avery saw their bodies slam into the walls beneath the weight of her force.

Wind picked up around them, the night warm in comparison to the chilly interior of the building. Avery clutched her arm, blood pooling between her fingers in a flow of warm liquid.

Her stomach—what about her stomach?

She rubbed her hands over her midriff, a sharp stab shooting through her bicep in protest. There was nothing there. No wound at all. Only the shot to her arm.

Realization dawned as her eyes snapped to the others. Syla was bent over herself, her teeth bright in the night in an agonizing grimace. The pain had been hers.

You have to move. Qav held a hand to her elbow. The breeze whipped his hair around his face, obscuring his features. She tried to stand. Her miserable hissing rent the air, cutting straight through to Avery's core. Qav tensed.

They were still connected in the merge, and yet Avery had felt nothing that time. He had shielded them from Syla's pain. But she could barely move, her knees giving way as she fell to the ground.

Left! Nova's warning was almost too late.

Avery jerked around, sending out another barrier that blocked the blastfire aimed directly at them. She shuddered at the impact this time. Her strength was waning.

Where did they come from? Grigg was firing his own blasts out to the group beyond.

There had to be at least five new guards atop the building. The elevator was meant to be the only way in or out of the building—unless these had come from somewhere else.

As if in answer, a cruiser pulled down out of the sky, bright spotlights centered on them as it pressed down.

Shit. There was no way she could hold up a shield strong enough to deflect a blast from that thing.

Syla cried out behind her, and Avery whirled. Qav was lifting her into his arms, silver eyes cutting through the night. *We have to move.*

They saw Rem's mind as he and Ennis raced toward them in their ship. They could still get out of this.

No. Qav's single word brought the command of the So' along with it. They all froze beneath its weight. *Stay back, Ennis. If you come close, the building's defense system will blow our ship to space dust, and then we'll all be screwed.*

Every muscle in Avery's body tightened. They were trapped.

They'd have to make it the half mile back to the ship to be out of range of those guns. *Don't think, just move.* Just move. They had to move.

They surged backward as one unit, Qav barely slowed by the added weight in his arms. Avery kept up her shields around them as they turned, running full speed toward the edge of the roof.

"Jump!" Avery called out, her voice strained to the point of breaking.

And they did.

This time, they ran through the sands on swift feet, already advancing up the first dune that would lead them to coverage and safety. Avery used her power to bolster the shifting surface, giving them a solid base for their footing. They were out of the range of the blasters, which freed Avery to let down her barrier. But the ship pursued them, pressing down its bright spotlight, pinning them within a relentless circle of white.

The wind picked up around them, sand billowing beneath the air of the cruiser as it drew ever closer. Fear struck forcefully through Avery—Linderly's. They were no longer protected by Qav's filter on their emotions.

Her eyes jumped to him. Qav's head was down, his breathing labored as he shifted a now unconscious Syla in his arms. He was losing control of his barriers.

Avery didn't dare glance above her.

She could hear the engines as their heat warmed the air over their heads, pressing in. Her heart leaped into her throat, choking a cry. That ship was going to crush them beneath its weight. An efficient way to take them all out in one blow.

A shot of light seared through the darkness of the sky, slamming into the side of the ship with a loud crack. It reared sideways over their heads, pulling up and away from them just as they crested the dune.

Avery concentrated on their escape, willing her resolve to the others as they slid down the sand. She had no idea if they would feel her—she still had no claim on her telepathy—but it wouldn't hurt to try. They had to keep going.

Two ships rose into the sky above them, their fight mere flashes that lit the darkness above. One as black as the night itself.

Ennis. Rem.

They had come to their rescue after all. They disappeared, up and away into the clouds, even the sounds of their blastfire fading away in the distance.

They didn't slow until they had reached the bottom of the next dune. Qav fell to his knees, bringing Syla down with more gentleness than Avery would have thought him capable. His hands were shaking as he drew them away. They were covered in blood, visible by the light of the full moon that had crested from behind the clouds. It was so much clearer here than in the cities; even the stars were nearly visible in the sky. Syla's hair shone like neon against the pale sands, her pink eyelashes vibrant against her dark cheeks. She didn't stir.

Linderly dropped to the ground, panting in short gasps. Nova rested beside her, reaching a hand to her shoulder. Grigg stood watching the sky.

Pain flashed through their bond. Anguish. Fear.

Avery looked at Qav in alarm. He was somewhere far away. Images surged through the connection, pure ice freezing a trail through her body.

Ground level of the city. Rain—it was raining. A torrential downpour, so loud it cut out all other sound. The lights of the buildings shimmered against the water gathered on the street. A girl. She lay in one of the puddles, facedown, head twisted. Her body still. Lifeless. Those bright amethyst eyes were wide and open—open—*always open. She saw everything. She always had.*

Grief stabbed, cutting Avery clean through. She gasped aloud, clutching at her chest.

Qav's eyes jerked up to her, awareness reaching their silver depths as Avery stumbled backward. He locked his memories away from her, sealing her off. He hadn't meant to leave himself open.

Qav pulled back Syla's dark coat to reveal her white shirt soaked entirely through with blood, staining most of it red. He ripped it away, the sound of tearing cloth loud in the night around them. A wide gash had shredded a hole in her side, and Qav pressed his hands to it, desperate to stop the flow of blood that poured outward.

"Syla?" Qav said, watching her face. His voice was that same soothing calm. He regained some of his control. "Syla, you need to stay awake." He laced the command with his power, willing her back into consciousness.

Syla jerked awake, gasping as her dark eyes opened, frantic and wild. She grasped Qav's hands. He drew her eyes to his, something passing between them as her breathing came out in pained spurts. Qav tensed, his entire body going rigid as Syla relaxed, letting out a long sigh of relief. She let her head fall back against the sands and stared up at the sky.

Avery knew then.

Qav had taken her pain.

And Syla was going to die.

CHAPTER
THIRTY-FIVE

Blood seeped between Qav's fingers, making them slick and warm where he pressed into Syla's wound. He pushed harder, pain surging through his body with the effort, his abdomen clenching in excruciating spasms.

There was too much blood.

Even if Ennis got here in time, Qav doubted even the med bot aboard his ship could repair the damage.

It was happening again—he was going to lose her. Syla was going to die here in this blazing desert in the middle of nowhere.

He had made a wrong choice in coming here. Qav rarely doubted himself, but he did so now. He had let his ego run away with him, and he hadn't listened to Ennis's warnings this time.

But she was right. Things were changing in the world that irrevocably pushed them into a new reality. Qav felt more pressure than ever to maintain his hold on what he had built and to fortify their place there. And he needed the clout this job would bring.

But was it worth Syla's life?

It did belong to him, after all. She was his to control—to command. She would willingly give it to him, if he only asked.

And he had asked someone before.

Something stirred, awakening deep within the cavity of his chest where he so rarely shed any light. That decision still haunted him. That price.

No—he wouldn't pay it again. He couldn't.

Avery drew closer and kneeled by his side, her features drawn. Her eyes were golden and bright in the night. Pure, unfiltered power. Without even looking into her mind, he knew.

She would never ask for that sacrifice of those who followed her. Of anyone.

Images flashed through his mind—her memory. Qav watched it play out in her head, standing by as she transported them back to the Port Station some months ago. Finn lay on the ground, bleeding out before her, her hands pressed against his side in the same fashion as Qav's in this moment.

But no, it wasn't the same. Not the same at all.

Something changed in her, within that memory, sprouting out from the very depths of her being. Light filled her, pouring from her hands and into Finn. A searing blend of pain and primal power pierced her, but she pushed through it, welcomed it, answered its call. And bit by bit, she wove his flesh back together, willing life back into him until she had nothing more to give. She had paid the price herself.

Qav blinked. Avery had healed him. A human. She had used her power to bring him back from the brink of death—perhaps even death itself.

Qav ripped out of the memory, nearly coming to his feet as he reared forward, dragging Avery to him. He pressed her hand against Syla's wound, fingers entwined, slipping against the warm blood.

You can heal her.

Her eyes widened at his thoughts. Terror surged through her. It was nothing compared to the physical pain he bore for Syla.

You did it for Lunitia—you can do it for her.

Avery blanched in the moonlight, pulling at her arm. He tightened his grip. Nova rose to her feet, but Qav reached the bright tether of her mind and held fast. She froze. He followed suit with Grigg. Linderly would give him no trouble—she watched them from her knees where she had collapsed in the sands.

Avery would heal Syla. There would be no interference. His word was absolute.

Do it! He reached out for Avery's mind, ready to force her if he had to. His power met that electricity within her, bright and fierce and liquid gold. He tried to tame it, bend her to his will, but it would not catch.

He could not control her, no matter his strength. No matter his discipline.

She reared back, and he let her go. She stood, looking down on him, the moon casting a silver halo around her head, her face in shadow.

Syla stirred in his arms. Even with his power numbing her, the pain was finally reaching her. Her light was fading; her essence dissolved from his grasp like dry sand sifting through clawed fingers.

Not again—he couldn't bear it.

That hidden restless thing surged up and out of his chest like a violent vise boring down on his heart. He grimaced, nearly crying aloud.

Whatever Avery saw on his face moved her. Even through the haze of pain, Qav could feel that. She saw her own agony—her own grief—painted across his face. She would help him; she yearned to. But she was scared, full of fear for what it would mean.

But fear he could handle.

Qav yielded to his power, embracing the ice that fueled him, letting it flow through his body as he surged outward, straight into Avery's mind.

He took that fear from her. And her pain and her grief—all of it. His power was a black hole absorbing everything in its pull, and he staggered beneath her emotion. The weight was enormous, dragging against his chest, writhing in protest. It was a part of her, molded her, and it wouldn't go quietly.

He pressed harder, bearing down until it had no choice but to surrender. When it finally fell away from her, dropping effortlessly into the chasm within him, he locked it away in the dark where it couldn't touch her. He wouldn't let it.

And in its place, he suffused Avery with his energy, gave her his strength, filled her with his power. He soothed those raw parts of her with the cold touch of calm that governed his every decision.

She straightened, eyes wide and pinned on him.

"Now do it," Qav grit out, the weight of her emotions and the pain of Syla's death wound dragging him into the dark with each haggard exhale. "Do it! Save her, damn it!" he yelled. He had no more power left to command her. His next words were a near plea: "You saved him. You can save her."

"Qav." His name was broken on her lips, pity in those sunset eyes.

"No," he denied that look, shaking his head. "You can do it."

"Even if—I don't know how."

Syla started to convulse, her body fighting with every last bit of energy to hold on to her life force. He was losing her. Qav snaked his power around her light, gripping it with everything he had left. If only he had Avery's power. If only he had those gifts. He would never have to suffer again. He couldn't go through this again.

Qav lowered his head.

"Please," he said simply. "Just try."

For a moment, he thought she hadn't heard him. Thought she had given up entirely. The only sound was the wind whipping across the desert, tearing at the ends of their clothes. It had been a miscalculation to come here.

He felt her power a moment before one of the others gasped. Qav jerked his head up, awe washing over him in a rush of candescent light, like the sun surfacing along the rim of a planet.

Avery kneeled beside Syla, her attention fixed and severe.

And she was glowing.

So subtly that if they had not been in the dark of night in the desert, he might not have noticed. Every inch of Avery's exposed skin gave off that faint light, as though her power was rising to its surface.

She pulled Qav's hand away from the wound, replacing it with hers. Her breathing was steady, deep. And when she closed her eyes, the light began to shift, moving down to her hands, pouring out from her in waves of brilliance, directly into Syla.

Qav had no strength left to enter her mind, to see how she did it. It was all he could do to keep Avery's feelings at bay, and he had long since lost his grip on the others.

He could only watch in wonder, as helpless as the rest of them.

And then Syla's light began to change. Qav could feel that at least. Her life force infused with Avery's, mingling with the very atoms that made up her being. Qav could no longer tell if he held Syla or Avery in his power; he couldn't keep their lights separate.

But as soon as it began, Avery's essence melted away until it was Syla—only Syla—left in his grasp.

Avery fell backward, sharply gasping, then lying prone in the sand. She stared up at the sky, her chest heaving. Nova was at her side in an instant, pulling her head into her lap.

Qav looked down at Syla's wound. Where once had been mottled flesh, there was now only smooth skin, darkened further by the still wet blood across her midriff.

Moons above. Avery had done it.

Relief surged through him on swift and terrible wings. What he would pay for that power. What he would do for it.

A boom sounded through the air, and they all looked up as the two ships came barreling to the surface. The sky was just beginning to lighten, harkening the arrival of dawn, and Qav's black cruiser stood out in relief against the pale beige sky. It maneuvered a tight spiral, piercing across the horizon, pursued by the larger Federation vessel. They hadn't been able to outrun them.

"Shit." Grigg's curse was biting and aimed behind them.

Qav looked over his shoulder. *Shit, indeed.*

The remaining guards had mounted their own sand bikes, speeding across the desert at them. Klein must have kept her guards well paid. Qav twisted his mouth. Under normal circumstances, he might admire the management skills. The bikes crested the first dune, careening down into the valley, where they disappeared from sight.

"They'll be on us in minutes," Nova said sharply. She pulled Avery to her feet, motioning to Linderly to do the same.

Syla was still unconscious. Qav shook her shoulder roughly.

"Syla." The word was a command. He had no power left in his reserves to force her awake. "Syla!" Not so much as an eye twitch. He slapped her face, the crack swallowed quickly by the soft sands around them.

"I'll take her," Avery said, her voice unyielding. She pushed his hands away and scooped Syla up into her own arms. She was nearly drained, her eyes sunken and tired. How she retained any power after what they had gone through, after what she had done, was beyond him.

She was much shorter than Syla, which made for an awkward image that would be burned into his brain for all eternity. He resisted a grin. Syla would hate it. He'd have to share the memory later.

"Let's move." Avery didn't look back at him as she took off through the dunes.

CHAPTER THIRTY-SIX

Avery was in agony. Every muscle in her body screamed for her to stop. But she pushed forward through the pain, dragging each foot through the sand in an endless repetition as she approached the horizon. They weren't out of danger yet.

Qav still kept a firm rein on her terror, holding that shadowed weight at bay. For that, at least, she was grateful. She was a cloud, floating through the air on the weightless euphoria that defied the exhaustion in her limbs.

The others followed, keeping pace with the slow jog Avery fought to maintain. She didn't have anything left to harden the sands beneath them, and their feet sank deeply, her calves groaning in protest with each stride. But it wouldn't be enough.

"They're gaining." Nova's warning was punctuated with a few rounds from her blaster. It did nothing to slow their pursuers.

They weren't going to make it. After all this, Klein was going to win. She would use this to her advantage for certain, sullying Avery's name and voiding her testimony. Another stupid mistake, and Avery was entirely to blame. She had dragged more people into this, risking the fate of something far larger than herself.

"Look out!" Grigg grabbed Linderly's waist, pulling her out of the way with a hooked arm. A blast mark scorched a hole in the ground where she had just stood.

Damn it—they were within range.

Avery glanced back, the specks of the sand bikes growing into large shadows in the dawning light. They would never be able to out-run them.

Avery slowed, panting heavily as her mind ran through options. But there was only one.

She couldn't outrun them, but she *could* give the others a chance.

Avery stopped, turning to Grigg, who pulled up beside her, passing Syla into his arms. Sweat poured down his temples, his forehead glistening. But he took Syla without question, maneuvering her body onto his back. Nova frowned.

"Keep running," Avery said, wiping sweat from her forehead. She gestured to the horizon. "And don't stop. I can give you time."

"Hell no," Nova protested. "We're not leaving you here."

"We don't have time to debate this, Nova. I'm giving you an order. Your duty is to follow it."

Nova held her gaze for a moment, refusing to back down. There was something in her eyes. Something unsaid. They shifted to Qav, then back again.

"Down!" Grigg shouted, seconds before blastfire rained over them, peppering the ground with scorch marks. Nova pulled Linderly beneath her, dragging the girl to her feet as she tried to judge the distance and weigh her options.

But Avery knew what she would see. Right now, in this moment, there was only one choice.

"Go!" Avery used a small surge of power to push them away. They stumbled back, and Nova resisted a moment longer before turning. She took off into the sands, pulling Linderly along with her, Grigg close by her side with Syla still in his arms.

Qav lingered, his sharp chin tilted in hesitation.

"You, too," Avery demanded. "You're no use to me fully drained. But you can get them on that ship. You can get them out of here."

Avery turned away from him, dismissing him as she faced the approaching guards. She wiped away the sweat that gathered above her lips, fighting to slow her pulse. She needed them closer.

She planted her feet, bracing her body as well as she could atop the shifting sands. Her hands lowered in front of her, palms up to the sky. Overhead, the two ships wove in and out of the clouds, a dancing pursuit of metal and speed. She could barely feel the arm that had been shot—whether from blood loss or adrenaline was anyone's guess. Not that it mattered anymore.

The bikes were closer now, nearly upon her. She could do this.

Avery closed her eyes, reaching deep within herself to that well of humming light that lived beneath her heart. If she had been able to call upon it to heal Syla, then she could damn well do it again.

It started small, a barely there ember within her chest, the glowing remnants of what was left after she had used her power to exhaustion. She followed the humming warmth, leaning into its path, showing her a way in. In a flash, that small spark ignited, a trail of fuel catching fire and burning its way through her veins, across her skin, white-hot and electric and alive.

A chill ran through her, its frozen grip mingling with the cells in her body, doubling her power. Her eyes flew open.

Qav stood next to her, his head lowered, eyes closed. He had left the others to continue on alone. He had left them.

Don't look back. She couldn't look back. They were strong. Even without Qav, they could still make it. She had to trust that they would be able to.

Another boom cracked through the air.

The Federation vessel sputtered, smoke billowing up around its guns in a dark trail through the sky. It slowed, long enough that Ennis was able to get ahead of its pursuit. Qav's black ship pulled around in a wide loop, heading on a course aimed straight for them, decelerating and drawing closer to the ground, the access door opening. Ennis intended for them to jump aboard in midflight.

But the Federation vessel righted itself, pulling around behind them. There wouldn't be enough time. Not for her and Qav to get aboard with the others. It would be them or their friends.

"Tell Ennis to pick up the others." Avery looked to Qav, his eyes opening at last to reveal dark storm clouds, their glow dimmed. "I can handle the rest."

His power was spent, but there was enough to reach Ennis. And they didn't have time to debate it. Avery would have to trust him to relay the message.

She looked back to their attackers, to the black ship heading straight for them. It would be fast. She would have to time it perfectly.

She exhaled slowly through her teeth, gathering electricity into her fingers. It built atop itself, pressure bearing down on her until her hands were shaking, gripping desperately to a lid trapping immense force. A bead of sweat dripped down the center of her back, tickling her spine. She clawed her hands, holding that energy, keeping it at bay just behind her barrier.

Ennis zoomed over them, a slash of black that carried a hot draft in its wake. Sand billowed up around them, thickening the air and blocking out their line of sight. Even the Fed ship disappeared into its veil.

Now. It was now or never. Her eyes flew open.

And Avery let go.

Relief was immediate as her power unleashed itself, snapping away like an unstoppable force. It spread out in a circle around her, a deep wave digging into loose sand, spanning outward, a ripple carving through the earth itself. It moved like lightning, clearing the view around them in all directions, and Avery went with it, following her power in its desperate rush across the dunes.

It reached their pursuers. One after the other, sand bikes flew into the air, arching away on the wall of pure energy. Bodies fell, dropping toward the ground, like harmless chunks of meteorite falling to the surface.

The air cleared, and Avery tensed at what the open horizon exposed.

The Federation vessel was heading directly for them, low enough to the ground that it would ram straight through them. Avery shook on unsteady legs.

But the ripple of her power was still moving, stretching outward across the sands. The ship slammed against the wall of energy, its nose flipping backward, spiraling away and out of control into the ground. It tumbled over itself, a harsh cacophony of screeching metal and billowing sand. Finally, it met silence on the ends of a muted explosion, careening into the immovable expanse of a tall dune.

Avery watched for a moment, the release of the power still coursing through her veins, intoxicating and pure. But the others—she whirled, tracking the black ship.

"They made it," Qav breathed.

No sooner had he said the words than the ship shuddered, wobbling in the air as it tried to right itself.

Avery drew in a gasp. Her power was still moving—had hit them, too.

She took a few steps forward, reaching for them, trying desperately to latch on to the energy, to control it. The ship couldn't right itself. It flipped, spiraling off and up into the sky, disappearing into the bright clouds.

Her stomach dropped, panic flooding her. "Can you reach them?" she asked Qav, her voice cracking and dry.

He didn't look at her, and when he replied, his voice was ragged. "They're too far away, even if I had any power left to use."

Avery fell to her knees.

Her limbs dragged, sluggish and heavier that she could support, fingers digging into the sand. Darkness crept up the edges of her vision, turning the sky spotty and black. She fell to her side, sand filling her mouth.

But there was no pain in the darkness that overtook her. She let her eyes close. There was no suffering, no mistakes.

So she gave into it, slipping into the blissful nothingness, where even her nightmares couldn't bear to dwell.

CHAPTER
THIRTY-SEVEN

The sun woke her, its rays grating against her eyelids. Avery tossed her head. But there was no relief from it, and her forehead quickly began to burn. She pulled her arm across her face, seeking shade.

Pain pierced her shoulder, and she hissed, rolling to her side. "You're awake."

Qav stood a few feet away, looking at the horizon. He had pulled the fabric of his scarf around his head again, providing some shelter from the sun.

"How long have I been out?" Her voice was raspy, her tongue a rough sponge that fought against her words. She swallowed, choking on the dryness.

"My best guess is a few hours. We were both unconscious—too much energy expended." He sighed, turning to her. "I explored a little of the area, looking for that wrecked ship or castoffs from the guards, *something* we can use for comms. Not much luck. Either it was cleaned up, or the sands have already covered everything."

Sand. She was coated in it.

Avery sat up, brushing the loose grains off her clothes, her face, her hair. Even her scalp was thick with a heavy layer caked beneath her braid. She came to her feet, every muscle antagonistic and stiff, as though the sands had even seeped beneath her skin and settled into her bones.

"You still can't sense them?" Avery was almost too scared to ask the question. His dark ship had gone careening into the atmosphere at the ends of her power.

Her throat seized. If they had been hurt—if they were dead because of her—

Qav stalked toward her, interrupting her thoughts. "It'll take some time to regain our power. For both of us. Until then, we're operating blind."

"What about your wristport?" Avery asked sharply.

"What about yours?" he countered, his half smirk indicating he already knew she didn't use one. "I don't need one most of the time since my mind allows me to communicate with whomever I need. And Rem takes care of the rest."

Her mouth twisted. A fine pair they made. Powerful beyond measure but essentially worthless without those they could control.

She scanned the skyline, covering her eyes from the glaring sun. The desert was positively liquid as heat rose up from its surface, rippling sands dancing against a wide expanse of beige sky.

"What about returning to the facility?" Avery suggested.

"They'll be waiting for us," Qav said darkly. "And like I said, we are no better than your average human right now. We wouldn't stand a chance at getting anywhere, even with your combat training. It won't be enough."

"But we could at least try—"

"If we go back there, we'll end up dead. Or worse—in Klein's grip. And I know you'd rather die than play into her hands. I've seen the things you want, Avery. Seen the future you envision. And I'm the one who brought you here—I'm the one who put that precious future in jeopardy." He lowered his chin, his voice gravelly and dry. "It's why you're glaring at me right now, as though you would kill me if given the chance."

Avery looked to the ground, focusing on the white-hot sands. She didn't have the energy to fight despite the anger that churned behind her ribs, tight and aching. It would do her no good now.

"Besides, leaving us out here is as good a method as any to dispose of us. Less messy, at any rate."

Avery shuddered. She heard what he didn't say; the facility didn't need to bother chasing them down. They had no comms, no water, no food.

The desert itself would be enough to finish them off.

Qav removed his shemagh, shaking out the sand that had gathered in its crevices. His loose hair whipped up around him. The ends were stained a red so dark they were almost black. Syla's blood.

Avery's throat tightened as she looked at his hands.

They were tinted that same rust color, his fingernails dark crescents where it caked underneath. Avery knew hers would look similar.

She would never be able to forget the look on his face as Syla lay dying in his arms. The grief etched there.

It had been so familiar to her, the personification of what she felt inside, her nightmare given life. And nothing in all the galaxies could have prevented her from trying to heal Syla.

It was in that moment that she knew—Qav cared.

He may not admit it to himself, but that agony that had surfaced from the depths of his soul was proof enough. Avery had felt his truth, while his power had entwined with hers, when she caught a glimpse of his memory, his past.

The girl in the rain.

He carried a weight that was not dissimilar from hers.

The sound of fabric ripping brought her back to him. He shredded his shemagh into two long strips, then held one out to her.

"I'm willing to guess you haven't had any solar pills lately—you'll burn easily out here. Those freckles have already multiplied by the thousands."

She snatched the cloth from his hands, hating the way his words made her feel less than. She took her time wrapping it around her head, the process made slow with the use of only one arm.

He didn't offer to help. She wouldn't have accepted it if he did.

"So if we're not going back, then what's your brilliant plan?" Avery asked acerbically.

He gestured to the expanse of sand stretching out endlessly in front of them. "The mountains to the north. We'll find coverage, recuperate, and wait for the others."

Avery peered out to the horizon. A blue-gray line of craggy peaks beckoned, hazy and wobbling in the rising heat, like a holovid with a bad connection.

It was miles. Miles upon miles. She tried to swallow, her throat sticky and dry.

Qav was already walking, and she hurried to catch up to him. But his pace was slow, his dark boots dragging with each step. He was more drained than he let on.

What energy Avery had used in those moments to stop their attackers had not been entirely her own. Qav must have expended a great deal of himself to keep their connection alive as well as bolster her power. It was because of him that she had even been able to call upon that primal energy to begin with. His cool presence was a balm, soothing the scars of her mind that she once thought were burned beyond salvation.

She imagined it was why so many followed him—seeking the relief he could offer.

So she trudged along after him, praying his power would regenerate before they hiked all the way to the mountains ahead. She tried to lick her lips, her fuzzy tongue running over rough cracks, amplifying her thirst. Sand crunched between her teeth. Her arm throbbed with every movement.

And she didn't voice the thought that ricocheted through her head: was grateful Qav couldn't read her in that moment.

There was no way either of them would last long enough to make it out of there alive.

The minutes dragged on into hours, and Avery did her best not to keep track of the sun overhead. It had well beyond reached its highest peak by the time she noticed a change in the air. She could barely keep her head up, focusing instead on her feet, desperate to just keep moving. Qav had fallen behind her ages ago, but she refused to slacken her pace. The sooner they reached shelter from the heat, the better.

The breeze picked up, teasing the sweaty skin of her neck each time it lifted the cloth covering her face. Avery had removed her black jacket, realizing just how quickly it absorbed every ounce of heat the sun poured over them. Qav warned her she'd regret the short sleeves of her shirt, but she couldn't bring herself to care, even as her sticky arms became bathed in grains of sand.

But something in the air changed as they walked. Imperceptible at first, the wind built on itself, minute enough that she could have been imagining it. After a few minutes, it had strengthened until it picked up sand, twisting and whipping around them, lashing out in a frenzied grasp.

Avery ignored it. She looked ahead, focusing only on the view of the mountains before her—still out of reach. Ever on their blazing horizon.

Maybe Qav had sent them on a fool's errand, trying to distract her from the inevitable. Maybe the others were dead after all. Maybe no one was coming for them.

"Avery!"

She barely heard Qav, his sharp warning muffled by the din of blood rushing through her head. But she couldn't stop. If she did, she'd never find the strength to start back up again.

Still, there was urgency in his voice. Avery had enough presence of mind left to register that something was wrong. She slowed, hazarding a glance over her shoulder.

Her heart stopped fully in her chest.

Qav was sprinting straight for her.

And behind him, a wall rose up into the sky, spreading the length of the horizon.

No, not a wall—a cloud. A billowing dark wave of living sand rolling over itself in a careening tumble, picking up speed as it consumed everything in its path. She could hear it now, the hissing approach of spitting debris moving fast on the wind. And it was heading directly for them.

Avery choked on a gasp. Should they run? They'd never be able to outpace it, even if she had energy left to aid their speed. Their best chance would be to weather it, although she had no idea what that would look like.

Qav was still racing to her, the cloud close on his heels and gaining. If he was enveloped before he reached her, they'd never find one another.

She took off toward him, every instinct protesting as she raced for the approaching sandstorm. The wind whipped up around her as she neared it, the swirling sand sending a thousand stings across the bare skin of her arms. She pulled her shemagh closer, squinting against the grains that pelted her eyes.

Qav didn't slow his pace as he reached her. He slammed into her body, arms going around her, bringing them both to the ground in a heap.

He glanced behind them, judging the storm. His hands were on her waist, fumbling fingers working at the jacket she had tied there.

The storm descended over them, swallowing them whole in a rush of hissing winds.

The sky disappeared until there was only impermeable beige in every direction. But she could still see Qav in front of her, his eyes half-closed against the biting dust. He freed her jacket, pulling it over their heads, a sad defense against the howling desert. Darkness moved in quickly, the light dissolving into near blackness as the storm raged around them.

Avery squeezed her eyes shut, the dryness behind her lids stinging nearly as badly as her exposed arms. She couldn't bear to breathe, worried the sand would filter into her lungs and suffocate her from the inside. The sound was overwhelming, gusts of air blasting around them in a fury, tearing at their clothes even as they huddled together for protection.

They couldn't keep going, not in this darkness. They would be lost, walking aimlessly. She peeked over her arm, wondering at the distance between them and the mountains that she knew were somewhere out there in the black.

The air around them shifted, fading in the next few seconds to an eerie red, like being inside the belly of the sun itself. Still, she could not see beyond a few feet of the blood-tinged wall of dust. Going forward would be impossible.

She sank back on her knees, meeting Qav's gaze, cool and direct. His brows were drawn low over his eyes, his expression bare. He knew it, too: they couldn't go on. For the first time, she saw an uneasiness in him, an uncertainty. Her stomach dropped.

Perhaps they would die out there after all.

Tears sprang to her eyes, piercing against the dryness, unable to fall. She had been a fool to leave Finn behind. Now she would never see him again.

A light penetrated the sands, the beam of white shining starkly against the vibrant red that encompassed them. Avery straightened in alarm, all of her muscles stiffening in response to threat. Qav merely craned his neck, unwilling or unable to care.

And then the ship appeared, materializing through the sands as though via some portal in the storm. Avery squinted as she traced its lines, devouring the familiarity. It descended on them, the ramp already open and ready.

She choked on a dry sob.

It was Finn.

CHAPTER
THIRTY-EIGHT

Finn knelt at the ramp's end where he gripped the edge for support, dark goggles covering his eyes, his hair whipping about in a riot of sand and wind. Avery's heart somersaulted as she stood, reaching for him.

And then his hand clasped around her arm, strong and warm and pulling her up beside him. She glimpsed Tai beside him, garbed in similar gear, reaching for Qav.

Finn pushed her upward into the belly of the ship, and all she could do was stumble to the grates at her feet. She retched, gagging on the sudden coolness of the ship, ripping off her head covering as she spat up bile and sand. Markes was there, shoving a glass of water into her hands that she devoured quickly enough to make her sick.

She glanced behind her. Finn helped Tai pull Qav in behind her. As soon as they cleared the door, Finn ripped off his goggles and slammed a hand on the control panel. The ramp shuttered behind them, leaving all traces of the storm and the sand and the heat behind.

And then he was there, kneeling on the ground with her, his arms folding around her in an embrace. Finn cradled her head, and she tucked her face into his neck, leaning her weight fully into him. For once, he felt cool to her touch.

"I'm here, sweetheart. You're safe."

His fingers curled into her hair, his hand pressing into the small of her back. Shock ran a strangling course through her body, dry panicked sobs bubbling up from somewhere deep within her. Still, she clung to his arms.

Finn's words were a soft refrain in her ear as he repeated in a raspy whisper, "I'm here." And he held her, letting the waves flow over her, keeping her steady.

Qav struggled to sit up, brushing away Tai and Markes, who tried to help him. He had taken off his shemagh, wiping the grit that covered his face with equally dirty hands. A band of grime ran across his face, the opening where his eyes had been exposed, making him look like some bandit. Avery supposed she had a similar mask on her own. But he did take the water, downing it as voraciously as she had.

She pulled back, looking up at Finn.

His eyes raked her face, running over every inch of it before he claimed her lips in a fierce kiss. His skin was smooth and clean against the dirt that caked hers.

He pulled away, brushing a thumb against the crest of her cheek. His mouth tilted up on the edge, that look telling her what was coming next. "I told you so," he joked softly.

Avery let out a strangled laugh. "If I had any strength left right now, I'd throw you across the room."

"I guess I'm lucky you nearly killed yourself in the middle of a desert sandstorm, then." He smiled, resting his forehead against hers. For a moment, they stayed like that, breathing in each other's air.

"And the others?" Qav's question was stilted, from pain or frustration, she couldn't tell. He leaned heavily on Tai as he struggled to his feet, looking every bit as beaten as she felt.

Finn pulled away from Avery in a rush of movement, rising to his feet, whirling on Qav. "You don't get to ask questions," Finn bit out, standing between them.

"Are they alive?" Qav's voice had frozen over once more, each word cold. Aloof. As though he couldn't have cared either way about the answer.

And yet, Avery knew that he ached inside, a piece of his soul hanging in the balance of Finn's response. Despite what he had told her in the desert, he was unsure. It bothered her.

Avery's limbs protested as she pulled herself to her feet. Finn noticed, at her side in an instant, and placed a large hand on her arm to support her weight.

"Are they?" She echoed the question, afraid. In that moment, she wouldn't have been able to say whether the fear was hers or Qav's.

"They're fine," he said gently, reading the worry on her face. Her eyes flickered to Qav and back. "Stranded somewhere near the mountains while they wait for a repair bot from Beijing. Something blew their ship right out of the sky—know anything about that?" He raised a brow, his mouth twitching.

"I didn't mean to. It just sort of . . . happened," she said weakly. She could feel Qav watching her. She resisted a shiver.

"God, Avery, you look horrible." Megan trailed down the stairs from the upper level, drawing everyone's attention. Avery tucked a matted strand of hair behind her ear, suddenly self-conscious. She pulled away from Finn.

"It's not that bad," Finn assured her.

"Have you looked at her?" Megan's eyes sliced to Qav, hardening as she took in his state. She sneered, "You're even worse than she is."

Qav didn't reply, but a coolness seeped out from him, a hint of his power that was barely present. His gifts were returning. Perhaps hers would soon follow.

Shit, Avery did look horrible. Finn could have pummeled Qav for that alone.

His gut wrenched at Megan's words as she bounced down the stairs to them. It was all he could do to blurt out that it wasn't that bad. But he had lied.

Avery's bare arms were red and blotchy, covered in scratches and mottled with dirt. Sand coated the rest of her, turning her golden-streaked hair into a dull matte, gathering in the folds of her clothes. Her face was burned, her nose positively red, her lips cracked.

He never should have let her leave without him. Nova had caught him up as best as she could during their flight across the ocean. And they hadn't even been able to get ahold of Nova and the others until they were a few hundred miles out. Whatever that facility was, it had some serious tech-blocking comms.

Thank the galaxy he hadn't waited back in Sanctum. Not that Avery knew that little detail—yet. When the sandstorm showed up on their radar, he had nearly lost his mind. And despite Megan's current nonchalant attitude, she had been inconsolable only minutes earlier.

They had been searching the desert for hours. Thanks to those blazing tech blockers, their scanners were limited at best. And once the storm started up, they had to scour the surface, combing over every foot, relying on the sensors alone to show them heat signatures.

He'd never forget the hope that surged through him when those two blips appeared on Petra's screen. Nor the way his limbs went weak as he saw Avery huddled there in the sand, those golden eyes peering up, her hand reaching for him.

It had been a long time since he had seen her so vulnerable—he had forgotten the way it affected him. Even now, with her in his arms, it was difficult to breathe.

And Qav had done this to her.

He had stripped her of what power she still had, dangling the promise of fixing her over their heads. But he was using them—using Avery. And Finn refused to stand by and watch it happen. They should leave as soon as possible; she had to see that now. They had already lost so much time, but they still had hope. They could return to Echo and fight Leviathan there. He wouldn't abandon the humans in his care. They still needed them. Avery would regain her power in time.

They had gotten out of worse scrapes before; they could figure it out once they were back on Echo soil.

"Let's get you cleaned up."

Megan's voice pulled Finn back to the loading bay, his eyes drifting to hers. He knew without speaking that she was thinking the same thing he was. Enough was enough—Avery was out of her depth.

"What about Qav?" Tai's question was nearly a squeak, as though he had dreaded asking it. And rightfully so—the bastard could rot for all Finn cared.

He opened his mouth to say so, but Avery spoke before he could. "Show him to one of the cabins."

"No need," Qav countered. His back straightened, as though his strength was returning. "We should head for the others. I'll clean up on my own ship."

Finn frowned. "We need to get the blazar off this continent as soon as possible. They can come back behind us."

"My ship can cover the ocean twice as fast as yours. We don't have time to take both."

"And whose fault is that time lost?" Finn snapped. His patience was hanging by a thread. "If we had listened to you and stayed in Sanctum, like the useless pet humans you see us as, you'd be dying in that sandstorm back there. Be grateful we followed you out here instead of sitting on our asses."

"You did what?"

Avery's sharp question rang in his ears.

Finn's stomach dropped, running over the words that just came out of his mouth.

Shit.

He whirled. "Avery, it's not a big deal—"

"Not a big deal?" she scoffed, a frown pulling her freckles together. "You didn't trust me, Finn. You lied to me—you stood on that roof and lied to my face. And what's worse, you dragged the rest of them into this, too."

Tai and Markes shrunk away from her outstretched hand, as though they hoped to blend into the shadows.

"I didn't lie to you, I just—"

"I think it's pretty blazing obvious what you did," she snapped darkly. "You as good as said it to Qav just now. You never had any intention of staying behind, did you? You just charged straight ahead, not thinking anything through. Just like always."

Finn tensed. "What's that supposed to mean?"

"So what you said to me that night—was that a lie, too?" Her eyes were glassy, her body shaking. She swayed on her feet, and he reached a hand out to steady her. She flinched away.

"Never," Finn whispered. His eyes darted to their audience. "But if I hadn't—"

"And now you're defending yourself?" Avery laughed softly.

He lowered his chin and stepped closer to her. "If I hadn't followed you, you'd be dying out there right now."

"I had it—*we* had it under control."

She looked to Qav, and something ripped inside Finn. Whatever followed was dark and ugly, twisting its way up through his belly, clawing at the edges of his chest, constricting painfully around his heart. He nearly snarled.

Megan moved between them and placed a hand on Finn's chest. "Okay, I think we should all just take a step back. Finn isn't the only one to blame here."

Avery's eyes snapped to Megan, to her hand on Finn. "So you're saying none of you trusted me to handle this? What about Petra?"

Megan's silence was answer enough. Avery's jaw locked. She looked away, ignoring the way her eyes began to sting.

Softly, Megan said, "Avery, you're exhausted. And hurt and disgustingly dirty. We can talk this over once we get you cleaned up. And if Qav wants to wait for his fancy ship, then we'll just drop him off and be on our way."

Avery let out a short laugh. Finn knew what was coming even before the words left her mouth. "I'm not going anywhere." She nodded to Qav. "I want to know what's on those vids and who you're selling them to. If Klein's involved, then things just got personal."

"Klein?" Finn twisted to face Qav, seeking confirmation. "You put Avery back in that maniac's line of fire?"

Qav raised a brow—he actually raised a brow—his face hardening into the picture of haughty apathy. That bastard had it coming, he really did.

Finn strode across the deck and slammed his fist into Qav's face.

The pain that radiated up his knuckles into his hand was mollified by the vision of that arctic-haired asshole flying feet up onto his back. He rolled to his side, smearing fresh blood across his nose until it blended with the dirt coating his face.

"Finn."

Avery's voice behind him was a tense warning as she latched fingers around his arm.

She was livid, angrier than he had ever seen her before. If she had her powers right now, she would have thrown him across the ship. Finn would have to apologize again, even if he didn't mean it. She needed to hear the words form him. But not here—not in front of that smug asshole who had dragged her into this mess.

Finn had made the right choice, had listened to his instincts and acted on them, the same as always. It was the only way he knew how to be. And acting on them had always given him a path forward before—they would do so now, too.

If Klein was involved, things were bound to get tricky.

Finn didn't get the impression that Qav did business with anyone they wanted to be involved with. Things were already complicated enough for them—they didn't need to add to Avery's responsibilities. They needed to keep moving.

Finn refused to leave the humans on Echo to face their fate alone. They had only come to Earth to restore her power, and Qav was wasting their time. Toying with them.

Finn had a responsibility to the humans on Echo that ran as deeply as Avery's own. He didn't look for the role, but it had been thrust upon him, and Finn would honor the weight it carried.

The way Nick should have done. The way their father had done.

Qav leaned on his elbow, staring at the blood that coated his fingers before leveling Finn with an icy glare that promised retribution. Let him try.

"Whoops."

The single word was all Finn said before he turned on his heel, stalking off to follow Avery and Megan up the stairs.

Tai and Markes could deal with the trash alone.

By the time they reached the others, the repair drones had already arrived, and the ship was back up and running. They arranged for someone to collect Finn's vessel while they would all return on the faster option.

Avery had insisted they ride together—she had to know what was on those vid files. Had to know who had purchased their retrieval. It hadn't been just a test for her after all.

Qav wanted her on the mission specifically because of her history with Klein. He knew she would be forced to stay and discover what was going on, if only from duty. He moved Avery about his board, a pawn at his fingertips.

Still—he had stayed with her in that desert.

He had given her the last of his power out there. She hadn't asked him to, and she certainly hadn't expected him to. Then again, it was his fault they were there in the first place.

A part of her had hoped that the reset would jumpstart her telepathy, but so far she felt nothing beyond her own presence. She was beginning to worry that Qav would never heal her. That maybe he didn't even know how.

She didn't need Finn to tell her that time was slipping through their fingers. She could feel that urgency riding him, pushing him to make desperate choices. They only had days left—maybe they *should* just leave.

But she couldn't abandon Earth now. Whatever was on those vids could be essential in the new government, an integral piece to the puzzle of connecting their two worlds. If Avery could do that without conflict, it would be worth any price.

After a shower and a pain blocker patch, she almost felt like herself. Despite the fact that she wasn't sure she'd ever be able to get all of the sand out of her hair. She kept a supply of her own clothes on Finn's ship and was happy to have those back. It felt good to have something comfortable. Familiar.

Rem laid out refreshments in the dining room, and Avery made a fool of herself shoving spoonfuls of different dishes into her mouth—although she kept grinding sand between her teeth with every other bite. She wondered how long that particularly lovely memento from the desert would linger.

Finn didn't eat a single bite, choosing to sulk near the corner viewing window, where he stared out at the clouds. Qav had disappeared entirely.

The rest of their crew sat around the table, talking in hushed tones. Ennis and Syla remained on the bridge to monitor their progress across the ocean. Rem only popped his head in occasionally to check on them.

Her eyes slid to Finn, her stomach clenching.

She had hardly spoken to him since they left his ship. She could barely look at him without feeling a stab of pain inside her chest. He had lied to her. *He didn't trust her.* It was like he didn't trust her. *Had he ever trusted her?* Her mind filtered through all the times in the past when he had dove headfirst into every situation. A part of her doubted that he ever truly believed she could handle herself. Even after she had saved his life—multiple times.

Then again, she was hiding something from him, too. Guilt mingled with the hurt deep in her belly, turning the food she had just eaten sour.

She needed to tell him about his father. But now wasn't the time. He was already fuming over being forced to stay here. Over just being near Qav. Another stress would only send him over the edge.

And besides, they could figure out his family's involvement in the Federation later. It didn't have anything to do with their current situation. He would understand that, surely.

He had called her selfish for agreeing to Qav's proposal to come here. Maybe she was. Maybe she was even hypocritical.

But Finn had lied to her face. Worse—he had made love to her in the process. Had taken something beautiful between them and distorted it in her memory, staining it with doubt and uncertainty.

Avery had proven her power a dozen times over. Finn had no reason to doubt her capability, and yet he had anyway.

He had always struggled to see the bigger picture. He couldn't understand. How could anyone, without her gift? Withholding the information about his father—about his family—was for his own good.

All of her decisions were for the good of those she loved. Because of her powers, she felt too much. *Cared too much.* Maybe it would be easier to be cold. Like Qav.

She let out a quiet sigh, pushing food around her plate.

She didn't have time to worry about it now. There were bigger events in motion that needed her attention. Once she had control of herself again, there would be time enough to deal with her own emotions. Until then, they would have to take a back seat to the matters at hand.

Avery leaned back in her chair. An ornate chandelier hovered above the table, twisted blue glass tangling around itself and casting lines of colored light across the ceiling. It was strikingly similar to the one she had shattered at the mansion and the one in their apartments. Qav must have loved the artist—no wonder he had been so pissed off at her about it.

Her mouth curved. What would he do if she broke this one, too? *She wouldn't touch it.* She wouldn't touch it. But still, it didn't hurt to imagine the look on his face.

Her eyes fluttered closed. And in the next breath, she was asleep.

CHAPTER THIRTY-NINE

"Are you sure you want to do this?"

Qav looked up from his chair as Ennis ambled into the living room. Her head was lowered, that knowing stare piercing and direct. She was always so insanely perceptive. It was exactly why he liked her. Why she was invaluable to him.

"Do what?" he asked flippantly.

From across the room, Syla watched them, her ears open. Where Ennis was perceptive, Syla was nosy. Qav could block her from the conversation, but he had agreed not to manipulate them ages ago. And he wouldn't renege on that now. He valued their candor too much to jeopardize it.

But Qav learned from an early age that his power could influence anyone around him, even unintentionally. As a result, he could never be certain that affection or loyalty wasn't forced. No relationship with him would ever be honest, would ever be untouched by his gifts. Not even with Ennis and Syla.

So he did his best to cultivate trust where he could. Even if it was a poor imitation of the real thing.

"I thought you didn't use your gifts to sway women," Ennis continued wryly, shoving both hands into the pockets of her dark pants. She frowned, her scar turning starkly white across her eye. "Didn't we already have this conversation when you hit puberty? It's wrong."

Qav let out a dramatic sigh, rising to his feet. "You know my tastes aren't so singular as to only include women."

"And you know that's not what I meant." Ennis turned to Syla. "Don't you have something to add here? Why are you so quiet?"

Syla shrugged, looking out the tall arched windows that were open to the gardens and the lake beyond. "It's his life. And we could use her."

"There, see?" Qav smiled over his surprise. "Syla says it's fine, so can we drop it?" He brushed a wave of appreciation up against her mind. She rolled her eyes and shook her head.

Ennis frowned. "She's a So', Qav. Sooner or later, she'll get her full power back, with or without your help."

"It's only politics. I thought you'd be proud of me," Qav drawled. He moved to the small glass bar against the wall, pulling out a bottle and pouring a glass of dark red wine. He didn't look up at the mirror that hung behind it.

Ennis was silent in that way Qav knew heralded some larger point. When she did speak, her voice was low. "We all saw what she did out there. In the desert. Messing with her mind would be . . . unwise."

Qav downed the wine in one swig before pouring another. He pivoted to her, the slick soles of his shoes making the movement fluid on the stone floor. "Duly noted, Ennis. And I appreciate your guidance. But as always, I make my own decisions." He paused, threading cold steel into his final words on the matter. "Particularly where Avery is concerned."

Ennis held his stare for a moment longer before dropping to the floor. She nodded.

He valued her—loved her, even. She and Syla were the closest thing to family he'd ever known, besides his parents. But they barely warranted thought at all. Had only ever made things more difficult for him.

Even if he valued Ennis and Syla as his confidants, as his sisters, they would never be his equals.

He was alone. He had always been alone, from the first moment he discovered his powers.

Strange, though, that Ennis had been able to guess what he was up to. After so long together, maybe Qav was getting too predictable.

And he hated being predictable.

But he needed Avery.

The raw electricity that surged through her veins was tantalizing, beckoning to Qav like some magnetic force. He needed to be near it. Needed to possess it for himself.

And she was the one who had come to him for help in the first place. He would be an idiot not to take advantage of an opportunity that fell into his lap. With Avery on his side, they would be able to change the world. No more hiding in the depths of the Earth, making deals in the shadows. Her support would grant them validity, and her power would prevent anyone from getting in their way.

Even tonight, her presence at this meeting would give them an advantage. Working with humans presented its own problems, and Ennis was often better at manipulating them than Qav was. Hell, even Rem could smooth-talk his way into their good graces; he had lived the majority of his life as one of them.

Besides, he *would* restore Avery's power, or show her how to do it herself. But not before she was soundly on his team. Not until she had relieved herself of the burdens she carried. She was meant to live for herself—no one else.

Qav ran a finger down his nose, brushing the now slightly crooked line. Finn had fractured it, badly enough that his med spa on board the ship hadn't been able to fix the break. His teeth clenched. He'd have to make a trip to one of the upper levels to get it taken care of.

But Qav would be the first to admit that he owed Finn his life.

If he had actually listened to Avery and stayed in the Sanctum, they wouldn't have lasted much longer in that sandstorm. Although it grated on Qav to be in his debt, he dismissed it in the next breath. Finn had ultimately played right into his hand.

Avery only needed a little push, a small nudge, and she would be exactly where Qav wanted her.

It was a pity he couldn't control her outright, but that wouldn't serve his ultimate purpose. If he wove his influence well enough, she wouldn't even notice the threads of it littered throughout her mind.

Avery would come to him, and willingly.

Curiosity brushed against him, and he glanced up. Syla was watching him.

He tilted his head. *Problem?* he asked.

"I hope I'm not interrupting," Rem said brightly, knowing full well he was.

"Sure you do." Syla finally tore her gaze from Qav, not moving from her post. Rem shot her an acerbic glare, fingers going to the side of his glasses in a nervous gesture.

Qav nearly laughed. "Don't give him such a hard time, Sy. You'd think after five years she'd have accepted you into the fold by now."

"Evidently not." Rem's emotions were spiky and bristling, sharp on the fringes of Qav's mind. "Cora just arrived. And she brought both Alex and Mayven with her. Exactly on time, as requested."

Qav brushed a finger over his lips. "Well, what do you know. She can follow rules after all. But did we invite the other two?"

Rem shifted on his feet. "She didn't run it by me. I figured with so much time already lost, you'd be amenable to the adjustment."

"It shouldn't be a problem," Ennis interjected. "I trust them."

A quick dive into her mind proved she was telling the truth. Although how anyone, especially Ennis, could trust humans was beyond him.

Trust was an illusion, a shimmering vision of an oasis in the barren wasteland that made up a life. Tempting to believe in, certainly, but all the more painful when that vision dissolved before your eyes. The only certainty—the only truth—was in control. To believe anything else was hubris.

He was doing Avery a favor. She had come to him seeking a cure for the block on her powers. He would free her of the rest, too.

"I suppose we'll know soon enough," Qav said. "Show them in, and bring Avery. Finn, too. Perhaps having a human on our side will work in our favor."

"Who are we waiting for, exactly?" Avery asked Ennis. Of all of them, she seemed much more inclined to provide answers.

"You'll see," Qav answered instead, a grin on his lips.

Avery shifted in her seat on the deep couch, Finn and Petra on either side. Rem had been adamant that their buyers would be skittish, so not everyone could be in attendance with her.

Surprisingly, Qav had been the one to insist on Finn's presence.

They had left the others on the back terrace of the mansion, which boasted a spanning rose garden and a pool, its edge extending to the lake, blending together until Avery couldn't tell where one began and the other ended. Not a horrible place to wait, all things considered. Not a horrible place to live.

"I believe Qav wants our guests to be a surprise," Ennis said, explaining the obvious. She threw him a wry look that seemed to censure.

"Of course I do," he confirmed, leaning back in a winged chair fully upholstered in a luxurious purple fabric. He really had a thing for that color. One of his long legs draped over a knee, his foot dangling, almost daintily. "The best things in life happen when we're surprised by them. Wouldn't you agree, Avie?"

Finn stiffened beside her. Even Petra's breath caught. Avery laid her hand on his knee. Qav was goading him on purpose.

Avery couldn't say she wasn't surprised. Although Qav's face showed no bruising, the perfect slope of his nose was now marred by a slight bump at its center.

"Have you opened the files yet?" Avery asked, attempting to bring the subject back around.

"He better not have, or his balls are on the chopping block."

Avery looked to the doorway where Rem led in three newcomers. The one who spoke strode toward them, her long red coat fanning out behind the swift pace. The stylish cropped hair and high cheekbones were familiar, but Avery struggled to place her.

"For God's sake, Alex, this is a business meeting," another woman behind her chastised. She smoothed a lock of curly black hair into the chignon at her neck. "Is a little professionalism too much to ask?"

Alex braced a hand on one narrow hip. Her full brows drew together as she stared Qav down. "We had a deal, Qav. We open those files together." She looked at the couch and who sat on it. She blinked. "Moon above, you're Avery Vey."

Avery shifted in her seat, glancing under her lashes at Finn. He was still, his face drawn as he met Alex's gaze. He recognized them.

"And Ambassador Lunitia," Alex noted, surprised. "Well, at least that addition will make Mayven here happy." She glanced over her shoulder at the third woman trailing behind.

Mayven's wide brown eyes were fixed on Finn, her bowed mouth upturned. She looked young—too young to be doing deals with the likes of Qav and whoever the other women were.

"It seems Mr. Qavarion has been keeping secrets from us after all," Alex mused.

Qav unfolded himself from his chair, sauntering over to them on light feet. His smile was a secret in itself. "As I was just telling Avery here, I like surprises."

"It would have been a professional courtesy to inform us beforehand."

"My apologies, Cora," Qav purred. "I assure you, this is the only revelation of the evening. Excepting, of course, whatever we find on those files. Can I interest any of you in a drink?"

Rem appeared beside him, holding a tray of glasses and a decanter of clear liquid. It sparkled against the dim lighting in the room, making the alcohol shimmer.

Finn was on his feet before Avery could stop him. "Are we just supposed to ignore the fact that Alex Pena just walked in here?"

All eyes in the room shifted to him.

On hearing her full name, a memory clicked into place. The trial. Alex Pena had been one of the leading representatives of Klein's opposition. She had even asked Avery a question during her testimony, although she couldn't remember what.

"I'm sorry, did I miss something? Are *we* a surprise, too?" Alex asked, waving an unruly finger between her group.

Ennis stepped forward to pour a glass from Rem's tray. "Since you all required low profiles with the association, we thought it best to keep details hidden from both parties. Now that we're all on the same page, I believe we can proceed." She took a sip, her mouth tilting up in a welcoming smile.

Qav's eyes met Avery's. His mouth twitched. As though she was in on some joke.

Aren't you? he mocked.

She resisted the urge to flip him off.

A grin did pull at his lips then, gone as soon as it appeared. A chill snaked against Avery's mind—not forceful, but enough for her to know he was there. She stood, hiding her shiver.

"I believe we are at a disadvantage," Avery said, using the tone she reserved for official meetings with the Elders. When she was trying to sound like she belonged. "I only know Representative Pena."

Cora stepped forward, extending her hand. "I'm Cora Najisuki. The quiet one back there is Mayven Thula." Her grip was firm, bordering on too hard.

"Najisuki?" Finn asked. "As in Najisuki Nano Tech?"

Her smile was feral. "That'd be the one."

Avery made no attempt to hide her shock, drawing in a shallow breath.

Najisuki Nano Tech supplied the building blocks for everything in global society, from toilets and doors to cruisers and wristports—even the Gate itself. Avery didn't know much about the company, except that its founder was a visionary in the field, and incredibly young when she started. She had moved the technology forward decades in a span of half that time.

She was also one of the top five wealthiest people in both galaxies.

Finn looked to Mayven, assessing. "And what's your role in this?"

"Oh, you'll like this one, Lunitia. Mayven here is our very own revolutionary," Alex said, wrapping a large hand over Mayven's bare shoulder, exposed by the elegant strapless top she wore. Even Megan would be impressed.

White fabric wrapped and folded over her, draping into a tunic over dark flowing pants. The look accentuated a silver choker around her neck, at least three inches wide, as well as the matching circlet encompassing her hair.

When she answered Finn, her voice was melodic and warm. "I'm here on behalf of the Citizens Liberation Front."

Finn frowned. "The CLF? The ones behind the bombings?"

Mayven bristled, her mouth setting. "That is a smear campaign designed by the Federation and the High Council at large to defame our cause. We weren't behind any of those attacks—*any* of them. Support is growing among the citizens of Earth, and that brings power. The Federation is desperate to snuff us out by any means possible." She cleared her throat delicately before continuing. "As a matter of fact, Ambassador Lunitia, your particular backing would mean a great deal to our—"

"Wrong place, wrong time, Mayven," Alex interrupted. "As much as I'm sure he wants to hear your pitch, you'll have time to woo the ambassador later. I'm on a tight schedule, and I'm far more interested in what we came here for."

"Which is what, exactly? I'm having trouble understanding why I risked my ass getting dirt on Klein for someone who is set to replace her anyway." Avery leveled Alex with a cool stare.

It was well known she was the favorite candidate of the progressive party. Once Klein was ousted, the leading party would rotate, ushering in a new era. Most likely with Alex Pena at its helm.

Alex smiled indulgently. "Unfortunately, we can't guarantee the outcome of the vote next week. And while your infallible faith is touching, it also tells me you're an optimist. But I've seen enough elections to know that the public is easily swayed. It makes the popular vote an extremely dangerous tool. I don't want to dwell on what the world would look like if we relied on votes like this for policy change." She laughed dismally at the thought. No one joined her.

"Unlucky for you, then, that you couldn't sway the public in your favor," Qav muttered from his chair. His boredom with the conversation was palpable.

"The vote of confidence was a necessary concession to draw attention to Klein's corruption, even if the methods are not foolproof," she lamented. "But I do always like to have a plan B. Which is why I finally agreed to chat with my favorite anarchist. Privately, of course—I'm not out to ruin my career."

"I think you know I'm not an anarchist, Alex," Mayven countered, all trace of warmth gone. "The CLF stands behind individual choice, progression, and peace via the union of our two species. The existing power structure does anything but support those goals, and in fact, it silences the people at large. The only thing we seek is a true voice. A reformation of government."

Avery considered her, meeting those eyes that were nearly too large for her face. Perhaps they were the reason she appeared so young. Like a child. *Her ideas are childish, too.* Were her ideas childish, too?

No government was perfect, even one that boasted the power of a So' to connect its people through understanding. Avery had worked diligently to build something on Echo that would last, something that would carry the Reanges into a new life of freedom and prosperity, finally able to make their own decisions and reclaim their world.

And in one fell swoop, Leviathan had destroyed it. She had destroyed it all.

Reanges were susceptible to manipulation and easily controlled by those who had the capability. But Klein and the Federation had already proven that humans were equally at risk.

Power was a bright, gleaming star in the expansive darkness of the universe. Its energy could be harnessed, converted into progress and unity in the right hands. But wherever power gathered, there would always be those in the shadows, waiting. Eager to devour the light.

And what was Avery except power incarnate? *Yes.* Yes.

She refused to let them consume her. To let anyone do so. Her fist clenched at her side.

Avery lowered her chin as she asked, "That's a lovely mission statement, but what does it mean? What do you want?"

Mayven smiled, the answer quick on her tongue. "The same thing as you, Miss Vey. The same thing as all of us here. Change."

CHAPTER FORTY

Rem poured drinks for everyone anyway, undoubtedly at some internal order from Qav.

Avery clutched hers, the cold glass numbing her fingers. *Drink.* She took a sip. It burned a trail down her throat, warming her from the inside, calming her nerves.

Finn watched her from the corner of his eye. She tried to ignore it—tried to ignore the current of uncertainty that crept along the bond between them. But it was there, the nagging discomfort of a spur just behind her ribs. She resisted the urge to rub her chest.

Finn downed his glass in one long swig.

The lights dimmed as Rem projected the files onto the wall screen above the fireplace. A small holofire burned within the hearth below, casting a gentle glow throughout the room. Avery imagined Qav spent quite a lot of time here, lounging in his ridiculous chair, sipping a glass of wine. Plotting.

It had to be lonely living in this huge mansion with no one but his own ego to entertain him.

Not too far off, Qav intruded on her thoughts. His attention remained on the screen. *But I rarely plot—I have Ennis and Rem for that.*

Avery bit the inside of her cheek to keep from rolling her eyes. She didn't reply to him.

But she didn't close him off, either.

In many ways, she had missed this—having someone in her head. She hadn't realized how forlorn she felt in her own mind. With only her thoughts and feelings to occupy her, it was like she wasn't entirely whole. A piece of her had been ripped away, leaving the quiet darkness of her solitude in its wake.

But with Qav . . . she could at least have that small part of herself back. Even if it was a pale imitation of the real thing.

"There's a total of six files here. We'll move through them in chronological order." Rem's words drew her attention back to the screen, where six blue cubes hovered, each featuring a time stamp beneath. He stood beside the mantel, a tablet clutched in his arms as he addressed Cora. "Per our agreement, your funds have been transferred to our accounts for the delivery of these assets. Before we proceed, would you like to view the contracts again?"

"Just play the blazing things already," Alex ordered. How such an aggressive personality became one of the world's leading political figures was a mystery. Avery had no idea how she cooperated on committees with this kind of attitude.

Rem said nothing but stepped out of view as he selected the first vid.

Avery didn't miss the satisfaction that skimmed past her, rippling throughout the room. Qav. Something had pleased him.

She glanced his way, but his face was unreadable.

The first vid began. As they had seen when Linderly first opened the files, it was a recording of the control room from the desert facility. Klein was seated at the main table, the chairs around her fully occupied.

Their initial discussions were of no consequence, the general conversation centered around the weather patterns and market compensations. Rem skipped forward. Klein stood from her chair, and he resumed normal playback.

"—asked for this meeting today to discuss the future of our world nation. You each have a vested interest in the continuation of our species, and the means with which to support your interests. It goes without saying that what we're discussing today must not leave this room."

"I would think we gathered that from the secrecy of this entire facility, Minister," one of the men commented.

"One can never be too careful. I'm certain all of you have your own strongholds that you'd rather I not know about." It was an expertly veiled threat, delivered with a warm smile. No one else spoke. "I aim to impress upon you all the importance of our conversation today." Klein paused, typing on her wristport as a holo of Earth materialized at the center of the table. A date stamp hovered above it.

"As I'm sure you all know, government funding has been studying the progression of climate change on our planet for hundreds of years. Any schoolchild knows that the impact of civilization and war has caused an exponential increase in the rate of soil contamination and rising water levels over the past century. As far as the average citizen knows, Federation resources developed technology to reverse this deterioration decades ago."

While she spoke, the land masses on the globe in front of her receded to rising water levels as the clock moved through decades, slowing its pace as they neared the present.

As she watched the vid, Avery's breath lodged in her throat, her eyes widening. She refused to move her gaze from the vid, begging Klein not to say the next words that she somehow knew were coming.

"Every schoolchild has been lied to."

The people seated around the table said nothing. One woman shifted in her seat.

"Our current estimations put end of life on Earth at another hundred years."

The globe changed, showing water levels moving out over the land at a rapid rate. The radiation fields expanded, encompassing every major city.

Klein continued, "That's our best-case scenario. Once our ozone layer depletes entirely, even the technology that currently keeps our major cities protected from sun flares and radiation will be worthless. Earth will be, in effect, uninhabitable."

"What are you saying, Klein?" a woman with stark white hair asked sharply. "You need more money to prevent this? Don't you tax us enough? I practically funded your entire reelection campaign."

"I don't see what the problem is," the man who initially spoke added. "I have plenty of estates on the colonies where I would be happy to live. Not to mention properties on Echo and my space cruise lines. Losing Earth presents no real threat."

"And I'm glad you have that option," Klein said delicately. "But we need to consider our species at large. You were asked here today because each of you holds a great deal of power in our society. And with that power comes responsibility—a responsibility to lead others toward a greater future. A future that small minds cannot fathom."

She tapped her wristport again, and the globe disappeared. In its place, the Gate hovered in a slow rotation. Echo could be seen through its ring.

"The Gate is a feat of human ingenuity. A symbol for what we can achieve through the spanning generations. We are able to travel across millions of light-years via the technology in this one device. But it remains a lax border. The campaign to rid Echo of Natives has dragged on for decades with little progress. There will always be threats as long as we are connected, from both sides. There will always be those who slip through, unnoticed until they take root, choking out our own resources."

The vocal man let out a short laugh, then looked at the others. "So, what, the Earth is dying, and you want to cut us off from the only habitable planet that we've found within a million light-years? Seems like a blazing idiotic idea to me."

"Let's imagine this for a moment," she said, walking toward him. "Say your arm were to become infected with the Mars Pathogen. It's a violent illness, to be sure, one that eats away at your flesh, spreading to your entire body before the end. It's quite painful, so I'm told, and a rather messy affair. But there is a way to stop it—you merely have to cut off your arm. I'd like to think everyone in this room is intelligent enough to not lament the loss of a limb if the reward is your life."

The man cleared his throat, flexing his fingers on the table as though reminding himself his own appendage was still attached.

Klein stopped in front of him, her point as dark as her tone. "This is a fight for our survival—we need to be willing to make certain sacrifices."

A beat of silence fell over them.

The white-haired woman said flatly, "You want to destroy the Gate. But you want us to be on the other side when you do it."

Klein smiled.

Ships appeared on the holoprojection, making their way through the Gate to the planet on the other side. "Your funding will guarantee you passage on the final transfer through to Echo. We will start selections for the best and brightest citizens humanity has to offer who will fill cruise vessels by the thousands, transporting them to their new home. And once we've accomplished this . . ."

She snapped her fingers. The Gate exploded into a chain reaction of spiraling debris and shrapnel as it followed the circular formation of the device.

"Of course, this cannot be achieved without your significant contributions to—"

"I've heard enough," Cora said loudly, her voice pure steel.

Rem paused the vid.

Energy rioted in Avery's veins. She bit her cheek, focusing on remaining motionless. Finn brushed a knee against hers.

This was big. So much bigger than Avery had imagined it would be. Klein's testing on Reanges seemed small in comparison. Why would she care about finding So's if she wanted to take over Echo? It didn't make any sense.

Alex said roughly, "We always knew it wouldn't be good, Cora. This shouldn't be a surprise. Play the next one."

Another vid pulled up in front of the existing one, a nearly identical scenario to the first. Klein stood at the front of the same circular table, but the people sitting around it were all different. They watched in silence as she launched into the same speech as before.

Rem pulled up the others, one after the other.

The same. All the videos were the same scene, the same interactions, but with different players in each.

Klein was gathering people of influence. Humans with money and power and selfish tendencies. She was building her own army—her own government. In this new world she envisioned, she would have no opposition. And those who couldn't afford it, who were found wanting, would be left behind.

The final vid finished playing, and Rem paused it. Klein's face on the frozen frame was confident. Satisfied. Not one single human had said no to her proposition.

Something settled into Avery's gut, making her feel sick. *Selfishness was in their nature.* They would always be selfish—it was in their nature. The only certainty was in the influence she could wield over her own people. In control.

But still—didn't humans deserve the right to know what was happening? A part of her wondered if the average citizen would do anything differently than the rich humans in those rooms with Klein. Would they even care about destroying the Gate if it meant their own survival?

A shudder slid up her spine. She didn't know the answer—didn't want to know it.

Finn was the first to speak. "We have to distribute this. We have to make these vids public."

"This needs to be handled delicately," Alex replied forebodingly. "You can't just throw information like this out to the public. The mob can be feral once they've had a taste of blood, and you two certainly gave them that with the stunt you pulled last year. It has taken us months to settle the progressive parties. Months to actually get any real work done."

"Excuse me?" Anger surged through Avery, flaring out to the room around them. The glasses on the side tables shook, tinkling lightly in the quiet. "What we did was a last resort. Klein tried to have us killed. If the government truly cared for its people and the pursuit of peace, then they wouldn't make it so blazing difficult to seek and find justice."

Mayven cleared her throat delicately. "I understand your frustration, Avery; truly, I do. But I believe in this instance Alex has a point. We need to play our cards right in order to make this work. Completely destroying the government and its systems will put us at a greater disadvantage in the long run."

"Not to mention the time limit," Cora said, pinching the bridge of her nose. "A century or less. We're talking about planetary evacuation—millions of people. We'll need some kind of organized approach before sending the public into chaos."

"So our planet will be a life raft for you, regardless?" Petra spoke for the first time, heads turning to her. Her limbs were stiff, arms tight against her sides. "The Reanges owe humans *nothing*. We ought to let them all—"

Qav let out a low laugh, stopping Petra in the middle of her sentence. "Now, Petra, let's not say something we'll regret. We all have humans we care for, I believe."

Petra's eyes flared, her breaths turning shallow. In the next second, she found a sudden interest in the floor. Whatever Qav had said to her in mind had deflated her entirely. Avery frowned.

"If the vote goes in our favor, then we have nothing to worry about," Alex pointed out. "We can commission an investigation once new leadership has been installed."

"And you expect us to wait for the vote this week? You said yourself that you didn't trust the outcome. That I was being too optimistic," Avery countered.

Alex shrugged a broad shoulder. "If I'm wrong, then we have these vids as our contingency plan. We can still stop this from happening."

"For all we know, the Gate could be one rich person away from blowing to hell," Finn added. "Do we even have until the two days needed?"

"It can't be in motion yet," Alex reasoned. "Klein has had her hands fully tied since the scandal last year. I've made sure of it. And besides, her clearance is on probation during the trial and vote. She doesn't have access to the Gate systems."

"Until she's reinstated," Ennis said calmly. Her words were met with silence.

Cora sat forward. "I know at least half of the people in those vids, and most are still here on Earth. Klein wouldn't go through without her financing."

Hope fluttered to life in Avery's heart. "So maybe we have time to figure out how she plans to destroy the Gate. And how to stop it."

"Let's not forget the blazing situation we're dealing with back on Echo," Finn warned, his voice strained. "We don't exactly have space in our schedule to circumvent another corrupt government plot."

"What situation?" Alex asked, full brows drawing down over narrowed eyes.

Avery frowned at Finn for even bringing it up, her palms turning sweaty. It would be a disaster if Earth found out about the human camps on Echo. It could very well start another war—they were frankly lucky Klein hadn't exposed it to the masses yet.

Before anyone could say more, Qav interrupted them. "I'm afraid that's not really your domain, Alex. But we're running short on our schedule for today, as a matter of fact. If you'll just wire us the remaining fees for possession of the vids, I'll have Rem transfer them over fully to you."

"You're just *giving* them the files?" Avery snapped. They couldn't afford to let go of them, particularly not now. Not when the futures of their two worlds depended on this information.

"Not giving, Avery. It's called a transaction."

"Which we've already paid you good credits for." Cora raised a finger at Qav.

"Due to the nature of the facility, and the dangers my team encountered, the price for full delivery went up. You didn't say they'd be shooting to kill."

Cora didn't break from his stare. "Everyone looks quite alive to me."

Avery flexed her arm, the fresh wound there aching beneath her jacket. From the corner of the room, Syla's dark eyes were fixed on Avery, her features severe.

Qav said nothing. He took a long draw from his glass, silver eyes bright in the still dark room.

Cora cursed, loud enough for them all to hear. Alex laughed.

"We need those vids," Mayven said quietly, touching Cora's arm. "They are necessary leverage."

"Fine," Cora snapped. "But, so help me, Qav, if you do this again it will be the last time we do business."

"Don't make promises you don't intend to keep," Qav purred.

Alex and Cora stood, and Mayven followed suit. Avery felt the need to stand as well, uncomfortable with them hovering over her. Finn and Petra flanked her.

"I'll have my people look into this—see if we can root out what Klein's plans are specifically," Alex said, nodding to Avery. "The security on the Gate tech should be impenetrable, but if a back door exists, we'll find it."

"Who did you find to break into Klein's facility?" Cora asked, suddenly curious. "I'll pay good credits for their information. A mind like that would be invaluable on my team."

"She's not for sale," Avery said, offended.

Cora raised a brow. "No offense meant. But I couldn't even break into that code myself. Contact me if you change your mind—or if she does."

Avery gave her a short nod, turning back to Alex. "I'm returning to Echo, but I'm willing to wait until after the vote if you think it's the best course of action to maintain peace. The last thing we need is to cause more unrest."

Finn looked at her in surprise but said nothing.

"I appreciate the concession." Alex held out a hand, and Avery took it. Her long fingers were surprisingly warm. "I'm glad we met today."

"Likewise," Avery murmured. "It will be difficult, if not impossible, to get information through the Gate with the new restrictions."

Alex nodded. "We'll need to communicate directly—I'll see what I can do."

And then Rem was at their side, ushering the three women out of the room, his suit a blur of pink roses as the lights returned, chasing away the shadows.

Qav stood, walking to the large windows on the far wall. He watched Rem load his guests into a boat, taking off across the water in one of Sanctum's many canal taxis.

"I need another drink," Finn sighed, heading for the bar.

"Less than a hundred years?" Ennis breathed, a thin hand pressing against her buzzed scalp. "Moons above, this changes . . ." She went silent.

Qav hadn't moved from his position. His hands were clasped behind his back, knuckles white.

Avery couldn't feel him at all. He had withdrawn from her entirely.

Maybe now she could convince them to join her. Maybe this was the excuse they needed to force integration between humans and Reanges.

But Alex was right—that kind of change couldn't happen overnight. It would be difficult, grueling work that required planning and strategy. They would face opposition from both sides; Earth and Echo each had their separatists.

She needed her blazing powers back. She needed them fully and completely. If Earth was to face this monumental change, they needed Echo to be strong. They needed allies across the stars.

"So now what?" Petra asked, each word piercing the silence.

"Now?" Finn laughed, the sound strangled. He turned to them, popping a red candy into his mouth, pilfered from the jar lined up with the bottles of alcohol. He raised a glass of dark amber liquid to the room. "Now we sit on our asses and wait."

CHAPTER FORTY-ONE

"Earth is just going to, what—dry up?" Megan's words lifted to a raspy squeak on the end of her question.

"It seemed like more of a drowning and radiation overload situation," Finn explained around a mouthful of food.

They had left Qav's place hours ago, returning to their apartments where Avery explained what happened over dinner on the terrace.

However, she omitted certain details about Qav that Finn thought were essential.

Like how he conned his way into double the money for an operation he couldn't even carry out on his own. And how he refused to offer any sort of help to dismantle the Gate explosion.

Whatever happened in that desert had changed the way Avery saw Qav. She had always wanted to give him the benefit of the doubt, but this—this was different. She was different, somehow. Cold.

"We still don't know if it's fully true." Avery's fingers trailed along the edge of her glass. "It could easily be a ploy for Klein to gain cooperation."

"Regardless, she's still going to destroy the Gate," Megan uttered, her eyes glassy. "That will . . . That will change everything."

Petra's hand moved, her pinky barely brushing Megan's where they were placed together on the table.

"Which is why we are going to stop it," Avery said resolutely.

Grigg raised a hand. "I thought our hands were already full? You know, with the whole Origin-taking-over-Echo thing?"

"My point exactly," Finn muttered.

Finn ducked at the piece of bread Nova threw at him. Grigg wasn't as lucky, the slice hitting the side of his head.

"If the Gate is destroyed, we don't have Echo to go back to," Nova pointed out.

"The vote is in two days—we can spare that," Avery said, her voice surprisingly calm. "I still need to get my powers back, which Qav will do for us now that he's back at full strength."

Tai spoke, his voice quiet, not used to the group. "But if Klein wins this vote, doesn't that mean we'll be at risk here? Is it smart to stay?"

"He's right." Petra nodded. "I say we leave."

"That's not an option," Avery countered. "I gave my word to wait—so we wait. But we can still try and figure this out on our own. There's no reason to wait for Alex's people to figure out how to stop Klein. We've done it before; we'll do it again."

The group quieted. She had already made her choice.

And she was right, to a degree. Avery had given her word to wait until after the vote. Never mind that Finn had nearly taken back that promise himself when the words left her lips. This would be cutting it close, gambling everything on the outcome they wanted.

But working with politicians required concessions. They had given away those files and would have to rely on Alex, Cora, and Mayven to deliver when the time came. They now had the fate of both worlds to consider.

He wouldn't dwell on it. They could focus on rooting out Klein's plan to keep them occupied. And Finn would much rather have a strategy to focus on, something to work toward.

Avery was right in that at least. They had stopped Klein before—they could do it again.

Markes and Linderly were arguing in low tones, whispering in the corner while she tried to slap his hands away from her. Finn's gaze slid to them. They were up to something. Markes caught him looking.

"Tell them." Markes jabbed Linderly in the side hard enough that she squeaked. "Linderly has something to share."

Suddenly, all eyes were on her.

"Um," she tucked a lock of silky black hair behind her ear. "I think I can help."

Finn leaned forward, asking curiously, "With what?"

She cleared her throat, trying again. "When I was back in the Origin, we were working on something. It was, um, kind of all I was working on until Avery showed up. A hack. Into the Gate data systems."

Finn's hand froze, his fork forgotten. There was no way she had actually gotten in.

The Gate systems were the most secure in the entire galaxy; Alex hadn't been wrong about that. Earth governments spent centuries funding its conception, even before the High Council had been founded. The complex computing needed to power it was the most advanced, not to mention the most expensive, ever created. If even one small calculation was off, it could mean a ship was torn to pieces or sent billions of miles off course. They needed perfection, and so they had created it.

Which meant it was unhackable.

"Go on," Markes said, nudging her shoulder. His small grin was hint enough of Linderly's next words.

"I was close. Very close. If Avery hadn't arrived in the Origin, I would've been in, probably in a matter of weeks. Maybe days."

"Do you think you could replicate your approach? From here?" Avery couldn't conceal her excitement. "You carry your coding with you, right?"

Linderly nodded, the movement as slight as her frame. "I could try. The servers that control the system are located in this galaxy, which would make my computing faster. And if I had Megan and Rem to help—"

"It was a great idea until that one," Finn interjected, shaking his head. He caught Megan's offended stare and clarified, "Not you, Meg. The other one." There was no way they were going to invite Qav's lackeys to join them.

"We have to take every opportunity we can, Finn," Avery said stiffly. "If Rem agrees, then we could use his help."

Finn leveled her with a cool stare. "Let's say they do it—let's say they hack in. You really want Qav having access to that kind of power? Because that's what will happen. Anything his people touch is within his control."

"And what do you think he's going to do? Destroy the Gate himself? He wouldn't take out the only link to our home world."

"I agree with Finn," Petra said, her voice low. "We should keep them out of it."

"Will wonders never cease," Finn chirped, grinning. He raised his glass in Petra's direction. She rolled her eyes.

"Luckily for you two, I call the shots," Avery countered. Finn bit the side of his tongue to keep from speaking. "I'll ask Brehna to contact him. Hopefully you can get started as early as tomorrow morning."

"Actually"—Linderly set aside her napkin and stood—"I'd like to start now, if that's okay. Sometimes the code nags at me until I can't sleep. I'll feel better if I go ahead and dive in, refresh myself on my past work."

Megan was on her feet. "I'll join you. The sooner we get started, the better." She threaded an arm through Linderly's, disappearing inside.

"I've never seen someone who enjoys working as much as that girl," Grigg said as Linderly left. He turned a smile on Markes. "Is it painful for you?"

"Is what painful?" Markes asked, confused.

"Having a sister who makes your intelligence look like the size of a space rat's?"

Markes scrunched his face in mockery before grabbing a handful of mashed vegetables and throwing it straight at Grigg. The wet food hit its mark, sticking to the side of Grigg's face on impact. He didn't move.

Nova burst out laughing, Finn following suit as she clutched at his arm to stay upright. Avery was giggling beside him, the smile on her face startlingly bright. Tai looked shocked, uncertain.

"This is your fault for giving him ideas," Grigg chided Avery. He clawed at the dish on his face, slapping a handful onto his plate. Markes let out some sort of choking sound, and Grigg zeroed in on him. "If you laugh, you're dead, kid."

Markes eyes widened, his shoulders shaking.

"Don't do it," Grigg warned, pointing a food-covered finger across the table.

The gesture sent Nova into more hysterics, and Finn grabbed his stomach, the muscles clenching to the point of pain. Even Tai was laughing by then.

Markes let out a sharp pitch of sound, certainly laughter, before he launched from his seat and made a dash inside. Grigg pushed back his chair in a screeching wail, taking off after him.

"You better run, you little shit!" he yelled, his voice trailing down the halls as Markes made his escape.

Their laughter dissolved into the hushed sounds of the night. The breeze picked up, pushing through Finn's hair in a soothing touch of warmth. He looked to Avery. Her expression was distant—thoughtful. She was somewhere far away.

Something seized beneath his ribs, clamping his heart like a vise.

He reached out to her, his hand covering her knee. Avery looked down, as though surprised, and when she met his gaze, she smiled. But it didn't reach her eyes. He ignored the stabbing pain in his side, smiling back.

That night, for the first time, they slept without touching.

CHAPTER FORTY-TWO

"All three of you came?" Avery stood in shock the next morning in the living area where Rem, Syla, and Ennis waited for her. She had left the others in the gym, where they were still running drills.

"Qav thought it would be good to have us fully onboard." Ennis's gray eyes flickered to Syla. "That, and Syla would like to repay her debt."

Avery hoped they couldn't see the blush that flooded her face. "There is no debt," she muttered.

Avery hadn't allowed herself to think about that moment in the desert. There would be time later to dwell on that power she had felt, how deeply it had affected her. How familiar it had felt, that warm humming that opened straight into her soul. Time for reflection would come later.

"I'll take any help we can get," Megan chimed in. She had actually woken up before late morning, surprising even Avery with her enthusiasm. "Linderly has been working through the night, so I'm sure she'll be grateful for the relief. I was just bringing them coffee, if you want to join me, Rem."

He nodded, following her down the stairs.

"I suppose that means we need to work on some physical training," Syla said, already walking toward the gym. "You better not be drained from whatever you already did this morning," she called over her shoulder.

Avery swallowed her groan.

Ennis grinned, slapping Avery on the back. "Aren't you glad we came to help?" she asked sweetly, pushing her after Syla. "I'd like to see more of what your power can do. Did you really heal Finn? And from a mortal wound, like you did with Syla?"

Avery edged a look at her, a brow raised.

"I have a little obsession with Reange history and lore," she explained. "I've studied everything I can find on your powers, but I've never heard of any So' being able to manipulate matter the way you do."

"Really?" Avery was intrigued. It was the first she had heard from anyone that her powers were in any way different. Leviathan had certainly never hinted at it. "But don't we just have certain proficiencies? Mine is physical, while Qav's is in the mind, right? He's much more skilled at manipulation and control than I've ever been."

Avery didn't know how to interpret the small smile Ennis gave her.

"In most cases, yes," Ennis agreed. "But what you can do is unique. I imagine your telepathic powers would be equally as powerful if you worked with them more. Qav has been perfecting his skills since he discovered them as a child." She paused, considering, before adding, "And healing Reanges is a common skill for So', but to heal a human? I've never read of such a thing being possible."

Avery frowned as they approached the gym. No one on Echo had ever told her anything of the sort. It wasn't common knowledge she had healed Finn, but still. Someone on the Elder Council should have informed her.

What difference would it have made?

Even if she was powerful, she had still been bested by Leviathan. It hadn't been enough. Sometimes it felt as though it would never be enough. *She would be enough there.* Perhaps she would be enough there, in Sanctum. That was, if she didn't have obligations—didn't have people counting on her.

Qav was more honest than most of the people who claimed to want the best for her, not to mention he sent his closest confidants to aid her when she asked.

But he still hadn't restored her powers. Avery blinked. She had nearly forgotten about that. Had it slipped her mind?

She would have to confront him about it, and soon. He had to be back to full power by now. And Avery couldn't hide in Sanctum forever, no matter how tempting.

Because she did care about those who were still on Echo without choice or leadership. She cared about the fate of the humans whom she had foolishly handed over to the Origin with her plans to help them. She cared about the future of her people. That meant both Reanges and humans alike. She couldn't forget that was why she was here. *Couldn't she?* Could she?

No. No—she wouldn't.

A headache teased her, an annoying pain rooting behind her eyes, and she let the thoughts go. Right now, she needed to recuperate. They had already decided on a plan, and she would commit to that.

This haven beneath the earth was like a cocoon, sheltering its inhabitants in darkness and warmth and safety, but it wasn't meant to last forever. All cocoons were temporary, made for restoration, for evolution . . . but ultimately leading to one thing: ripping open into a new beginning.

Finn had never been good at waiting, especially when there was something he should be doing. And this was no different.

He leaned on the cool metal railing of the terrace, looking out over the waterways below, popping his fingers in the silence.

Syla and Ennis were diligent in their training, even Finn had to admit that.

Apparently Syla's family had been a part of an ancient fighting tradition on Echo, passing down techniques for generations. Grigg and Nova had nearly shit their pants when she mentioned it, like it was some kind of myth itself. Syla had laughed—actually laughed— and told them her mom would be happy to train them. She still lived in Sanctum herself, adapting to her life on Earth quite well.

But how could anyone adapt here, be happy here, living under Qav's totalitarian rule? Sanctum was privatized, owned and controlled solely by one man.

Qav. As if his money and influence didn't grant him enough power already.

Finn also had those things, but he certainly wasn't going around creating monuments to himself and exploiting those with nowhere else to turn. Finn tried his best to live up to the privilege he had been given in life. Even if—especially if—his brother had dragged their name through the muck. But he had made Nick pay for those crimes, perhaps the ultimate price.

The Lunitias had stood for something once. Their parents had fought for equality and justice on Echo. His father had always taught them that every person, whether human or Reange, deserved a voice. And he believed in that more than anything else.

Finn couldn't sit there and let his father's work explode along with the Gate. Because that's what would happen. It would sever ties between the two worlds for good.

Klein had been right about one thing: that Gate stood for something. And Finn would be damned if he'd let it be blown to the edges of the galaxy. Nor would he let the peace Avery had fought so hard for be stripped from her legacy, either.

The innocent lives there deserved a chance. The humans that were still held captive, only death awaiting them. And nothing—not even an arbitrary vote on Earth—should stop that goal. That family he had seen in the arena flashed through his mind. The memory of the little boy running his fingers over Linderly's tattoos, awestruck. The fear in his mother's eyes.

They shouldn't linger here. They needed to leave.

His eyes drifted out over the lake to the white mansion in its center. Its reflection mirrored on the rippling water in the afternoon light, distorting its elegance. Finn's hand closed into a fist.

Each hour that passed, the possibility of them being closed off from Echo forever grew larger. Despite their theories, they had no idea when Klein would detonate the Gate. Hell, she could slip through the portal without them knowing and close it behind her at any moment.

And it wouldn't be temporary. If the Gate was destroyed, it meant they would be cut off from Echo forever, as far as their lifespans were concerned. The original build had taken the better part of a century to construct, and that had been with coordination from the original human settlers on Echo.

Earth was dying.

It had taken a bit of time for that to sink in, but he felt it now, deep in his bones. Human civilization had ruined this planet beyond habitation. Society as they knew it was going to change irrevocably, for better or worse. Even if they were able to stop Klein and keep the Gate open, the political unrest that was sure to follow would be revolutionary in and of itself.

That was assuming Pena released the information at all.

Given their conversation, Finn highly doubted it. A body of people was much easier to govern if they were kept in the dark, particularly about truths that threatened their existence.

But if it came down to that, he'd release the information himself. His word would be good enough to launch an investigation. The people of Earth deserved to make their own choices regarding their future just as much as those on Echo. And as an ambassador, Finn had a duty to them both.

Avery felt much the same. Or at least she had at one point.

She was determined to stop the Gate from exploding, but she also didn't seem to be in that much of a hurry to restore her powers anymore. As far as Finn knew, she hadn't even brought up the conversation with Qav since their return.

He wanted to talk to her, to explain what was going through his mind and hear what was on hers. But she could barely look at him right now.

She was still angry with him, furious that he had disobeyed her, that he had followed her. Finn would eat his own boot before he apologized for that. The choice had saved her life. She claimed he didn't trust her, but it wasn't as simple as that. Faith wasn't always black-and-white.

He didn't know what to say to her anymore. For somebody known for his loud mouth, it was damned inconvenient that he lost use of it when things really mattered.

Maybe it would be easier to just concentrate on the political unrest of one planet. They both had responsibilities there, had people counting on them. They couldn't afford to worry about Earth right now.

But he'd be better off asking the moon to stop its orbit of the Earth than he would be for Avery to stop caring for both worlds. It was what he loved most about her. She was kind and brilliant and strong and passionate about those she loved. Loyal. Sometimes to a fault. She would never leave her people behind.

But she was still hurting, more lost now than she had ever been before. And he didn't have any blazing idea how to help her. Didn't even think she'd accept it if he did.

He ran a hand through his hair, blowing out a sigh.

"I hope you don't expect me to ask what's wrong."

Finn glanced over his shoulder as Petra sauntered out onto the terrace toward him, hands shoved into her pockets.

"I think I'd die of shock if you did," he muttered, returning to his stance.

Petra rested her elbows on the railing beside him, giving the vista her back. For a moment, she said nothing, her green eyes squinting against the generated light overhead.

Which was fine with Finn. He wasn't particularly in the mood to talk to anyone. Her least of all.

When she finally did speak, her voice was low, almost soft. "We need to leave here."

Finn released his breath on a short laugh. "Of course we do. But you heard her yesterday. She calls the shots. I thought you, more than anyone, would be okay with that."

Petra's jaw set, her eyes hardening to jade stone. "You know this idea of waiting for the vote is insane. If the Gate is at risk, then we need to be on the other side of it. Avery is . . . she's not herself. Not here. Not around him."

She didn't need to say Qav's name for Finn to know of whom she spoke. He avoided looking across the water. Even now, he could be watching them, looking out through Petra's eyes.

Qav had no limits.

He had told Avery he couldn't control her, but what if that had been a lie? How could they trust someone who only looked out for his own interests, all others be damned?

Finn forced a casualness into his words he didn't feel. "Last I checked, you worshipped the ground she walked on, and now you're trying to get me on your side against her. What's changed, blueberry?"

He knew exactly what had changed: it had blonde hair, great taste in clothes, and a mind sharper than a Plutonian mining laser.

Petra stiffened at the nickname, sliding a glare at him that promised retribution. In the next second, she let out a swift breath, looking to the domed sky above. "What are we supposed to do?" she asked somberly. He wasn't even sure the question was directed at him. "We can't save her from this."

Finn's entire body locked, some unnamed emotion clawing up from the depths of his belly. He closed his eyes, forcing it back down, deep into the shadows. His rushing blood sounded loudly in his ears.

"I know," he bit out. It was all he could bring himself to say.

"We can't leave them, Finn," Petra said resolutely. "Those people back on Echo need us—they need all of us. Even the humans. I won't abandon my home." She slid covert eyes to him before amending, "Our home."

"Avery won't, either," he assured her, shaking his head. "Just give her time."

"We don't have time. That's what I'm afraid of—and you should be, too."

Finn's wristport lit up, signaling an incoming message. He hadn't received a direct comm in ages, at least not from someone close enough to have priority notifications. He read the sender, his pulse skipping as recognition skittered down his spine in a furious scramble.

"What is it?" Petra asked, brows furrowing.

"Nothing." Finn flipped his wrist back over in a hurry. Nausea boiled up his throat, choking him from the inside, robbing him of air. He pushed off the railing, flashing Petra a grin. "Let's go see if our women have found anything of use yet."

Petra grimaced at his words, stalking away from him on a huff of disgust.

Relief poured through him as he followed behind, her attention to the message forgotten.

But Petra was right. They needed to leave.

And fast.

CHAPTER
FORTY-THREE

The day of the vote came sooner than Avery would have liked.

They had been able to gain access to the Gate system at large, which had caused a great deal of excitement since they managed it within thirty hours. But that celebration quickly dissipated as they realized there was no hint of malware in the unending lines of code. They couldn't find a trace of anything Klein had planted there.

Alex hadn't sent word of any discoveries, either. Either she hadn't made any progress, or she was keeping it to herself. Avery wasn't sure she blamed her. It was difficult to govern, even when endowed with powers seemingly designed to do so.

Not that Avery had access to those powers.

Qav stood across the room in their apartments, talking to Megan. He had shown up that morning to watch the vote results, trailing in behind Ennis, Syla, and Rem. At least it was more neutral ground than his mansion. Avery clung to the sorry semblance of control that offered.

And she was grateful that Qav had agreed to her request to borrow Rem in the first place, albeit a tad surprised. He didn't strike her as someone who made concessions lightly. Or at all.

Avery took a swig of her drink. Her palms felt sweaty on the glass. Regardless of what happened, it wouldn't change their current plans.

The goal was still to prevent the Gate's destruction. At all costs.

And she still had to face Leviathan. Had to face whatever was waiting for her back on Echo.

The past two days had been a blur, training with Syla and Ennis, learning what they could from one another. They seemed ready, even eager, to help with the mission ahead. Avery was even starting to like them.

But they rarely, if ever, spoke of Qav.

Avery wished she could learn more about him, understand him better. A part of her worried that she understood him all too well. What did he think of his closest friends—if he called them that—helping her? Why had he agreed to it at all?

On the end of her query, his eyes snapped to her. He had been listening.

She waited for an answer.

It's their decision, he said to her in mind. *You should know by now that Syla doesn't take debt lightly. What you did for her will be repaid, one way or another.*

I'd rather you repay me first, Avery replied, gathering the courage to demand he fix her powers right then and there. But a twinge stabbed the base of her skull, and the thought flittered away from her. She frowned.

His only reply was a barely present smile as he turned to Megan. He noted the slinky gray dress she wore, found in one of the boutiques on the main street during their outing the night before, complimenting her taste in clothing on the end of some joke. Megan laughed, blushing.

For someone who claimed not to trust humans, Qav certainly flirted well enough with them.

Petra stood nearby, watching the two. Her eyes were unusually bright, almost a glassy shade of green. It was a look that felt unfamiliar to Avery from her friend.

Avery felt a pang of loneliness. She missed being able to confide in Petra. When things had been bad for her on Echo, when she had first discovered her powers, Petra had been there for her. And now she felt far away. Unreachable. Changed.

Maybe Avery was the one changing. *For the better.* For the better.

She glanced to Finn where he laughed with Grigg and Markes on the large couch. Something tugged beneath her ribs, a flash of familiar pleasure that swiftly extinguished on the edge of another headache. She flinched, frowning, trying to recall the feeling. It was just there. Wasn't it?

She shook her head, clearing it of whatever anxiety was troubling her. A soft coolness brushed her neck, and she let it calm her nerves, soothing away the worry. She moved to the couch, sitting down beside Syla and Ennis.

Her mind was clear, like boiled water frozen into ice, ready for whatever came next.

Avery only grew colder.

The vid screen took up nearly the entire wall of the living area, the percentage results displayed in the form of a simple bar graph. There were only two options: for reinstatement and against. Three newscasters discussed the changing bars, their images floating beside the results, their overly excited voices grating.

The polls were open throughout the day, votes tallied immediately upon reception via registered citizens' wristports and verified by a nonpartisan program. Results were made public instantaneously upon each submission.

While the two options held fast at a close tie over the morning, things had gotten progressively worse as the sun set. Much worse.

Avery could hardly breathe.

With only a half hour until the polls closed, the majority of citizens had placed their votes already. In effect, it was over. Their efforts of the past year, the interviews and the testimonies and the campaigning, had all been for nothing.

Klein was going to be found competent for leadership.

They sat in tense silence as the outlook continued to degrade. Avery was unable to move. Finn paced along the windows, disappearing outside for minutes at a time only to return on a string of curses. Petra had left the room entirely, brooding on the terrace.

Ironically, the only people who seemed unfazed by the results were the ones who lived on Earth themselves. Qav lounged on the far end of the couch, sipping on a glass of sparkling wine, his long silver hair piled atop his head in a loose bun. Pieces fell down around his face in a way that appeared artful. Intentional. Even when he was out of place, he wasn't.

His face in the desert flashed through her mind, distorted with pain—with fear. That memory of his, and the guilt. The girl with amethyst eyes.

Qav's body stilled, almost imperceptibly. As though he was remembering it, too.

"This is utter shit," Finn said for the thousandth time. His arms crossed over his broad chest, his normally laughing face drawn and tense.

"It's not over yet," Megan offered up, her voice a pale imitation of its usual verve. She didn't believe her own words. None of them did.

Finn carried on as if she hadn't spoken at all. "Didn't these people watch that vid from last year? All the work we did, all that time I spent apart from . . . and for what? This is such shit."

Avery winced at his words, each one accentuating the pain in her skull that had blossomed behind her eyes.

Finn was angry. She supposed she should be, too. But the only emotion she could muster was disappointment. It hung low and heavy in her belly, turning the food she ate earlier to an oily upset that teased sickeningly at her throat.

Why did she feel so ill? She had prepared herself for this outcome. Or at least she thought she had. This popular vote was not a sentencing—the trial had already taken care of that. The committee had already confirmed Klein's direct involvement with obstruction and duplicity against the World Nation and its Council. Not to mention numerous violations of peace treaties between worlds. No, this vote was merely for her reinstatement after having been convicted of those charges.

Which meant the citizens of Earth—the humans—didn't care.

They knew what Klein had done. And they were voting to keep her in power despite her crimes.

It would mean an effective acquittal of any wrongdoing. She would never have to pay for her crimes. She would be given her full powers back, bar none.

While Avery was still stripped of her own.

She stood, blood rushing to her head in her haste, accentuating her migraine. Energy fired up her arms, making her skin tingle as she fought to control it. Her veins were lightning, stinging her from the inside out, threatening to burn straight through her.

The news casters were still talking, their incessant voices too bright, too unaffected by the brevity of what was happening. Avery couldn't bear it.

She shot out a hand, frying the lights in the building. Everything went dark. The fading light from the terrace windows cast long, soft shadows, haunting the room with a lurking melancholy.

A small smile pulled at Qav's mouth.

"Is something funny to you?" Avery asked between clenched teeth. She still felt nauseous enough that she might vomit. Maybe it would bring some measure of relief.

"Not at all," he replied quietly, his silver eyes running over her. "I just like watching you ignite."

Avery thought she heard Finn growl from the corner. "You owe me," she hissed, taking a step toward him, energy cracking at her fingertips, her head pounding. "You promised to help me—now do it. I'm sick of your games."

Qav lifted a finger to his lip, brushing it lightly as he considered her. When he spoke, his words were careful. "You're upset."

"Of course I'm upset! Klein is about to be given every bit of control back. My job is going to get a hell of a lot harder, and that's not even considering what I have to deal with when I go back home."

An emotion she couldn't place crossed his face before it disappeared into a mask of boredom. "Your reaction to this is overblown.

Klein going back into her seat as minister will make no difference in the grand scheme of things. If you think *anyone* in a position of power, Klein or otherwise, is anything more than selfish, you're lying to yourself. Your naivete does you a disservice."

Avery couldn't speak at first, the din of her pulse drowning out sound. Her eyes flickered to Ennis, who looked away. Only Syla was brave enough to hold her gaze.

It was some seconds before Avery spat out, "Then why do business with them? Why go through all that trouble to provide Alex and the others with the files they needed to bring her down?"

"That was a business transaction. I have no qualms about dealing with selfish people—in fact, I find they usually make the best partners. I know exactly where they stand."

"Is that supposed to be a surprise?" Finn interjected sharply. "Takes one to know one."

Qav leveled a stare at Finn that chilled even Avery before continuing, "Let's consider it, shall we? You are extremely powerful, Avery. If I were to return your powers, what guarantee do I have that you won't take what's mine?"

Disbelief shot through her, cutting like a knife. Her skin tingled, vibrating in response to the fuel he just threw on the fire raging within her. The table sitting low before the couch vibrated, jostling the glasses placed there, a jarring chorus of sound.

Her next words were low. Lethal. "If you have to ask that, after all I've done for you—after all I've done for your—"

"You're right," he stopped her, rising to his feet. She tilted her head back, following his gaze. *Of course you're right. I meant no offense.* "But as much as I want to help you, gnima, I'm afraid it's not that simple."

"What the blazar does that mean?" Finn asked forcefully, stalking over to stand beside her. "The entire reason we're still here is for you to unlock her powers. You're not going to back out of this now."

"Finn," Avery chastised, bristling at his interference. *Was he trying to make decisions for her?* Was he? She could make her own decisions. This was her problem to sort out, her burden to untangle. She didn't want, nor did she need, help. From anyone.

Qav answered regardless, his words slow. Careful. "It means that I cannot undo what has been done."

"What?" Avery breathed.

Megan stood from her seat, watching them carefully. "What about how you healed Tai?" Tai sunk farther into the couch, his shoulders drooping, trying to disappear. "Surely this is a similar issue."

"Tai's memories were compromised, a complex infestation of negativity centered around a single traumatic experience. Once that seed is planted, it grows, spreading throughout the mind like the roots of a weed. I was able to reverse that by pruning out reality from fiction. In essence, restoring his perception." He ran a finger over his lower lip, his eyes drifting over Avery. "What's wrong with Avery is something I've never seen before—something I can't find the origin of. It's almost as if it's . . ." His stare went distant.

"As if what?" Avery demanded, scared she knew where his mind was going. Scared she knew the answer inside herself—had known it all along.

Linderly spoke up, surprising them all with the urgency in her voice. "Guys, something's happening." She frowned at the tablet in her hands, where she had been monitoring the Gate systems, waiting for movement.

Rem was beside her in an instant, peering over her shoulder. "She's right."

Qav stiffened beside Avery, already understanding via their thoughts.

Avery bit the inside of her cheek. "What is it?" she snapped, stepping toward them.

"Klein's credentials are back online," Rem explained. He glanced at his wristport. "They called the results. She must have been granted access again immediately."

"But Cora was certain. She said Klein wouldn't move this quickly—not with her investors still here on planet," Avery pointed out.

"Looks like she was wrong," Megan said darkly, looking over the tablet herself. "Damn, they're moving through the database already."

Linderly frowned. "What are they . . ." Her heart-shaped face tilted on the inquiry, eyes narrowing as she followed the user's movement.

"Moons above," Rem said, his voice strangled.

"Oh no," Megan whispered.

Qav looked to Ennis, who was already on her feet. "I'll make some calls." She nodded, then headed for the privacy of the terrace. Syla was already on her feet, pacing near the staircase in the foyer.

"Why don't I like the sound of that." Finn moved closer to Avery.

"Tell me," Avery said.

"They started a countdown," Linderly said, looking up at Avery with wide, frightened eyes.

"A countdown to what?" Grigg's shoulders were tense, his head lowered, as though he were ready for battle on the answer.

"I think we all know the answer to that," Nova answered him. Her eyes caught Avery's, a question within their blue depths.

"How long?" Markes question was quiet. He reached for Linderly's hand, his grip tight on her fingers. Tai stood close behind them, his head bent low, expression shuttered.

"The Federation is here—they're here in Sanctum!" Petra burst in from the balcony, her eyes wide, panicked. Qav brushed past her at a run as soon as she appeared, followed close behind by Syla and Rem.

"They're here," Petra said again to the room. Her gaze bounced off Megan, landing on Avery. "Avery, we have to go. Now."

The shocked silence quickly evaporated as loud sirens broke through the air, a wailing cry of invasion, heralding danger. Avery forced her body into action, running for the terrace along with the others. She ground to a halt, watching in horror as at least a dozen warships rose from the depths of the dark waters, heading straight for the city itself.

No. No. *He wouldn't let this happen—they would pay for even daring to set foot here.* She wouldn't let this happen. She would make them pay.

Her lips pulled back in a feral grimace, cold rage pouring through her in a rush of pure adrenaline. Avery embraced it, letting her power flow up and through her, a chilling rush of ice filling her veins. If this was how Klein wanted to handle things, then so be it. She had made a mistake to send her people here, to attack this place.

It only took seconds. The ships hovered for a moment, remnants from the lake pouring off gray metal in virulent streams of white, disturbing the surface until waves sloshed up through the canals.

Sanctum clung to those few precious seconds of quiet, holding fast to the normalcy of the evening. Pedestrians halted, faces turning up to the sky, fingers pointing. A solitary cry floated up on the air, reaching the terrace.

The city held its breath.

And then their world combusted into utter chaos with the same violence of an exploding star.

CHAPTER FORTY-FOUR

The first shot took out an entire floor of the building across from them. Avery staggered back on the screech of tearing metal and shattered glass. A wave of heat billowed outward, slamming into the terrace, striking her face.

She braced herself, fingers tightening as she called upon her power.

The building burned, orange flames licking their way up its sides while dark smoke curled upward, choking the sky. From somewhere below, someone screamed.

But the ships held, their shadowed masses eerily still and equally quiet.

Grigg stepped forward, his hands gripping the railing as he leaned out, angling for a better view. "What are they waiting for?"

"It's a message," Finn said, his voice flat but braced. As though he had expected this. The lines of his body were taught, matching the intensity on his face.

Qav's eyes cut to him, silver slicing through the air sharper than any laser. "A message for who?" His words could have frozen the sun.

Avery barely had time to process what he meant before Nova's warning, "They're priming again."

"It will never hold," Markes said, his voice shrill as he pointed at the structure burning before them. He stood beside Grigg, fixated on the ships. "Another shot from one of those guns, and that building is going down."

"There have to be hundreds of people still inside," Megan breathed.

"Three hundred and fifty-four," Qav bit out, his eyes fierce and cold and trained on the destruction. A bead of sweat built at his temple, the only sign that he was using his own power to maintain a hold on the people inside. "Avery." Her name was a plea on his lips, though he didn't look back at her.

"Here it comes," Markes whispered, barely loud enough to hear.

Avery ground down through her feet, raising her hands to hurl a surge of energy that poured out from her body on a wave toward the building. She had never blocked anything this large, and she sent up a prayer to whomever was listening that it would work.

The ship fired.

The blast slammed into her shield with enough force to shudder the molecules in the air, the harmful rays dissolving on ripples of transparent waves. Avery winced, hissing, the impact knocking the wind from her chest. She struggled, grimacing as she regained control of her lungs. But it had worked. It had held fast.

"Moon above, Avery," Megan breathed from somewhere behind her.

"You okay?" Finn's voice was tight, withdrawn. He didn't look toward her.

Nicely done. Qav's admiration washed over her, his power infusing her with renewed determination and steel.

But she wasn't finished yet. Oh no—she was just getting started.

Are they—

They're fine. The ones that are left are fine, he amended.

"Avery." Finn was in front of her then, a large hand on her shoulder, his eyes as dark as midnight.

"I'm okay."

"Shit." Grigg's curse was low on the air, pulling their attention back to the water.

"They're moving to street level." Syla's voice was stone, her long fingers clamped around the blaster strapped to her hip.

The ships piloted down the water's edge, opening onto the sidewalks as legions of Fed soldiers filed out and into the streets. But whatever Qav had done, whatever he was telling the Reanges, they had already made their way inside. There were no pedestrians left in the open.

Avery hoped it would keep them safe. Long enough for . . . long enough for her to stop this.

"I don't understand," Megan murmured. "Wouldn't it make more sense to just fire from the ships?"

"Not if killing isn't the only objective," Petra replied, her green eyes far away. Tai moved close to her, silent, standing arm to arm. "They want this to hurt."

Avery would die before she let Klein hurt more of her people.

And these *were* her people, in many ways even more fragile and in need than those back on Echo. She would rather die than see them suffer, than feel them suffer.

Qav's back was stiff, immovable, dark brows drawn low over his eyes, casting them in shadow. Whatever he saw through his power, it wasn't good. Whatever he felt was even worse.

Lavender eyes, lifeless in the rain. Red hair. Krez's devastated face. A life force being ripped away from her, tearing out a part of her soul.

And then nothing—always nothing.

Panic seared straight through her, burning a hole through her chest, turning her limbs into useless weights. Her pulse raced, a silent scream drowning out all sound.

Finn was holding her shoulders, saying something, shaking her. But she couldn't hear him, couldn't see him.

She wouldn't go through that pain again. It would break her.

Qav's head turned to her sharply.

Stop, he commanded, brokering no protest, accepting no alternative.

She had no option but to obey.

His power chilled her, frozen energy flooding up and through her, pouring into that gaping wound in her chest until she felt whole, healed by pure ice.

She could do this.

Yes. Yes. She was power incarnate. Hadn't he been telling her so all along? She would not let this happen. She would not let the Federation take anything else from her. *They would pay.* Yes. *Yes.*

"They will pay for this," she uttered, the words a dark promise.

Finn released her shoulders, eyes widening with something like fear. He took a small step back.

And then she sprinted for the edge of the building, vaulting effortlessly over the railing.

Someone called out behind her, drowned out by the wind in her ears.

She embraced the weightlessness that carried her down, the way her stomach curled, her body bracing for the impact of the ground rising to meet her from seven stories below. The force of the impact thundered through her bones, paved ground cracking beneath her as she landed on a bent knee, spreading the energy out in an imprint of fissured concrete.

She stood, her body immediately in motion, running full speed at the invading forces ahead, ready to face the darkness.

CHAPTER FORTY-FIVE

Avery jumped off the building—she jumped off the blazing building.

Finn moved as soon as he realized her intention, the railing digging into his ribs as he threw his body against it, reaching for her, fingers only grasping air. He watched her fall with wide eyes, his heart halting in a painful lurch as though she took it with her. She threw her arms out, as though bracing against gravity itself, her braid lifting up behind her like the tail of a kite whipping on the wind.

She hit the sidewalk, a striking crack echoing up to the terrace, ricocheting through his ears.

He didn't breathe—couldn't.

She stood, her head whipping up just before she took off in a sprint over the bridge, out of sight into the winding buildings beyond.

Finn let out a rush of air, his hands shaking.

What he had seen in her eyes . . . the icy rage that consumed her . . . . He could have sworn their golden depths had shifted, flashing silver. But it was gone as soon as it appeared, and she was over the ledge before he could blink.

"That blazing *idiot*." Megan was beside him, her voice trembling.

"We have to help her," Petra ground out.

Qav turned on his heel, stalking toward the apartment on long strides. Rem was at his side, face studied in concentration as he typed into his wristport with furious fingers.

"Hey!" Finn barked, but Qav was already out of sight. He whirled on Syla and Ennis. "Where the blazar is he going?"

Nova took a step toward Syla. "We need weapons."

"If you had let us keep our weapons in the first place, we wouldn't be in this mess," Finn snapped. Adrenaline coursed through his limbs, making it difficult not to take off after Qav. Avery was out there somewhere. He needed to get down to the street—needed to find her.

Syla shared a quick look with Ennis before she nodded. "Follow me," she replied tersely, heading inside, their group close behind.

"You're staying here." At Petra's stilted command, Finn looked back. She faced off against Megan, who tried to follow.

"I have every right to try to help you—"

"The only thing you'll do is get in the way," Petra hissed. Megan flinched. Her next words were softer. "Rem is gone, and Linderly has combat training—we'll need her. You'll be more of a help here monitoring the Gate feed."

"I agree with her on this one," Finn added apologetically. "Besides, Avery would kill us both if you got hurt."

Linderly handed her the tablet. Megan took it reluctantly, her movements slow. Finn didn't have time to dwell on it or look back as he rounded to follow the others to the elevator.

Syla passed her wrist over the panel, which lit up with a purple glow before descending. It kept moving past the lobby floor, the doors finally opening on some lower level shrouded in darkness. The room beyond illuminated slowly as they entered, soft blue lighting revealing what it held.

"Moons above." Markes was the first to take a step forward.

Even Finn grinned.

The room before them housed the most spectacular collection of weaponry he had ever seen. State-of-the-art blasters lined the walls, all shapes and sizes, nano nets spread across the table in the center, along with an entire collection of dark-matter grenades. . . . He even caught sight of a laser sword mounted on the wall.

"We have armories littered throughout the city," Ennis explained, pulling a gun from the wall, checking the scope and priming its charge. "Qav is nothing if not prepared."

"There's a reason people don't mess with Sanctum," Syla added.

"Let me guess," Finn drawled. "It's because of the nondisclosure agreements?"

Syla grinned at him—she actually grinned—before charging the blaster in her hands, its core glowing a bright blue in the dark. "I'm going to enjoy seeing if you can back up all that smart-ass talking."

He caught the gun she threw at him in one hand. "I do well under pressure."

Ennis ignored their banter, already at the door in the back of the room. "This corridor leads to the surface. Qav is dealing with the evacuation across the canal. Once that is handled, he'll connect every Reange in the city—including you all."

Finn tensed. He clearly wasn't included in that summation.

Syla was next to speak, her voice the detached monotone of an experienced soldier. "Until then, we'll need to take out as many of those Fed pricks as we can. Head for the central markets—they'll be spreading out from there."

And then they were both gone, disappearing into the shadowed hallway that led to the city above.

"You heard her," Grigg said, his smile lethal. "Let's go kick some Federation ass."

Once they surfaced, Finn led their unit directly into the heart of the city, following the winding canal pathways into its twisting maze. There were no boats on the water, no pedestrians strolling down the banks. Whatever Qav had done to warn them, the Reanges were prepared and staying out of the way.

"Listen," Petra said over her labored breathing beside him.

They slowed. And then he heard it, too.

Blastfire. Distant screams. An explosion, too loud for a single gun. It had to have come from one of the fighter ships.

Panic surged through his veins, launching his legs into a full sprint as he tore off down the arched bridge in front of them, not bothering to wait and see who followed him.

Avery—he had to get to Avery. She couldn't take on that many soldiers alone, no matter how much power she had gained.

"Finn!" Nova's call pierced the air, and he paused long enough to look over his shoulder.

A Federation ship pulled down between the buildings, its hulking mass threading into the narrow space, cutting him off from the others. Wind picked up under its engines, bursts snapping through the air, tearing at Finn's shirt. The water in the canal rippled away in violent waves beneath its approach.

It was headed straight for Finn—and it wasn't going to stop.

He was here.

Somehow Finn knew it. That message he had received in his wristport days ago seemed to ignite, a phantom pain burning a line up the tendons in his wrist, straight to his heart.

I'll find you. Nos sanguinem simul.

Nos sanguinem simul—we bleed together.

A favorite phrase their father had used, borrowed from an ancient language, adopted as their pseudo family motto. It meant their blood was shared, that family never left one another behind. And after their father died, Nick had loved throwing it in his face.

Nick. His brother was alive.

He had sent that message, and now he was here, following through on his promise.

Finn doubted it was in the hopes of some glorious family reunion.

Petra drew his attention as she sprinted for the ship, heading straight for it. Finn tensed. She was going to try to slide beneath to reach him before he was completely alone and cut off from the rest of their crew.

But the ship was still dropping. She would never make it.

Finn knew the vessel wasn't after the others—it was targeting Finn and Finn alone.

He took off in a sprint down the bridge, veering onto the pathway and deeper into the city, away from the others, away from Petra. As he hoped, the ship pulled up to pursue him, a dark metal beast that hovered close, licking his heels on the sound of sloshing water and scraping metal as it grazed the surrounding buildings.

He turned down a narrow side alley, the momentum of his sprint slamming him into the far wall, narrowly missing a recycling pile with a swiftly placed jump. He pushed off, propelling him forward and deeper into the shadowy space between structures.

The ship couldn't follow into the thin path, pulling up and overhead, trying to give chase as Finn continued toward another main canal. He didn't stop to check its position—he would have more luck trying to lose it in the maze of the city.

If Nick was in there, Finn didn't want any part of it. Avery didn't have time for his blazing family drama right now.

A ridiculous thought rioted its way through his mind. Maybe the attack wasn't about the Reanges or Sanctum or even Avery.

Maybe it was about Finn—maybe Nick had come solely for Finn.

The idea was so insane that Finn let it go, leaving it behind him in the trail of watery muck that littered the alleyway.

He barreled around a corner onto the edge of the main canal, ramming straight into a group of pedestrians. They rounded on him, pulling up their own weapons, charged and ready and aimed directly for his head.

He holstered his weapon, raising his hands, holding his ground.

"I'm not one of them," he said quickly. The sound of the ship roared above his head, his eyes flickering up to the sky above them, to the people in front, to the alleyway behind.

"He's right," a girl said firmly, lowering her weapon. She was young, maybe even younger than Linderly. "I saw him with the tsek in the markets last week."

"You guys need to get back inside," Finn urged quickly.

An older man frowned at him, hands clenching his own lowered blaster. "We will defend what is ours. We've lost too much already to go down without fighting."

Finn tensed. They wore equal faces of determination and anger, feelings he had seen in many Reanges before. Feelings he had shared with them. He prayed Qav would be able to help them soon, or that they had training of their own to rely on.

And suddenly the ship was on them from behind, rushing along the wider canal, headed straight for Finn. It flew so close to the water that waves sloshed up and over the sides, flooding the pavement at least two inches deep. The surge reached them, soaking Finn's boots straight through.

The young girl raised her blaster, aiming directly for the oncoming ship. Her form was impeccable, precise, as though she had been training her whole life. And he supposed she had.

Even on Earth, Reanges were forced to prepare for war. Their lives were a battle. This was what the Federation did.

They didn't just take lives and land and free choice. They took peace and safety and youth. They took a belief in a better world. They took hope.

She fired, a blast of energy bursting out from her gun and flying through the air toward the massive ship. It would never be enough to take it down. He had to get them out of the way, had to get them to safety.

Think—think, *dammit.*

But the ship shuddered on the end of the blast, its tail jerking in a violent struggle to right itself. Its engines sputtered, smoke billowing up from the exhaust vents, whipping around to reveal a wide blast hole in the rear.

Finn was speechless. How had her gun reached the back of the craft?

A loud familiar whoop filled the air as Grigg and Markes surfaced from around the corner several blocks ahead. Markes held a grenade launcher on his shoulder, having just sent it straight into the ship from its rear. Grigg smiled beside him, his teeth a white banner even at a distance.

A loud pop rent the air, the ship finally giving way and swinging around to begin a direct descent for the sidewalk.

Straight for Grigg and Markes.

Finn yelled, a warning cry rising to his lips as he tore out ahead, sprinting in an impossible attempt to reach them. To do something.

To stop what he knew was coming.

He reached a hand out, desperate and clawing.

Grigg looked up, his smile fading.

He glanced behind, at the ship barreling toward them. He grabbed Markes's shirt and pulled—

The vessel careened into the walkway. Finn only had time to throw up a hand, protecting his face as he hunched away, the explosion radiating enough heat to singe the hairs from his forearm.

No.

No. No. No.

"No!" He choked on the word, his body seizing as something dark wrapped around his soul and bore down with the weight of a thousand planets.

Grigg. Markes.

They were gone. Bile curdled in his stomach, threatening to drown him.

He slowed his breathing, willing his limbs into motion. There was no time to feel. He had to keep moving.

Years of training took over, and he welcomed it—welcomed the control needed to finish the job. He pulled out his blaster, hand straining until the metal cut into his palm.

He looked to Reanges behind him. One of the older men nodded shortly, his eyes solemn, before taking off into the alley. The others followed, the girl's gaze lingering.

Syla had said there were armories all over the city. If Qav was worth anything as a So', he would bring the people together. He would fight. Maybe he already was.

Something teased the back of his mind, a knowing pulling at his brain.

Finn whirled.

There, across the canal, strolling down the bank at a leisurely pace, was Nick.

He was completely dry, as though he hadn't even touched the water in his jump from that careening mass of metal. Not a spot marred his blue coat, not a single dark hair on his head was out of place. As though he hadn't been in the ship at all.

Finn's hand shook with rage or something else, something desperate and hopeless and menacing. He locked the distraction away, pushing it down to mingle with the grief that roiled through his belly. There was no room for it here. There was never room for it.

Nick reached the bridge and paused, toeing the line of its threshold.

Finn raised his blaster, aiming straight at his brother's heart.

This time, he would make it count.

CHAPTER FORTY-SIX

"You killed them," Finn rasped, his arm stiffening as the words passed through his lips.

"Who?" Nick asked simply. He regarded the wreckage farther down the canal. "Ah. Let me guess—your friends got caught beneath my ship. I don't see how that's my fault, Finnegan, since they were the ones trying to kill me. Perhaps they should have minded their surroundings better."

Finn saw Grigg smirking and grabbing Markes's shoulder. Neither of them had kept their focus. Neither of them had seen—

Finn reined in his mind, fighting back a feral snarl. "Why are you here?"

Nick smiled, that indulgent one he always used before explaining something that he found obvious. Finn could have shot him for that alone—should have. "Because despite what you did to me last year, despite the state you left me in, you're still my little brother. Did you think I wouldn't come for you?"

"I thought you were dead," Finn corrected.

"Did you?" Nick pondered, as though just having considered it. "That would mean you thought you had killed me. Is that what you want, Finnegan? For me to—"

"Don't call me that," Finn spat, taking a step forward. "You're working for Klein, is that it? That's been it this whole time?"

"It's more complicated than that. Let's call my association with Rebecca . . . a familial predilection."

"You know I hate big words. You'll have to dumb it down for me." Finn's mind raced. *Rebecca.* He had called her Rebecca—like she was a friend. A close one.

"I really don't have time to explain every little detail to you." Nick sighed, glancing over his shoulder. "I came here to take you with me. As much as you hate me now, I'm not going to leave you behind here to rot on this planet. After the Gate is gone, there will be no leaving this galaxy. No going back."

"Yeah, no shit. Which is why we're going to stop it."

"Don't be a child," Nick growled.

"Are we really doing this again?" He griped in a tone that he knew would trigger his brother. "Didn't I already tell you no? I seem to re-member doing so twice before."

"The Lunitias are anything but quitters. Don't make me the bad guy here, Finnegan. I *will* make you see reason."

"Reason?" Finn laughed, the sound hollow to his own ears. "There's no reason for any of this. No reason for what you're doing—for the choice you made. I don't understand. I don't get how you can see what the Federation has done, what Klein has done, and still claim it makes sense. Dad didn't raise us to make such a—"

"Our father was a liar, Finn. Every word out of his mouth was a lie," Nick said calmly.

Finn braced himself, readying for whatever came next. His finger squeezed slightly on the trigger, arm shaking.

"I suppose I've hidden it from you as long as I could. But you . . . you idolized him. And I really did just want to protect you, despite the villain you've painted me out to be. But I can see that keeping the truth from you may have been a mistake."

Finn kept his features blank. "I'm getting pretty damn bored of this conversation. In case you didn't notice, I'm kind of in the middle of something."

The corners of Nick's mouth turned up. "That infallible sense of humor. To be honest, I missed it."

"Sure you did. Get to the point."

Nick held his gaze, dark gray eyes nearly identical to Finn's and just as familiar. When he spoke, each word dropped like a stone. "Our father was one of the leaders of the Lares project."

Finn felt the words strike deep, piercing his gut. He lowered his gun. "You're lying."

"I wish I were. There is so much you don't know. So much he kept from us." Nick took a step forward. "But Rebecca has never hidden anything. She has only ever been honest—only ever been truthful. They worked together when they were both young. Did you know that? She and dear old Dad searched for an answer to the powers of the Elites side by side. Looking for a solution to the problems both our worlds face." Nick took another step, his eyes flaring. "But we've found it, Finn. We've actually—"

Finn jerked the gun back up. "Take another step. I dare you."

Nick had to be lying. This had to be some new scheme, some way to throw him off or hurt him. No way, in any universe, would his father have worked alongside Klein. No way he would have experimented on innocent people. On Reanges.

"Finnegan." His name was a plea. "Why do you think he worked so hard to undo what he had brought upon Echo in the first place? He was a hypocrite consumed by his own guilt."

Finn staggered back, putting space between them.

His mind sifted through memories, sorting them like a desperate space miner picking through moon rocks in search of riches. Visiting a ravished village after a Fed raid . . . meeting survivors in Milderion . . . the lectures and the talks and the belief that their position held meaning. That it held purpose. Had it all been a lie?

No.

No, Finn wouldn't believe it. Their father had been good and true and honorable.

Nick was wrong.

An explosion rocked through them, the ground shaking so violently that the bridge itself began to sway beneath the shockwaves. Finn fought to maintain his balance, kneeling to the ground to keep from being thrown into the water.

His eyes caught movement ahead in the canal: a flash of yellow hair—Markes! Finn nearly sobbed. He was alive, swimming for the walkway on the opposite side of the city, the strokes of his arms long and sure. Finn scanned the water for another body. For Grigg.

But nothing. He was gone. It had been a miracle enough that Markes survived. Grigg had pulled him away, had saved him and—

Another blast sounded, and he looked toward it, back the way he had come. The waterside market.

Avery.

His heart lurched with a violence that had him tearing up and into a sprint, desperate to reach her. Finn wouldn't let the Federation take her. Not again. Never again.

He gripped his gun, synchronizing his cadence in a jabbing repetition of exhales and boots on concrete. The streets passed quickly as a fine sweat broke out across his brow. He tore through an alley, opening up onto the other end of the main canal, where he slowed to a jog.

Bodies littered the walkways. Federation soldiers—dozens of them.

The buildings lining the water were battered as though their outer walls had been shaved away or melted in the result of some kind of massive blast. Finn ducked his head beneath a live wire that reached out into the air as sparks skittered over him.

There were a few Reange casualties, identifiable by their civilian clothing, lying lifeless alongside the soldiers. An older woman with a wound to her chest, slumped against a wall. A teen boy with his eyes still open, staring at nothing, a blaster clutched in one hand. And more that Finn chose not to notice, experience teaching him he couldn't afford the luxury. But he was still thankful that none of the faces he saw were from that alley.

Finn gripped his gun, the metal warm in his hand. Nothing he hadn't seen before. He kept running.

As soon as he cleared the buildings and reached the lake, he saw her.

Avery floated above the tents of the market, her boots clearing at least five feet above the tallest of them. Her arms were outstretched, teeth bared. Behind her was a battalion of Reange fighters, armed to the teeth and ready to do battle. But she was focused on something in front of her. Her head was pulled low, determined and angry.

Finn dragged his focus away to the large group of soldiers who were headed for Avery and her army. A shadow passed overhead, and Finn whirled around. Another ship approached from behind, speeding through the air—straight for Avery. She would never see it in time.

"Avery!" he yelled, knowing there was no way she could hear him above the sounds of the jeering Reanges beneath her feet.

But she started, glancing his way. His stomach dropped as their eyes connected. Then she looked up, noticing the attacking ships, and pivoted her body in the air, ready to take it on. The Reanges beneath her surged forward, heading to fight the soldiers in combat. He caught sight of Nova and Petra at their front, Syla close beside them, a glowing red laser sword in her hands.

Avery shifted her arms, placing them together above her head before she brought them down in a swift slashing motion. The ship rocked in the wave of energy that hit it, spinning wildly out of control and directly into the shadowed waters below. A second later, wind whipped Finn's face, pushing him back on his feet, the aftermath of her strike reaching him.

When he looked back to her, those golden eyes had gone wide, shock rocketing her face as she looked past him. What was she—

He turned on his heel.

"I told you, Finn. We finally found a solution."

Nick moved toward him, only he wasn't walking.

Instead, he floated, held aloft by his own power.

CHAPTER FORTY-SEVEN

"How?" Finn demanded, aiming the gun at his brother, hands steeled.

"We both know you aren't going to shoot—"

Finn pulled the trigger.

Nick threw up a hand. His energy deflected the blast in a sizzle of harmless fire. He laughed resentfully. "I didn't think you'd have that in you."

"It seems there's a lot of things we don't know about each other," Finn drawled, stepping back as Nick advanced. He had stopped that shot, but it hadn't been without effort. Finn had seen the way his hands flinched on the impact. "When exactly did you sign yourself up to be a government lab rat?"

"Oh, it was sometime after you beat me to a bloody mess and left me for dead," Nick explained, his smile savage. "I was in an induced coma for a good while before they tried to wake me up. Only I didn't wake up. I guess they decided there's no harm in running tests on a dead man."

Finn grimaced, unable to process the impact of his words.

He should shoot him again. But they needed more information. What if there were others like him? Just how far had Klein taken this? He needed to keep Nick talking.

"But you're—"

"Human? Yes, of course. Why did you think they were experimenting on Elites, Finnegan? As a matter of fact, if it hadn't been for your little Avery—and her perfectly adjusted genetic codes, courtesy of her grandmother's tampering—then we never would have made a breakthrough like this. In a way, I guess she saved my life."

A shadowy blur flew past Finn, and Nick went down with it, sliding a good fifteen feet down the docks, dragging a deep imprint into the concrete. Avery flipped up and over him, landing on her feet. She braced herself in an expertly trained stance, arms up and ready for a fight.

Nick pushed himself up from the ground, blood trailing down the side of his face from a fresh cut on his forehead. The dark red contrasted sharply with the powdery concrete dust covering his skin.

"Avery." Nick spit on the ground. "We were just talking about you."

"*You*," she got out, her eyes glowing with pure fire.

She wasted no more words on him. One was enough.

Avery launched herself in a frontal attack, leaping through the air with an arm pulled back for a blow to his face.

And Nick didn't move.

Finn's stomach dropped.

Instead, Nick held up a hand. He caught Avery's fist with it, and with his other hand, he grabbed her jacket. Then, using her own momentum, he swung her into the ground.

But she recovered quickly. She countered with her own energy to lessen the impact, swiping her leg to knock his feet from under him.

When Nick fell, Avery took the opening and sent a crushing blow to his face. But her fist didn't reach him. His hands were up as he grimaced, holding her fist inches away from him with his power.

Her eyes widened. "What have you done?" she whispered, her voice shaking.

"Only what is necessary," Nick hissed.

That's when Finn saw the wound on her abdomen. Dark red staining the white fabric of her shirt. She was bleeding. Badly. It must have happened earlier, but she would be weaker now. Who knew how much power Nick really commanded?

Finn wasn't willing to take that chance. He fired off a round of shots, one after the other, straight at his brother.

Gray eyes sliced to him, and a barrier rose, deflecting each of the blasts. Nick grimaced again before his face hardened into a resolute glare. Finn knew the expression well. His brother was furious.

Nick gripped Avery's side and dug into her wound, twisting it.

She screamed, pulling away from him.

Energy radiated outward from Nick, throwing Avery away from him and sending her rolling toward the docks, perilously close to the water.

Finn was already on his feet, but something grabbed hold of his body and froze him in place. His muscles tensed as he tried to fight it. He roared through clenched teeth, raging against Nick's control.

"Did she tell you about her conversation with Rebecca?" Nick asked, breathing heavily as he sauntered past Finn to Avery. She was struggling to stand. "Avery here has known for a long time the truth about our family. But I'm guessing she kept you in the dark."

Finn flinched. It wasn't true. Nick was a liar. This was more of his game.

Avery would have told him. If she had known anything about this, she would have told him.

"You really like to hear yourself talk, don't you?" Finn observed dryly, trying his best to keep the panic out of his tone.

"She doesn't deserve you anyway." Nick reached for Avery and pulled her up by her hair, dragging her to her feet.

She snarled, a sound of pure fury and spat at him, splattering blood across his face. He jerked away, and Avery moved.

She jumped into the air, wrapping her legs in a choke around his neck and flipping backward, upending Nick's body. He should have slammed into the ground, but he caught himself on a pillow of air while Avery kept moving. She fell behind him, air whooshing from her lungs in a wheeze.

Nick got to his feet, his eyes sweeping to the fight behind them.

Finn ripped his gaze from Avery. They were advancing—the Reanges were actually beating back the Fed soldiers. They were going to win.

Silver flashed in the corner of Finn's eye, and he looked to the shadows. Qav. Just beyond the line of the first buildings. Watching them. Why was he just standing there?

"Finn, I'm afraid we're out of time," Nick said quietly. He touched his wristport and held out his hand. "Stop this stupid game of yours and come home."

Finn bared his teeth, growling, "*She* is my home."

Nick studied him, something painful passing over his features before he gained control. He opened his mouth once, shutting it just as quickly, as though thinking better of saying something he'd regret.

"So be it." The only words that surfaced.

And then Nick turned. He ran for the water and dove in, disappearing through its dark depths. Finn wondered if he would ever see his brother again. If it even mattered.

Avery coughed, and blood spattered onto the pavement beneath her fingers. Finn ran to her side and cradled her arm as he helped her up. She winced, pressing one hand to her wound, clasping the other tightly to his. His heart twisted, chaos and grief burning through all the air in his chest.

A cheer sounded up behind them, signaling their defeat of the invasion.

Finn couldn't muster any sort of enthusiasm to contribute.

The cost had been too high.

CHAPTER FORTY-EIGHT

Avery limped over to the others, Finn hovering at her side. Her mind was reeling.

Nick was alive—and he had powers.

She glanced at Finn. His face was steel, unreadable. He always kept such a tight hold on his emotions, always trying to shield her, to save her. She didn't understand why he couldn't get it.

She didn't need saving.

Something teased her mind, the barest hint of feeling, like the brush of a butterfly's wing against the base of her skull. Her heart skipped, and she stumbled. But Finn was quick to catch her. He was frowning down at her, worried.

But she looked up at the Reanges who had fought with her, gathering among the destruction around them. Many were wounded, some able to walk, others not so lucky. Most of the buildings by the water had been pummeled. The crumbling structures were now open to the air, huge hunks ripped away from the outer walls, entire rooms gone altogether. The city had endured its own battle, sustaining its own wounds.

More Reanges were surfacing from the shadows of the canals, approaching on boats toward the market center. There were cries of joy as loved ones reunited and wails of sorrow for the dead. Tears filled

Avery's eyes, welling up from some deeper place within her. Finn held her hand firmly.

These people hadn't deserved this. They had been safe before she arrived. It seemed that she brought destruction with her wherever she went, no matter how hard she tried to help. At least they were safe now. At least they knew the danger had passed, thanks to Qav's connection.

Qav.

She found him immediately in the crush of people. They surged around him, hands reaching out to touch his sleeves, his shoulders, his hair. Some were crying, while others bestowed words of gratitude. Her blood seemed to slow. They had been able to defeat the Federation forces because of him.

Qav had opened the merge to the whole city during the fight, connecting those who could defend it, allowing them to take on the soldiers as a single mind. And the others, the ones who were too weak or too feeble to contribute, he had kept safe from the dangers. Theoretically, Avery knew connecting this many Reanges was possible, but she had never imagined what it would be like. What it would feel like.

Sharing her mind with thousands was different than with just a few comrades on a smaller mission. Even with her gifts fully restored, she doubted she would be able to harness that much raw power and control. It had been incredible—*Qav* was incredible.

Avery clutched her side, the pain from her wound mingling with something deeper that spiraled up her spine and into her core. *Sorrow.*

She could feel it now, entwining with her emotions, its roots spreading throughout her mind. A dark rivulet of shadow, carrying with it the anguish of hundreds, staining everything it touched, darkening her soul.

Avery's pulse quickened. She halted, trying to stop its poisonous spread, squeezing her eyes shut in desperation.

But it was reckless, this shadow, like obsidian lightning moving through her veins, threatening to choke the life from her. And she couldn't control it, couldn't stop it. She had forgotten how.

And then it was gone, dissolving away from her as soon as it had appeared. There was no trace of it left within her, only a cool mist that seeped into her, a frigid ice in its place. She opened her eyes.

Qav watched her.

His next words were for her mind only. *You and I . . . we're different than the others. Those feelings—that darkness—will overtake you if you let it. We must maintain a separation, a balance. If not, their emotion will consume you.*

Avery frowned. He was wrong. His words went against everything she had learned about her gifts—everything she was, everything she believed.

And yet . . . and yet . . .

You cannot make decisions for their good if you allow yourself to become influenced by their feelings. It will only lead to suffering. You should know that better than most. He showed her an image of her dream that first night, of Fiora fading away, of the emptiness that was left.

She shuddered.

"Are you all right?" Finn asked, his voice thick and gravelly. She looked up at him, studying his profile, his dark eyes scanning the crowds. "You need a blazing doctor."

Something was wrong.

Nick was alive, and yet Finn had barely responded to it. She didn't know what he had been through during the fight, but it couldn't have been pleasant. He was strung taut, as though one wrong move would wholly break him.

She had heard what Nick told Finn in those moments before she attacked him, desperate to stop him from talking. Avery was the reason he had powers at all. It was her blood, her time at the Port Station, that had given them the key to unlocking this. If Klein had the power to create So's—human So's—then what would be able to stop her?

If only Finn had told you when he received that comm days ago, we would have known. We could have prevented this.

Avery looked at Qav in shock, sweat beading on her brow.

Qav only raised a brow at her. *Nick sent a comm to Finn's wristport, warning him. I only just learned of it from the security feeds in your quarters. This is what happens, Avery, when we trust without control.*

Her eyes snapped to Finn. There was no way he had known. For days? No—he would have told her. Finding out Nick was alive would have been too momentous to hide, too important to keep secret. He wouldn't have done that to her. He wouldn't have betrayed her that way.

Unless . . .

Unless he didn't trust her. Had he ever trusted her? Even when she told him she could handle herself, that she could save herself, he never believed her. *He had come after her in the desert.* That's right, he hadn't even trusted her in the desert. Had come after her against her direct orders. *Did she really know him at all?* Avery was beginning to think she didn't know him at all. Maybe she never had.

She jerked her arm out of his grasp and stepped away, snarling.

Finn's eyes locked on her, widening at whatever he saw. "What's wrong?"

Her voice shook as she asked, words slow, "Did you know he was alive?"

Finn turned to stone at the question.

"Did you get a comm from him? Did he warn you he was coming?"

His look told her everything she needed to know: the surprise that lightened his gray-blue depths, the quick glance to the ground. His mouth opened to speak, but nothing emerged.

Avery grimaced, pivoting away from him and letting loose a sound of anguish, giving her pain a voice as it clawed up her throat. She couldn't bear the misery that weighed her down at the sight of his face.

It was true. He had hidden this from her—he had lied to her. Again. And this time it had cost lives. Reange lives.

She clutched her hands to her abdomen, willing the truth away. Begging it to leave her.

Finn reached for her shoulder. "Avery, don't—"

"Don't touch me!" She whirled back, slamming her good hand against his chest, hard enough that he staggered backward. "You lied to me—you lied! Look around you, Finn!" She threw an arm out, spanning it across the destruction. "Look at what your deception has cost us! The price we've paid because you didn't—you couldn't—trust me!"

He was silent, his eyes turning glassy and bright. He closed them slowly, his throat working against some emotion. But when he looked at her again, those same eyes were unbreakable, as hard and solid as his next words. "I did it for your own good."

She let out a groan of disbelief. "Are you seriously trying to say—"

"You knew about my father, right?" he asked forcefully.

Yes, she had known, but she couldn't say that. She couldn't admit to it. That truth had been festering inside her for days. And it wasn't the same. It wasn't.

Finn continued, taking a step toward her, "You knew about my father, and you didn't say anything to me. But I know why you did it, Avie. You didn't want to see me in pain. You wanted to protect me— to give me space for other things."

That was true—wasn't it? Pain seared her head, just behind her eyes, driving a migraine through her skull. Tears welled, and she pressed the heel of her hand into her temple, trying to soothe its fierce burn.

"That's exactly what I was trying to do for you," Finn went on. "To protect you."

Her eyes flew open, that icy rage that had fueled her through the fight surging through her body, straightening her spine. Her limbs went cold, her fingers unfeeling. But there was a strength in the ice, an otherness that comforted her.

And when she spoke, her words were stilted, as glacial and frozen as the way she felt inside. "I don't need protecting."

Something shifted within her, locking into place, numbing it all.

Qav smiled, kind and knowing. He was right. He had been right all along.

They weren't like the others. They were different.

For their good, and for the good of those in their care, they need-ed to maintain that barrier. That numbing otherness was their sal-vation. They could control feeling, and they were above it, where it couldn't touch them.

The only protection she needed was within her control. The only guaranteed safety was in her power.

But Avery couldn't control her power, not yet. And if she went back to Echo, she would be fully vulnerable without it. The people there had already betrayed her, just as Qav had said was inevitable. She had lost her ability to control them, and they had turned on her at the slightest provocation.

At least on Earth she had Qav.

She had control through him. She could regain her power through him. He could teach her even more. Even if the Earth was dying, they could find a way to survive in the burgeoning new world. And by Qav's side, she would never have to hurt again.

The emptiness—the nothingness she had felt—would never threaten her again.

Finn grabbed her arm and forced her back to face him. His eyes were darker than she had ever seen them—almost black. He frowned, almost confused, looking over her in a full sweep.

He lurched away, slashing a glare at Qav. "What are you doing to her?" Finn snarled, his head drawn low.

He is jealous of your power, has always wanted to affect change in the way we can. Even from the first moment you met. He is using you.

"You've always been jealous of my power," Avery breathed, the words flying from her as though they had a will of their own. "From the moment you dragged me to Nos Valuta. The moment you forced me into your cause. You've always tried to use me for your own purpose."

The others in their crew began to surface from the crowds, drawing near. Petra stepped forward. Megan was beside her, Tai's arm draped over her shoulders. Nova and Linderly were close, leaning on each other.

But once Avery started, she couldn't stop, like she was sliding down the ice that now lined her veins, toward her freedom and her power. "You have never lived up to the idea of your father, and you— you *needed* my power to do that for you. To give you purpose. You're right that I kept that from you, the truth about him. I knew it would break you. Because you are weak. *You* are weak—not me. I don't need your protection. I never did."

Finn wasn't even looking at her.

His eyes were fixated on Qav, blazing with a darkness that made the void of space tremble. He strode forward, a blaster suddenly in his hand, then pressed against Qav's temple, his finger shaking on the trigger. "Whatever you're doing to her, I swear to the moons—if you don't stop, I'll kill you. Right here, right now."

Qav smiled. "You can try. But I don't think Avery will like that much."

"Don't talk about me like I'm not here," Avery screamed at both of them, ignoring the pain in her skull and clinging to the blissfully numbing cold. "I *will not* be used!"

She raised a hand, channeling the fury inside of her, letting it flow out from her in a ripple of pure energy—at Finn.

CHAPTER FORTY-NINE

It hit Finn with the gravitational force of a black hole, knocking the breath right out of him.

His body sprawled across the pavement, into the tents lining the market, and he rolled with the momentum, letting it carry him into a stall rather than fighting it and risking more injury. He took out a couple tables, the brunt force stabbing into his arms and back. He would be bruised but not more seriously injured than that.

It could have been worse—much worse.

He pushed up onto his elbows, glancing back at Avery and Qav, his blaster lost somewhere in the tumble.

Whatever that bastard was doing to her, he had worked his way in deep. How in the blazar were they going to get out of this one? Qav was in complete control here, an army of weaponized Reanges at his back.

Not to mention Avery.

He may not be controlling her directly, but he had done something to her mind and messed with her thoughts. The words coming out of her mouth, the blow she had just dealt him, none of that was her. That flash of silver he had seen in her eyes on the terrace . . .

Avery would never hurt him—never. Finn knew that as well as he knew his own name.

She stared at him from across the square, a fine sweat at her temples. Her hands were shaking, her eyes glazed over and vacant. Numb.

She took a step toward him, arms low and out, bracing for another attack.

"Avery, stop!"

Megan pulled away from the crowd, ripping her arm away from Petra's grasp. She ran to Avery, planting herself directly in the line of fire as a physical barrier in front of Finn.

"This isn't you, Avie." Megan staggered on a sob, hands clasped in front of her chest. She shook her head, and her long blonde hair swayed across her back. "Look at me and tell me this isn't you."

"Maybe you don't know me," Avery countered coldly.

"Of course I do." Megan stepped closer. Some instinct pulled at Finn, warning him she shouldn't. She should keep her distance. "You're my best friend. You're kind and loyal and brave. And you know us—you know Finn. We'd never hurt you, Avery. We're on your side. We've always been on your side—you know that."

"Do I?" Avery scoffed, energy crackling at her fingertips. Finn pushed himself to his knees, halting as Avery's eyes cut to him. "You're just like *him*," she spat. The fury in her words stopped his heart. "Both of you are liars, hiding things from me just because you can. Because you're human. And I'll never be able to trust that. To control it."

Megan frowned. Another step closer. "We're not liars. Qav is filling your head with this—"

"You've all got secrets from me! You're all hiding things from me," Avery accused desperately, her face contorting into a chaotic frown as her eyes snapped to Petra.

Megan faltered.

"All I've ever done since gaining these powers is protect the people I love. And all that seems to keep happening is that I get hurt because of it—stabbed in the back." She looked up at the domed ceiling, her golden eyes wild. Finn winced at the sight. "Why should I even return to Echo if they're going to betray me? It was never my home to begin with. Maybe if Gran had allowed me to claim my powers earlier and opened my eyes to this place, my life would be entirely different. Would be better. I never would have met Finn or you or Petra. It would have saved me a lot of pain."

Megan shook her head fervently. "You don't mean that. Trust *can* be painful, Avery, but it's the only way to love. And I know you love us. *I know it.* As much as we love you."

Avery paused, tapping her palm against her temple, her eyes closing tightly. "Then I'm going to ask you this again. If you love me so much, why are you keeping secrets?"

"I—I'm not." Megan glanced to Petra.

"You are," Avery accused, pointing a livid finger to Petra, electricity crackling on the end, lighting up the air around her. "You and Petra both are. All I've ever done has been for you—for both of you! And this is how you repay me? By hiding things from me and sneaking around behind my back like you think I can't see what's going on? What else are you hiding?"

Petra was already moving, sprinting for Megan as Avery stepped forward, her fist raised and crackling with power. Her face was unrecognizable, distorted and seething and vengeful. It was Avery but not Avery. She was gone.

"Avery, no!" Petra's yell was almost a gasp, filled with terror and fear.

Finn, too, was on his feet, launching forward at Megan, reaching for her, trying to get to her before—

Avery struck her hand down.

The wave of energy slashed across Megan, jerking her head sideways and fissuring throughout her body, carrying her across the square. She slammed into a pile of storage boxes, her body lying still in the mess, a glimpse of her gray dress between metal. She didn't get up.

"No!" Petra screamed, tearing across the pavement to her. She reached Megan at the same time as Finn. "No, no, no," Petra repeated, turning Megan over with infinite care, pulling her into her lap. She cradled her head, hands shaking, wiping at the blood that came away on her fingers, staining Megan's temple a deep red.

Petra trembled, tears sliding down her cheeks, her fear striking Finn as heavily as any physical blow. He had never seen her so unhinged. So vulnerable.

He dropped to a knee and felt for a pulse in Megan's exposed neck. His composure was shattered. Even his fingers shook. It was there. Faint but steady. He nodded to Petra. "She's alive."

Linderly knelt beside them, clasping Megan's hand to her chest. Tai was with her. He placed a hand on Petra's shoulder. Linderly was frightened, caving in on herself. He caught sight of Markes in the crowd, limping to Nova with blood and grime spread over his face.

Enough. Finn had had enough.

He stood up, ignoring a twinge in his leg as he faced Avery. There it was again—he was certain this time: A strike of silver cut through the golden depths of her eyes.

Qav. He had a hold of her.

"Avery." His chest rose and fell rapidly. "Don't do this. Don't make us choose."

"Make *you* choose?" She laughed. "It always has to be them, right? You said that to me yourself! You've already chosen. I've always known it would never be me."

Finn went still. He watched her face work through emotions. He saw her struggle against it. There were tears in her eyes despite her words and her anger. She was fighting—he could see it inside her. He could feel her heart beneath it all, tied to his own.

"Fight it, sweetheart," he begged, stepping forward.

She braced herself and lifted her hand.

Finn stopped. He couldn't put the others at risk, not like this. He had already lost Grigg today, and nearly Markes along with him. He didn't know how he would tell the others. Didn't know how to. . . . They were stuck.

This was a situation that had no solution. No exit. His chest was a vacuum, the pressure collapsing over his heart until he thought it might burst.

Finn couldn't save Avery from this.

She would kill him if he tried, and take the others out with him. If he let that happen, she would never recover from it. It would break her a million times worse than losing Fiora ever had.

But the humans on Echo, the thousands of innocent lives depending on them . . . . There was still a chance to stop that. Even without Avery, they had to try. For her sake, they had to try.

But they needed to save the Gate first, and who knew how much time was left? Linderly had said there was a countdown—it could already be too late. Nick's sudden appearance trying to drag him away couldn't have been a good sign. They were out of time.

Finn had to make a choice. Now.

"Dammit, Avery!" Finn bit out, his eyes stinging. His world was breaking, his stomach turned to rock. "Don't make me do this."

"You're already doing it," Avery cried, shaking her head. Tears poured down her face now, and Finn shattered.

He glanced at Qav, who watched them. That bastard smiled. Finn's hand fisted at his side until he saw spots.

"Just leave." And Avery turned on her heel. Like he wasn't worth the effort of more words. She disappeared into the crowd, taking Finn's heart with her.

He didn't know how he stayed on his feet. His limbs were so heavy, they would have dragged down the moon. But he was numb and somewhere far away, watching himself as he stared at the spot where Avery had left him.

And he felt nothing. He was empty and hollow and hauntingly cavernous.

"Rem," Qav said sharply, the man in question appearing at his side. Even he was dirty, his striped suit torn at the shoulder. As though he had fought, too. Maybe he had. "See to it that they are taken to their ship. I want them out of here by nightfall."

And then he turned to follow Avery, disappearing after her.

"Are you going back home? Through the Gate?"

The question came from behind him, and Finn turned. It was Bedria. She stood beside her sister, hand in hand, that rat pet perched on her shoulder.

Finn said nothing. He didn't trust himself to speak.

"We're going with you." Bedria's eyes were fierce.

He nodded, a single short movement. The air had turned to lead, heavy and dense in his lungs.

Petra stood up, holding Megan in her arms. Her blue brows were drawn low. "We're not staying here, either."

"Me neither," Linderly said. "I've had enough of this place, I think. It's not so much like home after all."

"I'm staying." Nova had reached them. Her words cemented to the ground. Markes was beside her, sobbing silently as Linderly took his hand. "You told us to look out for her, remember? To be there for her when you couldn't be. Well, I'm not going back on that promise. And I'm not going to give up on her."

"I'm not giving up," Finn snapped, having found his voice.

"Of course you're not." She laid a hand on his arm. "But you can't stay here. Someone has to stop Leviathan and keep that blazing Gate from blowing up. And I'll take care of our girl. I'll do what I can from here to help."

Finn's throat worked, and his eyes welled. He had to tell her. He had to let her know. The words were bile in his throat. "Grigg. He was—"

Nova shook her head once, squeezing his arm to stop him. "I think I know. But not yet—I'm not ready yet."

Finn cleared his throat, then nodded. He looked at what was left of their crew—the few they had added to it and remembering the ones they had lost. Their family was broken.

"Then let's go." His words sounded alien to his own ears.

And when he walked away, he didn't look back.

CHAPTER FIFTY

Avery felt nothing.

There was an emptiness, a cavernous void expanding in her chest as she peered out over the lake toward Sanctum, sitting on the window seat of Qav's living room. It was the same room where they had all been together only days before. The same room where she had sworn to stop Klein's plans.

She had been so fervent then, so enraged and determined. But now . . . now all she felt was a heavy shadow. A disinterest that permeated through her very soul, its gravity dragging her down into the earth itself.

And she was tired. Too tired to care anymore.

What Qav offered, his perspective on their place in the world, was a relief. Like he had seen her drowning beneath the weight of that responsibility and thrown a lifeline, a refuge from those unrelenting waves. He was right. She didn't belong in the water, beneath that emotion and pain and grief. She was above it.

They had left her. Finn had left her.

She bit the inside of her cheek and tasted blood.

But she had wanted it—she had told him to leave. Hadn't she? *Yes.* Yes, in that moment, she had.

A throbbing pang pulsed behind her eyes, and she closed them, pressing her fingers against her lids, trying to dull the pain.

She couldn't even tell what she wanted anymore.

Any attempt to sort through her feelings, to dig into her memories, resulted in a massive headache that threatened to bring her to her knees. The patched-up wound in her side was nothing in comparison, that gash only a dull ache against the constant pounding in her head.

But she knew one thing for certain with a clarity that astonished her.

She was angry.

That icy rage was fixed upon her heart, a safety vest that she clung to and kept her afloat.

"Are you okay?" Nova asked quietly, setting down a mug of tea on the windowsill.

Avery didn't open her eyes, and she didn't answer. Nova. She still had Nova. At least one person hadn't left her.

"Must be the blood loss. That was one hell of a gash in your side," Qav answered flippantly from across the room. "It would be convenient if you could learn to heal yourself."

"I told you before, I don't know how I do it."

"Well, we've got plenty of time to figure it out." Qav leaned back in his chair, crossing a leg over his knee as he unwrapped a candy and popped it into his mouth. He gestured to Ennis. "Do we have a report on the damages yet? I'd like to begin plans for rebuilding as soon as possible. Gather a team."

"Already on it," Ennis replied, perching on the edge of the couch.

Syla stood near the corner, her focus on Sanctum, lost in thought.

"And can someone tell me why I spent millions of dollars on security protocols only for it to fail? I want to know how they got in, and whatever we're spending on security, double it."

Ennis nodded. "Understood."

"If Rem is right and the Gate really is going down in the next forty-eight hours, then we'll need to make sure our borders are secure. The surface world is going to get nasty, and quick."

Something stuttered in Avery's veins at his words. She had nearly forgotten the countdown Linderly found just before the attack. She hadn't realized it was so soon. Two days. Or less, if they had already lost so much time.

"So we're going to let it happen, then?" Syla finally spoke, turning to the room.

"It won't make a difference to us either way," Qav countered, dipping his chin until a few loose strands of silver hair spilled over the slate gray of his shirt. "Everything we've built is here. Everything we have—everything that matters."

"But we always said we'd go back," Ennis pointed out delicately, her gaze bouncing off Syla. "You always said that once things slowed down, we'd offer it as an option to those living here. That was our goal. To restore the balance. To give them that choice."

A muscle ticked in his jaw, eyes flashing. "With Klein out of the picture, and the Gate sealed, Alex is next in line to lead the human government. With her and the others in our pocket, we will be able to create a new world. One where we don't have to hide beneath the surface. Where we can expand Sanctum across the globe. And with Avery"—his eyes slid to her, a smile tugging at his lips—"no one can challenge us. Not even the Federation. Or whatever's left of it after all this."

"But Earth is dying," Nova said, her words unusually soft.

Avery looked to the floor.

"She's right," Ennis agreed. "There won't be a globe to spread across if it's uninhabitable."

Qav waved an elegant hand. "Then we'll spread across the stars. We've lived beneath the surface for more than a decade. I think we can manage the challenge of a few space colonies."

"But Qav—"

"Enough," he snapped. Ennis glanced at Syla again. "Don't worry about things that haven't happened yet. Besides, the others may prevent it entirely. Either way, it's out of our hands."

That's right—the others. And Finn.

Something stirred in her belly, a low tug, the edge of pain. Petra was gone and—Megan.

Megan.

Something had happened to her. Hadn't it? Avery's stomach dropped. Something she had done. Something bad. What was it?

What was it?

She needed to remember something—something important. It was there, hovering just out of reach. Avery grasped for it, the memory slipping through her hold the harder she tried. Like a dream teasing the edges of her mind.

Why had they left? Finn and the others were gone, but why had they left? Avery couldn't remember.

Hadn't she known just moments ago? But it was gone—it was all gone. She couldn't remember anything.

Pain stabbed her skull, and Avery grimaced. She must have made a sound because Nova placed a gentle hand on her arm.

That tug beneath her ribs pulsed, pulling at the center of her being. That thread that connected her to something dear, something irreplaceable, was being stretched beyond its limit. It was drawn tight and in danger of snapping.

What would happen when it did?

Qav suggested she go lie down, and Avery let Nova lead her from the room.

Yes, sleep sounded good. She would feel better when she awoke. She would remember once she had rested. She was just drained from the battle and her wounds.

Even as she fell onto the bed, her eyes closing as she succumbed to the demands of her mind and body, Avery could hear a voice somewhere deep within. Small and weak and quiet, but still there—still present beneath the impermeable emptiness.

And it screamed.

CHAPTER FIFTY-ONE

"How is she?"

Petra looked up as Finn entered the med bay. Her throat closed up at the pain she saw in his face. She squeezed Megan's hand.

There was no sign of his humor there. No trace left of him at all.

She knew how he felt. He was fractured. It was enough that they were still breathing.

She let out a shuddering sigh, clinging to the facts as she updated him. "Her arm was broken, but I've set it and reinforced the bone with a nano splint. The gash on her head was superficial, and no internal bleeding, but she has a concussion. I gave her a patch for the pain."

"She hasn't woken up yet?" His voice almost cracked.

Petra couldn't speak. She merely shook her head.

What Avery had done . . . Petra wasn't sure she'd be able to forgive her. Even if Qav had been inside her head, he hadn't been controlling her outright. He may have manipulated her thoughts, but Avery's actions had been her own.

Finn had begged her to fight it. Even Petra had seen her try. They could see the way Avery struggled against Qav's hold. But it hadn't been enough.

Avery hadn't tried hard enough. She had failed them—all of them.

In the seconds she had once Avery raised her arm against Megan, Petra had felt her world shift. Megan mattered to her. Deeply, irrevocably. She was already half in love with her.

A human.

It was almost comical. In fact, if anyone had told her this would happen a year ago, even six months ago, she would have laughed in their face. And probably punched them for the insult.

But when she saw Megan lying there in that metal, her body unmoving and still . . . Petra gritted her teeth at the memory, her heart skipping a beat.

She had already made her choice.

Finn moved farther into the room, fiddling with the supplies laid out on the cot across from Megan. The soft clicking of the med tubes he touched was the only sound beyond the hum of the engines.

He wanted to say something. He tried to find the words. This had to be a first. Finn's smart-ass mouth was the thing she liked least about him. But seeing him this way, struggling to speak—she liked that even less.

"Oh good, you're both here." Linderly saved them from further awkward silence as she peeked her head in the door. Tai kept close behind.

Her brother's eyes softened on her, then trailed to where she held Megan's hand. For the first time, Petra realized Tai wasn't a little kid anymore. He saw more than she realized. Remembered more than she knew.

"Any luck?" Finn crossed his arms over his chest.

Linderly let out a tired sigh. "I was able to isolate the code controlling the countdown order, but unfortunately, there is no way I can manipulate it remotely."

"What does that mean?" Finn asked, too sharply.

Linderly flinched.

"It means she can't stop it unless we get to the source," Tai explained, glaring at Finn.

Petra's muscles tensed, her pulse stopping. "The Port Station."

Linderly met her gaze. "Exactly."

"So what," Finn scoffed, "we have to break in and get you access to their control room? How hard can that be?"

"It won't be that simple," Petra countered. "Their security will have doubled since we were there last time. There's no way the four of us can handle it. Not without her."

Finn was quiet. He stared at the wall screen, watching the rhythms of Megan's monitors dance on squiggly blue lines.

Tai cleared his throat. "We already sent the codes to the others."

"You what?" Finn sneered.

Linderly studied her feet. "I—I sent the codes to Rem."

"What blazing good is that gonna do? You think Qav will let them leave—will let them stop this? It's probably what he's wanted all along."

"Finn," Petra said sharply. He only glared at her, unused to being chastised by her. "Contacting them is worth a shot. Even if we wanted to try this alone, we don't have time. We have to make a choice. And we all know it."

"Earth or Echo?" Linderly's question was barely more than a whisper. Tai moved closer to her.

Finn's breath grew heavy. "I won't abandon her." His voice did crack then, and he turned away.

"We can't leave Echo to Leviathan. She is going to kill those humans, Finn," Petra stated. It was fact, whether they wanted to admit it or not. "If we stay here—if we wait to see if we can somehow stop the destruction of the Gate—then we are as good as condemning them to death. Are you seriously telling me you're willing to take more risks? After the galactic disaster we just went through?"

When Finn turned back to them, his eyes were red. "There has to be another way. If we go through and that Gate explodes—"

"There isn't another way," Petra ground out. His eyes clashed against hers, the grief in them identical to what she felt inside. It was enough to make her voice shake as she added, "I know you, Finn. If those humans die, their lives will be on your head. And you'll never forgive yourself."

Finn looked away, barely holding himself upright. He ran a hand through his unkempt hair. "He may have taken Avery, but I trust Nova. If Rem can be convinced to help, she'll make it happen. I'll try and send her a comm—we'll have to pray it gets through."

"You need to trust Avery, too." Linderly stepped toward Finn.

"When she first came to the Origin, she adapted to it, bending us all to her will without force. And she defied Leviathan, something I didn't think was possible. She is stronger than you give her credit for, Finn. She *will* find a way to break free of him."

Petra looked down at Megan, her nose prickling. Finn was silent.

"She will," Linderly repeated in a whisper.

Petra wanted to believe her. And two weeks ago, she would have. But now . . . after what Avery had done to Megan . . . .

There were limits to her power—a danger in her gift that Petra had never acknowledged.

She prayed to the moons that Linderly was right. Avery was more than Petra could have ever dreamed, a bright star that had brought direction and hope into their dark world, freeing them from the shadows of oppression and fear.

But if she couldn't free herself, then there would be no going back. They would have to stumble on blindly without her somehow.

And Avery would be lost to them forever.

Finn stared at the Gate before him, hovering just outside the nose of the ship, a wide ring beckoning him to the other side of the universe. There were no restrictions passing through from this side beyond his credentials. With a pass of his clearance badge over the reader, they could be through the portal and into the next galaxy before anyone was the wiser.

The Port Station loomed ahead, the large metallic structure floating miles away that monitored the Gate traffic. It was hard to imagine that he had met Avery there, all those months ago. He had nearly died there.

There was still a chance.

He could change course right now and just go for it, planning be damned.

But if things went wrong . . .

Petra's words echoed through his brain. All those lives, all those deaths, would be his fault. Was Finn willing to gamble on it this time?

No.

His answer was swift and final and immovable.

He had the opportunity to do something for the humans left on Echo, and he had a crew willing to help him try. He wouldn't leave them to suffer certain death if there was a way to prevent it. It was his duty. It always had been.

It had been his father's duty, too. And Nick's. And they had both failed.

The man who raised him—the father Finn loved—would have never worked with Klein.

Maybe Nick was right, and Finn didn't truly know who their father was. The image he treasured in his mind was infused with a particular infallibility. He had been strong and honorable, everything Finn hoped to be. Never once would the father he knew second-guess himself. Never once would he have made a mistake.

Which was stupid—no one was that perfect. No one.

Not even Avery.

That tether that he felt beneath his ribs, connecting them, tying them to one another, was frayed. They had tested it, maybe beyond its limits. But still it pulled deeply on him, leaving his chest sore. Raw and open and bleeding.

His eyes drifted beyond the Station, to Earth.

It always looked so small from space, so insignificant. And Finn had always craved that distance. No matter what he saw or experienced on the surface of the two planets, when he was this far away, he could focus on the bigger picture. He could always find a solution.

But this time was different.

He couldn't see an alternative path to what they were about to do. And even if there was an option, Finn wasn't sure he'd have the gumption to pursue it. He had finally gambled more than he could back up. The price had been too high. And he had already paid enough.

Grigg was gone. And Avery soon would be, too.

But Linderly was sure she'd free herself, was sure she'd find a way. There was some solace in her confidence, and Finn would cling to that.

Avery's fate was in her own hands, just as she had always wanted.

Finn typed in coordinates on the monitor, initiating the launch sequence that would activate the Gate. There was no turning back now.

Avery *would* find a way. She had before, and she would again. Finn steeled himself as he piloted the ship forward, suddenly shaking. She would find a way back to him. She would—he had to believe that.

Earth blurred away into a smear of blue as they took off, launching into the folds of the universe on the wings of this final leap of faith. Something ripped away inside of him, the pain visceral enough that he cried out as the planet disappeared before him, leaving him clutching desperately at his chest.

They broke through on the other side, and Finn gasped, struggling to catch his breath. His body hurt, agony spreading outward from his torso like the gravitational waves in the wake of an exploding star. He didn't think he could bear it.

"Finn," Markes said sharply, his warning chasing away the edge of Finn's anguish.

"Oh no," Linderly rasped. Her hand grabbed Tai's beside her.

Finn looked up.

And whatever remained of his heart stopped entirely.

CHAPTER FIFTY-TWO

A very lurched up in bed, a searing pain tearing inside her chest, robbing her of breath until she gasped, sheets tangled between sweaty fingers. Her inhales were a repetitive hiss in the night, air whooshing out through her teeth.

Finn.

Finn—Finn—Finn.

He was gone. She was alone. Her heart bled, filling the empty cavity within her chest until she thought she would drown in it. That warmth she carried there had been taken from her, stripped away in a violent lurch that left her half alive.

Avery covered her face with shaking hands, fighting to control herself.

She had done this—he had left because of her.

She was so close to remembering. It was there—right there—just beyond her reach. If only she could . . .

She poured over her memories of the last few days, most of them too blurry to be of any real use.

No—not blurry but fractured. Out of order.

Something glimmered on the edges, a flash of silver that carried the brisk touch of frost. She reached out, testing where she had felt it, looking for that same glint.

Avery gasped aloud as pure ice speared through her mind, driving a headache straight to the backs of her eyes.

It was the same—this pain and the headaches she had been having. Every time she had tried to make sense of her place here and her next steps, that pain had driven into her, a barrier she couldn't cross.

She pushed through it this time, testing the limits of that silver coldness threading through her memory. She grabbed its frigid tether, just like the Reange minds she once controlled so easily. She wrapped her power around the ice, holding fast. And it began to unravel beneath her touch, a glittering thread coming loose of its seam.

Avery jerked, following the silver trail, infusing it with the heat of her own power until it melted away from her entirely. Memories locked into place, the icy pain dissolving until there was none left, until Avery could feel herself again.

At last she was alone in her mind.

The headache had ceased, leaving her with only clarity, crystal and pure and absolute.

Her eyes widened in the darkness of the room, nothing but shadows lingering on the expensive furniture, curling at the windows.

Megan. *Megan.*

It came crashing back to her. Avery remembered what she had done, only hours before, could see Megan's lifeless body strewn into the ground. Could see Petra kneeling over her, crying. Could see Linderly watching her, fear in her eyes.

Avery clenched her hands to her chest, crying out in silent agony as her unshed tears finally surfaced. They poured down her face, sobs racking her body as she cowered in the bed, curling over herself, trying to contain the pain.

That agony condensed within her, bringing along a surge of power that blossomed in the pit of her belly, feeding on her misery, leaving her raw. But as it fed on her emotion, it offered an outlet, taking away the stinging bite of anguish that threatened to extinguish her.

And so she fed it, pouring all of her guilt, all of her pain, straight into the source, welcoming the chaos, like radiation consuming her, poisoning her, swallowing her whole.

"Avery!" Nova burst into the room, the door slamming against the wall as she yelled, an arm held up over her face. Syla was close behind her, her mouth open in shock.

They were far away. Below her.

Avery realized she was no longer in the bed but hovering above it, suspended in the air as the lights flashed, throwing them in and out of darkness. Her arms were outspread, a violent wind whipping through the room, objects swirling around her like a tempestuous storm of destruction, and Avery was its center.

Finn's face appeared in her memory, broken and painful, his beautiful eyes full of tears. Every trace of laughter was gone. Every sign of the man she loved had been stripped away from him. And she had caused it.

She had told him to leave. She had told him she didn't trust him. She had hurt him. And Megan. Avery bit down on her fist, the look Petra had given her driving a hole through her gut.

Qav.

Qav had done this.

There was no mistaking that silver thread she found lingering throughout her mind. He had wormed his way inside her head, planting his blazing thoughts straight into her consciousness. She could see every manipulation, remember every thought that hadn't been her own.

Nausea roiled through her, threatening to come up her throat.

And so she screamed, a wailing howl of pure hatred erupting from her throat like a wounded animal. She hated Qav—and herself for being duped by him. The sound of her cry carried through the house and farther, through the open windows and out across the water, drifting to the city itself.

Avery followed the echoes of her scream, sending her mind out along the water. Something broke inside her, along with her heart, a wall cascading down around her as she finally opened her eyes.

She could feel them—all of them.

The Reanges throughout Sanctum called out to her, living beings that were both a part of her and not. Some were still awake, celebrating their life, others were lamenting their dead, watching over their wounded. And some were sleeping in their beds, grateful that the day was finally over. But she could feel them: their relief, their sorrow, their joy, their pain . . . .

She could feel it all.

Tears poured down her face as she laughed, a sorrowful cackle that cracked on lamenting sobs. She was finally whole—finally free. Her shoulders racked as she welcomed the presence of every Reange beneath the dome, taking their feelings inside of herself and treasuring them, the joy along with the sorrow.

She would never take this for granted again—never regret her powers or her gifts. They were a part of her, for better or worse. Not to be used lightly, and certainly not to be exploited. They were hers and hers alone.

Her tears dried as she came back into herself. Awareness returned in degrees while she lowered her body to the ground, her feet touching the stone in a soft descent. But she kept the storm up around her, relishing in the feel of her power restored, needing an outlet for her rage, that familiar white-hot electricity that was all her own.

She had allowed Qav to take advantage of her and completely overestimated her own ability to judge him or remain unaffected by his power. She should have welcomed the help Finn had offered. The others, too. They had all tried to tell her, to warn her. And she hadn't listened.

She was so sure of her gifts, so enamored of her own ability, that she had been oblivious to her weaknesses.

And Qav had known that—had seen it. He had used it to his advantage.

A quick sweep of the building told Avery he was not on the mansion's island, nor were Ennis or Rem, or any other Reanges.

Good. That would make the next part easier.

"Avery, don't!" Syla cried. She reached out for her, but Nova held her back.

Avery flung her hands out at her sides, letting that condensed ball of energy within her go, the surge that followed flowing outward in a wave of destruction that took out everything in its path.

She shielded Nova and Syla, encompassing them in a bubble of protection as her energy tore through the walls of the mansion, ripping through stone and glass and steel, demolishing it as though it were made of nothing but sand.

Avery flung her head back, letting out another scream of rage as she poured everything she had into that blast.

And when she was done, there was nothing left around them but rubble.

An aftershock billowed out across the water, the wave traveling swiftly over the lake, surging onto the docks where they had fought only hours earlier. It hit the bright lights of Sanctum, shuttering the city into darkness.

She felt the cold brush of Qav's presence seconds before his black ship arose from the water, nearly invisible in the blackness of an underground city without power.

As though her thoughts activated it, generators kicked in and the backup power was restored, bathing the city in the green lights of an emergency system. The false moon in the sky powered on, the constellations of stars winking back into existence, casting shadows on the dark lines of the ship as it descended, illuminating the debris that remained of the mansion below.

The vessel hovered above the courtyard before the docking ramp opened. Qav emerged seconds later, storming down to the ground. Ennis followed him, her face rigid with worry, scanning the damage. Rem took one look at Avery and slowed, lingering on the ramp.

Qav stalked forward without breaking his pace, boots crunching on the shattered remains of his home, his eyes pure silver in the dark.

"Shit," Syla breathed, the single word full of panic.

What have you done? His voice ripped through her mind, confusion and anger clashing against her, pure ice forcing its way into her head.

Avery smiled.

And let him in.

CHAPTER
FIFTY-THREE

Qav realized his mistake as soon as he entered her mind.

Avery felt the second he tried to pull away, but she refused to release him.

This time, she was the one in control.

Avery opened her head to him, embracing the frozen energy that she was now so used to, the presence that had become a natural part of her own thoughts. She brought him into her memories, let him filter through what she had seen and what she knew, luring him deeper until his power was wholly encompassed by hers. She used his own tricks, lacing her energy around him, knotting it until there was no hope of him pulling away.

And then she constricted her grip.

Shock crested over his face, his body stiffening as he halted his approach. He knew what she had done, and there was no avoiding it.

Avery forced her mind out to him in a rush.

The world around them melted away as they both fell into that other place, into the reality that lived within their heads alone. Only it wasn't his mind this time.

It was hers.

There were no carefully crafted fields of lavender, no rolling hills of tall grasses, no gentle breeze or blue skies. In her mind, there was only shadow, only darkness. A vast and endless emptiness that threatened to consume her—and now him.

"What is this place?" he asked shakily, desperate to orient himself.

"Don't you recognize it?" Avery asked, her voice nearly as dark as the void around them. "This is what lies inside of me—this is the cavern you have carved out of my soul."

"This isn't your soul, Avery. It's your fear," he countered, some semblance of his balance returning.

She was on him in the span between heartbeats, her hand at his throat, lifting him above her as he clawed at her fingers. His eyes were twin orbs of silver glowing in the dark, narrowing on her, threatening to wink out entirely in the black.

"My fear?" she sneered, her grip contracting. "*You* brought what I fear most down upon me! You took everyone I've ever loved away from me! And for *what?*" She dropped him, and he sputtered, coughing and gasping for air at her feet. "You think you are so enlightened—that you have everything figured out. Well, I think you're full of shit, Qav. And I'm going to prove it."

She reached into the icy fortress of his mind, breaking his barrier with a mere touch of her power, stepping straight into his memories.

He was crying, begging for the red candies from the street market that had been laid out at just his height, easy for him to reach. They were his favorite, the flavor rich and juicy and sugary sweet. He wanted them.

But Mother said no.

They didn't have the credits, he knew, but he still wanted them. Why didn't he ever get anything he wanted? It wasn't fair.

He was suddenly angry, the emotion crawling over him and lashing outward with . . .

Mother's eyes went blank. She grabbed the bag of the treats from his hands, ringing it up with the seller, handing over the credits, and giving it back to him.

It was hours before she was fully aware again, but by then they were already back home. He had eaten half the bag at once, unable to return it. His stomach had ached for hours. It was then that Qav realized he was different.

She sifted through more, pulling out the ones that were important to him. The ones that meant something. They jumped forward.

Qav looked for the two girls every time they came to the markets. He had run into the one with purple eyes again last week—she was so pretty that it hurt his chest sometimes to look at her. He wanted to see her again, to talk to her this time.

The girls were both orphans, he knew, part of the group of street kids that ran free in the Underground.

Maybe he could help them. Maybe they could be friends. . . .

And another, years later.

He winced, touching his busted lip as he inspected it in the mirror over the sink in the seedy bar he loved.

Syla had nearly beaten him into unconsciousness. She was livid. Ennis and her big mouth. He should have stopped her from saying anything.

Qav supposed he couldn't blame them. He had hidden his powers from them for long enough.

Ennis had been the one to figure it out first—not a huge surprise. She had always been the smartest out of all of them. She had clung to her own education like a lifeline from the horrors of her life.

Qav had never revealed his secret to anyone. If his parents suspected, he did his best to alter their memories so they would never know.

He wasn't stupid.

He had heard the stories of the So's back on Echo, the way the refugees spoke of them, like they were some kind of saviors. He knew what having that power would mean. What his parents would expect. They were such worshippers of the old ways, they'd put him on the first ship back, desperate to sacrifice him at the altar of their cause.

Qav didn't want to save anybody. He liked Earth. It was his home—the only home he had ever known.

And he would live his life for himself.

But each year, his powers became more difficult to control. And he had finally slipped, big enough that Ennis had noticed.

Honestly, he was surprised she hadn't figured it out sooner. Was surprised she didn't remember those early days with . . . No, he didn't think of that—he wouldn't.

He'd have to buy Syla something expensive to get her forgiveness for this one. Maybe that laser dagger she'd been eyeing the week before . . . .

Avery paused, the memory fading away as Qav fought against her to maintain control of his mind. She bore down on him, stilling his protests, digging deeper, searching for another.

For the memory he kept hidden, even from himself.

For the one he refused to look at, even as it sat in the center of them all, like a coveted treasure he dared not touch for fear that it would bring everything crashing down around him.

He was drenched in the rain, but Qav couldn't feel anything beyond the emptiness that had ripped through him as she died, as her life force had floated away into the dark, where he couldn't reach.

She was gone. Veena was gone.

She lay there in the street, her body lifeless, those gorgeous amethyst eyes devoid of any light within. She was dead, and it was his fault, and a part of him had died along with her. That emptiness had shredded a part of his soul, taking it with her as she went.

A dry sob racked his body as he fought for air.

Movement drew his eye, and he whirled, body tensing, ready to fight.

No—not a threat—Ennis.

Ennis!

No . . . no!

Qav ran to her, dropping to his knees in the puddle where the small girl lay, looking so much younger than her ten years. Blood matted her dark hair, the same shade as Veena's, turning the water red beneath her, a vicious gash running down the side of her face. She was unconscious but breathing. He pulled her into his lap, hugging her to his chest, rocking against the steady downpour.

His power was a curse. He knew that now.

It had taken the person he loved most in this world. It had taken a part of himself. He would never forgive that.

He would never lose control again.

He may have failed Veena, but he would never do so with her sister. Ennis would be safe. He would keep them safe this time—always.

Avery released Qav, withdrawing her power and letting him go, returning to her body and the world around her. The lights were turning back on in the city, blues and whites filling up the darkness of the dome as it twinkled back to life.

Qav was on his knees, eyes squeezed shut. His chest rose and fell in rapid repetition, his breath harsh in the quiet that surrounded them. Syla knelt beside him with a hand on his shoulder.

Ennis stood farther back. She tore her eyes away from him to meet Avery's.

"You are a hypocrite, Qav," Avery said, turning her attention back to him. "All this talk about superiority and control when it's really just to save your ass. You're afraid of your own power, of the toll it takes, of the way it influences those you love." He peeled his eyes open, silver glinting at her through narrow lids. "And you do love, Qav. I've seen it. You love them." She nodded to his companions. "You chose your family—just like I chose mine. And I will do everything in my power to protect them and the things they hold dear."

She lifted her body into the air, propelling forward, then lowered to the ground before him. Her next words were as cold as the energy Qav possessed. "If you ever—*ever*—try to use me that way again, I swear to the moons that I will make you regret it. And I won't just stop with making you relive bad memories. I'll make it count."

Avery held his gaze for a moment longer before she started walking to the ship that remained open behind them, coating her bare feet with a light layer of energy to protect them from the sharp rubble underfoot. Nova was suddenly beside her, head held high, pride emanating from her in a warm, effervescent glow.

They reached the ramp, and Rem scrambled down to the island, eager to get out of their way. Avery almost laughed.

"I'm taking your ship," she tossed over her shoulder. Then quietly to Nova as they ascended, "Can you fly this thing?"

Nova's voice was scratchy as she replied, "I'll wing it."

Avery didn't spare a backward glance to Qav, leaving him on his knees in the ruin she had left of his life.

The bridge of Qav's ship was just as dark and sleek as the first time they had entered it, but the impression was wholly different. As soon as they stepped foot across the threshold, grief slammed into Avery, the intensity so deep that tears sprang to her eyes, her chest seizing.

Nova.

Avery looked to her friend. She had pulled up short, focused on the couch where they had sat on that trip to the desert. Grigg.

Avery squeezed her eyes shut against the onslaught of pain and dove into Nova's mind. She saw Finn, the agony etched on his face as he tried to tell Nova—the loss. And Markes, eyes red with tears, broken and crying.

And Avery hadn't been there for them. She had dismissed them.

Her fists shook at her sides.

Her inability to let them in—to accept their help—had led to this, and it had nothing to do with her missing telepathy. They had offered, they had tried, and Avery had refused to listen. She had been convinced she could handle it alone.

She had overestimated her power. Again.

And again, she had lost a member of her family.

All of the growth she thought she had learned, all of that power she claimed, and yet she had taken it for granted.

She wouldn't be so foolish a third time.

Avery took in a slow breath, letting go of Nova's grief, pushing it away. Tentatively, she reached out for Grigg, bracing herself for the hollowness that would come. That knowing—the emptiness—the weight she must carry from here on out.

She froze, her head jerking to the windows at the front of the ship.

"Nova." Avery stumbled forward on unsteady feet. "Look."

There, in the middle of the lake, a boat was heading straight for them, its sole rider seated low at the back, his broad silhouette cast blue in the lights of the city.

Nova let out a sob, her shoulders collapsing as she fell to her knees beside Avery, clutching at her thighs.

Grigg. He was alive—and headed straight for them.

Relief crested over Avery in a wave of rapture, and she couldn't tell if it was hers or Nova's. But she wasn't sure it even mattered. She let out a choked laugh, the first real joy she had felt in weeks lighting her from within and soothing the pain that still lingered.

Avery pulled Nova to her feet, wrapping her arms around her in a fierce hug as they cried together, sharing this strange mix of terror and happiness that combusted within their chests, overwhelming them both.

Finn would be euphoric. It was all Avery could think about, all she could focus on.

They had to let him know Grigg was all right. He had to know as soon as possible. That broken look he had given her, the tears brimming in his eyes, the way his face had shattered on those last words she threw at him . . . she had to see him. Had to beg his forgiveness. If he would even speak to her.

She let him leave—let them all leave—to stop Klein alone. To face Leviathan alone.

A part of her knew they had already passed through the Gate. That distance had severed something inside of her, like her connection had severed. They had returned to Echo without her.

Her stomach heaved, shame wriggling its way into the lining of her belly.

She couldn't linger on the feeling, or it would swallow her whole.

If Finn had taught her anything, it was that there was a time and a place for emotion. When they needed to fight, nothing else mattered. Avery would let it go and push forward—for him.

There was still work to be done.

CHAPTER FIFTY-FOUR

Avery felt Grigg reach the island, beckoning him to the ship and preparing him for what state Nova was in. He sprinted up the ramp, not even looking at the others on the island who now crowded around Qav like he was some kind of wounded animal.

And then he was there, lingering just inside the bridge, his broad chest heaving from his mad dash, sporting a black eye and a wicked gash to his head. His once-blue shirt was now stained with grime and blood, and his left sleeve had been ripped away completely. But he was there. He was alive.

He grinned, lopsided and innocent. "What did I miss?"

Nova's tears started again as she covered her face with a hand, grimacing against the emotion that overwhelmed her.

Grigg was there, moving across the room in moments, folding Nova into his arms as she cried. It only took a few seconds for her sobs to quiet, but her breathing remained heavy as he stroked her blonde hair. At last she pulled away, shoving Grigg hard enough that he landed heavily against the couch, barely catching himself.

"Don't you *ever* do that to me again, you incompetent ass."

He chuckled, looking to Avery. "That means she's glad I'm alive, right?"

Avery laughed, wiping at her eyes. "Yes. That's exactly what it means."

His grin softened as he stood. He let out a low whistle, surveying the island from the windows. And what was left of the mansion.

"Damn, Avery. Remind me never to piss you off."

"You should have seen her," Nova said, her voice still shaky. "It was like being inside of a black hole, tearing away at everything in its path. She leveled it in seconds."

"Finn would be laughing his ass off right now," Grigg muttered. "This one might even pull a smile out of Petra."

Avery's heart wrenched.

"We need to get out of here," she said firmly, and threw a wry smile to Grigg. "Any later to the party, and we would have left without you."

He shrugged. "What can I say? My timing has always been impeccable."

Nova snorted.

"So, what was the plan? You were gonna let Nova try to fly this thing?" Grigg laughed.

"Is that funny?" Nova ground out, hands on her hips.

"I know you've never seen tech this advanced. You'd be lucky to get out from under the water, much less the atmosphere."

"Then I guess it's a good thing I'm coming with you."

Ennis stood in the doorway, hands raised in a show of peace. Avery dove into her mind immediately, searching for any sign of Qav, any indication he had sent her.

"I'm here of my own volition," Ennis said quietly, doing her best to keep them calm. "Qav learned a long time ago he couldn't influence us and still keep us around. Syla and I have always been free to make our own choices."

"And your choice is to come with us? Not blazing likely." Grigg moved his body just in front of Avery. Still protecting.

"I'm a Reange, too. I may have grown up on Earth, but it has never been my home. I always dreamed of leaving and returning to Echo." Her pale eyes grew distant, as though lost in the thought of a moment.

Avery conjured an image of that girl in Qav's memory. Veena. She had been Ennis's sister. And she had died the same night Ennis got that scar across her face. Life hadn't been easy for her here.

"I don't want that Gate destroyed any more than you do. And I'm the best pilot you've got."

Grigg let out an amused grunt, crossing his arms over his chest. He nodded to the hallway. "And I suppose she's here for you?"

Ennis whirled, true surprise on her face as Syla joined them. Her features were hard, immovable. One brush against her mind told Avery that her intentions were authentic, too.

"I'm here to repay my debt." Syla met Avery's eyes, always direct. "And because . . . what Qav did . . . it wasn't right. He isn't a bad person. He's just . . . "

"Lost," Ennis finished for her. They shared a look, pained and vast. His actions had wounded them. Leaving him would be even worse. They cared for him. Deeply.

Avery knew he felt the same way. She only hoped he would realize it someday and would open himself up enough to reach his own potential. And when he did, perhaps she could find a way to work with him. Echo needed more than one So', and these people living in Sanctum deserved to decide their own fates.

Avery looked to Grigg and Nova, questioning. *What do you think?* she asked them, opening their minds to one another.

I think we don't really have a choice. Nova shrugged.

Grigg raised a brow. *Nova's got a point. And Ennis is right—we'll need her to fly this thing.*

Avery nodded and looked to Ennis. "Okay. But the first sign of Qav in your heads, and I'm locking you both up in the med bay."

Ennis strode forward, heading for the controls. "We need to contact Cora immediately. A few hours after they left, Linderly sent Rem a comm detailing her findings to approach the issue with the Gate. Stopping Klein is on us now."

"What?" Avery snapped, her eyes narrowing.

"Qav kept it from us, too." Syla followed Ennis, moving to her position at the navigation panel.

"Is that supposed to make us feel better?" Nova ground out. Grigg rested a hand on her arm.

Ennis typed in a call, pulling the ship up and to the water. "Linderly found the vulnerability, but we'll need to be on that Port Station to implement it." The nose of the ship dipped, sending them straight into the dark depths below. Cora picked up the call almost immediately.

"I was wondering when you'd contact me." Cora's dark hair rested in tight curls loose around her shoulders, contrasting with her cream suit. A pair of coding glasses were perched on her nose, like she had been working.

"I assume you've seen the countdown," Ennis replied, cutting straight to the point.

"Of course," Cora confirmed. "My tech makes that Gate function. You can bet I've got a handle on everything that happens in that code."

Avery stepped forward quickly. "Does that mean you can stop it?" Her voice was desperate, all trace of control gone.

"Unfortunately, no. Is that girl with you? The one who got through Klein's tech? It's a similar system, so she should be able to handle it. But you'll have to be—"

"Directly patched in, we know," Ennis interrupted. "There's no way around that? You're saying we have to be *on* the Station to make this happen?"

"Precisely. But you'll need to hard code it on the fly once you're in."

Avery's blood froze. "Are you saying we *need* Linderly?"

Cora frowned. "Is that a problem?"

"She's not here anymore." Ennis saved Avery having to respond. "But she sent us her protocols. Do you think that will be enough?"

Cora let out a long breath through red lips. "Possibly. Can you send them over to me? I'll take a look and make adjustments from here. I'll get back to you."

"How long?" Syla leaned forward into the frame.

"Where is Qav?" Cora frowned, roving over the others in the room.

"Not part of the equation," Syla replied tightly.

Cora's only response was a bemused raising of her eyebrows.

"Give me half an hour."

CHAPTER FIFTY-FIVE

Once they reached space, they hid their vessel on the dark side of the moon, planning their approach to the Port Station. The winking lights of the lunar mines flashed in the darkness, the only sign that anything other than shadow resided on its surface.

As soon as they emerged from the water, Nova had received a comm. Avery had nearly cried when she told them it was from Finn. But all excitement faded as they realized the signal had just been delayed from the distance, and the message was actually hours old.

He hadn't sent a vid, only text, urging her to get the code from Rem. There wasn't much more beyond that. Avery tried not to let it weigh her down. She had to stay strong. There was still a job to finish.

Of course, it would have helped if Rem himself were with them, but he had chosen to stay with Qav. Syla drawled out that she wasn't surprised. Rem was little more than a hired tool, in her opinion.

Ennis remained silent on the matter. Avery suspected it was more complicated than Syla cared to acknowledge.

Their time was running short. The countdown loomed over them, mere hours to spare before the Gate detonated. But Cora had assured them Klein was still on Earth. It didn't make sense for her to cut them off and still be on this side of the universe. Maybe it was all some plan to confuse them.

Regardless, they couldn't take the risk. They would have to storm the Station, make their way to the control center, and input the cancellation codes manually, locking out any external manipulations that could block them in the process. It would be a difficult task to accomplish, even if they had one of their experts with them.

Cora had called them back with her approval on Linderly's bot programming, although she had made a few adjustments. She had also provided them with a direct link to her server, suggesting that once they were in the control room, she could patch in and work on the code remotely.

Until then, whatever coding skills Ennis possessed would have to do.

If only they could send a message through the Gate and get in touch with the other side, then she could let Finn know she was here. She hadn't abandoned them. She was going to stop this from happening. Maybe there would be time in the control room to open the comm channels, and she could tell him that herself.

What it must have taken for him to leave . . . she didn't want to think about it—couldn't.

"Are we ready?" Avery asked, looking around the room to those who were left.

"As we'll ever be." Grigg slid his blaster into the holster at his hip, the black metal resting against the tan of his trousers.

"We get in, we implant the code, and we get out." Avery adjusted the fit of her black jacket, checking her own holsters for her weapons for the hundredth time.

Syla let out a sound of amusement, pulling her hair into a heavy bun that rested on top of her head. A few pink braids fell down the side of her face. "Do things usually go that way for you guys?"

"What way?" Grigg asked.

"According to plan."

He didn't answer, and instead rubbed the back of his neck. Nova cleared her throat.

So Avery replied, "It had better this time."

"Right," Syla said. She strapped her large gun to her back and double-checked the laser knives hidden in her tall black boots.

Ennis cloaked the ship, pulled up and out of the shelter of the moon, then headed straight for the Station. It took them only a few minutes to reach the structure, and Ennis maneuvered around, sailing them smoothly into the hangar that took up the entire bottom level. Qav's tech was more advanced than the scanners the Federation used on their most secure facility. Bizarrely, they were able to slip in entirely undetected.

She was blazing glad she decided to take his ship.

Avery opened the channel of the merge for them as they landed, making their way down the landing ramp and into the hangar itself.

The last time she had been there, Avery had changed irrevocably.

Finn had nearly died—she had nearly died.

Petra had been the one to save the Reanges being held, filing them onto a ship in that exact room, getting them away from danger while Avery went after Finn. While she saved his stupid ass from his own impulsivity. She smiled sadly.

It seemed like an entire lifetime ago. In many ways, it was.

They were into the main corridor before any guards appeared, stealth absolutely essential. Avery wanted to prevent any more casualties at all costs. The sheer body count she had leveled back in Sanctum made her shiver. Qav had been influencing her, certainly, but that rage . . . that power . . . that had been all her own.

She never wanted to use her gift like that again.

They moved swiftly as a unit, working down the white hallways one after the other to clear each new section. Avery vaguely remembered the layout of the building, but they were relying on Petra's knowledge from her time there and the map on her wristport to guide them.

They rounded one of the final corners, with Syla, Ennis, and Nova moving forward to clear it as Avery and Grigg hung back, watching the rear. Her stomach dropped. There were four guards ahead, posted at the main hallway.

They had no option but to engage.

Grigg grabbed her jacket, pulling her entire body to the side as blastfire sounded loudly through the hallways, a burn mark sizzling in the wall where her head had once been. Adrenaline spiked through her body, her eyes connecting with Grigg's before jerking to the two soldiers who had snuck up from behind.

There was no shelter from them, nowhere to hide. The soldiers fired again, and Avery held up a hand this time, deflecting the blasts. The guards paused, giving her an opening.

Avery rushed forward, sliding on the ground toward one to whip her leg around and knock them off their feet. She swiveled on her back, bringing her leg down with added force to the soldier's head, knocking them unconscious. Grigg fired at the other, his body dropping to the ground in a slump. Avery didn't look at his face.

We've got a problem, Syla warned.

Avery could see through her and knew immediately. The other guards were moving.

Alarms sounded through the hall, the shrill noise grating her ears, triggering old wounds. The lights changed to a vibrant red, turning the white hallways into a flashing nightmare.

So much for stealth, Grigg said through the bond, already running to the others alongside Avery.

He was right. They would have to be even faster now that the element of surprise wasn't on their side.

Which was why Avery didn't waste any time.

She ran at a full sprint around the corner, passing Syla and Nova, who covered her with their own weapons, heading straight for the soldiers ahead. She held up her hands, using her power to send a wave of energy that knocked all four of them off their feet. Their blasters fired harmlessly at the ceiling.

We'll take care of them, Nova assured Avery, already pressing forward. *You and Ennis keep pushing. This is our only shot.*

Avery didn't hesitate, trusting them to follow through. If anyone was capable of handling themselves, it was Nova and Grigg. And Syla had proven herself an excellent fighter, better than them both.

They would be able to hold off any other attacks. They needed to keep that hallway clear—it was their only exit back to the hangar.

Ennis pulled up beside her, and they ran together to the control room. Two more guards appeared ahead, large blasters tucked into their shoulders. They didn't hesitate, firing directly at them.

Ennis didn't even slow her pace, her trust absolute.

Avery raised both her hands, erecting a wall of pure energy that would withstand fire from any Fed warship. The blasts hit her shield, the air giving on the impact, making the floor shudder beneath their feet, deflecting away into the wall.

The soldiers had seconds to stagger backward before Avery and Ennis were on them. Avery's single blow knocked one down immediately, while Ennis landed three expertly placed hits to take the other out.

Ennis paused, sharing a smile with Avery before she rushed on ahead.

Avery was beside her in an instant as they reached the final door. It had been locked and fully secured to prevent any kind of attack. Ennis crouched beside the panel, already withdrawing her tablet to hack it.

Some seconds passed, and she was still getting nowhere. The door's coding was more advanced than they had anticipated. Ennis wouldn't be able to get through on her own, and there was no way to contact Cora for aid until they had access to the main control panels.

It's not working. Ennis fixated on her tablet, dark brows drawn down over her eyes. *I'm sorry—I don't think I have the skills to take this one out. They've changed the algorithms.*

Avery nodded, her mind working fast. They didn't have time for this. Any longer and Klein would be able to lock them out, even if they did get into the control room.

Back up, Avery told her, and Ennis complied immediately.

Avery braced her legs, pulling an arm back and infusing it with enough power to take down a building. She controlled her breathing, and on the exhale, let her arm fly, her fist slamming directly into the center of the reinforced white metal. It gave immediately beneath the pressure, crumpling inward and flying across the control room to clash against the blast windows that offered an unobstructed view of the Gate.

I didn't know you could do that, Ennis said appreciatively.

Avery grinned. *I'm full of surprises these days.*

The room contained a few frightened engineers, huddled in a corner, and three other guards beside them. Their eyes widened, pulling away from the crumpled door where it sizzled against the crushed monitors.

Avery held her hands out, letting electricity spark at her fingertips, ready to do battle.

They dropped their guns, backing away to stand with the others. She let out a huff of surprised laughter.

Ennis was already at one of the main computers, plugging her tablet into the hard connection as she typed in commands. Avery stood guard over her, energy sparking and ready, watching the others in the room for any sign of attack. Adrenaline was lightning through her veins, begging to be released. She bounced on her toes, trying to dispel the agitation.

I'm in, Ennis said, her fingers moving furiously across the holo-controls as she worked. She cast the work up to a screen above them, the countdown appearing in an ominous blue time stamp, ticking down. Forty-five minutes. They sure as blazar had cut it close.

I'm connected to Cora now, Ennis said, running swiftly over the code in front of her, watching the tech genius work for them. Thank the moons she had answered and was willing to help. They wouldn't have been able to do this without her.

Avery checked in on the others who were holding off a new surge of soldiers, pushing them farther back down the corridor. If they lost any more ground, their path out would be blocked.

Avery's eyes flickered to the blast door in the control room, near the back. It led to a private docking station—Captain Harding had tried to use it before to escape from her. Before she had slammed him into it, breaking his neck. She wondered if Ennis could remotely pilot the ship to get it around here in time. They should have considered it in their plans, a casualty of haste.

How are we looking? Avery asked. She did her best to shield Ennis from her worry, giving her the space she needed to finish the malware with Cora.

Almost there, Ennis replied, shooting Avery a compressed smile.

It was going to work. It was actually going to work.

She got it! Now I just have to approve the sequence from here! Ennis exclaimed, typing in the final command from the control pad, activating the code.

The Station went dark, the lights crashing as the power source reset.

One of the guards tried to rush them, and Avery flung out her hand, swiping him away with a whip of energy that threw his body against the wall. He lay there motionless and groaning.

"Anybody else want to try?" Avery asked ominously, shifting forward. One of the engineers whimpered.

Avery, look.

She swung her head around. Ennis pointed at the screen.

The countdown had stopped. It flashed once, before an error code appeared, along with a warning that the program had been terminated. Avery let out a tight breath, her heart opening for the first time since she had broken free of Qav.

She smiled, wide and full of hope. *We did it,* she called down the bond to the others. *We actually did it.*

"Great! Now let's get the blazar out of here." Grigg barreled into the control room, Syla and Nova close behind.

"What are you doing here?" Avery asked, panicked. She had been so ecstatic about the success of the code that she forgot to check in with them. "We need that hallway open!"

There were too many, Syla added, kneeling at the entrance, ready to defend the narrow space. *Way more than the specs led us to believe. They've been reinforced.*

Avery frowned. Klein had expected them or had at least prepared for them in some fashion. She shouldn't have been surprised after that debacle in the desert. Even if her authority had been limited, she had still prepared for an attack.

Shit, Avery cursed. They weren't out of danger yet. If Klein trapped her here, the results for the peace treaties could be catastrophic.

You've got that one right, Grigg agreed, taking a place beside Syla and firing off a few shots as more soldiers approached.

Can't you hold them off? Syla asked Avery, taking down two more.

I don't have enough control of my power to keep it contained. If I tried to take out that many, I might end up blowing the whole Station apart, including us. You saw what happened in the desert.

Avery grimaced, her mind working through options. She could surrender herself, she supposed. If she took off into the approaching guards, she could possibly distract them long enough that the others could get away. It could work.

No way, Nova said, leveling her with a dark stare. *I know that look, and you're not going off alone again. We do this together or not at all.*

Avery's nose tingled as she held Nova's gaze. She nodded.

Avery moved to the hallway, raising her hands in front of her, ready to go down swinging. They had stopped the Gate from being destroyed, and that was all that truly mattered. If Klein took her prisoner again, then so be it. She could reason her way out of this in the courts.

She lowered her chin, channeling her power as she charged forward.

A twinge of ice brushed against her mind, testing the merge. Avery tensed, halting as her eyes glued to the windows behind them.

A dark ship emerged, pulling around in front of them and heading straight for the side dock. Its cloaked windows dissolved as it passed close, revealing a silver-haired pilot.

Qav.

He had come for them after all.

CHAPTER FIFTY-SIX

Well, don't just sit there gawking, Ennis. Activate the docking sequence. His words were sharp and cold in their minds, outside of the merge but still able to pass his own thoughts through.

Ennis jumped into action, typing in a new command as Qav sidled the ship up beside the control room. The door hissed as the air lock activated, sliding open to reveal the dark interior of his ship, beckoning them to safety.

They didn't waste any more time, running for the vessel as fast as their legs would carry them, leaving the Station behind. As soon as they crossed over the threshold, Syla slammed her hand against the control panel, and the hatch locked shut behind them.

Avery leaned against the wall of the ship, her shoulder digging into the metal as she let go of the merge, leaving them all to their own heads. Grigg started to laugh, and it was contagious. Avery joined in with Nova soon behind her until they were a trio of lunatics sobbing from hysterics on the floor.

Ennis was grinning as she walked to the bridge. Syla rolled her eyes.

When they entered the bridge a few minutes later, Avery pointedly ignored Qav. But Ennis's eyes were red, and Syla's were distinctly glassy. She didn't want to know what had been said in their time alone.

Rem stepped forward sheepishly, brushing hair off his face. "Qav thought you might need our help—my help, I mean—with the coding. But it seems Ennis handled herself just fine in there."

"We have Cora to thank for most of it," Avery explained, her voice cold. "But looks like we needed you guys after all."

"Your timing is impeccable," Grigg drawled.

When Qav finally spoke, his voice was low and lilting. "I think we all know you would have figured out some way to get out of there. But I wasn't about to let you have my ship."

Avery scoffed. "Just when I thought you were going to be decent and—"

Something beeped on the monitor, signaling an incoming comm, and Avery halted, her heart in her throat as she saw the name and the smiling face in the ID picture.

Finn.

But he was on the other side of the universe. Wasn't he? The comms were blocked through the Gate, and they didn't have time to do anything to fix—

"A little surprise for you," Ennis said, smiling as she ran to the controls. She had removed her jacket, and Avery caught sight of another long scar slashed across her left shoulder blade, extending from beneath her green tank. "I opened the communication blockade while I was in there. So you could let them know—so you could be the one to tell them we stopped it."

Avery couldn't speak, shocked by the gesture and its thoughtfulness.

Her stomach was in knots, and her eyes were bouncing off Grigg and Nova. What would she say to him? She ran a hand over her hair, pulling the braid around to the side of her shoulder. She probably looked like absolute death.

Her breath was short, and Avery paused, taking a deep draw of air to steady her nerves.

She looked to Ennis. "Patch him through."

It was loud, so loud that they all winced, their bridge filled with the sounds of warning alarms rioting through Finn's ship.

And when she turned back to the screen, when she saw him, her heart stopped.

Blood poured down the side of his face, and he was sweating, covered in some kind of smoke residue, an absolute mess. The image flickered in and out on the spotty connection, and Finn went with it.

Avery stepped forward, tensing as she braced for a fight, ready to defend him.

"Hello?!" Finn yelled at the monitor. Something exploded down the hallway, and he ducked, glancing behind him. "Avery? Avery, are you there?"

"I'm here," Avery said, barely above a whisper. He didn't respond, and she stepped close to the screen, repeating herself, louder this time, "I'm here—I'm right here, Finn. What's happening? What's wrong?"

His eyes locked on her, that familiar muted blue going wide as he realized she was herself again. She had no idea how he could tell, but he knew. As soon as he saw her. He knew.

"Avery." His voice was pained, and his face equally so. His eyes welled as he laughed, wiping at his nose. "I hope you showed that bastard what real power looks like."

"You know me. I handed his own ass to him." She laughed, too, tears surfacing. She choked on her words. "Finn, I'm—I'm so sorry about what I did. The things I said to you—I didn't mean it. Any of it."

He gave her a crooked smile, that dimple deepening in his cheek, making her stomach flip. "Never doubted you for a second, sweetheart. Well—maybe a few of 'em. But I knew you'd figure it out—you're my girl."

"Finn!" Petra yelled from the doorway, a blaster in her hand and blood coating the side of her arm beneath her dirty shirt. "We're out of time. We've got to go—now!"

Avery frowned, true panic surging through her. She tried to see around Finn.

"Finn, what's happening? Wait there—we'll come through and get you—"

"No!" he said forcefully, his eyes going wide with terror. "Stay away from the Gate, Avery. Do you hear me?"

"No, Finn, it's all right," she assured him, confusion amplifying the dread that was building inside of her. She glanced at the huge ring still floating in the distance, their only portal to Echo's galaxy. "We stopped it. I told you, we stopped the countdown."

"Finn!" Petra cried sharply, disappearing down the hallway. Finn was already on his feet, backing away to follow her. He was limping.

"Avery, we're out of time. Are you up there now? Are you near it? Moons above, get as far away as possible—"

"But we stopped it, we—"

"Leave! Get the blazar out of there!" he screamed, pleading with her, tears running down his face. "Avery, whatever happens, whatever comes next, just know that I love you. I've always—"

The screen jumped, freezing before going dark.

Avery looked to Ennis, panic causing her power to surge out of control. The lights flickered. "What happened? Did the connection cut out? Get him back! We have to go through. We have to help him!"

"You heard what he said," Qav reasoned dismally beside Ennis. "Get us out of here," he commanded.

"Where?" Ennis asked.

"As far away as possible—"

"No!" Avery said, forcing her mind into Ennis's. *No*, she commanded. "We can't leave them, we have to do—"

Something hit her, some invisible wave that shredded through her body, igniting every instinct she had ever had to run. Qav felt it, too, stiffening as his head whipped to the Gate.

Avery whirled, watching in horror as her only link to her home blasted apart, dissolving into a million pieces along with what was left of her heart.

"No," she whispered. She reached her hand out as though she could stop it.

There was no time to think, no time to breathe, before a gravitational wave surged to them on the heels of the explosion. A portal of that size, with an open connection to a live wormhole, wouldn't go down easily. The hole it left in the fabric of the universe clapped together, sending a shockwave that would do incredible damage to anything in its wake.

It reached the Port Station ahead of them, tearing through the massive structure as though it were made of nothing more than recy-cled plastic. A flash of fire glowed as the oxygen ignited, extinguished immediately by the vacuum of space, chunks of metal and glass dis-solving into nothing but remnants flying out at them. All those peo-ple—all those lives, gone in an instant.

Avery's eyes widened, her tears drying up in the next second. It would do the same to this ship. There was no way they would be able to avoid it.

She looked to Qav and grabbed his hand, opening her mind to him. *Help me—I need your power.*

He nodded, closing his eyes and holding fast. That ice flowed into her, feeding directly into her connection with her power. Their energies twisted around one another, locking into place and amplify-ing. Avery could feel that pulse inside of her, that warm hum within her soul, calling to her. The glowing source she had channeled to heal Syla, to save Finn, to send the crushing wave across the desert and take on an entire Federation fighter.

She could use it now—to shield them.

Spread your energy out, encompass the ship as best you can, she told Qav, doing the same with her own. She went with it, fortifying layer after layer of energy, pulling as much matter as she could from within herself, coating the ship, praying it would be enough.

And then the wave was on them, bearing down on her with the force of a million stars, threatening to tear her apart from the inside out. She screamed, squeezing her eyes shut. Qav gripped her hand, cracking her bones, the pain a mere blip compared to the forces that clawed at her, threatening to rip her power away from sheer force.

But she held fast, and Qav stayed beside her.

The seconds dragged on in agony, bleeding into an eternity of pain, an onslaught that refused to end. And still, she refused to let go. Together, they weathered it.

The wave was past them, the blissful relief releasing a sob from Avery as she dropped to the floor of the ship. Qav fell beside her, his free hand gripping the ground to stay upright. He spat up blood, coughing and sputtering beside her, refusing to let go of her hand.

Ennis was yelling, Syla standing beside her, gripping the seat, her face fierce.

Avery realized they were spinning, careening through the universe, entirely out of control. Nova was on her knees, pulling Avery toward her, shaking her, saying something.

Avery couldn't hear beyond the pulse of the universe, echoing within the vast infinity of her blood.

Time came slamming back to her, along with the sounds and sights of the room. Alarms were going off, a sharp warning from a calm AI voice repeating the same message. The computer couldn't calibrate. They would rip apart within their own force if it continued, spinning out into the galaxy beyond.

She had nothing left.

But that humming started again, that warmth in the center of her soul. It was soft and comforting and familiar. The energy from Echo, the one that had led her out of her prison. It was calling to her. Somewhere far away, she heard Fiora's laugh, bright and full of her light.

There was more she still had to give.

Avery raised her hands, Qav still grasping at her fingers, and her eyes closed once more. Pain speared her skull, a sharp and stabbing throb as she called on whatever she had in her. And with the last of her energy, she slowed the ship. Not much, but enough.

Ennis regained control of the engines, the computers taking advantage of the grace Avery offered, finally powering back on to stop them.

Avery released everything, falling into Nova's arms, black spots threatening to take away her consciousness.

"What happened? I thought we stopped it?" Grigg's voice was stretched thinner than Avery had ever heard him. Her heart ached. The Gate was gone.

"We did." Ennis panted in the silence. It was so quiet that Avery thought for a moment she had blacked out entirely. "That explosion was from the other side."

Avery sobbed, choking on the pain in her heart radiating like a poison throughout her body. She thought she felt Nova's arms close around her, felt Grigg's large hands cover hers.

And when the blackness claimed her, she let it, calling to the emptiness that haunted her dreams, begging it to take her too this time.

She wasn't afraid of it any longer—she was ready.

CHAPTER FIFTY-SEVEN

Rebecca watched the news coverage of the Gate explosion from the comfort of her living room, enjoying the glass of champagne she had opened especially for the occasion.

When the report of Avery's appearance on the Port Station came through hours earlier, she thought everything had been ruined. She could have killed Nick herself for not following through and dealing with her when he took off on his little unsanctioned adventure to the underground city.

He was too damned obsessed with his brother. It was beginning to be a liability.

But in the end, the Gate had been destroyed anyway. From Echo's side.

Rebecca wanted to laugh at the coincidence—it was too perfect. She had always planned to blame the explosion on the Reanges, and they had played straight into her hand. This would work flawlessly, absolutely ideal for her plans.

And Nick was already showing promise developing the rest of his skills. If their tests continued on this path, they would be well on their way to being able to realize her dreams.

Humanity had a future, all thanks to her.

She took a sip of the bubbling liquid, letting the sparkles run over her tongue in a delightful tingle, relishing in the expensive bottle.

The door beeped, heralding Nick's entrance before he appeared. His eyes drifted across her face down to the glass in her hands.

"As much as I love to see you happy," Nick said carefully as he approached, "I thought the point was to be on the other side when you blew it up."

She smiled lazily, leaning forward to hand him the glass she had already poured, waiting for him. "I suppose you'll have to trust my vision, darling."

He took the glass, pulling a deep swig, his strong throat working as he tilted his head back. "My brother was on the other side," he said tightly.

She let out a little tut, scooting over and patting the empty spot on the couch beside her. He raised a brow but obeyed, taking the seat.

"One day, you will have to choose between him and me." She leaned forward, claiming his mouth in a deep kiss. She nipped his lip as she pulled away, hard enough to hurt. He didn't so much as flinch. "I hope I can count on you to make the right choice." She tilted her glass, clinking it against his, taking another sip.

"He's changed now," Nick replied cryptically, his tone bleaker than she'd ever heard it. The lights flickered, the news blacking in and out on her screen. She said nothing, and he looked up to the news reports, adding, "There has been significant damage. The cities at lower sea levels are dealing with a surge that could be irreparable. Do you have a plan for dealing with it?"

"Did you see the riots? The looting?" she asked gleefully. "My speechwriter is preparing a statement now—I'll be making an address within the hour. We'll have to come together as a species to fight these Native terrorist attacks. I'll build my whole platform on it. They'll be so obsessed with their fear, with fighting one another, that they won't even notice when we slip away in the night."

"Which begs the question, Rebecca," Nick said slowly, like he didn't think she had heard him before. "How are we going to get to Echo if the Gate is gone?"

"Darling," she said indulgently, rubbing at his lips where her lipstick had smeared on his face. "Did you know my father was the precise definition of an Old Earther? He was the most paranoid person I ever knew, always going on tangents about Natives and how they would take over our planet if we weren't watching. He was so afraid of it, in fact, that he picked up a very peculiar hobby. He liked to build safety vaults on our land, or whatever of it we had left." Nick stared at her strangely, like she was out of her mind. "I always thought the obsession was crazy, not to mention embarrassing, God knows I never brought any friends home. But it did teach me one very important lesson."

She stayed silent, taking another sip.

"Okay, I'll bite," he said on a sigh. "What lesson was that?"

She smiled, her next words delivered in a whisper: "Always have more than one way out."

Avery opened her eyes, blinking at the ceiling's familiar floral etchings.

She tried to sit up. Her entire body screamed at the movement, making it excruciating but not impossible. She was alone in the room.

Her mind was foggy, slow to catch up as she swung her legs over the side of the bed. Her feet touched the cold floor.

Sanctum. The apartment. *Finn.*

Where was Finn?

Her heart seized, and she clutched her chest, gasping at the pain that radiated outward through her limbs, shifting her bones. She collapsed inward, hot tears spilling down her cheeks as she tried to contain it, tried to wrap her control around the grief.

He was gone.

The Gate was gone.

Finn was cut off from her forever, trapped on the other side of the universe with no way back. Her mind conjured that last image of him, hurt and scared, tears running down his face as he tried to tell her goodbye.

He had known. He had known they were going to destroy it.

They had been fighting someone, he and Petra and the others. Trying to prevent it. She knew they would have done everything in their power to keep it from happening.

She thought of what occurred afterward, that gravitational wave that surged around them, destroying everything in its path. If Finn and the others had been anywhere near that on their end—

No. She wouldn't consider it. She couldn't.

He wasn't dead.

She would know if he was dead. She would feel it, even across the stars, if his light had gone out.

Avery forced her body to sit up, rising from the bed and shrugging on a silken gold robe that had been left for her. She padded downstairs to the living room.

Nova rose to her feet as she saw Avery. Grigg was halfway across the room by the time she reached the foyer.

"You shouldn't be out of bed," he chastised. He took her by the arm, taking some of her weight as she limped to the couch.

Qav was there, and Ennis, Syla, and Rem. He watched her, his face drawn, unreadable. The pity that emanated from Ennis was cloying, as was the uncertainty from Syla. Avery pushed them out of her head.

"How long?" she asked, her voice a veritable croak.

"Two days," Nova answered softly.

Two days. She had been out for two days.

Avery blinked slowly, her mouth going dry. "Do we know what happened?" Her fingers gripped at the edges of her robe, the silk cold between her fingers.

Ennis answered, the calm tenor of her voice steadying. "Klein is blaming it on the extremists and the refugees. An act of terrorism."

"But it was from Echo, right?" Avery felt heavy, her breath a solid thing that dragged her down with each inhale.

Nova hesitated before answering simply. "Yes."

"That gravity wave was catastrophic on Earth," Ennis said, explaining more. "The cities are in turmoil. Our water levels in Sanctum rose, but not enough to cause any serious damage. We're equipped for flooding threats. The CLF has stepped up their efforts on the surface, taking advantage of the confusion, hoping to force the avenue of a new government. We've already been contacted to—"

"I don't want to talk politics right now, Ennis." Avery was embarrassed at the way her voice cracked. Nova moved closer to her and took her hand. Avery did choke on a sob then, quiet tears surfacing and rolling down her cheeks.

Qav spoke, his voice soft and smooth and cold, a balm on the inflamed wound that was her heart. "You need time, Avery. Nothing is going to help, but the days ahead will make you stronger. You'll learn to bear it." She looked at him, his silver eyes piercing and fierce and for the first time, honest. "I promise you," he whispered, as though for her ears alone.

She wanted to throw his words in his face. Wanted to rip that silver hair from his head and scream at him that it was all his fault. If only he had helped them sooner. If only she had listened to the others.

If only . . .

If only . . .

And even despite all that, she hoped he was right. She hoped she would find a way out of this darkness that lingered at the edge of her vision.

But right now, she couldn't think about anything. Not her next steps or what her future held or what this new world would look like. She could think of nothing beyond the grief and its weight that pressed on her chest, holding her entire body in its grip, making even the next breath pure agony.

And in that moment, she couldn't see any world, any future, where it would ever be bearable.

CHAPTER FIFTY-EIGHT

But Qav was right. Time did help.

Not with the pain itself, but with Avery's ability to shoulder it. The first week, she barely touched her meals, keeping to her room. By week two, she was moderately hungry, spending a few hours on the terrace each day. By four, she ventured out into Sanctum with Nova and Grigg, shocked at the progress they had made on the rebuilds.

She was careful to keep her feelings away from the others, worried that her grief would burden them. But she knew Nova and Grigg mourned in their own way. They had lost Finn as much as she had. They had lost their home.

Megan and Petra and Gran. They were gone forever. Everyone in the universe who was dear to her heart. It had been her fault—entirely her fault. Avery had no one to blame but herself.

But that was her burden to carry.

And Finn wouldn't want her to give up. He would want her to fight.

It had to be them. She always had to choose them.

She would honor his words and the memory of him that she held in her soul by spending the rest of her life fighting for her people.

Avery couldn't have her happy ending, but she would damn well give the other Reanges left on Earth that chance.

By the second month back on Earth, Avery asked Qav to arrange a meeting with the CLF. Mayven's group was hard at work gathering forces and establishing their own government, separate from the High

Council and the Federation at large. They had public support via Alex and significant financial backing, most likely due to Cora's influence.

Things were finally changing—really changing.

But that didn't mean it would happen easily.

She braced herself as she sat in the living room beside Qav, waiting for the meeting that would determine her next course of action. The next steps in her path toward finding some semblance of herself again.

Not the same, never the same. But different. Evolved.

The wounds that had opened would never really heal, but they would become bearable. A constant reminder of mistakes she had made and the lessons she had learned. Of what she had lost and gained.

And for that, at least, Avery was grateful.

Often times evolution was only birthed into existence on the tides of force, in the wake of open wounds, still bleeding with wisdom learned.

The door to the apartment slid open, and Mayven entered with two other humans and a Reange, none of whom Avery recognized. Mayven smiled, her deep brown eyes lighting with excitement as she nodded in greeting.

Avery stood, extending a hand, satisfied with the evenness in her tone as she welcomed them. "Mayven—it's good to see you again."

Change was here, walking into the living room, shaking her hand with the grip of someone equally ready for the metamorphosis.

And this time, Avery was ready, too.

ACKNOWLEDGEMENTS

There is a truth universally acknowledged that sophomore novels are a difficult beast to slay. Throw in the stress of a global pandemic, and I had a hell of a fight on my hands to get this one finished. Without the help of those humans in my life whom I cherish, I'm certain I never would have been able to complete it.

I owe so much to my husband, Leo, for continuing to push me with understanding and patience as I wrestled with the complexities of this story. I wasn't the most pleasant human to be around through the process, I'm sure. Thank you so much for keeping my embers burning, even when I feel they've gone out forever.

Immeasurable thanks goes to my miraculous, phenomenal, and insanely skilled editor, Marinda Valenti. My work would be merely a pile of sloppy repetitious adjectives without you. Thank you for making it shine—you are incredible.

Ashley Sharpe, you already know how precious you are to me. Your unwavering support means the world, not to mention your attention to detail at the end of every book. I wouldn't be the same writer, or the same person, without you.

I am ever grateful to Allie Preswick, who once again captured the heart of Avery in her unique and beautiful style for this gorgeous cover. I'm in awe of the way you bring her world to life.

And to the others who have made my words and story better, with feedback, teamwork, and early readings. As always, my mom is one of my biggest cheerleaders with my dad close behind. To my brother, Tom, for always answering my strange texts about spaceships and gravitational forces and planetary disruptions. To my family and friends who offer fabulous early feedback: Elizabeth, Alice, Lacie, and Olivia. I love you all so much!

My deepest gratitude goes to all the healthcare professionals and frontline workers who have done so much to keep us healthy and safe during this strange time in which we're living. This new world has been difficult for all of us, but especially you, and I appreciate everything you've given and continue to give as we fight the global pandemic.

And finally, to the readers, for your support and excitement for Avery and Finn and their story. I never expected anyone else to love them as much as I do, but I'm glad they have found a home in your hearts.

JESSICA LYNN MEDINA has spent the better part of her life sacrificing sleep to devour good stories in one form or another. When she's not writing or reading, she is watching the newest k-drama or digesting extrapolated theories from her latest fandom. Jessica lives in Seattle, Washington with her husband and one quirky hound mix.

READ A FREE BONUS SCENE ONLINE

www.JessicaLynnMedina.com

@medinajlynn